LONDON COUNTRY

JOHN KING is the author of ten novels – *The Football Factory*, *Headhunters*, *England Away*, *Human Punk*, *White Trash*, *The Prison House*, *Skinheads*, *The Liberal Politics Of Adolf Hitler*, *Slaughterhouse Prayer* and *London Country*. He has also written the novella *The Beasts Of Brussels* and numerous short stories. He lives in London.

JOHN KING

LONDON COUNTRY

LONDON BOOKS BRITISH FICTION

LONDON BOOKS
39 Lavender Gardens
London SW11 1DJ
www.london-books.co.uk

A catalogue record for this book
is available from the British Library

ISBN 978-1-7396983-0-0

Printed and bound in Great Britain by
CPI Group (UK) Ltd, Croydon, CR0 4YY

Cover design by Benedict Richards/Graphicacy

Cover map illustration by Charlie Peel
Contains OS data © Crown copyright (2018)

Typeset by Octavo Smith Publishing Services

To the humble, shy and handsome,
To the outcasts with no friends,
To all the unsung heroes,
If you are near the end,
To the ones that nearly made it,
To the ones that never will,
To the ones who live in squalor,
At the bottom of the hill.
Be proud of where you come from,
Be proud of who you are.

'Proud', Lee Wilson / Infa-Riot

HERBERT MANOR

Winter, 2015

JOE MARTIN BLEW at the steam coming off the top of his mug and sipped his too-hot tea, put it on the table to cool and studied his friends sitting opposite, their backs to the cafe window. Dave's eyes were following the woman who'd brought them their drinks as she returned to the counter, while Chris was scrolling through what looked like an extra-long message on his phone. Dave muttered something about Polish blondes as Chris muttered fuck. Neither heard the other and nor did they notice Joe watching. Dave thanked God for the East Europeans and Chris added cunt. These were Joe's best mates. His oldest pals. Dangerous Dave and Sherlock Chris. A right pair. Herberts, basically. And Joe made three.

Looking past them to the stalled traffic outside, through the gap between the back of a black lorry and the front of a white van, he zoomed in on his car parked down a side street and was pleased to see it was still there, even if the sort of person interested in thieving it would have to be a purist, a collector of clapped-out bangers, the rarest of rust-bucket runarounds. His relief came from knowing what was in the boot, and as rain dotted the cafe window and a rush of wind smeared it across the glass, he was reminded that this was the perfect weather to be indoors chopping up sounds.

When the clouds opened and a sunbeam filled the room, Joe raised his face and closed his eyes, savouring the natural light and warmth as figures formed and danced across his lids, silhouettes straight from the shadow-puppet shows he'd seen in Bali. He'd bought fifty of these and had them shipped home, focusing on Rama and Sita as he knew their story best. They'd all sold inside a month with a family in Southall taking five of each, and when he delivered them personally he'd been invited to stay for the meal Auntie was putting on the table, one of the best of his life. Those fifty puppets had more than paid for his flights, as well as introducing him to Terry White.

Bali was a memory and a promise, his tickets booked that morning for a return at the start of December. He was going to swerve next winter and see in the new year on a beach in the tropics, and after a month in Bali head for Darwin. The Northern Territory was meant to be on another level when it came to the monsoon, and he was looking forward to seeing Kakadu during the rainy season, remembering how free he'd felt sitting on top of Chungking Mansions watching the thunderstorms, back when he was living in Hong Kong and pouring drinks to pay the rent.

Now it was Dave's turn to work in a foreign bar, Chris winding him up in the pub two nights earlier, insisting he was the New Joe Martin, that soon he'd be wearing tinted contact lenses so his eyes were the same colour as Joe's. Next they'd be sharing dirty underpants. Like Ant and Dec. Chris was drunk and going on about plastic surgery and fake fingerprints, a facelift and knob extension, a fresh set of teeth and memory implants. Dave had laughed along at first, but it wasn't long before his smile flickered and turned to a scowl. Worse was the drawn-out glare that followed. Even so, a bit of piss-taking couldn't be the reason for the tension Joe was sensing.

He knew these two, and especially Dave, who joking apart was more like a brother – a living brother – and anyway, even if what Chris said was true it was normal for people to copy each other. Life was all about repetition, the passing on of knowledge. There were no year zeros. Nothing was new. That was a con, part of the Big I Am. Dave was living in Palma for another reason, one that went by the name of Micky Todd, and while Joe loved going away for a few months, having a break from the West World, he loved coming home just as much. He'd hate to end up in exile like Dave and was going to sort things out with Micky, and he was going to do it soon.

Joe had been thinking about going to Darwin and the Top End of Australia for years, but it was reading Alexis Wright that had made up his mind. The landscape looked incredible in its own right, but the Dreamtime added another dimension, and when he saw pictures of the Outback now he imagined sleeping kangaroos and crocodiles and snakes. He could never feel someone else's ancestors or stories in the same way, but Wright's fiction had given him a glimpse of another way of seeing the world. He'd always loved the sound of the didgeridoo, while Aboriginal painting was just as psychedelic, the truth that nothing was solid where science met the spiritual. After Kakadu he would drive down to Alice Springs and Uluru, take The Ghan to Adelaide and return to England via six weeks in India, travelling through Gujarat, Rajasthan and the Punjab, part of a loop that would start in New Delhi. That was the plan.

The clouds closed and the dancers faded, Joe opening his eyes and waiting for his vision to clear, returning to the sampler in the boot of his car. Two cups of powerful black coffee and an hour talking with the man he'd bought it from had boosted his excitement. Electrician Jack had a healthy reputation locally and at thirty-two had probably built up enough goodwill to keep him in work until he retired, but it was a sideline buying and tinkering with turntables, mixers, speakers, amps and samplers before eventually selling them on that had linked them up. The MPC2500 was a fine-looking machine, and this one had even had its black pads replaced with sixteen slabs of flamboyant, yellow rubber.

– I wouldn't mind shagging that, Dave remarked, turning to the others now the woman he'd been watching had gone into the kitchen, drawing on a terrace classic for his punchline... Shag her senseless, shag her rotten.

Same old lines, same old Dave. Nothing changed, everything changed. Digital Dave. The tempo was slower, the rhythm faster. Dave remixed. David versioned.

– Did you see the G-string when she bent down? Riding right up her arse it was. Did you see? The G-string? Jesus.

Joe pursed his lips and slowly shook his head in mock disgust.

– She can come and work in my bar anytime she likes, Dave continued.

Chris was elsewhere, right index finger frozen above his phone, bent at an odd angle, confusing it with his pinkie, as if he was holding a bone-china cup at an upmarket tea party, waiting for the help to bring him a crustless cucumber sarnie instead of the Full English he'd just ordered. This was hard even for Joe to imagine, as while Chris was tall and thin, he ate like a horse.

– No need for a formal interview.

Chris kept staring at his phone and Joe waited for him to blink, which he eventually did, but that was it, and when Joe inched forward to see what he was looking at the mobile slowly tilted away while the eyes remained blank and still.

– I'll bend her over the Estrella pumps and do some pumping of my own. Minimum wage, maximum shagging. That G-string, crack of the arse. One up the bum, no harm done. Dear oh dear.

Joe shook his head even more slowly, exaggerating the sadness, the distaste he felt for this outdated, sexist language. The culprit merely smirked, job done in the traditional manner. Joe leaned over the table, keeping his voice low.

– That's her husband behind me.

– Whose husband?

Joe put a finger to his lips.

– The lady you're talking about. That's her husband there.

Dave glanced at the two shaven-headed lumps sitting at the next table. More Poles by the looks of them, their clothes and the dried cement telling him they were builders. These men were busy demolishing their all-day breakfasts and he doubted they'd heard him. It was rude to talk like that in front of a husband or boy-friend, a father or brother, but it had been a private conversation and he was only mucking about. How could he have known the woman's husband was sitting there? Even so, he was more than happy to apologise, joke his comments away, but that would be it as he wasn't the sort to get into a big discussion on this sort of thing.

– The one with the eye, Joe added. He's not happy. Not happy at all.

Dave shrugged. He wasn't scared of violence, would do what-ever was required to win a fight, but the cafe was a friendly place and he didn't need the hassle, never mind the police turning up. He couldn't be embarrassing Sherlock, not in front of his Old Bill mates, aware that he had to be on his best behaviour after his pissed-up confession the other night. That was a major concern, not Mr and Mrs Lewandowski. He couldn't remember exactly what he'd said, but was sure of the subject matter, just didn't know if Chris had heard him over the music, and if he had, did he remember?

They'd had seven pints in the pub and between the three of them done most of a bottle of Tanqueray when they got back to Chris's house with the Chinese. Their host had put on some right-eous sounds as they demolished the chow mein and gin, the thundering voice of Prince Far I doing its work, as once Joe had gone home Dave started talking about the secret that could never be shared. There was no rest for the wicked with that old-school reggae and dub, records regarded as tougher than tough, proper Old Testament fire and brimstone, prison-house rock. Hard labour was demanded and the rod of correction delivered. What the fucking hell had he been thinking? It made no sense, and Joe would do his nut if he found out.

– Her name's Joanna, Joe said. Nice lady. Much too good for you.

Dave knew that when it came to the conscience department he was lacking. Not that he was a psycho or anything like that, knew his right from his wrong, just preferred the grey areas where he could operate more freely. He had never felt guilt in the same way as the majority of people did, had little time for the law, while Chris had moved in the opposite direction, joining and then leaving the police when he became sick of dealing with scum, discovering a knack for technology after working as a computer salesman, starting and building and selling his own business for a lot of money. Set up for life, he had gone full Sherlock and rejoined the force, putting his new skills to use with the dedication of a religious convert, one who'd strayed before returning to the fold twice as determined. He was ashamed of the theft and burglary of his youth, keen to make amends.

– When are you painting that box room? Joe asked, changing the subject.

Dave frowned and sipped his tea. That fucking room. His confession…

– Once we buy the paint you can knock it out quick enough.

Chris had been angry about something, so Dave had responded and ended up spilling his guts. He tried to remember what Chris was upset about, but couldn't. It didn't matter. At least he hadn't gone all Catholic, standing there full of beer making a grand speech, but he was still a fucking idiot and couldn't ask Chris straight out as that might trigger the memory or pose a question. Coppers and computer geeks loved a mystery, which meant Sherlock was double trouble, wouldn't rest until he had an answer. It would gnaw at him the same as it was gnawing at Dave who was never going to go to prison, and especially not for killing that bullying cunt Gary Wells fifteen years ago, an historical event best left in the past.

Chris was his mate, but they'd drifted apart and the bloke was funny about things these days. He was Old Bill and therefore a threat, a copper who could easily destroy his life, and when Dave looked back over at the builders he had the urge to hurt someone, although it wouldn't be these two, and it wouldn't be over a Joe Martin wind-up.

– When does Operation Bambi start? he asked after glancing at Chris and seeing that he was lost in his phone.

Dave didn't want to think about the Wells confession or talk about his promise to paint the box room at his sister's house, a thank you for her letting him stay there the last couple of times he'd come home. Joe was on at him to do the right thing, even offering to give him a lift to B&Q so he could buy the paint. Dave hated decorating and again wished he'd never opened his mouth.

– If it's this week it will probably be Saturday night, Joe replied. Clem will let us know. He'll go for a drive and see if he can spot the car.

– I've only got this Saturday night left before I fly back and I don't know if I want to spend it sitting around waiting for a phone call from some pikey who's off prowling in the woods, even if he is our mate. Can't we do it another time?

– Clem reckons they only go out on a Saturday. At least as far as he knows. It's not regular. Once a month maybe. You'd think they had something better to do.

– It's about time we found out who killed Bambi.

– Something like that. You don't have to come.

– No, I'm fine, the women can wait an hour or two. It'll do them good.

Dave's phone vibrated and he picked it up off the table.

– Fucking hell.

– What?

– Nothing, he said, bringing his screen closer so he could see the picture more clearly. It's private.

Martina might have been five years older than Dave, but she looked a decade younger, especially topless sitting on a table in Vista after locking up for the night. She was also tickling the end of a Heineken bottle with her tongue. This selfie was seductively lit by the light coming from the fridge behind the counter, and he wasn't going to moan about the angle, his cock stirring as he moved to the next image. She must have used a timer on this one as it was a longer-range shot and she was leaning back on the table, legs raised and open, the green bottle ready for insertion.

– I've got to get out of this dump, he muttered. What the fuck am I doing here with you two when I could be sitting in the sun with a cold lager?

– That's not very nice, Joe responded. Anyway, it must be cold over there this time of year. What has Palma got that we haven't got?

Martina for a start. His boss had a great body, but Dave was as attracted to her face, those wisdom lines carved into tanned, soft-leather skin. She was glamorous and sultry, smelled of perfume, incense, tobacco, wine. Martina attended church three times a week and was horny as fuck when she came home, the classic mix of religion and sex, nun and whore. Not that she was a tart. Only in the bedroom, or Vista after closing. She was a classy lady. Dave regarded himself as a man of great style, which had always surprised Joe, but Martina seemed to agree, which surprised Dave.

Maybe there wasn't that much difference between a genuine Gucci handbag and a snide Lacoste polo.

Joe was mulling over the Bambi comment and what had happened to Clem, how he'd found two men in the woods next to the Oaks where he lived, a pair of cunts straight from the Berkshire Hunt rhyme who'd shot a deer with their crossbow, one of those small deer that lived in the area. The arrow was near its heart, but it was still alive, and Clem was struck by the defeat in its eyes, the confusion, how they shone in the light from his torch which he turned on the hunters, giving them an earful and stepping forward. A crossbow had been raised, insults exchanged, Clem forced to walk away, returning half an hour later and finding the deer dead. It was a doe, and she'd been left to die by two sportsmen who weren't even killing for food. Clem was an easygoing character, but now he was angry and Joe didn't blame him. He had told Dave about this, but not Chris.

Dave moved to the next picture. Martina's face was hidden. She was on all fours with her bum in the air, the bottle doing what he should be doing.

– I must be mad.

The rain pushed harder, drawing Joe's attention away from Dave who was tapping out a text and joining Chris in cyberspace. The traffic outside had started to move, but slowly, headlights coming on as the weather became more grey and gloomy. He wasn't working today, but even if he had been he would be indoors, and being self-employed he looked at things differently to those on fixed hours and a wage. He had freedom, but that meant uncertainty. Even so, he was solvent and debt-free, owned his flat and lived within his means, had achieved his ambition to not spend his life feeling trapped. Money had to shape a person's mood more than the weather. Rain or shine, it was no fun being skint.

Easy borrowing was a short-term mercy and a long-term curse, the debt some people racked up insane, and while many had no choice there were those who just couldn't handle their finances. Look at Dave and his trouble with Micky Todd, the cash he'd owed and how that had shaped his decisions. The debt was paid now, but Dave still had to tread carefully when he came home. Chris was loaded and secure, Carol and the kids happy, but he was seeing some horrible crimes with the police, stuff that could never be unseen. True, it was his choice and Chris was doing an important job, and Joe admired him for that, but it had taken its toll. Even so, he had a good life, they all did, especially Joe.

He had never felt so fit, the training he'd got into addictive, and while he enjoyed a social drink that was his only real vice these days. Reaching for his tea he tried again, blowing on the mist-free surface out of habit. It had cooled enough and was the perfect cuppa, Joanna leaving the teabag in specially, and he saw her reflection in the window, the builders at the counter paying, heard Polish spoken and coins dropped into the tip bowl.

The two Poles walked back through the cafe, opened the door and pushed themselves into the wind, a cold burst of air shocking Joe and reviving Chris. The door was tugged shut and closed with a bang, and this brought Dave back. Four eyes were raised and focused on Joe.

– What did you say? Chris asked.

– I don't know. When?

– Who shot Bambi? Chris seemed surprised. Detective Sid Vicious is on the case, you know that.

Two plates appeared, Joanna placing one in front of Joe and touching his shoulder, before looking at the others.

– The Full English? she asked. With bubble and squeak.

– That's me, Chris replied, his voice automatically enthusiastic despite the text and photo he'd been sent.

He wasn't hungry now.

– Thank you, he said, as his food was set down.

Dave hadn't been in the cafe for years, and definitely not since the new owners had taken over, and after he admired Joanna's return to the kitchen to collect his food he looked at the sausages on Joe's plate and tutted.

– You've given up on all that vegan bollocks then?

– You're the one who's going to be eating bollocks, lips and arseholes in a minute. And if you get gourmet sausages, intestines as well.

It was Dave's turn to pull a face, but he messed up, trying for a nonchalant look that showed he had a cast-iron stomach and didn't care, but if anything it seemed like he was going to puke. Joe was glad he'd created a realistic picture, and that Dave had a soul.

– Thank you, darling, Dave said, as Joanna put his plate down.

To everyone's surprise, she patted his head like he was naughty boy, looking Joe in the eyes as she did so.

– You are very tanned, she said, referring to Dave. Is it natural? The other two laughed.

– Never used to be, Chris said. He was the sunlamp king before he went into exile.

– This one's a hundred-percent real, Dave announced, puffing up.

– He went on holiday and hasn't come back. *Can't* come back.

– Same with me, Joanna said. But I don't get a suntan in Slough. Not like this one's girlfriend.

She left them and it took Dave a few seconds to twig, and he had the decency to feel embarrassed, realising she had seen Martina posing on his phone. Despite this, he wondered which picture it was, hoped it was the last one. He loved foreign birds, but reasoned that they all did, every Englishman with a taste for the exotic.

– I'm starving, Joe said as he got stuck into his food, looking at Chris. How did it go with the Major?

– Yeah, it was good, Chris replied. First time he's come round the house. Usually I go and see him at the allotments.

– Dad said he saw you. Had a cup of tea and some of Mum's cake.

– They were the only two people down there.

– Winter's quiet, but Dad's into his green manure, been putting the seeds in.

– If I'm the New Joe Martin I suppose you're the New Major Tom, Dave said, seeing his chance and turning to Chris. Bet you two share your panties as well. Have you got the same notebook?

Joe 90, isn't it? Space-cadet coppers. Does he wash his Y-fronts before he lends them to you?

– Ha fucking ha, Chris muttered. Careful, or me and the Major will nick you. You're back on English soil and we have the power to put you away.

Dave jolted.

– Crimes against dress sense. You can serve your time in the rain like the rest of us.

Dave told anyone who asked that he was living abroad because of the weather. He hated the cold, went on to explain how he'd become addicted to the local tomatoes, that there could be no argument whether these were fruit or vegetables. It was definitely the climate that gave them their taste. This shifted attention and he never mentioned the Micky Todd business. The offer to work in Martina's bar had come at the perfect time, and looking back at his problems with Micky it really was pathetic, even if he had been off his nut at the time. He had taken the job with Martina and sorted himself out, and while he'd never wanted to travel like Joe, couldn't imagine bumming around on the cheap in those third-world shit-holes, it was a change of scene and he was happy. He did miss England, though, and didn't want to die abroad. This he also kept to himself.

He ran the bar while Martina created the atmosphere and managed the business. They drew in the locals as well as some tourists, and it was all very relaxed. The only time he'd messed up was when three Germans started insulting Martina after she told them they were drunk and had to leave. It was a quiet evening and he'd had a Heineken or two himself, over-reacting from a sensible point of view by using the baseball bat he kept behind the counter. The police had arrived, and it was only Martina explaining, arguing and finally pleading that stopped them taking him away. She'd kept Dave out of prison and he would always love her for that, knew he would crack up inside. Now there was his Wells confession. What the fuck had Chris meant about nicking him on English soil and putting him away?

While Dave worried, Chris brooded. He had lost his appetite, but couldn't leave a Full English untouched as the others would know something was wrong and he didn't want to be answering questions. In normal life the things you knew were true and didn't want to admit could be ignored, the ugly stuff you suspected dismissed as fantasy, but he had to confront the details in the text he'd received, the photos of acid burns on a woman's face. It was police business and he was past the shock and anger and into a hopelessness that was more like mourning. There was nothing normal about being in the police force. This wasn't his case, but DI Williams was a friend as well as a former colleague and had asked for his help.

Joe, meanwhile, was looking at his car again, thinking about the sampler and two boxes of records next to it in the boot. One held the albums he'd bought from an old rockabilly who hadn't had a turntable for years and was streaming his Johnny Cash and Carl Perkins these days, while the other was full of twelve-inch jungle picked up in a storage clearance. While Joe had been buying and selling records for years, he had started doubling up as a private crate-digger, one with plans and an expanding, more eclectic range of music. He had to learn how to use the sampler first, aware that the hard part was going to be mastering the machine in order to make the tracks half-forming in his head real, a series of mash-ups that would always be personal.

He seemed to be the only one enjoying his food, wondering why the others were so moody, reasoned that Chris was going to work soon and probably already there in his mind given his reaction to whatever was on his phone, while Dave had been dodging his box-room promise for too long and was narked he was being pushed to do the right thing. That made sense in theory, but Joe felt he was missing something.

– What's the matter? he asked, once he had finished eating. Aren't you two hungry? Unlike you Chris, you're usually licking your plate clean. I thought you'd be looking forward to a proper fry-up after all that fresh fruit and vegetables, Dave. Why eat your tomatoes off the vine when you can have them out of a tin?

– The tomatoes are fresh, Joanna said, her hand back on Joe's shoulder.

– I know, I was only joking, he said. That was lovely.

– You don't like your food? she said, turning to Chris and Dave. You've only eaten half. Both of you.

– No, it was great, Chris answered, regretting his lost appetite and knowing he would regret it later. I'm just not feeling hungry.

– Me neither, Dave added. Sorry.

Joanna took their plates away, and after Chris checked the time he said he had to get going, the three pals paying and leaving a generous tip, soon outside but not about to hang around in the rain. Chris shook hands with the others and hurried to his Audi, parked in the street right next to the cafe where he could keep an eye on it, while Joe and Dave crossed over the road to the Skoda.

– Isn't it about time you treated yourself to a new car? I can't believe this pile of shit still runs.

Joe knew this was coming and would have been disappointed if Dave hadn't said anything. It was the same with his clothes…

– Why don't you buy a proper Harrington instead of that cheap army-surplus job. Treat yourself to a Baracuta. A classic G9.

The food he ate…

– Can you have nuts? I mean, are they vegan? Yes? What about cheese? No? That's mad. You make life hard for yourself, don't you. It's not going to help. People are always going to eat animals.

The travel…

– What do you want to go to India for? It's all here anyway. Why risk getting malaria and cholera and fuck knows what else? What about when you were sick in Mexico? Bandits on every corner eyeballing the gringo. Why leave Europe? Come and live in the sun. Slough's a toilet. So's the rest of England. It's much more civilised once you cross the Channel. Summerland is waiting. You'll love it. Trust me.

– I'd go insane, Joe liked to respond, feeling that maybe Dave secretly agreed. No offence, but Summerland is boring. I'm happy here.

It was childish stuff, but that had always been their way, and each time Joe laughed it off and came back with a strong reply there was a relieved look on Dave's face, the glint of satisfaction.

It was as if he was testing Joe, pleased to be put in his place as it meant his friend was still the same person he'd always known, and this proved that Dave's own roots were solid. It was true that Joe had over-reacted once or twice in the past, even put Dave on his arse, but none of that mattered.

They stuck together, and while there were times when they'd fallen out they were always there when it counted, helped each other when it came to the crunch. Dave had killed Gary Wells to save Joe from prison, and that was something he would never ever forget. It was also something that was never mentioned, as if doing so would break a spell and leave them exposed. If Joe could properly sort things out with Micky Todd it would be as if he'd repaid some of the debt he owed, and once they were in the car and on the move he was tempted to play Black Grape's 'In The Name Of The Father' as a reminder of what had gone before, but instead asked Dave if he'd heard the Sleaford Mods album *Austerity Dogs*, not waiting for an answer and pressing play.

Moving through the foggy streets... speeding to the sounds of Satellite... following this big looping circle that takes me to my private place... I am one more shadow in the night... a blur on their control-room screens... bones clicking and heart ticking... spirit surging... flanked by houses... downstairs curtains drawn tight... shutting out the darkness... centuries of bedtime terrors... monsters imagined and real... mutating... but the people here are full of hope... it is a good place to live... to raise children... grow old... fabric glowing as widescreens pump out the positives... happy endings... good always defeats evil... love conquers hate... I believe this... never mind the weak moments... the doubt that creeps into us all... TVs delivering sport comedy movies drama... science-fiction films series documentaries... we need big bold answers to the big bold questions... supernatural extraterrestrial divine... one hero would be enough... the houses fading into the murk as I reach the edge of the estate... tripping past St John's... the Green Man... church gossip and pub sermons... voices merging... common land... common people... buildings shrinking... my skin steaming as I pause at the junction... a streetlight spreading magic through the haze... electric halos... gas rainbows... and I feel fantastic as the vapour wraps octopus arms around my body... bursts of thick cloud puffing past on the road in front... these wonders... day and night... sun and moon... hot and cold... here and there... now and then... from concrete to grass in twenty-three steps... and I am moving faster... picking up speed... listening for engines... crossing the road... taking care... faint beats growing louder... thousands of hearts accelerating... slowing... Satellite thinking... Satellite wondering... and I follow the path that runs behind a factory... single-storey premises... dirty brick... fifty or sixty staff... our short cut when the ground isn't muddy... I walk down here with my girl and my boy... taking them to school... we don't bring the car... cross the road holding hands... mustn't let go... the road I have survived... forklifts parked... dark and unlit... there is a flash indoors... a nightwatchman... the wall ends... wasteland... derelict sheds... rock-hard earth... frozen thistles... the fog here is thicker... haunting... and I see flickering lights... Jack O'Lantern wants me to leave the path... but I know the tricks he plays... this Will O' The Wisp... must keep moving... can't stop... dilly dally... mustn't be persuaded... keep a clear head... through the second gate and strolling along the side of the school... stop by the playground and put my palms on the fence... fingers through wire... squeezing the cold... my daughter and my son... leave the school behind... moving into the gloom... two football pitches... a black path... churned-up grass... dirty studs... Sunday morning and Wednesday evening... benches... bins... someone up ahead... a man sits on a bench... I can't see a dog... wary... mace in my pocket... in case... the one in a million chance... slipping my right hand in... ready... he's on his phone... silent... listening... could be a trick... Jack O'Lantern... Will O' The Wisp... but he doesn't look up... I pass... glance back... he is talking now... and I settle into an easy rhythm... it is the exchange we make... individual freedoms... the collective... I leave the football pitches... warehouses and offices... the older paths of the agricultural workers... labourers...

shepherds... right back to the animals... their original ways... into the brighter lights... a supermarket... takeaways... burgers and chips and onion rings and pizzas and kebabs and baked potatoes... passing through more houses... more closed curtains... widescreens pumping... the possibilities... forgotten remembered imagined... the curse of dementia... thank God I have so many years left to live... breaking away and tracking the edges of another person's story... my friend Grace... her bed at the end of the ward... by the windows... curtains pulled but never big enough to cover the glass... we learn to deal with trauma in our own ways... there comes a time when words mean little... more white noise... more white trash... garages and lock-ups... deserted now... busy tomorrow... mechanics head down... men loading and unloading... cash and carry... toilet rolls... detergents... pulses... everything we need... men drinking tea... smoking... eating cheese rolls... bacon butties... retired men wandering... lost... shrinking... small versions of their heyday selves... born-again infants... women growing stronger... new leases... running shops... teaching children... caring for the young and the old... all of us moving in these spirals... no drugs required... speeding... tripping... our natural highs... pounding limbs and joints... free will freewheeling... adrenaline rushes... adrenaline junkies... and I can't control my excitement... feel fantastic... sliding through the hole in the fence... a long strip of forgotten land... climbing the embankment... palms on gravel... reaching the top and loving the hum... the smell of petroleum... lights in the fog... diffused... and I walk along the ridge... slowly... catching my breath... strolling... pass the earth where the farmers grow their weed... it's years since the police came... destroyed the crop... made arrests... but time passes and the focus changes... farmers return... fresh faces... dead skunk stems as green manure... next year's harvest... not yet planted... and I keep walking until I reach my special place... dip into the bushes and take out my fold-up chair... open it and sit down... nobody bothers me here... soothing trance... motorway hypnosis... they say lonely people never live in lonely places... the gold ball at the top of a hill... the arc of a humpback bridge... thatched cottages

*and cream teas... Satellite speeding... Satellite tripping... Satellite
sounds soaked in fog –*

Ray English knew he was lucky leaving court with a Not Guilty,
and the first thing he did when he was outside in the street was call
his mum to give her the good news. It was only right. He had been
staying with her these last two months unable to hide what was
going on in his life, and while she had done her best to accept this
latest trouble and the possibility of prison, the end of his marriage
and the divorce, she was feeling the strain. Ray had only just
realised how fast she was ageing, the process no longer gradual,
felt terrible he hadn't noticed before. Ashamed that he might be the
cause. She didn't deserve to be fretting. Not at this stage of her life.

   She had started coming up and hugging him. Holding on and
squeezing tight. This morning she wouldn't let go and begged him
to find a way to control his temper. Maybe see a doctor. Someone
professional. An expert. She leaned back and looked up into his
eyes and told him he was still her little boy, that whatever happened she would always be on his side. He was her son. But he had
to grow up. And when he tried to explain that it was only threatening behaviour, a few months inside at the very worst, more likely
a fine, which wasn't going to happen as he would get off, she told
him not to talk as if he was a hard man.

   She hadn't raised a villain. He wasn't the sort of person who
went out and hurt people for money. Or sold drugs and ruined
lives. Did he think he was a gangster? The third Kray twin? He was
just a big kid who drank too much and hung around with other big
kids who did the same. He should be at home watching a film.
Reading a book. One of his George Orwell novels. Or trying to find
himself a nice woman who would look after him when she was
gone. Ray was reminded that she had carried him in her tummy.
Wiped his bum and changed his nappy. Cleaned his willy. She
could still beat him up if she wanted. Punched his arm. A hard
blow for such a small fist.

   – Careful, you'll crack a knuckle.

– I'll crack something, don't you worry, she said, punching him again.

Raising a hand as his co-defendants Ian and Darren approached, Ray gestured that he would catch them up, watched as they walked away from the court and into the high street. There would be a few of the lads in The Three Tuns, and with the pressure off he was in the mood for a pint. First he needed Mum to pick up her phone. He ended his call before it went to voicemail. Gave it twenty seconds and pressed redial.

– Hello. Ray?

– Not guilty. I'm an innocent man.

– Thank God. I was praying for you.

– The boss was listening. About time as well.

– Don't you blaspheme.

She sounded younger. Healthier.

– You were lucky. You know that, don't you? Fucking lucky.

– Please don't swear, Mum. There's no need for foul language.

– Fuck off. You got lucky.

– I didn't do anything wrong. Not really.

– It's a fresh start. Another one.

– Everything's fine, don't worry. A new beginning.

– Promise me. Swear you won't get into trouble again.

– I'll do my best, I promise.

– Your best isn't always good enough, though. You've got to promise.

– It *will* be good enough, Mum. I can't do any more than my best.

He pictured the expression on her face, the way she rolled her eyes to show she was dealing with an idiot. It was part of their humour. She hadn't rolled her eyes last night or this morning, though, apart from when he'd banned her from coming to court. He couldn't have handled that, but felt she was secretly relieved to be staying at home, even if she'd argued the toss. Ray knew that he really did have to sort himself out. For her sake as much as his own.

– What time will you be home? You're not going into work, are you?

– No, I'm having a drink with the others.

There was another pause, and he felt her worry returning as she imagined what could happen. She didn't need to be concerned. Not anymore. It was all in the past. A quiet pint with family and friends. Maybe two. Definitely no more than four. Nothing serious.

– Uncle Terry will be there, he reassured her. He was in court. I told you he would be.

Ray could almost hear her relief in the silence. She trusted her brother. Terry had always been there for Viv and her boys.

– Shall I make you something nice to eat? For when you get home.

– Make it tomorrow, Mum. I don't know what time I'll be in. I can get a curry if I'm hungry. Do you want an onion bhaji if I do?

– George's or the takeaway in Iver?

– I might not have one, but probably George's.

The Iver Tandoori was famed for the size of its onion bhajis.

– Will you bring me a bottle of Guinness from the pub? The Export.

– A bottle of Guinness Export and an onion bhaji. Anything else?

– Well…

– Go on. Have anything you want. My treat.

– Maybe some chana masala? The side dish. I couldn't eat a main.

– Of course. Mum…

– Yes?

– Thank you.

– Don't be silly. Go and have a drink with your friends and say hello to Terry for me, but remember, stay out of trouble. And mind you don't spill anything on your clothes. That's your best shirt you're wearing and you've only got the one suit. I won't be able to get the stain out if you do. Especially if it's curry.

– I'll be careful. No fighting, no stains. Promise.

Ray rang off and wondered whether he should go home instead of the pub, let his mum cook him dinner. Bangers and mash with tons of gravy. Bread and butter on the side. He was innocent in the eyes of the law, but feeling guilty about what he'd put her through, and while he had previous and it was ages since he'd been arrested, this time it felt different. Nobody wanted to go to prison, but it could have killed Mum. And he thought about Chelsea and April. What his daughters would have thought if they'd known their dad had been nicked for fighting in the road. It wasn't exactly setting a good example. He'd been fortunate it was only threatening behaviour. Lucky the CCTV wasn't working.

There was nothing wrong with having secrets. A person would go mad if they had no privacy. It was like a form of sleep deprivation. Some things were best not shared. Never known. If he'd gone to jail his girls would have found out and he'd have hated that, but this ending was a happy one and it was only right that he enjoyed the victory. It was time to wash the negatives away. He deserved a couple of pints. Had to get back to normal. Started walking. And while he wasn't one for formal clobber and wished he could ditch the suit and tie, he did feel taller and stronger than ever in his Crombie and brogues.

– Where did you get to? Terry asked as Ray came into the pub and down the steps and into the back bar. I thought you'd be straight down here.

His uncle was ready with a pint of London Pride in one hand, Guinness in the other. Ian and Darren were to his left with their mate Stan. Hawkins and Laurel to his right. Handsome and Gary had been involved in the fight but not arrested, and it was agreed they shouldn't come to the pub let alone court.

– I had to call Mum and let her know.

– I bet she's a happy woman.

– Very happy. Same as me.

– Here you go.

Terry passed over the Guinness and Ray made a show of holding it up and examining the body and head, sniffing the top and licking his lips.

– Onwards, Terry announced, and everyone raised their glasses.

– The first of many, Darren added, once everyone had had a celebratory gulp. Result or what? I knew we'd get off.

Ray wasn't so sure and considered the two younger men he'd ended up with in court, how the old girl was always telling him he needed to start acting his age. His ex had been saying similar for years before not just kicking him out again but filing for a divorce. He didn't blame her, although Mum did. In his mother's eyes he was always right even when she knew he was wrong. Did she really think he was an overgrown child or was she trying to shame him? A lot of the men he knew were the same, but that was logical as they were the ones who were out and about.

There were plenty of blokes who got married and disappeared, ended up with no friends and no life that he could see. Fuck that. He'd made mistakes, that's all, and whatever happened he couldn't stop living. He enjoyed a sociable drink and that was healthy. Good for the brain. Like Mum said, he'd never done anything terrible. Couldn't kill a person. Maybe in self-defence or if one of his daughters was raped, but not for money or in cold blood. The idea made him feel sick. He wasn't that sort of person. Didn't want to be either.

– It's wrong none of that other lot got nicked, Darren was saying. They started it as well.

– That's not strictly true, Ian replied, but they definitely got away with one.

– Maybe they didn't start it, but it was down to them. We owe those cunts.

– Nice to see you suited and booted, Terry said, moving things in a more peaceful direction. Crombie, brogues and the usual smart barnet.

– Thanks to Angie, Ray replied. I hate wearing a suit and tie, though.

– Offer's still there. I'll take you to see Threadneedle Man when you're ready. Sort you out. My treat.

Ray raised and drained the rest of his glass in one go. He was a big man with a big thirst, but while he wasn't going to get pissed, the first couple wouldn't touch the sides. He knew to pace himself. Four pints maximum. He would make the last two last. It was the right approach on a school night. With work in the morning.

– Same again?

– We'll get our own round, Ian said, indicating Darren and Stan.

– No, Ian. I want to buy everyone a drink.

– Thanks, Ray.

– I remember when you were a lager man, Terry pointed out, as he often did.

It was one of their two main wind-ups, Terry coming from a generation who'd seen lager as a girl's drink when it was introduced, European and therefore effeminate. The other was who controlled the Rock-Ola in the Union Jack, whether ska or Oi was the proper skinhead sound. Terry owned the club and the jukebox, so he was the one making the decisions.

– Lager's gone flat, Ray replied. EU regulations.

– We can't blame everything on Brussels. You could be right, though.

Ray's strong anti-EU beliefs were well known. He passed the other drinks out as they were poured, his second pint of Guinness tasting as good as the first. More or less.

– Same old Chelsea, Hawkins was saying, once Ray had paid and was back with the others. We beat Swansea 5-0 away then Bradford knock us out of the FA Cup at home.

– Fair play to Bradford, but that's rare these days, Terry replied.

– I'm still buzzing from PSG in Paris, Darren added. That was a proper tear-up.

– It's been a lively start to the year, Ray admitted. Thumped 5-3 at Tottenham, then we do the Scousers in the League Cup and get another go at Spurs in the final.

– Fucking wrong getting done like at Three Point Lane, Darren said angrily. Fucking Yids.

His hatred of Tottenham was one of the worst Ray had seen, which was saying something. Them and Liverpool. Ray felt the same way.

– Still didn't knock us off the top of the league, though, did it?

– We'll win the title this year, I reckon, Stan said. Now the

Special One's back and we've got Costa up front. It's what we've needed since Drogba left.

– Costa's no good to us if he goes around stamping on people and getting banned.

– He's a nutter. No offence, Ray.

– None taken, Ray said, letting the eye contact linger.

– Diego just did to the Scousers what they've been doing to everyone else for years. You need that sort of player up front. Didier could put it about, but Costa's on another level.

– He's more Mark Hughes than Didier Drogba, Hawkins said. Everyone hated Hughes until he came to Chelsea. All the people slagging Costa off would buy him tomorrow if they could. It's the same with any player.

– You wouldn't want Ronaldo at Stamford Bridge, though, would you?

– He's brilliant, but you might be right on that one.

Ray was reflective by the time he was sipping his third pint. Things were on the up. While he'd put on a brave face, this last week had seen him seriously worried, but now he was in the clear his anxiety had vanished. There were only good times ahead. Mum could relax and get on with enjoying her life. Chelsea and April had no nasty surprises in store. The drink was flowing and he was in good company. George's was a short walk away. Plus he had a ticket for the League Cup final against Tottenham. And there was even the chance of a referendum on the UK's membership of the EU. It was hard to believe that might happen after all these years, but UKIP had spanked the main parties in the EU elections and Farage had Cameron and his Coalition bum chum Clegg on the run. Ray was excited about the future.

His fourth pint saw him talking to Handsome on his phone before discussing the differences between Ed Miliband and Bob Crow with Lol, while his fifth coincided with Ian searching for the lead magistrate on Google, Hawkins wondering if the three defendants should chip in and leave some thank-you roses on her doorstep.

As he raised his sixth pint of Guinness to his mouth, Ray was starting to feel the effects, and Darren's suggestion that they drive over to the pub where the fight had taken place and have a drink there didn't seemed as much of a no-no as Stan and Terry made out. But the young firm soon forgot this idea and were off, Hawkins shaking everyone's hand and heading back to Slough. The time had flashed past.

– Do you want another one here? Terry asked. It's my round.

– Let's go somewhere else, Lol suggested.

They were down to core family now, and the three English men walked around the corner to the Queen's Head, Terry getting the drinks in and bringing them over to the table where Lol and Ray were sitting. The pub was low-ceilinged and local, Windsor Street a window into how Uxbridge looked before the shopping centres were built and the high street closed off. Lol had only had the one pint and been drinking lemonade since, while Terry had bought himself a bottle of Heineken, which cracked Ray up as he started on his seventh pint of Guinness.

– What time are you leaving tomorrow? he asked Lol, conscious he might not want to stay out too late.

– Ten or thereabouts. There's no rush.

He looked so young. Little more than a child. Ray was proud of Lol but had worried about him in the past, knew this was nothing compared to what Terry must have felt when he was fighting overseas. Grandad George was the one who had inspired Lol to join the Army. He had never met George as he'd passed away before he was born, but knew all about him, the fact he was a gunner in a Lancaster and been taken prisoner when it was shot down. Neither Lol nor Terry knew that George had been tortured by the Germans. That was one of Ray's secrets.

– It will be good to see the lads again, but it's been great having some time at home, Dad.

Ray knew part of Terry regretted passing on that side of the family history in the way he had, never thinking that his son would act on it and sign up, but hopefully those more dangerous deployments were in the past now.

– Careful with that lager, Ray told Terry. It might make you feel dizzy. A half as well. Served in a bottle.

Terry mumbled something about volume.

– What was that band you were going to form with Kev The Kev? Ray asked Lol. I was trying to remember the name the other day. I don't know why. It just came into my head when I was at work driving.

– The Thinkers.

– Tinkers?

– *Thinkers*. We'll do it one day. Kevin's in love and got no time to form the new Rancid at the moment, and I'm still serving. We'll do it one day, don't worry.

Lol remembered how they'd thought to call themselves Rage And Love, tapping into Green Day and Ray's character, which hadn't changed as much as it could have done. He was still switching between the two. And Lol got out his phone and showed them photos from when he was out with Kev The Kev and the others last week, boys being boys, young men being young men.

– You want to get those printed, his dad said.

– I know. You're always telling me.

– Honestly, though, if you don't print them they're going to get lost. You'll get to my age and have no photos.

Ray was drinking fast, soon off to the bar to order a round. He felt a tap on his shoulder. Turned and was face to face with Priscilla.

– Hello, Ray, I thought it was you.

He must have looked surprised. Maybe even shocked.

– Don't be scared, she laughed. I'm not going to zap you with my phaser.

The longing he'd felt last year returned.

– I'm not. I know you won't. Sorry. How are you?

– I'm good, Ray, she said, touching his arm. I almost didn't recognise you. Have you been to a wedding?

He couldn't tell her about his court appearance.

– I'm out with my uncle and cousin.

She glanced towards the table when he pointed over.

– I was just leaving, Priscilla said, conscious he'd avoided her question and not about to pry. My friends are outside waiting.

Ray wasn't sure what to say. Her eyes were staring into him, the look she had that made him want to reach over and lift her up and kiss her on the lips, unzip the jacket she was wearing and wrap his arms around her waist and pull her in close. It wasn't sexual. Well, it was. Sort of. But different.

– Look, I've got to go, Priscilla said, after waiting a good twenty seconds for him to speak. We've got a cab coming any second. Give me a call. You've got my number. I hope you've still got it. Seriously, don't be scared.

And then she was moving through the pub and out of the door and into the street and stopping to look back through the window and blow him a kiss. She took her time doing this as well, as if she wanted him to know it was meant. Then she was gone. And Ray was disorientated. His thoughts confused. The last drink of his round was placed on the bar. This was his eighth pint of Guinness and would be his last.

– Who was that? Terry asked, once Ray had put the drinks on the table and sat down.

– Priscilla.

– Unusual. Her mum and dad Cilla Black fans?

– I don't know. Could be a family name I suppose.

– Priscilla likes you.

Ray shrugged. For some reason he felt embarrassed.

– I mean she *really* likes you.

The feeling was mutual. They'd clicked the moment they met, but only been out three times. They had kissed. Nothing more.

– You can't tell seeing her once, Ray said, hoping Terry would continue. Angie had her eye on you for ages before you twigged.

– That's very true, but Priscilla fancies you. No doubt about it.

– He's right, Lol agreed. How do you know her?

– I got talking to her in here as it happens.

Despite the attraction it hadn't worked out. He needed a simple life.

– I'm hungry, he announced. George's is a minute away.

Terry had been using The Taj for years, but a fire in the kitchen had gutted the place and owner Harry had used the insurance money to do it up and sell the property on. He still had Chapatti Express, which went from strength to strength, but what The Taj had done for Slough, The Raj was still doing for Uxbridge. Slough had Harry, Uxbridge had George. And Ray had always preferred the Indian down the road.

– Shall we have this one and go for a curry?
– It would be rude not to, Terry said.
– Sounds good to me, Lol agreed.

None of them had eaten since breakfast apart from some crisps in The Three Tuns, so it was an easy decision. With their taste-buds fired up, the English family hurried their drinks and Ray took the empties to the bar, bought a bottle of Guinness Export and slipped it into his coat pocket. They headed towards George's, past the old police station on their right and a busy Metropolitan on their left, the smell of those Raj spices increasingly pungent as they neared the door, a final blast engulfing them as they entered a local institution, Ray reminding himself not to forget Mum's onion bhaji and chana masala, and not to get curry on his best white shirt and only suit.

Joe stood in the doorway and admired the room, especially the shelves he'd built, the cupboards down below, and even though he still had jobs to do he let the satisfaction flow. From the outside the building looked more like a village hall than a church, which meant it blended into the surrounding streets, so it was important to make the interior special. If there were any boy soldiers present he hoped they were pleased. He had to admit that those shelves were the bollocks, and his turntable, mixer and speakers fitted into the platform he'd constructed with space to spare. He was hoping to finish off tomorrow if he stayed late tonight, but wouldn't rush. It had been a lot of hard work, and this deepened his satisfaction.

He had removed the pews and other furniture – including a

heavy mahogany cabinet with the help of a boxer from the con-gregation – taken down cupboards and curtain rails, filled holes in the walls, ripped out carpet, peeled off wallpaper, treated mould, sanded the door and replaced a section of skirting. A skip had been ordered, filled and removed. He had also stripped and varnished the floorboards he'd been surprised to find under the carpet. That had meant extra time and money, but Lou spoke to the lady paying for the work and she'd said to go ahead. He had then thoroughly cleaned and painted every surface apart from the wall to his left that had needed plastering by a professional. All this before he got to start on the fun part.

Joe had never taken on such a big job before, was an occasional builder of shelves and cupboards, but he'd been offered good money he could do with earning, persuaded by the friend of a friend. A bit of carpentry suited him in the winter, broke up the buying and selling of records, driving around in the rain, meant a lump sum and a change of scene. It also helped keep him physically and mentally fit, stretching his mind as well as his muscles as he pondered life in a different sort of way. He was picky, charged properly and asked for something up front on top of the materials.

This was another hobby that paid as far as Joe was concerned. He had first become interested in the process when he was thinking to have his own shelves built, the cost and hassle sending him down the DIY route. He was drowning in records, his stereo and speakers on the table where he ate, and knowing exactly what he wanted he went and did an evening class, bought what was needed and got stuck in, the end result a lot better than he'd hoped. Chris asked for some, then Chris's father-in-law, and other requests followed. He only made two or three sets a year, and by the end of each job he was refreshed and keen to get back to dealing vinyl.

Working alone, Joe took the chance to think – *really* think – something everyone did but rarely thought about. People thinking but never thinking about thinking... Too much thinking could drive a person insane, but so could being alone all the time. He broke things up by tuning into the World Service, liked hearing about the places he had been and the places he hoped to one day go. He'd known about the reputation of the World Service before he first went off travelling, but the reality had struck when he heard those BBC voices on the other side of the planet.

The focus was so different from the mainstream, and it was one of the things that had made him realise that the centre of the world depended on where you were at a given time. There was always the pull of home, his roots which he could never escape, but it hadn't taken as long as he'd thought it would for his own axis to shift. He also liked the World Service for its impartiality, and while the journalists were precise in their use of the Queen's English, it was the lack of emotion that showed up the bias of other news programmes, and even within the BBC itself. Despite its formality, the World Service had a dreamlike quality, an eccentricity he hoped it would never lose.

There was a kitchen at the front of the church, and while it was small it had a kettle, fridge, cooker, toaster and microwave, as well as a table and two chairs. It was a short walk to a parade of shops for supplies, around ten minutes to the high street and two shopping malls with takeaways, cafes, diners, restaurants and an indoor market. If he left home early enough it was a twenty-minute drive in the morning, and as he was doing his own hours he could avoid the traffic on the way back as well. Joe was left alone and didn't have to worry about making a noise. There was nothing not to like.

The detached wooden building stood on one level in its own little garden halfway down an Edwardian terrace, and at first he'd thought the gap must be down to a bomb destroying some of the houses during the war, but the church dated back to the 1920s so there had to have been something else there before, maybe stables or a yard, or just a patch of green the owner had refused to sell to the builder. Joe's first impression of the inside of the church was that it was gloomy and smelled of damp and gas, but Lou's enthusiasm was infectious and she'd made him see the possibilities.

Lou was in her late twenties or early thirties and didn't look like the medium she'd turned out to be, but there again, he was going on the stereotype. She was always smartly turned out and he could see her running an office, an upbeat character who got people working hard through her positivity, just as she had Joe. He had never felt spooked in the church, not even when it was dark outside or the couple of times he'd heard voices, knowing it was people walking in the street. There was one evening, though, when he'd seen a face in a window, actually turning around to look and finding nobody there, but Joe didn't believe in ghosts. He had to admit that a shiver passed through him, a sensation he hadn't felt before, but the window was open to let the air circulate and the glass must have reflected a passerby, the angle playing tricks on his tired eyes. He respected Lou and how the church mixed memory and prophecy, offered comfort and hope. There was nothing wrong with that as far as he could see.

Joe stopped admiring his work and went into the kitchen, put the kettle on and made himself a mug of strong black coffee, holding his hands near the kettle to warm them, the only real negative the cold first thing. He had an electric heater for when it got too much, but hadn't used it yet, as once he was working he soon warmed up. Taking his loaf of bread out of the cupboard he stuck a couple of slices in the toaster, added thick layers of apricot jam from the fridge when they were ready, took his breakfast into the main room and put it down on the portable table he had set up for his paint and brushes, next to the propped-up *Aladdin Sane*, *Diamond Dogs* and *Station To Station*.

It had been difficult choosing which records to bring in, but these were three of his favourite Bowie albums and, as De La Soul rightly said, three *was* the magic number. It had been hard leaving *Hunky Dory*, *Ziggy Stardust*, *Low* and *Lodger* at home. Early Seventies or late Seventies? That had to be the greatest decade, a fantastic time to be young with hard rock, glam rock and punk rock among so much other brilliant music, while Bowie had left Los Angeles and moved to Berlin to reinvent himself, getting into Kraftwerk while Dr Dre was still at school.

He checked his phone as he ate his toast, found a message from Dave asking if he thought something was up with Chris. It was an odd text, but they didn't see much of each other these days so this quieter, more introverted Chris must be a surprise. He had his family and was strong in himself, but it was a tough job trying to police the sick side of the internet, and dealing with the perverts and nonces and dregs of society was bound to have an effect. There were also messages from his dad on the allotments and Luke in Brighton, and he answered these before finishing his breakfast and getting to work on the wall that had been plastered.

He arranged his ladder, opened the paint and gave it a good stir, went to the shelves and turned on his turntable, amp and speakers. Lou had this idea to install a decent but affordable sound system so the church could be rented out for talks and children's parties, things like that which would help raise money in the years to come. While it made sense, he could see a Spiritualist hall scaring the kids and freaking out some of the adults, although he supposed others would rent it for the novelty value. His thinking was that it would be handy to try the shelves with some equipment in place, test the acoustics, but really it was an excuse to play some of his records in this empty hall at the end of the Uxbridge Road.

The city end had the Sex Pistols and The Clash, the country end The Lurkers and The Ruts, and these were the four main punk bands as far as Joe was concerned, the beats of West London, big parts of his Herbert Hi-Fi. The chance was too good to miss, and he loved it when things fell into place like this, yesterday dedicated to *Never Mind The Bollocks*, *The Clash*, *God's Lonely Men* and *The Crack*, albums with tracks that still made his skin tingle. There was a quality about some music that meant the thrill remained however many times a favourite song was heard, an addiction that was right there in the repetitions of tune and chorus, the digressions into solos and verses, the joy of something returning to the beginning, and he kept coming back to these four bands and these four albums, thinking about his sampler.

Every day there were individuals out there making music, a tradition that would only end when humans died out, but birds chirped and dogs barked and horses brayed and the animals would keep the songs coming. In music he saw the perfect analogy for life itself, everything new coming out of something old, and that was why he was an analogue man, interested in hip hop but especially trip hop, the Bristol sound and Mo' Wax, how history and its repetitions were respected rather than dismissed. Everyone had similar going on, just it was buried inside their everyday lives, and this had to be the core of every person, the characters he had met, the friends he had made.

He had his family, his oldest friends, drinking friends, music friends. Some crossed over, others didn't. He had friends who didn't fall into any of these categories. There were the people he lived near, worked with and for, bought from and sold to, bumped into here and there and everywhere. There were those he'd met on the road when he was travelling who he regarded as some of his closest pals even though they'd only known each other briefly and would probably never see each other again. Despite this he had yet to meet his soulmate, a woman he could spend his life with, and he didn't expect to now, knew he was set in his ways, a loner who would remain alone.

He had asked Lou if he could play some records before he brought them in, didn't know if it was sacrilegious or insulting to the congregation, asking her if the spirits would be upset hearing the voices of Rotten, Strummer, Wall and Owen; the guitars of the Jones boys Steve and Mick, Glen Matlock, Pete Stride and Paul Fox; the drums of Cook, Topper, Esso and Ruffy; the bass of Simonon, Moore and Segs. Lou didn't know these names, but said it was fine, that one of the positives about Spiritualism was that it wasn't a stuffy religion, had always been about resistance. Mediums were respected for their abilities rather than their social standing, and she had explained its popularity in the aftermath of the First World War as a nation mourned the loss of a generation of young men slaughtered in France. The people were desperate, sick of the established Church, and Joe thought about that desperation and what it meant, but said nothing, preferred to listen.

He had started with *The Crack*, remembering how he'd seen The Ruts locally and in Central London at their peak, meeting Paul Fox in the early 2000s in The General Elliott, lucky enough to have had a drink with him on several occasions, this brilliant guitarist influenced by Hendrix living on the canal at the back of the pub. He thought about Malcolm Owen's voice living on in 'Something That I Said', 'SUS', 'Savage Circle'. He had seen the re-formed band in Islington shortly before Paul passed away with Henry Rollins on vocals, and later there had been the cremation, the drink after in the Crown And Treaty.

Joe had played *The Crack* several times, hearing it in new ways, more appreciative of what made the record so special after learning about Segs and Ruffy's tastes in music, their funk influences, the sort of stuff he'd hated as a kid when life was more tribal and violent, saw it as the sound of the Community Centre and Pied Horse, permed men in dungarees and Hawaiian shirts, and yet *The Crack* was a punk classic, as alive today as it had ever been. The records that had inspired The Ruts' rhythm section were some of the building blocks of trip hop, and Joe found that exciting.

He had followed *The Crack* with *God's Lonely Men,* and while The Lurkers had none of the sadness that surrounded The Ruts after Malcolm died, there was a longing in the music of Ickenham's finest. The title said it all, even if the sound was upbeat and the lyrics understated, a humour in songs such as 'I Don't Need To Tell Her' that he saw in The Ramones but not many other bands. The Lurkers dealt in outsiders. Not the rock 'n' roll cliché, but locals who worked and struggled to fit in, hesitant men who worried too much and lived in the shadows. Some were branded misfits for refusing to agree, for drinking too much, for living at home with their parents.

He thought about his best friend Smiles who had committed suicide, how Smiles had found his mum's body in the bath after she cut her wrists, eventually hanging himself from the loft outside the bathroom where she'd died. Joe wondered if Smiles's dad was still alive, knew his brother was about, but his link was Smiles's son Luke, and for a few seconds that time returned more vividly than he could ever remember it doing so before, his feelings as much as the events, and despite his scepticism he felt sure it was this Spiritualist church that was responsible.

Joe had put *The Clash* on his turntable next, more worn vinyl to follow *The Crack* and *God's Lonely Men*, felt the same excitement he had when he was a kid hearing the introduction to 'Janie Jones' for the first time. The amount of music The Clash had created in such a short space of time was incredible, and while they improved and mixed genres, had come up with the brilliant six-sided *Sandinista!*, it was their debut that had made its mark on Joe. It was the first of these records to be released, and from the thumping start of 'Janie Jones' he was changed. 'What's My Name' was his favourite song on the album, and while 'Police And Thieves' was maybe the easiest to sample, he was determined to do things differently.

The Sex Pistols had released one album and it was perfect. *Never Mind The Bollocks* was punk – job done. He didn't mind the *Swindle* stuff, but it was a film tie-in and there was no Johnny Rotten so it didn't really count. 'Pretty Vacant' and 'Holidays In The Sun' were the two best tracks, rightly released as singles, the introductions alone enough for Joe to build new songs around. 'New York' was another one he'd always liked, but there were no fillers, and as usual he wondered why the brilliant 'Satellite' was only ever a B-side on a single, but then so were 'Did You No Wrong' and 'I Wanna Be Me'.

Yesterday had been noisy and different to how he'd been working these past few weeks, and he'd gone home buzzing, his brain full of ideas, what he could do with these records, but this morning as he set off in the car he felt defeated before he'd even started, that this would be another dream that was going to fizzle out and go nowhere. He had to learn how to use the sampler properly and wasn't technically minded, didn't have the right sort of personality to really focus and not give up, and yet by the time he was parking outside the church his confidence had returned, the shelves an example of something he had conquered.

While Joe Martin was a punk, he was also a Bowie nut. It wasn't just the music but the changes in direction that put Bowie on another level, and again, over time Joe had grown to appreciate his records in new ways. These shifts were what he admired about Paul Weller as well as The Clash, bold moves and a refusal to be categorised. They had just gone out and started again, the creative drive more important than the money, the process as interesting as the result. If anyone was the king of the suburban and new-town sound it had to be Weller. Everyone loved Paul Weller. David Bowie as well. Joe took *Aladdin Sane* out of its sleeve, placed the record on his turntable and lowered the needle, climbed his ladder.

This second coat would finish things off nicely, brilliant white and the brilliance of non-drip technology, and when 'Watch That Man' played he was lifted up further as the Reverend Alabaster danced on his knees, taking care of the room as Joe heard about a mirror cracking in shame and bleeding bodies on a screen and that he must be in tune, the cover image of Bowie powdered and zapped by Ziggy Stardust lightning. The face of Jesus on a cross, the lad gone insane, this wall the one at the front of the church, losing himself in his brushstrokes and the final surface.

He was off the ladder as he listened to *Diamond Dogs*, the spoken 'Future Legend' at the start with its Hunger City and no more big wheels, the ending 'Chant Of The Ever Circling Skeletal Family', which could have been written for the church. How would he sample Bowie? It had already been done by the man himself, and he thought about William Burroughs and his own cut-outs, how Bowie had brought him into the mix, and that was something Joe should do, but he would use English voices, Londoners who were hardly known, forgotten, never known. He was sure he had sprayed DIAMOND DOGS RULE OK on an underpass wall when he was a mouthy teenager wanking his life away, repeating Bowie's delivery as he did it, although this could have been his imagination. He kept working until the side ended and it was time for a break.

– Hello, a voice said as the needle gently clicked, making him jump.

The idea that this was the church ghost may have been fleeting, yet it still popped into his head, and turning he saw a woman he recognised, remembered her sitting outside in a car when he came in early to show Lou the floorboards he'd found. This was the person paying for the work, and she was looking around the room in the same way he had been doing earlier. He wondered how long she'd been standing there, if she had heard him repeating David Bowie's lines and talking to himself.

– Is it okay if I come in? she asked. I'm Mrs Day. Maybe Louise told you about me?

– I saw you sitting in your car.

She looked embarrassed.

– I didn't want to get in the way. I don't want to now either.

– It's fine, everything's dry apart from that wall, Joe said, conscious of the turntable spinning. Lou said it was okay to play some records and test the acoustics, but mainly I wanted to make sure there was enough space on the shelves before I screwed the last bits in.

He lifted the arm off the record and turned the Technics off, thought about it and did the same with the mixer and speakers. Mrs Day was standing opposite him when he turned around again and he jumped for a second time.

– I was going to make a cup of tea, Joe said. Would you like one?

Lou had told him the person paying for the work wanted to remain anonymous and hadn't mentioned her by name, so he was surprised she was here now.

– Only if it's no bother. I don't want to be a nuisance.

– It's no bother.

She crouched down and ran a hand over the floorboards.

– I was so happy when Louise told me what you'd found.

She stayed there for a while feeling the grain, and he moved back to give her space. When she stood up again her eyes focused on the shelves and she walked over.

– They're beautiful. Louise said you're a craftsman, and she was right. You've done a great job.

Joe laughed because he was an amateur.

– I'm no craftsman, he said, wishing he hadn't laughed as she might think it was directed at her rather than himself.

She seemed to understand.

– You're being modest. The room looks fantastic.

Mrs Day walked along inspecting the shelves.

– There's a nice little library. Some of the books are quite old. Plus prayer books and Bibles. Pamphlets. And CDs. Music, talks, that sort of thing.

She went over to a window and he realised it had been raining.

– Milk and sugar? Joe asked. I've only got soya milk.

– That's fine. Milk and two sugars, please. I didn't come before as I didn't want to be one of those people who asks lots of questions when someone's trying to work. Sorry I sat in the car that time. I felt silly after. It was rude not to introduce myself then, but we can have a cup of tea together to celebrate.

– I'll make it and bring it in.

As the kettle boiled Joe looked to see if there were any biscuits left, but they were all gone. He felt a hand on his arm and jumped for the third time. Mrs Day was standing next to him. If Lou didn't fit the medium model, then he supposed this lady wasn't far off with her jet-black hair and chunky rings and this ability to move around quietly and read his mind.

– Don't worry about the biscuits.

Joe felt awkward with her being so close and a hand on his arm, now being removed as she smiled and stepped away. He had the idea that he was in the presence of a witch who could read his thoughts, which was a worry as she would know what he was thinking, but this was ridiculous, and he wondered where these barmy thoughts came from, and anyway, what would a witch be doing in a Christian church?

– Sorry. I've only got bread for toast.

– What have you got to put on the toast?

– Soya margarine, apricot jam. There's some miso. That's nice if you burn the toast and put it on quickly so it melts.

– Margarine and jam sounds good. Go on, spoil me.

Joe made the tea and was about to take the bag out.

– You can leave mine in. Thanks.

He handed Mrs Day her mug, put the toast in and did the business as she went back into the church proper. When it was ready he followed her and they sat talking, watched by David

Bowie as an insane lad and a diamond dog and a thin white duke, while next to Bowie God's lonely men lurked on the Battersea side of Wandsworth Bridge, and next to these Lurkers some clash city rockers flashed a Union flag, and next to The Clash a crowd gathered in Beatles-Bailey fashion, while next to The Ruts the Sex Pistols made their point with some black words on a yellow background. Mrs Day said that her first name was Helen and he could call her that if he liked, now that they were friends.

– My mum used to come here, Helen said. She loved this place, came every Sunday and to some of the evening services in the week, the daytime healing as well. I often brought her, but I'm not a Christian, not like she was. She passed over a year ago, and I kept coming along every now and then, then I was at a service and looking around at this room and it just seemed so run-down, so I talked to Louise and here we are.

Joe was surprised, had assumed she was a regular or a medium, but it made her donation an even nicer thing to be doing.

– Don't get me wrong, this place is full of spirits, just I'm not sure I want to be stuck in heaven forever doing nothing.

– Me neither, Joe agreed, but if the spirits can come here then they can't be stuck. I know what you mean, though.

– It would be more fun going to hell I think. Not the real hell, but a fun version where I could have a drink and a cigarette.

– That would be okay.

– This place is different to the mainstream churches I've been in. Not that I'm a big churchgoer, but it's personal here. Not just to me but everyone who comes, they're all looking for a part of their lives, the people they love on the other side. They want a direct link not some idiot preaching at them, saying they have to have faith. People need to know there's an afterlife. None of us wants to think we die and that's it, that we'll never see those we love again.

She took a bite of toast and stared at Joe.

– I can't believe that's what happens, he said, but I don't know what does. If we're reincarnated we wouldn't know who's who when we return, unless we follow our DNA somehow, end up being reborn in families. But what about karma?

– That's just another version of heaven and hell.

– There must be some sort of natural justice, though, don't you think?

– I suppose so, Helen said, but she didn't sound convinced. It might just be wishful thinking. Do you want to pay for your sins forever? I know I don't.

Helen talked until she finished her toast and tea, telling Joe about her husband and children, her mother and father, the sort of spirits that the mediums drew, the circle Helen had sat in briefly, the witches who were everywhere even though the women concerned wouldn't describe themselves as such, the difference between white and black magic, animal totems, stone circles, those people who didn't know or accept that they had died and how their souls drifted endlessly. Didn't Joe think that was sad? And she ended up saying that *Ziggy Stardust And The Spiders From Mars* was her favourite Bowie album, that she had seen his show at Hammersmith Odeon when he killed Ziggy off. She was young, twelve or thirteen, had felt terrible and cried her eyes out, but needn't have worried.

– Thanks for the tea and toast, Helen said. Give me your plate and I'll wash up. I better be going as I'm meant to be babysitting later.

– I'll do them, don't worry, he said, standing up.

– Are you sure?

– I like washing up.

– Seriously?

– Seriously. It's like finishing the job, leaving everything neat and tidy.

– Thanks. I'll see you again. I need some shelves made if you're interested, but you'll come to a service here, won't you? I'll give you a call if that's okay, get your number from Louise. I love what you've done.

Helen left and Joe cleaned up, didn't know what he thought about the details of an afterlife, and while he was interested in Buddhism as a philosophy, could accept the teaching that all life was suffering due to human attachment to things that were impermanent, the belief that there wasn't even a self wasn't what he wanted to hear. Hinduism had a lighter take on this, but again, he wanted his soul to survive and remain aware of who he was and who he had been. As a secular Christian raised in the West he needed some sort of heaven.

Returning to work, he paused in the doorway again, scanned the room and imagined it differently, no longer empty but full of spirits, but only when a medium was present. He tried to picture the souls who would respond, and if he was receiving a message it would be from one of his grandparents or maybe Smiles, but that would be hard, he didn't know how it worked with suicides, or stillborn babies like his twin brother, or the murdered Gary Wells. That term was stark and brutal like the reality, and Joe drove those last two spirits out of his mind, put *Station To Station* on, losing himself in the chugging start.

If he was going to make his own songs he had to draw on his life, old enough not to have to raid his parents' records, while the vinyl he bought to sample had to connect. He had more than enough music and stories, references that would make whatever he did personal, and he was definitely chopping up those albums he'd played yesterday, his goal an Uxbridge Road soundtrack, and as he worked he was struck by how much his view of Spiritualists and this church had changed, as if the people and building had been broken down and reassembled in his mind.

Later, when he was polishing the pews before moving them back in from the hallway, he was listening to 'We Are The Dead' and the rest of *Diamond Dogs* again, thinking how the song didn't really fit how he felt. This place was positive, rooted in the present and not the past as he'd assumed, imagined it as a recording studio with a classic console at its heart, an oddball house of psalms and versions where punk met trip hop and the Army bands of 1918 could hear the pound of their marching drums, King Tubby talking through Lou as Shadow and Tricky sat in the congregation with members of the Sex Pistols, Clash, Lurkers and Ruts, Bowie standing at the back with Mrs Helen Day, and as Joe rubbed and sweated he knew he'd have to come in again tomorrow but didn't mind, wanted everyone to be happy with a job well done.

We sit on top of the hill... watching the snow fall... loving the way it shimmies... dances... just the two of us... me and my daughter... listening to the silence... while down below us the fields stretch out in all their patchwork glory... watercolour greens running into the horizon... no black line where earth meets heaven... and we are doing our best to stay warm... wrapped up tight in our favourite coats and scarves and hats... two pairs of socks... new shoes with no holes in the soles... mittens and gloves... we can't let our fingers freeze and snap off... mustn't lose our toes... and we have come here in the car... singing songs... a special road that is very straight and very long... we can see our hill in the distance... at the end of the strip... a church with a gold ball on the tower... catching the sunlight... the glow dull compared to summer... but every season has its beauty... the sphere on the skyline... gold leaf... a landmark... spectacle... embers in a wooden belly... I don't tell my little girl about the lords who gathered there... once upon a time... the legend says they saw the Devil... she will worry about demons... monsters... I hate the thought of her being scared... don't mention the mausoleum either... the caves... chalk and flint... she's excited enough... this adventure... travelling on our perfect highway... the road plays its part... deliberately fashioned... easy driving... leaving it halfway early would be disrespectful... my speed is modest... means we reach the foot of the hill safely... the slope and its trees hiding the church... my daughter wants to know where it's gone... tugs at her seat belt... sits back when I reassure her... we'll see it soon... starting up the lane to the summit... slowly... concentrating hard... low-hanging branches... the threat of ice... we will slide sideways... over to the right... the higher we are the further the fall... snowflakes... glitches in a scan... signs of a stroke... my mother... lights up ahead... another car moving fast... I slow right down... this narrow lane... bent and twisting... thorns scratch the doors... blood through skin... engine groaning...

I can't see the driver's face as he passes... a child sings but it's not my little girl's voice... I stop... stall... red lights in my mirrors... the other car... vanishes... I put the gear stick in neutral... turn the key... right foot down... left foot up... listen for the purr... confidence soaring with the perfect start... another minute... coming out of the trees and into the light... the roof of the world... and we are alone... the universe is ours... transparent... eternal... arching over our heads... my daughter claps her hands... celestial swirls in a frozen sky... greys and whites and blues... church tower... gold ball... I park and our focus changes to the view in front of us... my little girl undoes her belt... kneels on the seat... palms on the dash... the edge of the hill... a slope not a cliff... but it is dangerous and my tummy turns... she is young... brave... naive... I make sure she's buttoned up... check the handbrake three times... scared the car will roll forward... scared I won't know the way home... scared I am lost... muddled... forgetful... but the fear passes as I hurry around to my daughter's side and open the door... in case she jumps out... wanders... she is a clever girl... knows to wait for her mummy... who loves her like nobody else ever could... apart from Daddy... Charlie loves her... we both do... I hold her hand... adjust my grip so it is firm... we walk forward... sit on a log and look across the fields... again... back where we started... my hand empty... panicking... want to scream... but she is still here... I wasn't concentrating... can't make mistakes... this is my child... if anything happened... she slips her mitten into my glove... we squeeze at the same time... she leans against me and I swap hands... put my left arm around her shoulders... reach across with my right... we sit like this for five minutes... until the snow falls faster... thickens... settles on the grass... a breeze... fields turning white... we don't speak... enjoy this time together... but the temperature keeps dropping and we shiver... stand up... return to the car... stop for a second moment to look at the church... gold ball black... back in our pod I turn on the engine... the heater... there is hot soup... sandwiches... we have time... I think... it would be a shame not to enjoy our picnic... the food I have made... opening the flask... cream of tomato... the snow stops... starts... I am sure we have time... eating our sandwiches... crisps... the sun sinking... light fading... darkness dropping... we can't linger any longer... have to leave... you can eat while I drive... preparing... ready for lift-off... but my daughter is gone... no... she is right here... she seems so faint... flickering for dear life... what's wrong Mummy... I look upset... no... I am happy... and we are the only people on top of the hill... mother and daughter... Mum reversing... driving forward... back down the lane... we mustn't slide... maybe the other car is waiting... the man with no face... mustn't panic... mustn't rush... helter skelter... we reach the bottom... returning to that very straight and very long road that will take us home... away from the church and its gold ball turned black... singing as we go... happy as can be... but I can't stop thinking about what will happen to the child sitting next to me... my darling daughter... my lovely little girl... in the years to come –

It was as if Lady Penelope had coaxed Joe into one of her *Thunderbirds* scenes, mistaking him for her puppet chauffeur Parker, a servant she could boss about, but he didn't fancy the role and was thinking about packing up his records and leaving, moving on and finding O'Mara. It was the condescending tone as much as what Her Ladyship was doing and saying that had given him the hump. He would forget the money, the hour spent hanging around as she lowered and raised the turntable needle, releasing short bursts of sound, searching for faults, repeatedly inspecting the sleeves. She'd started in on the agreed price five minutes after he arrived, openly haggling when he had enough and pulled her up. The real Lady Penelope was better than this. He was dealing with an imposter who pranced out of the room and left him alone with Shosta-kovich's *Leningrad*.

The house was the biggest he had ever been inside apart from those belonging to the National Trust, and he'd never met a person like Penny before. He saw and heard her daily on the news, in TV series and films, but not in the flesh. She was loaded, and what difference did twenty or thirty pounds make? The price was a fair one for ten Shostakovich albums in excellent condition, six with covers that were works of art in their own right, but he guessed this was how the rich stayed rich. They weren't shy about spending on high-end goods for themselves, her attempts at bargaining more about the value she placed on him and what he did for a living, but his time was precious and worth more than she imagined. He had places to be and people to see, and so maybe he should just accept that last offer and take the pink Rolls to make up the difference, leave his Skoda behind to even things out.

He doubted she'd see this as a fair trade, but there again she could be an old-banger fanatic, the sort who left her house late at night and headed into the suburbs and new towns searching for the ultimate clapped-out motor, taking her time choosing the right one for Parker to break in to so she could drive it home. The standalone garage outside was probably full of scrapyard bargains, breaker parts stacked high, a luxury lock-up where she could put on a boiler suit and turn into the superhero Petrolhead P, dismantling and rebuilding engines, tuning and respraying and turning dead cars into living classics. Drew from *Salvage Hunters* would turn up with a camera crew and beg to be shown around, only to find she preferred *Iron Restoration* and American imports and be turned away.

The Roller would look nice parked next to Charlie Boy's pink Cadillac, if only Joe's mate from those Satellite nights hadn't been forced to sell his prized Yankee to pay the bills, and while Joe loved a customised car and the effort that went into it he was happy driving his Skoda around, enjoyed sticking its nose into traffic and hearing the screech of brakes, a trick he reserved for the flashiest owners showing off their thirty-grand toys, these mainly men terrified of the smallest scratch while he didn't give a toss if he had a prang and added to his collection of dents.

Joe knew Lady Penelope's alternative lifestyle was unlikely, that he had to get back into the real world, instead saw himself hand-cuffed at the side of the Western Avenue in Parker's stolen uniform, marionette strings glistening as a police spotlight picked him out, an LAPD helicopter hovering overhead as he starred in the latest rap video. He also knew that it was the recently bought *Gerry Anderson Presents: Thunderbirds & Captain Scarlet* album shaping his thoughts, along with *No Strings Attached* and its 'Parker, Well Done' track which he'd had for ages and only just rediscovered in a box of ten-inch vinyl. He preferred *Gerry Anderson Presents* for the narration, but 'Well Done' did make him smile.

There were some interesting overlaps between the Lady Penelope recordings, similar tales built around her relationship with Parker and the importance of the Rolls – upper- and working-class characters, mistress and servant, exaggerated accents and roles undercut by a mutual respect and subtle humour. Class was up front in so many of those old TV programmes and films, whether the root of the comedy or something more critical of a snobbery that was seen as outdated and ridiculous at the time yet barely touched on today, as if the class system had suddenly been erased.

The M4 and London Airport were mentioned, and he'd gone back to listen again as Parker explained that he had lubricated the canon and polished the gun, wondering if the ex-con was servicing Penny on the sly. It was said posh birds liked a bit of rough, a serious length off one of the plebs, but Joe knew this was wishful thinking by deluded shaggers such as David Barrows, that the *Thunderbirds* set-up was purely professional. Joe's Lady P had the same blonde hair, bone structure, glowing skin and mannerisms as the original, but a sharper edge than the puppet version, lacked the good manners of the better-bred marionette.

His thoughts shifted to his sampler and how he could use these records, the Barry Grey Orchestra themes an obvious place to start, and then there were the effects – machine-guns on the Rolls, tyres skidding across a motorway surface, the crashing of a car driven by the Hood or another enemy agent. He would add voices, especially Parker's – 'You rang, my lady?' 'Home, my lady?' 'Yes, my lady'– and Lady Penelope's brilliant, enthusiastic 'Parker, well done'. That was the right tone. Respect for a task completed by a working man. A pat on the head. Joe was grinning as his strop faded.

As well as the *Thunderbirds* theme he had *Captain Scarlet*, *Stingray* and *Joe 90* to investigate, and he would definitely be using the 'this is the voice of the Mysterons' line from the first of these. That Supermarionation series from the 1960s was pretty special, the fact the programmes had been filmed locally, created by Gerry and Sylvia Anderson and shot on the Slough Trading Estate, adding to the attraction. Electronic creations with a solenoid to connect their lips to the dialogue, he realised he didn't know who spoke for Lady Penelope and Parker, but would find out.

He had told his Lady Penelope – Alex – that she was being rude and talking down to him, that the price was fixed, and the change was instant. She offered him a cup of tea, said she was going to have one herself, explaining that the albums were a present for her husband, that the hi-fi system belonged to him and she wasn't used to vinyl. Maybe she was being over-fussy, and if so she apologised, but if she could just check the last one again they could proceed. The money was waiting for him in an envelope upstairs. The full amount in cash as they had agreed. Lady P left the room before Joe could reply, leaving him alone with a system based around the McIntosh turntable, a piece of kit that on its own would have cost thousands.

He tried to lose himself in the music, aware of the irony of listening to 'Symphony Number 7' in this grand house on a top-end system, a work rooted in communist Russia and the siege of Leningrad, the era of revolution and utopian slaughter, the execution of the wealthy and the betrayal of the masses by a new leader. Being here was an experience and an education, the chance to see how the controllers lived, and he thought about the Spirit-ualist church, how brilliant it was to have space, a chance to play his albums in a big empty room, his boundaries extended, a one-off that was routine here. He should have brought the Pistols, Clash, Lurkers and Ruts along and treated Lady Penelope, seeing as he was in Ealing and had come down the Uxbridge Road via a curry in Southall.

Shostakovich took him back to his journey on the Trans-Siberian Express and how the scale of Siberia and the weight of

Moscow had struck him at the time. People here seemed to have forgotten what the Russians had been through, the decades of communist rule only interrupted by a fascist invasion. If he ever went to Russia again he would try to visit Leningrad Cemetery, where half a million victims of the siege were buried. Knowing something about the history added so many extra layers to the music, and while that was true of any recording this one was on a different level. He didn't know much about classical music but wanted to learn.

Penelope wasn't a real Lady, but she was posh enough and had that air about her, the superiority of those who had always known privilege, believed it made them morally and intellectually better than the rest of the population. It didn't matter that their good lives were inherited rather than earned, the sense of entitlement too deep-rooted, the preferential treatment meaning they ended up in positions of power which many of them couldn't handle. The goal of a genuine meritocracy felt as if it was part of an imaginary past, gently dismissed through deflection and distraction, fading as the plebs bailed out the bankers, everyone in it together, a Big Society moving forward.

He didn't know what Alex and her husband did for a living, but seeing that photo of His Lordship on a nearby table meant Joe had him down as one more stuck-up cunT. There again, the man might be rich but decent like Tony Benn, say, and he knew he was dismissing someone without ever having met them, which was wrong. If Alex was buying vinyl for his birthday he had to have something about him, and there must be specialist record dealers around, their own kind charging extra for some of that special Eton brain power, so maybe P wasn't as stuck up as he thought. More Joanna Lumley than Lady Penelope, posh but nice, out there campaigning for the Gurkhas, demanding fair treatment and settlement rights.

The record ended, and he felt the silence as if it was a weight, stood up to turn the vinyl over as Lady Penelope returned.

– I can do that, she said.

Alex went to the McIntosh and removed the album, turned the

system off and put *Leningrad* back in its sleeve. She turned and walked over to Joe.

– Here is the amount we agreed, she continued, handing him the envelope she had brought down from upstairs. Thank you for delivering them and for your patience. My husband will be thrilled. Now, I must press on. I have a dinner this evening and much to do before then.

The expressionless face and dismissive eyes were fixed in Joe's mind as he drove away from the house. He had been put back in his place, instantly forgotten like one more tradesman, but it was part of the experience and he was having fun imagining himself as Parker, repeating 'yes, my lady' over and over as he tried to mimic the chauffeur's voice. His marionette track would have something extra about it as he moved from his Parker impression to Eminem, asking the real Lady Penelope to please stand up, please stand up. In truth, once he had been shown in and met the woman he hadn't expected much, but had come away with a headful of ideas that spiralled and expanded as he drove.

It took Joe half an hour to reach O'Mara, the difference between P-Brain's street in Ealing and this one in North Acton dramatic. He parked near a pub, looked in through the window as he passed and saw the usual suspects hard at it, continued towards the flats, found the right entrance and pushed the relevant buzzer, heard a muffled voice and identified himself. The door unlocked and he was inside, walked up to the second floor, knocking on a door left slightly ajar.

– Come in, a woman said.

She was waiting at the other end of a dark hall, no more than an outline.

– I'm here to see O'Mara, he said.

– You've found me. I'm O'Mara.

He'd expected a man, had never thought of a woman only using her surname, and he followed her into the living room and the light. She was forty or thereabouts, roughly the same age as Lady Penelope, but that was it as far as the similarities went.

– Would you like a cup of tea?

– Thanks, Joe replied, realising that Lady P hadn't brought him his drink. Black no sugar, please.

– Did you find the place okay?

– Easy enough. I parked near the pub.

– The albums are on the floor by the window if you want to start looking.

Joe went over and picked up an armful, brought them over to the coffee table and sat down on the sofa. Sometimes he was in and out, other times he was invited to have a drink and hear about the records, where they came from and what they meant.

– I'll make the tea, O'Mara said as she went into the kitchen.

Joe started going through albums by Jelly Roll Morton, Cow Cow Davenport, Brownie McGhee and Sonny Terry – together and solo. Joe loved their 'Stranger Blues', and there was that line from '1977' by The Clash, on the flip side of 'White Riot', where it warned 'danger stranger', telling the outsider or maybe a local he had better paint his face. Those two were made for each other, an easy blending as McGhee and Terry met Strummer and Jones.

– Did you say no milk? O'Mara called.

– No milk, no sugar. Thanks.

All of these records would sell for decent money if they were in good condition. Going on the scuffed covers they had been well played, but taking them out of their sleeves it was clear the woman's dad had looked after his vinyl.

– Here you are, O'Mara said, putting his tea on the table. Do you want some biscuits?

– I'm okay, thanks.

– Are you sure? It's no trouble. I only have to open the packet.

– I don't eat anything with dairy in it. Sorry.

– They're vegan. I can't eat dairy.

– Go on then.

– Do you want me to make you a sandwich? I don't mind.

– No, really, it's fine. I had a curry earlier. A biscuit would be nice. Thanks.

There were albums by Bessie Smith, Leadbelly and Bill Monroe, Joe sure O'Mara's dad would have compared 'Black Girl' and 'In

The Pines', the reason the bluegrass man from the Appalachians was next to the blues man off a Louisiana plantation. Huddie William Ledbetter meets William Smith Monroe. Joe thought Nirvana's acoustic version of the song with the cello was pretty special as well.

– In the pines, in the pines, where the sun never shines... he mumbled to himself, with O'Mara back in the kitchen.

– What did you say?

– I was talking to myself. Words from a song.

– Did you answer?

– I'm not sure. The voice sounded different. A lot deeper.

She came into the room with the biscuits and a couple of plates, sat down and opened the packet and held it out to Joe.

– Help yourself, she said. Go on, don't be shy.

He took three and put them on his plate, sipped his tea, picked one up and took a bite. They had a sharp lemony tang about them and were very nice. He told her so.

– Special offer. So what do you think about the records?

– You've got some great stuff here.

– There's lots more, but I want to play them all first, make a list and remember my favourites. I'm starting with Dad's blues albums. He loved the blues. Country and western as well. Soul. He had good taste.

– He did, Joe agreed.

– I miss him. We all do.

She lowered her head and was silent, while he tried to think of the right thing to say.

– I'm Joe, by the way. Joe Martin.

– I know. Hello, Joe.

He waited for her to tell him her first name, but instead she leaned forward and offered a hand, which he shook, feeling the bones and realising how gaunt and tired she looked, guessed her dad wasn't long dead and it was to be expected, but then he remembered she'd said in her email that he had passed away three years ago. Maybe selling his records was too much for her, although it could have been anything, work or a relationship, everyone trying to earn a crust, wanting to be loved. He returned to the albums – Sonny Boy Williamson, Memphis Slim, Montana Taylor.

– My brother's got a load of cassettes he wants to sell, O'Mara said eventually. Early acid house, jungle, hardcore, drum 'n' bass. He used to make his own mixes. They're in the loft at our mum's. He asked if you'd be interested.

– I might be. I couldn't really sell them on, but maybe for myself. I'd need to have a listen and a think. They won't be worth much, though.

– People don't play tapes these days.

– I've been thinking about that. Let me know when he's got them down.

They drank their tea and talked for an hour as Joe checked all the records, O'Mara pleased with the generous price he offered, promising to give him first refusal on the rest of her dad's collection if she went ahead with selling them, and as he lugged forty-three albums back to his car he glanced in the pub again and saw the same men in the same positions and wished he knew them and could walk in and say hello and have a pint, but even if it had been Dave and Chris sitting there he'd have had to press on, had two more stops and was running late.

From North Acton he joined the Western Avenue, an arterial road he had been up and down countless times, a quick route into Soho and Camden when he was a kid, and while the roundabouts had been removed and the journey was smoother the speed limits drove him mad, especially coming into London. It was seventy on the M40, sixty from there to the other side of the RAF base and Polish War Memorial, fifty until well before Hanger Lane, then forty to the Westway and beyond. Central London took it down to thirty, but at least he was heading out now, picking up speed rather than losing it, and while it was busy the traffic was flowing.

He came off at the start of the motorway, circled back under it onto the Oxford Road, took the first turn towards Denham village but only needed the first street on his right, an estate of semi-detached council houses with long gardens that would only be built for the private sector these days. He found the address and rang the doorbell.

– You're late, the old man who opened the door barked.

His name was Norman Smith, and despite the ancient face he was fit and lean.

– We said between five and seven.

– What time is it now?

– A quarter to seven.

– You're cutting it fine.

– Fifteen minutes to spare.

– Are you trying to be funny?

– No. What do you mean? No, I wasn't.

– Take your shoes off.

Joe was tempted to salute, but resisted.

– You can sit on that stool over there while you undo your laces. You're not wearing slip-ons are you? I can't stand slip-on shoes. At least not on a man. And I hope your socks are clean.

– Fresh on this morning.

– I change mine twice a day.

Joe followed Norman into the front room.

– I suppose you want some of this cider?

He pointed to a table covered in bottles.

– I'm driving, but I'll have a taste.

– Will you now. I make it myself. Been brewing my own cider for sixty-five years with a gap for the war and one spring when I was busy shagging a tinker girl. Never too old to go scrumping. Never too old for nookie. Whoever invented Viagra deserves a medal. Same goes for the internet and all those porn sites.

Joe didn't know what to say. This bloke had to be well over eighty.

– I'll be ninety-two next birthday, he said.

Joe looked around the room and was surprised to see an iMac on a glass desk, more so by the frozen image on the screen, the contorted face of a woman with a cock in her mouth, shocked that Norman hadn't tried to hide it and was instead laughing at the expression on his visitor's face.

– You should see what happens next.

– It's not hard to guess.

– Right, here are the records.

They were 78s.

– These are 78s, Joe said.

– Of course they are. Look, Fats Waller.

This was meant to be a quick stop, a handful of records not worth much but some of them interesting to crate-digger Joe.

– Sorry, but I can't use these.

– Why not?

– My turntable can't play them. I can't sell them either. There's very few turntables around that they'll work on.

– I need the money, son.

Norman looked as if he was about to start crying and Joe felt terrible, then thought about the iMac and how much they cost. It was an easy mistake to make and more his fault than Norman's, plus twenty pounds wasn't much.

– Tell you what, throw in a couple of bottles of that cider and I'll give you the twenty quid.

Norman perked up.

– Make it thirty and I'll give you ten bottles. It's a bargain, believe me. Here, have a taste.

There was a mantelpiece and Joe looked at the photos as Norman went into the kitchen and opened a bottle from the fridge. One stood out, Norman in a uniform standing next to a Daimler.

– Is that a chauffeur's uniform? Joe asked when his host returned and handed over a small glass of the cider.

– What are you talking about?

– In the photo. A chauffeur's uniform.

– That was my sixth life.

Joe drank the cider. It was refreshing but strong.

– It's the same for everyone. Seven lives. First I was a baby and a child. I like to lump those two together. Is that okay?

– Fine by me.

Norman's delivery changed, became more formal, as if he was giving a guided tour, which Joe supposed he was in a way.

– I was born in the village in 1923. My father was a farm labourer, illiterate until the day he died, but a good man who did his best. My mother was religious and sang in the church choir, and while I shouldn't really say so in case she's listening, she didn't have the voice of an angel, if you know what I mean. Everyone loved Mum, though, as she was great fun to be around. Dad said little. He'd been on the Somme and never spoke about it of course. There were five of us children and we had happy lives.

Norman stopped and stared at Joe, making sure that he was listening.

– My second life was between the ages of five and eleven. Those years were also good from what I can remember. I loved going to school as I wanted to learn to read, enjoyed playing in the fields and climbing trees. My third life was as a teenager, and I'm sure you know what that's like, becoming interested in girls and having those first erections and wanking like there was no tomorrow. Fourth was the war and I served in the Army. That changed me, but it changes everyone, and I came out of it in much better shape that my father did.

– My fifth life was post-demob, labouring until I got into bricklaying through a mate. That meant better money and I was enjoying life again. My sixth life is in that photo you were looking at just now. It started the day I was officially employed as a chauffeur for the Wesley family and it lasted for twenty-three years, with another ten as an odd-job man for their children when it was decided I was too old to drive. They didn't have to do that, but they were very good to me.

Norman paused, and Joe urged him on.

– They were filming in the village, a series called *The Persuaders!* with Roger Moore and Tony Curtis. Well, I went down to have a look and later, when I was walking home, I saw that Daimler in the photo broken down. The bonnet was up and Mrs Wesley was arguing with my predecessor, a miserable git who had his jacket off as he tried to fix the problem. I knew a bit about engines and soon got it going, and before I knew it I was being invited to the house and Mrs Wesley wanted to know about my work record and where

I had served during the war, and she offered me the job of being her new chauffeur on the spot as she disliked the other chap. I couldn't believe my luck as the money was better again than I was earning and it was a much easier job. Do you know what I said when she asked me if I would come and work for her?

– Yes, my lady?

– She wasn't a lady as such, but yes, I accepted the job.

Joe was trying not to laugh.

– What's so funny? You don't think she made me her chauffeur, is that it?

– I do. I was just thinking about another chauffeur I know.

– Another chauffeur? What's his name?

– Parker.

– Parker? What's his first name?

Joe couldn't speak and Norman seemed perplexed, but he continued.

– They were the best years of my life. I was looking after Mrs Wesley, although on occasion I drove her husband, and I loved that car. Part of my job was keeping it clean as well as mechanically sound. Not the big stuff, but oil changes and suchlike. Honestly, the pride I felt when we were out was incredible. They were happy times.

He walked over and picked up the photo.

– She was very kind to me, Mrs Wesley. A beautiful lady as you can see. She was a fascist, mind. Loved Mussolini. The way he'd died upset her, and I didn't like to tell her about the Italians in the war. Classy, though. Loved sucking cock.

Joe was startled and let it show.

– Do you think the rich don't have needs? Are you trying to be funny? She sucked my cock for most of those twenty-three years. Not every day of course, but on and off as the whim took her, although once there was a gap of six months, which was a concern. I didn't know when she would ask, but I can tell you, I was never late for work.

Norman was smiling as he reminisced, suddenly reflective and serious once more.

– She had a fetish for uniforms, you see, but said the officer class left her cold. I was handsome and in good shape and she was smitten. It was the manual work I had been doing. Fit as a fiddle. She asked me to pull her hair sometimes, although that was rare. She spat, never swallowed, used a lace hanky and apologised, would never let me fuck or even finger her, but I wasn't complaining. I tell a lie, though, as she was always generous when it came to my Christmas bonus.

Joe felt as if he had been tugged back into one of Lady Penelope's *Thunderbirds* scenes, and it definitely wasn't the marionette original, not even the Ealing remake of earlier today, but a third porn version starring Norman Smith, directed by Norman Smith, produced by Norman Smith.

– This is my seventh life, making cider. It's quiet this time of year, obviously, but things will start happening soon. Happy days. Right, I can't be nattering with you all night, but it has been nice meeting you and I hope you enjoy listening to my records and drinking my cider. There's all these bottles to get through, so just give me a call if you need restocking. I can't do better than that, can I?

Joe drove away telling himself that it was a wind-up, the same wishful thinking he'd heard from Dave and others, but he wasn't sure, and for some reason it bothered him, so instead of returning to the motorway and circling back around he took the longer but quieter route, down into the village past the old farm cottages where he imagined Norman growing up, over the bridge by the weir and past mucky farms cleaned and converted and sold for sums no local could ever afford, into the main street with its church and Domesday Book tallies, a long row of tumbledown brick cottages, the small green, a tiny bridge over a tiny stream, the pond to his left.

When he reached the North Orbital he turned left and at the lights did a right up the hill to Tatling End where he stopped to pick up two record boxes left inside a recycling bin belonging to one of the secondhand car lots, payment already made through PayPal. Once he had these in the car, Joe rolled his seat back and turned the light on, opened the blue box first and flicked through the singles to make sure they contained what he'd bought, a nice selection of Britpop 45s including some hard-to-find Oasis and Blur plus Nirvana, REM and various other American bands. The red box included earlier indie from the likes of The Fall, Bauhaus and Theatre Of Hate.

The road was deserted when left the dealership, a minute later turning into the darkness of the country lanes that would lead him back to Slough. He travelled in silence, and when he crossed the motorway it was like a vision from another century, but this was gone inside two seconds and he was back in a parallel, timeless land that survived between the roads and towns, old paths barely visible when the black closed in. He slowed for the forge at the bottom of the hill, the water higher than usual, and when he rose up again he stopped at the junction facing the woods, avoided Iver Heath where he could join the dual carriageway, cutting through more lanes and not seeing a single car, finally on the road that led to the hospital, right past the crematorium, into the houses, nearing his lock-up. It was almost eight, and he wondered what Dave was doing.

– Where are you? Dave asked when he answered his phone.

– On my way to the lock-up to drop some records off, then I'm getting some food and going home to try this cider I've just bought. Shall I pick you up?

– You'll be doing me a favour. Things are tense here. What are you getting to eat?

– Samosas and chips.

– Horrible, greasy English muck. What about a nice bit of tapas? Some antipasti? Anyway, I've already eaten. Give me a shout when you're done at the lock-up.

Joe saluted and continued, thinking about Norman, O'Mara and Lady Penelope, the tracks they suggested, the titles that might suit them – *Norman's Daimler Breakdown, Stranger Dangers, Big Society* – but he was sure he could do better than that as the right name was essential, meant everything else would fall into place.

*

We stand in the middle of the bridge... staring into the water...
loving the way it shimmers... dances... just the two of us... me and
my son... listening to the silence... and when the wind blows it
mixes our reflections with those of the clouds... blue and white
oils... slivers of pink... it is impossible to see where the water begins
and where it ends... the depths and the heights... we are doing our
best... trying to stay warm... wrapped up tight... favourite coats
and scarves and hats... two pairs of socks each... new shoes with no
holes in the soles... gloves and mittens... we can't let our fingers
freeze and snap off... mustn't lose our toes... and we have come here
in the car... singing songs... stopping in a lay-by on a busy road...
leave it for the fields... a track through rough pasture... hooves and
paws marked in the mud... before long we are flanked by hedges...
towering hawthorn... wings flapping and a twig breaking... these
are the only sounds as the world is closed out... sun shaded... crows
watching... a mouse climbing... and when we come out the other
side we are in a remote land... another dimension that time
forgets... reaching the towpath... following the water... and I hold
my son's hand tight in case he slips... move around so I am next to
the canal... my life for his life... sun leaking purple... grey clouds
black... a rare light... more fields... these are frozen... stiff fairy
mounds... anthills... rabbit burrows and foxholes... the smell of
manure... horses in the distance... one two three... scrunching...
stone and ice... a wall of trees... and there it is... up ahead... my son
pointing at the white bridge... hazy visions... flaking...
humpbacked... my father brought me here when I was small... my
son knows this... he is as excited as me... we move faster...
concentrating... ever so careful... reach the bridge... walk up the
arc... stop in the centre and lean on the wall... but my little boy is
too short... he stands on his toes and still can't see... wants me to
lift him up... too dangerous... but he keeps asking and I can't
resist... can't say no... wrapping my arms around his waist and
heaving... we are together... laughing... staring into the water...
again... mesmerised by its glassy stillness... how it mirrors the sky...
our faces... ripples... a fish... big and brown... I don't know what
sort... my son keeps slipping... asks me please... can he sit on the

wall... a bad mum... useless... the terror when he falls... when I imagine him falling... he is safe... my arms are locked... the cold tightens and it tries to snow... fluffy specs that drift and hover and melt... we stay like this for several minutes... movement... a barge on the horizon... no black line... earth and heaven... this world and that... it is coming towards us... growing... smoke from a chimney... my son waves and the woman steering waves back... engine chugging... there is a man behind her... he raises a hand... and as the barge is about to pass our bridge the captain rings a bell... I lift my son down and we hurry to the other side... I lift him up again... the barge moves away... shrinking... and my son asks if we can live on a boat like that one day... he wants to have adventures... I hope he never leaves me... never goes away... joins an army... gets into trouble like so many boys do... never gets knocked down... beaten or stabbed or murdered... we watch the barge until it is a dot... gone... and I realise we are shivering... temperature crashing... clouds swollen and ready to burst... closing out the sun... darkness is coming and we need to leave... drink soup... eat sandwiches... no time now... panicking... is it this way or that... I am disorientated... my son knows... leads me off the bridge as the wind picks up and shakes the trees across the fields... rabbit ears pinned back... horses shuffling... we retrace our steps... down the towpath... and I am scared we'll be blown over... slip and fall... nobody to help us... bramble cuts... blackberry bones... inside the hedges... mustn't get lost... stuck in a maze... thunder... we reach the pasture and follow the track... start to run... a child's strides... footprints in the mud... I can hear the traffic... we will be back soon... climbing the steps to the lay-by... we get into the car... just in time... lightning and thunder... rain... fast and heavy... and I remind myself that it is fantastic to be alive... to experience these miracles... turn on the engine... the heater... and we drink our soup... cream of mushroom... eat our sandwiches... crisps... safe in our cocoon... when the rain eases... stops... we head for home... singing songs as we go... nursery rhymes... and I fight to keep these feelings of joy... standing on the white bridge with my father and my son... the hibernating land... thunder and lightning... the rain that feeds the

*earth... a barge on water... but I can't stop thinking about what will
happen to the child sitting next to me... my darling son... my lovely
little boy... in the years to come –*

Ray pulled up outside the hotel and lowered the volume on an
Infa-Riot classic. He looked around for his fare as an Uber came
up behind him, a Mercedes with a Somali or something driving.
The car must have cost a bomb and he couldn't work out the eco-
nomics involved. If the drivers took on huge loans or there was a
centralised plan to put every other cab company out of business.
He had asked some of the lads at work, but while everyone had a
theory nobody knew. That seemed to be the way the world was
going. Endless facts and figures. Information on tap twenty-four
hours a day. But fewer and fewer people had a clue what was true
and what was not. Himself included.

Despite Uber and the Asian firms, Estuary Cars was holding its
own, even if they'd had to drop their prices to compete. They had
their regulars, customers who knew and trusted the drivers, with
one or two refusing to give their money to Muslims, but that didn't
mean Estuary could ignore the realities. Cheaper prices for the
punters meant lower wages for the workers, which normally led to
higher profits for the bosses and shareholders, but this was a Terry
English operation, and he looked after his staff. Absorbed the
losses. This was rare. Made Ray proud. Terry might have been his
boss, but he was also family. Like most taxi drivers employed elsewhere, Ray hated Uber.

Turning his engine off, he watched the other cab slow, stop and
after a pause reverse. A couple hurried out of the hotel, thinking it
was about to drive off. The man seemed nervous. His head jerking.
He was several years younger than the woman, who Ray guessed
was in her early thirties. She was wearing high heels and struggling
to keep up, and he decided they'd been doing the nasty behind her
husband's back. He wondered why they'd picked this hotel. Going
on its appearance and location it wasn't exactly romantic, and
these two didn't look poor. Once they were inside the Uber the

driver left the same way he had arrived, his scowling face unseen by the relieved couple snuggled up in the back.

The last rumblings of 'Catch 22' faded and Argy Bargy took over, Ray raising the volume with his fare nowhere to be seen. He had said it before and he would say it again to anyone who was interested and some who weren't – he fucking loved this band. Watford Jon's lyrics and vocals put Argy Bargy right up there in the Oi Oi rankings with the brilliant Cock Sparrer. *Drink, Drugs And Football Thugs* was an album delivered by someone who lived the terrace culture of England. It was the sort of thing that couldn't be faked. Ray looked at a lot of bands across the different genres and too many of those involved were geeks. It was pathetic how nerds straight out of *The Big Bang Theory* posed on their record covers and tried to look hard.

There was movement at the front of the hotel. A tanned man came into the light and walked his way. Slicked-back hair. Neatly creased strides. Stone Island jacket. Brown loafers. He had a swagger about him and looked familiar, but Ray couldn't place the face. His suitcase was big and ridiculous. Didn't suit him at all. Or maybe it did in a psycho sort of way. It looked like he wasn't wearing socks. And this put the Estuary driver on edge. Not as much as the suitcase, though, which was plastic and coated in a shiny leopardskin finish. There were wheels so it could be rolled along, something his fare was doing without it wobbling or going off course. Ray wanted to laugh but didn't, glad when the head turned towards him and the eyes narrowed. It was Joe's mate Dave Barrows. Someone he did not like at all.

Ray lowered the volume again. Got out and opened the boot. On hand to help with the suitcase if needed. Barrows greeted him with an all right mate, but he didn't recognise Ray and that was a relief. His passenger lifted the suitcase into the boot and closed it himself before heading for the back seat. Ray waited until the door was shut and got behind the wheel, double-checking the address. As he pulled away he glanced in his rear-view mirror and found a pair of eyes staring straight back. These remained fixed, and Ray returned his to the road.

Argy Bargy could just about be heard. At least in the front. Otherwise the cab was silent. This was going to be a fare who didn't want to talk. Which suited Ray. There were punters who rabbited for the entire journey and punters who didn't say a word. He liked to chat, but respected the quiet types. There was one woman he'd been ferrying around for years. Not every day, but when she was running late for work. Maybe two or three times a week for a month, then nothing for ages. She always smiled and waved when she approached the cab, but said next to nothing once she was inside. He had tried to make conversation at first, and again she would smile, nod at the mirror, but hardly open her mouth. And yet it was never awkward once he knew the score and left her alone. Most of these silent rides weren't difficult. Unlike this bloke who when Ray checked his mirror again he realised was fuming.

– What a fucking dump, Dave Barrows announced.

Ray was working and had to respond. And if they talked it would make the journey pass quicker.

– The hotel? I've never been inside. Don't think I've ever picked up from there either.

– I was awake half the night. There was this couple banging away in the next room and they woke me up. I was knocking on the wall and they either couldn't hear or didn't care, so I went into the hall and thumped on their door. Nothing. Fuck knows what they were doing in there. Screams and all sorts. I went back to bed and an hour later they stopped, but I couldn't sleep after that.

Good. Serves you right, you flash cunt.

– Could be the couple I saw leave just before you came out, Ray said. He was a bit younger. Three or four years maybe. Hard to tell.

– I didn't see them, just heard the racket they were making. Then there was no hot water this morning. Worse than that, it was warm for about thirty seconds, enough time for me to get in the shower and cover myself with soap before it cut off. I'm not putting up with that, not here in the winter, but who are you meant to complain to? Who's going to sort these things out? They hire kids and give them no proper training, pay the minimum wage.

Ray nodded. That was true enough.

– I had a row with my sister. Her and the brother-in-law. I had to leave in case I lost it, so I booked a room and thought I'd have some peace and quiet. Shouldn't have bothered as it was only a family row over nothing, me being wound up about other things. She's got her family, and I phoned and said sorry. Everything's good. All friends again. I said I'd paint the box room. I'll be glad to get back to Majorca. I can't stand the weather here.

Ray thought he was living in a caravan near Bournemouth. Maybe he had that wrong. And wasn't there something about him being a knife merchant? Dangerous Dave. He didn't like people who used blades. Fist and boot was the skinhead way.

– I live in the sun.

Maybe Ray was wrong about the knife.

– Run a bar.

– Nice one.

– Yeah, it's just a shame that wanker Gordon Brown never joined the euro. I have to pay for the privilege of using pounds and pence whenever I come back. We'll join the eurozone eventually and it will make life a lot easier, but I wish they'd hurry up. It's costing me money.

– Not if we have a referendum and leave.

– Never going to happen. The government won't allow it. Not Cameron and Clegg. The European Union is the future.

Ray had never met anyone who was this positive about the EU before. Told himself it was important to hear different points of view. He was interested to see if this twat had a proper case to make or if it was just the Me Me Me angle.

– I tell you what, that hotel should be closed down. I had to get out of there before I clumped the manager. I saw him when I arrived. Tall and skinny, the spitting image of Ricky Gervais's mate. He had the same twang as well. I couldn't see him, though, asked at reception and the girl said he wasn't in, but I searched, found his office. I think it was his office. He's probably hiding in a cupboard, saw me coming on the cameras.

This threat of violence irritated Ray. Its target as well as the fact it was being shared with a stranger as he sat here doing his job. He knew the actor and battering a gentle giant like that was bullying. Ray was no angel, but he didn't like hearing this, and definitely not from someone who used to sell drugs for Micky Todd. Maybe he had that wrong. He wasn't sure. But Ray hated drug dealers. Thought back to the time Chelsea was found with ecstasy in her bag. Poor kid had no idea what the pills were, sold to her as sweets that would make her happy. He'd tracked down the scum responsible. Dealt with them in a supermarket car park. Fucking Alis selling drugs to white girls made him think about the Muslim grooming gangs. As bad were the lowlife who'd let it go on. What the fuck was happening to this country?

– It's not his fault really, Dave continued in a more reflective tone. They call him a manager but I doubt he's got much of a say. He isn't going to be making executive decisions, is he? He wasn't the right person. You have to take things out on someone, though, it's human nature. I don't know, I just feel mucky after staying in that hotel and need a hot bath.

The traffic had built up and they came to a halt at a crossroads. Ray didn't want to look in his mirror again, but couldn't resist. Dave Barrows was waiting. Smirked and winked. Did this mean he'd twigged who Ray was? He didn't think so. They'd only met each other in passing, and it had been a while ago. Ray stared at the cars in front, wondering how he could frame the sovereignty question. What did his passenger think about the laws being made in Brussels? Was he bothered that the EU wasn't democratic? Had he studied his George Orwell?

– Who's that playing? It sounds like Argy Bargy.

Ray was surprised. Verging on impressed. He had Dave down as a disco man. Soul-patrol sounds for the ladies. From the weediest jazz funk to the blandest house to the tiniest urban. But Dave had grown up with Joe Martin so it made sense he knew his punk. Argy Bargy had come along later and were one of those bands who never gave an inch. Oi at its very best. There was no sneaky shuffle into synthesiser pop. Maybe he was being unfair on the wanker in the back seat. Joe was a good man so his mate must have something about him. He returned to the currency question.

– You really think we'll go into the euro? Ray asked, turning the music up but not so loud that it would stop them talking.

– Only a matter of time. We're lagging behind the rest of Europe as it is. It's all about globalisation these days. Money, the internet, smooth transactions. Why am I paying commission? It doesn't make sense. We have to think about Fortress Europe not Little England.

– Give up your currency and a country's finished. Means you've lost control of your economy. A British prime minister won't get rid of the pound. They'd never be elected again.

– Nothing the average person can do. The euro's inevitable. So is a single European state. We have to enjoy it and take what we can, make things easy and help ourselves.

– What about democracy? We shouldn't have laws being made by people we can't kick out in an election.

– Fuck democracy. There's no such thing.

Ray could feel himself bubbling up, needed to control his reaction.

– I haven't heard this song before, his fare continued, sounding less confident and more wistful. It's an odd one coming home. I haven't lived here for years.

There was a long pause, the driver wrong-footed.

– I've got a good joke for you, Ray said at last, deciding to hold back on the EU.

– Go on.

– What have Watford Jon, Elton John and George Michael got in common? Apart from the fact they all come from Watford?

– Watford Jon's the Argy Bargy singer?

– That's right.

The reply was hesitant, just as it was with those who knew Argy Bargy inside out, as the obvious answer seemed impossible.

– They're all queer? Watford Jon's not gay, though, is he?

– Of course he's not. Answer is, they've all got a Christian name for a surname.

Dave chuckled, leaning forward as he listened to the rest of the song, Ray keen to get back to the EU, but they were on the move again and it wasn't a long journey. A pound coin was added to the fiver cost, Ray getting out and opening the boot, Dave slow joining him so he reached in for the suitcase. It was a lot heavier than he'd expected, but he reasoned that a tanned expat soulboy wasn't going to be travelling light. He would need a decent wardrobe and lots of scent. And shoes. Hopefully some socks. Those bare feet bothered him almost as much as the EU, Ricky Gervais's mate, the possible drug dealing and knife use.

– I'm outside, his fare was saying into his mobile in an exasperated tone. Can't you get up? I know you've only just got back from work. I haven't got my keys.

Ray went to roll the suitcase, but it tilted and started to fall.

– Yes, I know I threw them at the wall. It's my fault. Come on, it's cold out here.

Ray was quick. Kept the suitcase upright.

– There's a knack to it, Dave said, taking over and walking towards the house, turning his head when he reached the front door.

Ray waited for the next line.

– My boss bought it for me as a birthday present.

This confused Ray.

– My boss is a woman, Dave added when he saw the driver's expression. I don't mind working under a lady. The woman on top.

When he was back in the car Ray called the office and was given another address, glanced back at the house and saw that Dave was standing with his back to the front door as he waited to be let in. He was staring over, raised a hand and waved. The door was opened by a woman in a white dressing-gown. Words were exchanged that Ray couldn't hear. He pulled away and headed towards George Green, shifting to 'Smash The Discos' by The Business.

Those soulboys never changed. It was always about looking after number one. They listened to shit music so they could prance around in a nightclub trying to get their ends away, saying whatever was needed, no matter how gooey. This one wanted the euro because it would save him money. He would surrender the pound and control of the economy just like that, wasn't even pretending when it came to the question of democracy. Britain had fought two world wars to stop Germany building its empire. And yet part of him had warmed to Dave. Maybe it was the psycho suitcase, knowing Argy Bargy, growing up with Joe Martin – a combination of the three. He wasn't sure. Couldn't work it out.

Forced to slow down, Ray guessed there had been an accident as this stretch was never busy. At least the cars were moving. He didn't let these delays upset him. He was an experienced driver and they were part of the job. It wasn't good thinking about yourself when some poor soul had gone through the windscreen. He put these breaks to good use, had come to almost look forward to them when he was on his own between jobs as it meant he could play his music as loud as he liked. There were songs he didn't like to turn off before they'd finished, and sometimes he would keep going for a few minutes so they could end. He'd always been like that. One track led to another. This band took him to that band.

He'd first read George Orwell in 1984 – *Nineteen Eighty-Four* – been hooked and continued into his other books. The essays as well as the fiction. Orwell said everything that needed to be said about the country and those in power who wanted to see it fail. He'd been working over at Heathrow at the time, after laying tarmac with the O'Driscolls ending up doing nights as a security guard sitting in a hut on the perimeter. That had been a doddle and given him the time to read. Orwell had led to Alan Sillitoe and Aldous Huxley. Driving gave him the time to listen to his music.

The Business were followed by his favourite Cockney Rejects song 'The Power And The Glory'. This was one of the reasons he loved Oi, the sheer energy lifting him up, the words reflecting how he felt, making him strong and determined, backing up his belief that people like him mattered. This was the living side of punk, bands created by the fans and not a bunch of nostalgic old hippies who secretly hated the music and had been riding a fashion, only ever interested in fame and fortune. He saw his next fare waiting and pulled over.

– Can you stop at the shops? the woman asked a minute later.

It's on the way. I promise I'll be quick. I've got to top up the electric.

– Show me where, Ray said.

Three minutes later and he was parked and listening to Eight Rounds Rapid, a band from Southend that Joe was raving about, one of those London-on-Sea outposts dotting the east and south coasts of the Danelaw and Wessex. Joe had copied their album *Lossleader* for Ray, sure anyone who loved the Cockney Rejects was going to be impressed with the vocals of Dave Alexander on songs like this one, 'Steve'. Ray was Oi through and through, a skinhead who could dip into the better punk and herbert, as long as it had enough backbone. Eight Rounds Rapid definitely had a spine and something interesting going on.

'Channel Swimmer' was another cracker with its frantic delivery and mad YouTube video, a black-and-white film of the band wandering around the Southend seafront in their trunks, munching chips and roaming an amusement arcade. He pictured Dave Barrows sheltering from the rain in a caravan by the English seaside, sunning himself on a Spanish island. Something happened and a person's life changed. He thought about Priscilla. The text she'd sent this morning.

When his fare was outside and returning to the car he paused 'Writeabout', the fact Eight Rounds Rapid were halfway through this song making him realise how long she'd been gone. Banging her forehead with a palm she stopped dead. Looked at Ray and pointed to the shop at the end of the parade. Made a praying sign and turned before he could respond. Disappeared inside. This annoyed Ray. She had been quoted a fare and he'd done her a favour and stopped. Now she was taking the piss. He knew he was a soft touch. Especially when it came to women. Too much of a gentleman. Couldn't say no. But he had done with Priscilla. Last year. And he was going to do it again. Had no choice.

Priscilla was gorgeous and fun to be with, those times they'd gone out special, but there was a line, and she was way over on the other side. He had her number but there was no way he would call. He couldn't, it would be...

– Thanks for waiting, his fare said as she opened the door and got into the back. There was a problem with my card.

A bag was being passed forward. The woman's big beaming face filled his mirror.

– I bought you a doughnut. The woman who runs the shop makes them herself. I couldn't resist, but don't worry, I'll eat it after you drop me off. I don't want to get sugar over the seats. You keep your car very clean, don't you?

Ray was moved by her kindness. And the compliment.

– You didn't need to do that, I didn't mind stopping. But thanks.

He was conscious of how quick his mood had changed. He wanted to laugh. Selling his soul for a doughnut. It smelled great.

– Go ahead and eat yours. Just lean over the bag, please. I do like a clean car, you're right.

Back on the main road he listened as she told him about her card failing and the debts she was trying to sort out, the job she'd lost and the new one she was starting next week. She was worried about the three months of probation. What if they didn't like her and let her go when it was over, and then she had to start all over again.

– You'll be all right. Three months is normal. It will be fine.

It hadn't been a piss-take, her going in the shops like that, just her chaotic way. She had a big heart. A generous soul who would never be able to control money. Presents for her friends as well as the family at Christmas and on their birthdays. Small gifts for the children of relatives and neighbours when she saw something she thought they'd like. He would let her off the fare. This woman liked to talk and he let her, dropping in the odd line here and there.

– I'm going to have to eat mine as well, he said when she paused for breath. I can't resist it any longer.

Ray spread the serviette from the bag out on his lap, keeping his eyes on the road as he did this, took the doughnut out and bit into it, surprised by the amount of jam inside. He was impressed and told his passenger. His second bite sent a big blob of strawberry jelly falling into his lap and he jolted, tightening his one-handed grip on the wheel as he felt the car trying to veer right. He was in luck as the jam landed on the serviette and he remembered the grief he'd got off his mum when she found the curry stain on his white shirt, the one he was forced to wear to weddings, funerals and court. This was different. Jam on jeans. Easily washed out.

He slipped the doughnut back into its bag and put this down on the seat next to him. Would finish it when he dropped the woman in the back off. He shouldn't be taking chances. Eating while he was driving in traffic. Couldn't risk swerving into the oncoming cars and lorries. Killing himself and his fare and God knows who else.

Joe left the main road and entered the retail park, drove to the B&Q end and stopped, and with a break in the rain they didn't have to hurry inside, could take their time and saunter towards the entrance discussing the sort of cider that could blow a person's head off, how it was only ever going to be made by a seventy-odd-year-old scrumper in his nineties, a lollipop man posing as a chauffeur. Dave broke away to get a trolley, but it stuck to the one in front and this set him off tugging harder and harder, and when it still wouldn't budge he shook it and started kicking the frame, swearing and adding to the racket as Joe offered advice – a tilt to the right, a tilt to the left, ease the nearest wheels off the ground and charm it loose. He was happy to help for as long as it took, but seeing the fear on the faces of an elderly couple who speeded up as they passed he changed his approach.

– Take deep breaths and relax, David. Try to visualise the Buddha sitting in the full lotus position. Leave your attachments behind and move on. Let the next trolley come to you.

Dave scowled and stepped sideways to the parallel row and this one rolled out smoothly. Looking at Joe he mouthed the word 'don't' before grinning in his boyish way, the frustration gone as fast as it had arrived. His cockiness returned and Joe swore he was strutting as he took charge of the box-room raiding party, leading the way to the doors which parted neatly, the second set doing likewise and the store spreading out in front of them in all its pristine, shining glory.

– Welcome to paradise, Joe announced. The worker's dream 2015.

The two pals paused to take in the sheer scale of the scene, the brightness of the light illuminating an indoor stadium packed with goodies, aisles rising high above their heads in racked precision, the air clean and tasting of the new. Even though Joe made a point of using the smaller independent shops it was hard not to appreciate a superstore when it was cold and wet outside and most other places were closed.

– I should have brought my shades, Dave replied.

As Joe stood there deciding where to go he heard the music, unsure at first if it was real or in his head as it was so faint, imagined it filtering through from a hotel lobby next door even though this building stood alone at the end of a long car park on the edge of an industrial estate. It became clearer as he listened, easy-listening muzak for the consumers, a shoppers' soundtrack. He wondered who'd chosen this tune, sure it had to be a head-office decision based on professional research rather than a member of staff into garage or grime. It was meant to relax people and get them spending. He had never noticed music playing before, at least not consciously, and he put this down to his sampler and the new awareness it had stirred.

– My suntan lotion and shorts, Dave continued.

Joe was thinking about a twenty-minute mash-up involving the blandest easy listening ever recorded, lifted from those albums even the charity shops couldn't sell, although that description was his music snobbery talking. This was a popular genre and there had to be a lot more to it than the first-class travel, luxury hotels, plush cocktail bars and five-star restaurants he was picturing, although that sort of escapism had to be a big part of the attraction for Joe Public, a soundtrack for a world where there were no arguments and no nasty surprises.

– What are we doing? Dave asked.

– The paint's over on the left. Second-to-last aisle over there, before you get to the kitchens.

– You really know your way around, don't you? You're an interesting man.

– Fuck off, cunT.

– Cun*T*, Dave repeated, really spitting the T out.

Joe wanted to look at the wood first and guided them in the other direction, stopping to peer down an aisle of nails, tacks, screws, nuts, bolts, hinges, hooks and brackets. Men of every age stood in front of the shelves browsing, considering, comparing, calculating, deciding. Some came with a list of items needed the next day for work, others turned up with a more casual DIY approach, while Joe reckoned a few had no intention of buying anything and would leave empty-handed, here for the ambience and the drive over. Nobody spoke, not even when there were two or three of these characters together, and Joe ran his eyes over the faces, quickly checked his phone and shook his head.

– Come on, he said.

– Okay, Dad, Dave sang as Joe led the way, looking down each aisle they passed.

Dave didn't mind following Joe around, every minute spent here was one less doing the actual painting, and he felt relaxed and anonymous, waiting for Martina to answer his last message, the one with the photo where he was flashing his knob. Joe had put the pressure on about the room he was meant to be decorating, but it was easier getting the paint with him than his sister, and maybe they'd stop for a pint after.

– Let's go this way, Joe said, once he'd been along the timber aisles.

Dave followed him up and down racks loaded with building materials, coming back into displays of flooring, tiles, wallpaper, soft furnishings and finally lighting as he fiddled with his phone. Joe wanted to buy a lamp, maybe two, one to go next to his bed and another to light up the MPC, the sort that clamped on the side of a desk. A floor lamp might be better, though. All three best. He had seen some good ones at the IKEA in Wembley, but he was getting distracted, confused by the options, rows of bulbs in the full range of shapes and sizes, bayonet and screw tops, their ingredients and ways of measuring strength beyond him.

– Good, he mumbled as he came to a stop.

Micky Todd was standing in front of them examining a lamp. It was in the form of a rabbit, one of its front legs raised in the air with a shade attached to the paw, a flex running into the back of a hind leg, and looking at his trolley Joe realised that Micky must have arrived earlier than they'd agreed, already gone and bought the wood and materials Joe said he'd show him, seeing as he had to pick up something himself. It didn't matter and, if anything, made this chance meeting easier to explain.

When Micky sensed company he turned his head and smiled at Joe, registered the man with him, face tightening as he clocked Dave approaching with the trolley, head down as he studied the picture Martina had sent in reply to his last one, her face close to the screen, lips pouting, promising him the blow job he wanted if he would cut his visit to England short and hurry back.

– Evening, Joe, Micky said, eyeballing Dave who raised his face and failed to hide his surprise. David...

– Michael...

Dave stopped next to Joe and stood tall.

– Nice looking rabbit, he said after an awkward pause. Are you taking her home, Micky?

Joe winced at this opener. Dave's debt to Micky had been repaid and some sort of peace restored, and Joe had helped smooth things over there, but this was the big test. An accidental encounter that could go either way, and yet he was confident as they all knew each other from when they were young and more time had passed.

– He's done too many drugs, I reckon, Dave continued.

Micky studied the lamp, seemed bemused or irritated, put it back on the shelf, his features hardening further. Joe knew that if he'd said those same words the bloke would have laughed, because it was definitely one mad-looking rabbit with its blue-velvet fur and big green eyes, but there was that mention of drugs.

– He's taken a wrong turn, thinks he's burrowed his way into Wonderland.

There was another pause before Micky smiled, looked at the racks and appreciated the sweet smells of choice and prosperity, pointing to his trolley.

– You're not wrong there. I've gone a bit over the top. Double the shopping list I brought along. It's hard to resist once you come in here.

– Very true, Dave said, scanning his surroundings.

There was another brief silence.

– Nice tan you've got there, Dave. Is it real?

– All my own work.

– How's life in paradise?

– Can't complain, Micky. You should come over sometime. You're always welcome. Local bar five minutes from the sea. Fine wines and ales served by yours truly.

The tension eased as the two men swapped pleasantries, Joe staying where he was before giving them their privacy when they moved closer together, grinning and cracking jokes. He went to the lamps and inspected a few before picking up the rabbit. He ran a hand over its head and back.

– I'm not getting in the car if you buy that thing, Dave said. Its eyes just moved.

– Give you nightmares, he will, Micky added. Bite you when you're sleeping.

– A rabid fucking rabbit. Look at the size of its teeth. It'll take a chunk out of your car as well.

– You're not still driving that Skoda around?

– I've told him, Micky. Told him a hundred times.

The two of them stood side by side, united as they took the piss out of Joe, who couldn't care less as long as they were getting on. He put the lamp back. There were further friendly exchanges and handshakes before Joe looked at the wood Micky had bought and promised to come round with his tools, give him a hand with the shelves. Micky winked and whispered 'clever' and the two trolleys moved off in opposite directions, Micky towards the cushions,

Dave and Joe towards the paint. Nothing was said about this encounter as they discussed the options and made their choices, bought brushes and turps and a roller, Joe focusing on the job as Dave wondered.

They were quickly through the tills and back outside, hurrying towards the car as the rain fell, loading the tins and bags into the back seat of a car that started first time but stuttered as it moved away, the electrics damp, energy surging as they warmed up and Joe left the car park, stopping at the lights leading back to the A4.

– You don't think of Micky Todd going shopping for rabbit lamps, do you? Joe said, deciding now was the time to mention the man.

– I was ready for the fat cunt, Dave replied, reaching into his coat and removing an evil-looking knife, a small ultra-sharp blade that seemed more vicious because it was crafted from orange plastic and meant to slice fruit and veg.

– What's the matter with you? What are you doing walking around with that in your pocket? You've lost the fucking plot. Why do you need a knife? An orange one. Made of plastic. In B&Q. Fucking hell, Dave.

– Protection. Can't be too careful with these Muslim gangs running around with their swords and machetes. Forget the knife. It's in the past. Done and dusted. We're all friends again. Stroke of luck that, bumping into Micky. Couldn't have gone any better if some clever sausage had planned it ahead of time. Relax, there's worse things to worry about. Much worse things going on.

Joe was shocked and didn't know what to say, saw the lighting section soaked in blood *Zombieland*-style, the undead running riot, police responding, armed units piling into the store, and he gave up trying to find the right words, put on 'Midnight In A Perfect World' off *Endtroducing* as Dave stared out of the window and watched the buildings pass by, thrilled but keeping the feeling to himself. That handshake with Micky proved he was off the hook, and while he had known him since they were kids and wasn't afraid of Micky himself, he was part of something bigger that could have had him shot. He didn't have to worry about coming home now, but then he remembered that, like the cunt he was, he'd only gone and replaced one threat with another by blabbing to Chris.

Dave's emotions raged as he considered the time he had left in England, what he needed to do in the days before he left. Thoughts of Chris moved to Operation Box Room which reminded him of Operation Bambi, so when Joe glanced sideways he found a smiling face. At least his plan had worked, which was the main thing, Joe's faith in human nature rewarded. The knife was a worry, but only there for protection. He missed his friend even if he did his head in at times, and with the Micky Todd obstacle removed and peace restored he let his thoughts drift back to the rabbit with the blue-velvet fur and green eyes. It might look nice between his Yamaha monitors, lighting up the yellow pads of the sampler. He would go back and have another look at it later in the week, but this time on his own.

– Fancy a drink? Dave asked.

– Is the Pope a Catholic?

– Does a bear shit in the woods?

– Is this hot-rod Skoda good for another ten years?

Dave banged his palm on the dash.

– Class wheels guaranteed to pull a Polish lovely. East European birds love a classic Skoda. Nothing gets them wet faster. Seriously, who'd have thought we'd be driving around in this pile of shit when we were kids.

– I can drop you off here if you want. Anyway, it's got a VW engine.

Dave nodded as if he was satisfied with the response and returned to the streets outside as DJ Shadow played and Joe thought about his easy-listening mash-up, where to start looking for his building blocks. It was going to be hard sticking to his own stories when there were so many others out there waiting to be invented, but, there again, anything that came into his head had to be personal. He wasn't sure, the possibilities endless, exciting and daunting at the same time, Dave pulling him back.

– Where shall we have a drink? What about that lap-dancing

club out towards the airport, a nice little Latvian rubbing her tits in your face?

The listening there would be easy but more uptempo, light-weight Eurodisco that was cheerful in a trebly sort of way and meant to disguise the realities of the dancers' lives, relax the punters and get them spending their hard-earned. There was nothing exotic about those clubs as far as Joe could see, just nervous working girls from the East and lonely working men from the West, some bored lorry drivers from across Europe parked in the lay-bys outside Heathrow.

– Not my style, Dave, and we need to drop the paint off first.

– We can stick it in the boot. Don't tell me you don't like the idea of a Russian bird in a G-string rubbing her bum against your balls.

– Not really, no. And I've got to dump the car.

– Leave the Skoda outside the club and pick it up tomorrow. One of the girls might steal it for old time's sake and you can collect on the insurance. How much is it worth? A tenner? You might even get a score if you say you left your wallet in the glove compartment.

– I can't be fannying about in the morning. I've got a busy day. We'll take the paint to your sister's and I'll park the car outside my flat and we can go local. Call Chris, see if he's in the mood for a beverage. Call Clem as well. He won't answer, but try him. Come on, stop sulking you miserable cunT.

Dave smirked and did as he was told, or at least he called Clem and left a message, tried Chris for two rings then turned his phone off before he had a chance to answer.

– They're not picking up. Chris knows it's me.

– It's hard getting him out these days. He needs a nudge. It depends what sort of cases he's working on, I think. We can try him again in a while.

– Let him call me.

– It's not healthy him seeing what he sees. He needs to get off that computer when he's at home, forget about work and switch off. It's why we can't tell him about Clem and the berks. It's best not to mention anything like that as it just gets him going. A conflict of interests. He's not himself.

Dave mumbled something and was quiet the rest of the way to his sister's where they delivered the paint to a burst of excitement, but instead of heading back to his flat Joe decided they'd knock for Chris in person, ask his better half if he could come out to play. That way he would find it harder to say no. A good drink would work wonders.

As they pulled into the drive of Sherlock's detached home Dave's mind was racing. Joe got out and went to the front door, rang the bell several times, but nobody came. He stepped back and scanned the front of the house, could see a faint glow coming from Chris's upstairs office, but the alarm was on and the light would have been left to deter burglars. Chris and Carol were out at the same time and that was a good sign, so Joe got back in the car and started to turn around, Dave keeping his eyes fixed on the office window, saw the faint outline of a man at the edge of the glass, suspected Chris was no longer his friend and probably his enemy.

Moving slowly... taking our time... ambling through the streets of an English village... we are a family of giants... the four of us together... mother father daughter son... you see we came here in the car... Charlie driving... singing songs... parked next to a clean new church... in a clean new street... detached houses from an American suburb... long Astroturf lawns... blue-velvet gates... pavements fashioned from foam... and we enter the village as one... the path here crooked and cracked... days of making do... mending... it's freezing cold but we are invincible... wrapped up in our warmest clothes... the village idyllic... quintessential... when we reach the green we stop to watch the cricket... a promise of what is to come... lazy summer days... sun blazing... the purest white light... our family picnic in the middle of a meadow... but there is another promise... that this is the place where we will live when we are old... our working days done... there will be an invitation... please... retire here... good health... generous pensions... dignity and respect... labour rewarded... more than cogs... worn-out horses... the knacker's yard... anyway... we are happy where we live... it might be lonely in this village... if we were here all the time... peasant fantasies... welfare-state dreams... our little boy... our little girl... we stare at the bowler together... his hands in the air... appealing... LBW... stumps in place... the umpire is considering his decision... long and hard... for years... the batsman waits... patiently... second batsman running... wicketkeeper crouching... a slip diving in the wrong direction... another floating in the air... outfielders loitering... one man sprinting to the boundary... fours and sixes... cricketers out of sync... time muddled... an icy scoreboard... runs made and wickets taken... spectators... deckchairs... blazers... summer dresses... tiny glasses of beer and spirits... Charlie reaches for my hand and the love flows as we continue... our children running ahead... stopping... pointing at the approaching train... I call to them... wait for us... stay away from the tracks... bodies on the line... dowry suicides... young men... pensioners... the fast service into Paddington... out to Reading and the West Country... steel wheels and locomotive pistons... driving wheel in motion... steam engine at the front... coal effects... I wave... six coaches... a boxcar... the driver grinning... huge red lips... passengers in the dining car... guard at the back... and there is a station but the train doesn't stop... people wait on the platform... they've been waiting for years... chipped skin... flaking paint... the sound of the train fades as it heads for another village that doesn't exist... running in circles... nobody can get on... nobody can get off... we amble on... thatched houses... cottage gardens... miniature trees and flowers... birds and dogs and cats and horses... bigger properties held together by black beams... individual shops... there are no supermarkets here... the baker holds a loaf of bread in the air... the grocer cradles a cabbage... the butcher shows off a cleaver... and there is a pub... The Cross Keys... drinkers sitting outside immune to the cold... a post office from the days when Granny Smith was still loved... a postman carries letters to an almshouse... dinky bike at the gate... I see the vans of the baker and the grocer and the butcher... a sports car driven by Terry Thomas... and we cross a river in three steps... stagnant water and a boat that has sunk... there's a woman in the water... floating on her back like Ophelia... we pass a common... the yearly fair that doesn't move on... robin redbreast on top of the merry-go-round... almost as big as the horses... there are bumper cars and a coconut shy... stalls with goldfish and jars of sweets... fortune-teller Lola... a haunted house... caravans... crowds in the fairground... families like ours... and further on there is a Norman church... a graveyard with plastic yews and a memorial to the Fallen... next are the allotments... sheds and digging men... scarecrows... behind are out-of-scale shrubs that rise up as a forest... we stick to the path... a small-holding... farmhouse and stables... pigsties... three fields with sheep and cows and more horses... there is a man on a tractor and an unused plough... a worm that must seem like a python to the farmers... and eventually we are back at the village green... everything exactly the same as we left it... the umpire trying to make a decision... we leave and sit at a table by the entrance... Charlie buys hot chocolate... we talk about the village... what it would be like to live in such a place... the train is our children's favourite thing... and Charlie takes them to the big station... sometimes... they sit in the car and watch the locomotives flash past... there is a lane where we stop... we could go on the way home if it wasn't so cold... a lane with a bridge that crosses a railway line... a path down the bank... but I would never walk down there with our son and daughter... closing my eyes... listening to them chatter... smelling the chocolate... snow frost fog mist thunder lightning rain... suddenly scared they have left me behind... been snatched... injected... fallen off a hill... into water... killed by a train... my husband and children... dead or alive... hospital beds... but no... the good times... the best days are coming –

After an hour at the gym Joe was pumped up and ready for action, the energy flowing through his body and brain, but at the same time he knew he had to resist the urge to let the adrenaline lead him astray. He was determined to make this first pint of Ghost Ship his last, slowing his breathing down and drawing the air deep into his lungs, holding it there yogi-style, imagining a Hindu sage in his cave on the banks of the Ganges, the Buddha searching for enlightenment under the Bodhi Tree in Bodh Gaya. That was a place he'd love to see, and he wondered if he ever would. For now he was making do with the two Bengali collections in a batch of nine albums he'd bought from a bloke in Hounslow, four of them by Ravi Shankar.

He sipped his Ghost Ship and felt the citric tang of the East Anglian IPA in his mouth and mind, knew that a second pint would weaken his resistance, and once he had the taste he could end up moving to a pub where men he knew were gearing up for the daily session, local thinkers living the life he'd fancy if he didn't have his drives. It would be easy to get lost in the public-house bliss of too much beer and philosophy, where the humour and insights increased with the drink, but his willpower was firm and the pie and chips he was eating were enough to soak up this single pint. He had things to do and a place to be, his sampler connected and ready thanks to Luke helping him over the phone.

Smiles would've been proud how his boy had turned out. Joe didn't have kids, but if he did he'd have wanted his son to be like Luke. He was a true diamond, more nephew than his dead friend's child. Not that he wanted to replace Luke's uncle, but he had more in common with him than Tony did, and it wasn't just their natures but a shared interest in music, seeing it as a montage that kept building on itself, mutating and reinventing as it created the new from the old, a mirror of the wider society. Nothing was new, everything recycled. More than anything, Luke was his mate. He lived in Brighton and had his family and work, and even if they didn't see each other for a year it was easy when they did. They came from different generations, but for Joe it felt as if they were the same age, two analogue men in a digital age.

Seeing DJ Shadow at the Forum four years earlier had blown Joe away. He owned all of Shadow's work, his debut *Endtroducing* a revelation when he heard it for the first time. He'd been in Brighton, staying at the Albion across from the pier, walking through the Lanes when Luke took him into a record shop and pointed out the album before buying it as a present. He knew something about sampling and had bought the first Public Enemy LPs when they were released, knew his Cabaret Voltaire and On-U Sound, plus he was a Bowie man after all, but *Endtroducing* was different.

Eighty samples had been used, and while Joe admired the process and dedication required, the music and how he had come to hear it represented something bigger. In it he saw the nature of time and the past and how it made the future, Smiles living on in Luke, the three of them sitting together in the Cricketers sipping two pints as Joe read the credits and removed four sides of vinyl for inspection. The titles 'Midnight In A Perfect World' and 'What Does Your Soul Look Like' sort of summed up how he had felt then and how he was feeling now.

UNKLE's *Psyence Fiction* was another special album, Shadow working with James Lavelle whose Mo' Wax was well represented on Joe's shelves. He loved the look of the label, the way it drew on *Thunderbirds* and *The Man From UNCLE*, with covers based around the art of Futura 2000 who he had seen with The Clash at the Lyceum. He thought again about Lady Penelope in her grand house, the marionette as well as the human version whose rudeness was the price of some interesting insights. Gerry and Sylvia Anderson were the legends behind *Thunderbirds*, and he'd found out it was Sylvia herself voicing Penny, while David Graham spoke for Parker as well as Brains, Gordon Tracy and Kyrano. Joe wondered where on the Slough Trading Estate the audio had been recorded, couldn't help picturing his lock-up, the flat where he would be sampling their words.

Shadow's live performance was right up there with the best gigs he'd ever seen. A chainsaw graphic ran across the back of the stage and cut open this egg-like structure where Josh Davis was waiting, mixing and scratching and playing his drum pads. It really had been incredible. Hip hop or trip hop – intelligent hip hop as some preferred – DJ cut-ups or downbeat, it was all punk as far as Joe was concerned, but a version that didn't preach that Year Zero nonsense. Again it was Luke responsible. He'd bought the tickets and come up to London in the car so he could get back for work the next day, and talking in the Bull And Gate afterwards Joe had decided to buy a sampler, but when the drink faded so did his confidence. It had taken four years and his second DJ Shadow show two weeks ago before he got it back.

He finished his pie and pint, returned the glass and plate to the bar, left the pub and went outside, got in his car and put himself in the right frame of mind with *This Is PIL*, and that was what made punk different, the way it had spiralled off in so many directions, the reason he saw the likes of Shadow, Tricky and Eminem as punk rockers. Lydon would always be the originator, making that one perfect album with the Sex Pistols and a handful of unbeatable 45s before walking away from the bullshit, returning with Public Image Limited and a single that was more punk than punk. *This Is PIL* was brilliant, Lydon back on top form, Joe thinking of 'Time Zone' and his collaboration with Afrika Bambaataa, how so many of these things repeated.

He left the car park and headed for his lock-up, had been wondering if he should leave the Farnham Road and move to the Oaks, the old Webb place between Slough and Uxbridge. Clem lived out there, and while the Webbs ran their garage from the biggest barn and sold scrap on the side, there were the smaller buildings where he could rent something decent. Clem was a nightwatchman of sorts, while Bobby Webb lived in the main house with his family. Maybe he should keep the one in Slough that he used for his stock, the packing ready for posting, all the stuff he didn't want cluttering up his flat, and use the other as a glorified shed. He had his music gear set up at home, the shelves he'd built, but it was an idea. He knew he probably wouldn't do it due to cost, plus he suspected he wasn't driven or angry enough, lacked the spark that made a person create.

He thought about Lydon and what he'd said about anger being an energy, Johnny Rotten living in his LA mansion with space to spare, enjoying the good life, but best of luck to the bloke, he could do whatever he wanted as far as Joe was concerned. He spoke sense and had a humour working people understood. Mark E Smith and Morrissey as well. They said what they thought, didn't bend, and the more time passed the more Joe appreciated Morrissey, the fact he was a Cockney Rejects fan a bonus. He saw him sharing a pot of tea with Jeff and Mick, the Geggus brothers nibbling scones as Morrissey poured the Darjeeling. The Rejects' last album *East End Babylon* contained some of their best work, 'Your Country Needs You' near enough 'The Power And The Glory' standard, and while Joe had eclectic tastes it was impossible to better punk at its best. It was in his blood, and he knew he was lucky to be making a living out of something he loved.

When Luke was younger he'd had an anger that was normal enough given what had happened to him, the years in care before he went to live with Linda, never knowing his dad, but now he was settled, a mellow character very different to the Luke that Joe had first met back in 2000. He had a family of his own and a good job, children who depended on him, a wife who loved him to bits, and seemed content. While Luke liked his techno and trance, only a few people could make a living as a DJ, but that dream had been replaced with responsibilities and a solid future. Joe admired him for his strength as well as his personality. Luke had genuine grievances, but had conquered them, and when Joe felt sorry for himself he thought about that and knew he was blessed.

He returned to that second DJ Shadow gig at the Forum two weeks back, the Renegades Of Rhythm show with Cut Chemist very different to the first one. Luke had come up on the train this time and stayed at his place after, and Joe had supplied the tickets for a surreal trip into Seventies funk straight from the Pied Horse and Community Centre, the sort of music he'd hated as a kid. Shadow and Cut Chemist were using Afrika Bambaataa's own records as well, which was mental in itself, and despite being a teenage boot boy who'd wanted to smash the discos before Micky Fitz put the idea into words, the old hatred hadn't returned. He thought about the legendary Sully, hoped he still had his twelve-inch American imports, went from there to the sheer range of music in the Seventies, a decade regularly slagged off by Z-list celebrities who hadn't been born and didn't have a clue.

It had been a mad old time, which, looking back, was probably to be expected seeing as the older generations had been through two world wars, a depression and a period of austerity, while the battle between capital and labour reached some sort of peak under Thatcher, but for kids like Joe, Dave, Chris and Smiles they were brilliant days. Maybe not for Smiles exactly, but while things were more violent there was another sort of excitement, a maverick creativity it was hard to get across to those who hadn't been there. The same enemies were still taking the piss, but they did it from behind a shield of fake smiles and words they didn't mean. The Renegades Of Rhythm show had made him think hard about that stage of his life, and maybe Dave had seen the positives he had missed, the same as Mick Jones did with Strummer, but while Joe couldn't feel the same way as his friend about jazz funk and the weaker ends of rave and house that followed, at least he was being more open-minded.

Pulling up outside his lock-up he was soon inside and working his way through the orders that needed sending out. This week's highlight was a Parlophone copy of The Beatles' *Please Please Me* album, the stereo version with the gold lettering on a black label, and as he added bubblewrap and taped the cardboard packaging and fixed the special-delivery label he'd already bought and printed out to the front he wondered how many pints the Fab 4 would be buying him over the next few months. The Beatles were another one of those bands that had grown on him, because despite their superior songwriting and experimentation, that quirky Englishness they shared with The Kinks and Small Faces, he had always preferred The Rolling Stones. It had been a relief getting into The Beatles properly, and that was thanks to Oasis and the Gallagher brothers. He wanted to broaden his tastes and was making some progress with classical, picking up albums cheap on vinyl and making himself listen, particularly enjoying the great Russian composers, Vaughan Williams, Sibelius and Wagner. The biggest challenge was jazz, a form of music with huge range but one he couldn't feel. Not yet, anyway.

When the packing was finished, Joe took his parcels to the post office and dropped them off, was home by two o'clock, made himself a cup of coffee and went into the room where he had set up his equipment. There wasn't a lot of space, but this was a hobby and good enough. He was going to start with the records he'd played in the Spiritualist church in Uxbridge, his own little revival session – *Never Mind The Bollocks*, *The Clash*, *God's Lonely Men* and *The Crack*. He would save *Diamond Dogs*, *Aladdin Sane* and *Station To Station* for another day, wasn't sure where to begin when it came to David Bowie. He could bring in The Stooges, Lou Reed and Marc Bolan maybe, but despite the way Bowie mashed things up there was an English feel to what he did, and the first couple were too American. He supposed not all music suited the sampler, thinking about the need for clean breaks, and yet what did he know about any of this? Nothing really. He felt the confidence draining out of him, but if he could make one recording that he liked it would be enough. Nobody else was going to hear what he produced. The process was the pull, a place to go. He looked at the albums lining his shelves, the singles in boxes, piles of CDs and cassettes and was overwhelmed, but in a positive, excited way.

His marionette plans were further along and he was going to try and lift things off those ten-inch *Thunderbirds* records, dip into *Captain Scarlet* and *Joe 90*, inject some *Star Trek* wisdom and the building panic of Space Invaders, the insane drone of Suicide and especially 'Rocket USA'. The main element there had to be spoken word, the accents and humour of Lady Penelope and Parker, Joanna Lumley and Sid James. He had to get some Mo' Wax into it, needed to go through the label's albums and maybe avoid DJ Shadow himself, but it had to have something else, in a flash knowing it would be 'Leningrad'. He would think of a better title than *Big Society*.

Joe went to the section of his shelves where he kept his sound-effects albums, but maybe it would be better to mine The Members' 'The Sound Of The Suburbs', Gary Numan's 'Cars' and

The Jam's 'Eton Rifles', add some JG Ballard, lines from *Crash* and *Concrete Island,* Anthony Burgess and *A Clockwork Orange*, the novel and the film, phrases and single words, repeated mentions of droogs and devotchkas, but neither of these men were herberts, belonged to a different class. He had to do something with his *Stranger Dangers* idea as well, those lines from 'Danger Blues', a song that chugged along ominous and optimistic, would definitely use the 'danger stranger' clip from The Clash's '1977', his visit to O'Mara productive and lingering. These were only the bones, and he wanted more than single notes and bleeps, a clearer bastard-pop picture of what he hoped to get across, and turning his set-up on and sipping his coffee Joe focused on how he was going to make these plans work, had to get to grips with the machine, make sense of the storm inside his head.

Monsters imagined and real... mutating and adapting... it's not the spirits who scare me... the ghosts in the fog... unsure if they are alive or dead... not the pixies at the bottom of the garden... bogarts hinkypunks goblins... fields and hedgerows... not the crucified vicar in the churchyard... witches in the woods... women who cure the sick... herbalists tied to stakes and burned... not the men fighting for fairness... hung from oaks that still stand... traumatised... locals serfs pagans commoners branded scum by the rich and powerful... that land-grabbing class rooted in invasion... they don't know us... don't even speak our language... it's them we should fear... the accusers and dismissers... living humans who bully and smear... control the means of production... deceivers manipulating the system... betraying our trust... deciding futures... and the new breed have broken into our homes... trolls and bots... wi-fi nasties... phones laptops pads... say one thing do another... word manipulation... accountancy theft... those asset-stripping privatising milk-snatchers... locking onto easy targets... masters and servants... capital and labour... us and them... and there are streaks of sadness in this beautiful mind-bending fog... polluted patches... black smudges in the haze... warnings that something

terrible is coming... an unknown shadow at the top of the bank...
next to the motorway where I doze in my chair... Grace in the
ferns... freezing... our mental wounds... congealing... skunk
skeletons in dead earth... human hibernation... hedgehog men and
hedgehog women... dreaming... but spring is coming... loud bangs
like gunshots... crashing coaches and lorries and white vans... the
roar of heavy loads... long-distance drivers... airport trunk roads...
supermarket car parks... lay-bys and lanes... the great orbital
roads... avenues that flow into the heart of London Town...
railway rhythms of techno and garage... amphetamine basements
and herb-filled lofts... a derelict pub collapses... thud of Herbert...
police sirens and a pink Cadillac... burning rage meets melting
skin... chopping chopper-copper blades... the fog too dense for lift-
off... policemen grounded... you can't catch me... this CCTV
blur... a glitch on their scanners... town-centre cameras... warehouse security... horsepower... I don't need to run like I did when
I was younger... irrational fear... I HAVE DONE NOTHING
WRONG... God knows I'm good... smoke in the fog... I sit
forward and sniff and listen... it could be an accident... people
trapped in the wreckage... leaking gasoline... everyone is needed...
doctors and nurses... firefighters... hurry to the hospital... worst-
case scenarios... but the harder I listen the quieter the world
becomes... like I'm the last person left... locked out of heaven...
searching for a heartbeat with my hand on my chest... nothing... I
have never felt this way before... not in my special place... I stand
and stretch... need to get home... children's voices... I hide my
chair in the bushes and come down off the ridge... tentative steps
on a rocky slope... slipping and sliding so stones cut my hands... at
the bottom I wipe the blood off on my sweatshirt... start moving...
searching for the sounds of Satellite... along the base of the
embankment and over a ditch... turning back towards the town...
shops parading... terraces... car beams... another estate... pizza
scooters... houses lined up two-by-two... the pressure building
inside... curtains smoulder... it is late... there is violence and abuse
on those widescreen TVs... torture murder rape... revenge as happy
endings... concentrating on my path I am pushing my body...

moving as fast I can through the murk... repeating my mantra... people are decent... people are good... people are moral... few of us ever meet a murderer... hardly anyone... and while I am not the same as before I try my very best to be strong... don't look back... new beginnings... lives... the babies inside me... spirits conjured and bodies chosen... allocated... miracle conceptions... spirits born to grow think walk speak... to express themselves in the physical... these babies have always been with me... in my blood... DNA... but it is deeper than that... our spirits are one... with the joy comes dread... there has to be an opposite... sickness accidents predators... the fear that I won't be able to protect and feed my children... keep them warm and dry with a roof over their heads... we can't end up homeless... freezing on the streets and in the fields... the tough times are never far away... the worry of losing my job... what if I make a mistake or become ill or say too much... I speak out now... believe in my union... our defence... there are bad people out there... nature or nurture I just don't know... but nurses never turn their backs... never walk away... the paymasters know... especially when we have dependents... and these thoughts press in on me as I lift my eyes towards the upstairs windows where the curtains are open... a face watches me pass... child teenager adult pensioner... sweet dreams... bitter nightmares... insomniacs talking to strangers on the other side of the veil... planet... four walls... OCD decay... respect the past by living in the moment... that's me... Mum forgot bless her... didn't recognise her own daughter... her little girl... why do these things happen if God exists... but she's with me now... remembers everything clearer than before... Dad too... my father in heaven... reunited with his daughter... little girl... I am speeding through the streets with my parents inside me... pure spirits alive and dead... don't know... don't care... care too much... must stay in the middle of this empty road... stick to the path... they say nobody hears the screaming out in space and maybe that's true... but it's the same on Earth in the remote locations... busy locations... the forests and oceans... down on the farm... in the city... behind locked doors... blacked-out windows... high walls... orphanages asylums prisons slaughterhouses... few

people want to know the gory details... unless there is a cure...
redemption... forgiveness... life in a nutshell... karma and versions
of the same... some folk demand revenge... retribution... I am
almost home... hurrying to the warmth of the house where I am
safe... my husband... our son and our daughter... our dog listening
for my footsteps... these are the ones who will love me... forever...
head aching... doubts nagging... watch ticking... dice rolling...
time and chance... front door swinging... the fog... my big looping
circle –

Joe picked Dave up and drove out to the Oaks, parked near Clem's
caravan and followed him to the garages, climbed into his four-
wheel drive and set off through the old Webb buildings, past a line
of battered cars and a rusting tractor, across heathland towards the
woods. The soil here was soggy and would have swallowed the
Skoda whole, Clem's headlights picking out the firmer track that
was going to lead them through the trees. This tightened as the
brights were turned on, so it felt more like a holloway, as if the
earth had risen up and this was the only way forward, turning
back impossible.

Sitting up front, Joe played selector and chose 'Pretty Vacant' to
get them in the mood, drawing on the example of the legendary
Mike Huskisson who liked to play the Sex Pistols loud when he
was on his way to confront a hunt. Joe turned up the volume and
felt his emotions surge with Steve Jones's guitar.

– They've left their car on the lane next to the plantation, Clem
shouted, doing his best to be heard over the best introduction to a
punk record ever recorded. The one off the lane down from the
quarry. We could have followed them in from there, but it'll be
better this way. More of a surprise. We can stop at the earthworks
and walk. It won't take long.

– You're sure it's the right people? Joe asked.

– Same car, same place. It's them, don't worry. They've got a
fucking nerve coming back, I can tell you.

– You definitely didn't recognise their faces?

– Never seen them before. Could be local, but I doubt it. They weren't hunting for food. Nothing traveller or poacher about those two. They had all the gear, brand new and very smart, could have been kitted out by Dave when he was flogging designer gear. No, they're outsiders. Hobby hunters. Sportsmen.

– Berkshires who don't come from Berks or Bucks, Joe noted. Va*cunts*.

– Doing things here they wouldn't do at home. Same as the rich in their castles. The lords and ladies hanging their arses over the walls and shitting on the peasants below. They bring the bodies out at night and dump them in ditches, dig shallow graves because they can't be bothered with the full six feet, leave us to clean up their mess.

Joe thought about the brickworks in Iver and Langley, the Grand Union and Slough Arm spur. The bricks made there had helped build West London, been taken in on barges that returned loaded with rubbish. The kilns were long gone, the brickworks broken up and covered in earth and brambles, and yet the canal had been cleared and was a lot nicer than the one he had known, the dirty water that had changed his and Smiles's and eventually Dave's lives.

– There's plenty of deer in Richmond Park. They could go there.

– Protected, isn't it. Gamekeepers do the killing in Richmond.

Dave remained silent in the back. He hadn't said much on the way over either, and it was more than him being moody, almost as if he was sulking. It could've been because Joe'd told him to leave the plastic knife at home, only half-joking when he asked if he needed to be frisked, but Dave had brought up Chris again, probably narked he wasn't with them. That made no real sense, though, and Joe wondered why Dave had come. It wasn't as if he was obliged, while Chris didn't know what they were doing, couldn't know given his law-abiding ways.

– Lovely night for it, Dave moaned, speaking at last. I could be in the pub chatting up a Polish blonde, a beautiful East European. Perfect tits and bums those ladies. Instead I'm heading into the forest with a couple of lumberjacks.

– What are you on about? the driver asked.

Why *was* he here? Joe could understand Clem, who lived nearby and had been threatened, but Joe was the only one who didn't eat meat. It was right that the majority of people hated fox hunting, the killing of animals for fun, especially those big-game hunters who went to Africa and shot lions on safari, and yet they thought it was fine to torment a pig its whole life, lift it into the air and cut its throat, leave it to bleed to death, and if you could excuse the killing of a lamb, well, you could excuse most things. It was the madness of human beings, and he wondered if animals lied, and if so, did they lie to themselves?

– You're a couple of lumberjacks. Wood-cutters without your axes.

Maybe that was why this mission felt right and Dave was sitting in the back. Three men with different views had united around a single cause, as if they were part of an army or religion or political movement, and didn't the military, churches and trade unions all like their marching music? Nobody could resist 'Pretty Vacant'. Joe was pleased with his choice.

– How long are you back for, Dave? Clem called out. I bet you're missing the easy life. Has to be a shock coming back after getting used to things over there. You must miss England as well, though. Having a pint with the boys. A proper pint I mean, not that poodle piss they serve in Europe.

Dave decided to see the funny side. Soft-hearted Clem always stepped up and did the business when required. He didn't have to put up with some cunt in a hunter costume pointing a fucking cross-bow at him, and Dave was taking that more and more personally as the Pistols played, because while he might have been enjoying an extended holiday in the sun, this was still his manor, the place where he had been born and bred and wanted to be buried. Not these woods exactly, but near enough, and Clem was his mate, a man he could trust, unlike Sherlock Fucking Holmes Chris.

– Something like that, he replied.

Martina had been prick-teasing him, and here he was out in the wilds on a wet Saturday night when he should have been behind her bar serving the locals, nice and chilled as he chatted with civilised people who all spoke English. There was no guzzling, singing, fighting. Worse, this idyllic life was now at risk thanks to his big mouth, even if he was blaming Chris, that upright, law-abiding rich fucker who was going to send to him to prison if he wasn't careful. Fucking wanker sitting at home with the wife watching hours of Scandi noir, getting fat on pizza and popcorn, leaving Dave to come into the real darkness with Joe and their pikey mate, Dave loyal to the end.

– I could never live over there, Clem continued, shaking his head. I'd miss the family. My mates. Fair play to you, though. Each to their own.

The last pictures Martina had sent Dave showed her sitting on the balcony of her apartment, the place they shared, fully dressed and reflective, and he really did love her face, the shape of the nose and cheeks, brown eyes that never stopped sparkling, not even when she had a strop on. She could lose it as well, really give him an ear-bashing and deliver a punch, but while he gave it the big one about shagging, in truth he was loyal to her as well. Martina's personality was right there in her features, expressions he couldn't explain yet knew what they meant, and through these how she was feeling inside. They said a person's eyes the mirrored their soul, so maybe the face was the mirror of the mind. But what did he know? Just that he was out on the prowl, looking for a couple of horrible cunts he had never set eyes on before.

Chris, meanwhile, was sitting in an unmarked police car in Reading with an off-duty DI Williams, listening to the more relaxing rhythms of Scientist, a faint but steady throb that wasn't going to draw the attention of passersby. An arrest had been imminent, but that was three months ago and Abdullah was still free, turning up at the house of his victim Faiza on at least two occasions to taunt her and her parents. DI Williams had only recently shown Chris the photos, and while he had known about the case, the images were ones he was never going to forget. The young woman's nose and right cheek looked like melted plastic, while her right eye was white and blind from the acid.

Williams insisted a prosecution was unlikely, that Abdullah had got away with the attack, and imagine what would happen to any woman he one day married. Men who committed the most serious crimes were always going to reoffend, and while Chris didn't think this was strictly true, that there were even killings that were one-offs and could be justified, when it came to something like an acid attack he agreed. Abdullah's brothers had provided a false alibi, and while there was enough evidence to prosecute, DI Williams believed it was being used as the justification not to do so, the real reason being that the authorities feared they would be accused of racism, as that card was already being played.

The DI had thought about this long and hard while attending a family funeral in Jamaica, the idea that so-called honour attacks, the genital mutilation of girls, forced marriages and noncing could be regarded as sensitive areas – cultural practices best left to the communities concerned to sort out – was evil. That sort of thinking had no place in a modern democracy. It just allowed men to abuse women – nothing else. If the law wasn't enforced, England was finished. The way the large-scale rape and brutality carried out by racist Pakistani grooming gangs had been sidelined for political reasons was a disgrace.

Abdullah had to pay, couldn't be allowed to get away with what he had done, and it was important that he knew the reason for his punishment. DI Williams had little time for liberals, believed in retribution. Most stories were based on revenge, no matter the form they took. Again, Chris agreed. The house they were watching had a light on in the front room, the plan to either follow Abdullah when he came out or if he ended up at home alone go in and deal with him there. Either way he was going to get a good hiding. It was a loose plan, but there was a personal element to this Reading meet, as they hadn't seen each other for nearly a year and it was high time they did.

Their shared love of reggae and dub, added to the mutual respect they had for each other as professional police officers, had bonded them when they were out on patrol, back when Chris was in uniform, before scum like Abdullah had driven him to leave the force. He was strong again now, more dedicated than ever, and it was great to see his friend Williams, someone who looked at the world in a similar way, a lot different to Joe and Dave who seemed to drift through life accepting things in a way he could not.

Williams reached over and rubbed the inside of Chris's leg and he felt his cock stiffen. He leaned back as the DI undid his flies, lifted up so he could lower his trousers and pants, the hard-on revealed the best he'd had for ages, and while he felt bad about Carol they no longer had a sexual relationship, had become parents rather than man and wife. He felt Williams's tongue tickle the end of his knob, the sweet sensation intensifying as her mouth moved down his shaft, Chris closing his eyes as she repaid his earlier hard work in the back seat.

While Chris was enjoying a blow job to the steady rhythms of *Heavyweight Dub Champion*, Dave was putting his Spanish promise on hold as 'Pretty Vacant' ran into 'Search And Destroy', The Stooges spelling out what this mission was all about. Dave knew it was time to hurt a deserving stranger, to relieve the pressure he had been feeling with some old-school CCTV-free aggro.

– Over there, Joe said, pointing into the trees to their right.

Clem stopped and turned the engine and headlights off, a torch beam clear in the woods. He reached for a pair of night goggles as the music continued, put them on and looked at the selector.

– Impressive, Joe remarked, turning the music off.

Clem identified two men, one of them armed with a crossbow, opened his door and got out, the others following. The hunters were moving in the opposite direction and didn't know they were being watched.

– Don't bang the doors, Clem warned.

These were clicked shut and the inside light died, leaving them in the black, Joe unable to see anything at first, his eyes taking time to adjust to the light of a half-moon filtering through the trees shielding the track. When Clem turned his torch on he was holding a shotgun.

– What's that for? Joe asked, shocked and suddenly worried.

– We can't go up to them empty-handed, they've got a crossbow. Might even have a shooter of their own. Something fancy.

– You said you were bringing a taser.

– I know, but this is better.

– Makes sense, Dave agreed, pulling a small chopper out of his coat. These are the cunts who killed Bambi.

What the fuck was he doing with an axe? Joe couldn't really say anything, not when Clem had produced a shotgun.

– We can't be killing these rotters, Joe said, trying to hide his fear by joining in with the Sex Pistols reference. I thought we were giving them a warning. A slap at most.

– We aren't going to kill anyone, Clem said. But we do need some firepower. Words aren't going to work on their own. There has to be a threat. Think of this gun as our nuclear deterrent. Come on. And stay behind me. We don't want anyone getting lost. It's going to be boggy once we're off the track and I know the right paths to take.

Clem led the way with his torch pointing down at the ground, Dave behind him swinging the axe back and forward, while Joe followed at the rear. He needed his head seeing to, and really they should have just smashed up the sportsmen's car. Mind you, that wouldn't save the deer they were going to try and kill.

– I'm going to chop their fucking heads off, Dave said. Stick them on stakes. Drag their bodies to the lake and swim them out to the middle.

– Shhhh, Clem whispered. They're over there.

He stopped and crouched down, turned his torch off. The others did the same, and again it took time for Joe's eyes to adjust.

– They're watching something, Clem said. I think they've got their own night vision. They're facing the other way and still haven't heard us, the useless cunts. Let's go get them. Quiet as you can.

The two sportsmen didn't suspect what was coming up behind them until Clem shone his torch and they turned, dazzled by the light in their eyes. Joe saw that they were in their early thirties and wearing matching Barbour jackets and walking boots. Everything about these plums seemed out of place.

– Evening, sports, Clem announced in his attempt at an Australian accent. What are you doing here in the Outback?

The hunters had the same problem as Joe, took time to identify the three men, the crossbow starting to come up before they saw the shotgun pointing at them, William Tell's favourite weapon immediately lowered.

– Nothing.

– You must be doing something. Do you remember me?

There was no answer.

– You can't have forgotten me already. What are you up to? I thought I told you you're not welcome round here.

– We're hunting. There's no law against it.

– I don't know if there is or if there isn't, but I don't like you snooping around and killing deer, don't like you pointing that crossbow at me either. Do you think I'm some sort of cunt?

The sportsmen didn't answer.

– CunT, Dave remarked.

His smaller torch came on and he held it below his chin and directed the light up into his face, turning himself into some sort of mad serial killer, or at least trying to, as the effect was more trick or treat than *Halloween*, which only made it seem worse to Joe, more childish and therefore insane, the woods doing something to everyone's heads, the place where the worst fairytales came true.

– He asked you a question, Dave said, stepping forward, the chopper clear now in the beam of Clem's torch. Do you think my mate's a cunt?

– No, of course not, said the man holding the crossbow.

– Or a cunT?

– No, the other sport said, his voice wavering and unsure.

Dave was taking charge, and Joe realised he was just an observer and Clem not much more. Something very bad was about to happen. Joe wasn't a pacifist, but he *was* a lover rather than a fighter, and whatever the description he didn't want to see a maiming or a murder. Dave was capable, the memory of what he had done to Wells clear. That B&Q incident with Micky Todd had been his warning. A near miss that Joe had ignored.

– Don't 'of course' me, you wanker. Why are you trying to kill Bambi?

Clem's light showed confusion moving towards terror on the sportsmen's faces. Why was the axeman talking about Bambi?

– And drop the crossbow or my mate is going to shoot you in the face, and I'll chop your friend's head off.

The sport with the crossbow did the right thing, glancing back the way he'd come, telegraphing the idea that maybe he should try and make a run for it, while Joe noticed how his pal seemed to have shrunk now he was faced with this lumberjack who had remembered to bring his axe. Joe couldn't help feeling sorry for the bloke. No, fuck him. Dave was only having fun. He didn't mean what he said. At least Joe hoped he didn't.

– Chop it off and put it on a stick.

The fact they were in the woods on a winter's night was making everything seem much worse than it probably was.

– You two are deer hunters and we're headhunters. I'll cut your arms and legs off as well. Scatter them through the forest for the wolves.

An explosion rocked Joe inside and out, Clem firing a shotgun barrel into the air above the sportsmen, the hunter's torch thrown sideways as they ducked down, as if not having it proved they were defenceless. Joe moved sideways and waited for the shock to run out of his body, while Dave laughed and stayed where he was, pointing his torch up into his face again and turning it on and off.

– Go on, fuck off and don't come back, Clem shouted, lowering the other barrel so it was pointing straight at the main man's chest.

The sporting types were on the move, walking as fast as they could given the uneven ground, and when Clem sent another beam of torchlight after them they panicked and started to run, the hesitant one stumbling and falling, scrambling back to his feet and staggering, staying upright, his friend leaving him behind as he disappeared, quickly joined by the second hunter.

– That was easy, Clem said, picking up the crossbow. Too easy.

Joe felt nothing but relief as the three of them stood together not sure what to do next, but knew the others were disappointed, expected something more, and especially Dave who kicked and split a rotten log. Clem took charge again and started walking back the way they'd come, Joe and Dave following in silence. After a couple of minutes Clem stopped.

– Turn your torch off, he said to Dave, and did the same. Listen.

There was no sound and the blackness came right up to their eyes. It was cold and eerie, the sudden shift in atmosphere causing Dave to sigh and shuffle his feet.

– Shhh, Clem said. Keep still.

Dave did as he was told and Joe began to hear faint noises, some hisses and pops, a fluffy needle on scratched vinyl, except he was in the woods and the sounds were natural. Leaves rustled and twigs cracked and something with legs was breathing. He was sure they weren't alone, that eyes were watching them, but he wasn't going to imagine witches, guessed it was one of the deer they'd come out here to protect. A person screamed and Dave's torch flashed and he was on the move mumbling fuck this.

– It's a fox, Clem called after him. Dave, it's just a fox. And you're going the wrong way. Over here...

Joe was happy to get back to the moonlit path that would take them to the Oaks and the Webb buildings and the garage with its forgotten motors. He wondered if Lady Penelope had seen her chance with Clem away, studying the tractors as an ever-patient Parker waited in the mud-splattered Rolls. As Clem drove, Joe felt uplifted knowing they had saved some lives tonight, and probably in the months to come as well. He felt at peace as they came out into the open, their mission accomplished.

– Are we going for a drink? Clem asked, once he had parked and they were standing outside his caravan. It's still only nine. Ten past.

Joe drove them towards the chosen pub which was fifteen minutes away, and when Clem told him to do a right turn not long after they left the Oaks he assumed it was a shortcut, realising too late that this was where the sports had left their car.

– Slow down, Clem said. Can you pull over up here?

Joe did as he was asked, wondering what Clem was planning as he was the one who'd fired into the air and told the two men to leg it, but he had left the shotgun behind so it wouldn't be anything too serious, although there was still the mad axeman sitting in the back to worry about.

– What's the matter? Dave said.

– I wanted to see if those two had got back to their car yet.

Dave leaned forward, suddenly interested.

– No, Clem continued. They've gone.

The track next to the plantation was deserted, and Joe was relieved.

– I suddenly thought we should've done their tyres, Clem said. They got back before us, though, didn't get lost. It was just a thought.

Joe turned in the entrance to a field and drove back up the lane and joined the empty road that would take them towards The Plough. There were some huge houses along here, protected by electronic gates and metal fences, passersby only glimpsing them for a second or two through the conifers, a world he had seen in miniature delivering those records to Lady Penelope. These places were much bigger, though, new and probably home to a different sort of person again, where money alone counted. Leaving this road for a winding lane the width of a car, he sped downhill to avoid anyone coming the other way, reached the bottom and veered left ahead of the ford past old council houses and labourer's cottages, pockets of the past where families had survived for generations, the nature of their work changing but not by much, the quiet the same as when the dwellings were first built.

– What were you doing in the woods? Dave asked Clem, putting the phone he had been studying away and leaning forward between the front two seats.

– Hunting hunters. I was with you. Remember?

– No, when they shot the deer.

– What are you talking about?

– Fucking hell, Clem. Last time, when you first saw those

wankers in the woods. What were you doing out there in the middle of the night?

Clem didn't reply at first, and Joe had the thought that maybe he'd been doing some hunting of his own, but couldn't see it somehow, especially as he'd been so angry about that deer being shot. He waited for an answer, and when one didn't come he glanced sideways and saw Clem looking uncomfortable.

– I was going for a walk on the track we drove down earlier, saw lights in the trees and went to investigate, that's all.

– I don't know, Dave said. We've been mates for a long time, and that doesn't sound like you. A stroll in the moonlight? On your own? Sounds a bit iffy to me.

– It changes you when you're living alone in a quiet place like the Oaks. It was a nice evening. The stars were out. There's nothing else.

Joe pulled into the potholed car park at the front of The Plough and was soon opening the door and leading the others inside, the conversation dipping as heads turned their way, but only for a moment, several men greeting Clem as he passed. Joe hadn't been in here for a couple of years and was glad to see it hadn't been tarted up and turned into a restaurant like a lot of these isolated pubs. It was still a drinker's hideaway, which meant one or two people would be getting behind the wheel legless at the end of the night. Maybe the police didn't care, the lanes being deserted at night, and it wasn't like they didn't have more important things to be doing.

He bought a round and some crisps, went over and sat at a table at the far end with Dave, next to a fruit machine, Clem spotting his nephew and going to say hello, Joe calming down in the agricultural surroundings, the beams and horse brasses and framed rural scenes that had decorated the walls for twenty, thirty, forty years. The men who drank in here were largely middle aged with money in their pockets. Self-employed and self-made. Builders, plumbers, electricians. Buyers and sellers. Engineers. Directors of small limited companies. A locally famous nightclub owner. There was a table of nurses who would have driven over from Wexham Park or High Wycombe after a shift. The pub used to be known for its speed and coke, but he'd never heard of it being raided, and that phase felt as if it had passed.

There was a plush red carpet covering the floor, and rather than the usual faded, drink-soaked effort this one looked and smelled new, and as he relaxed the earlier glow returned. The hunters were long gone and no non-human or human animals had been hurt. It was a good night's work, and even Dave seemed happy as he sipped his Directors. Joe opened a packet of crisps and ate them one by one, took a mouthful of IPA. There were a couple of ska DJs at the Union Jack Club tonight and he'd been thinking to go over there later, but could feel himself settling in here.

– What was all that about with the torch? Clem asked, once he had come over and sat down, laughing as the image replayed.

– I don't know, Dave said. It just came from nowhere and felt like the right thing to do. Did you see them? I think that scared those two more than anything else.

– You could be right. It fucking scared me. I thought you were going mental. Your face looked like something out of a Punch And Judy show.

– When you've got the good looks I've got, messing them up is bound to be a shock.

Light drifted across their table whenever a car passed on the road outside, long white shafts that flickered across the three pals before fading with the faint swish of tyres. When a car slowed and pulled in and turned towards the pub their beams lit them up to the harder sound of crunching gravel. Once the engine was turned off there was a delay before the door opened and the arrivals entered. This happened three times as they sat drinking and talking, the reaction the same with brief dips in noise as the newcomers were noted.

– You should come over in the summer, Dave was saying to Clem. I keep asking Joe, but he still hasn't been to see me.

– I've got to work, Joe said. Anyway, you're always coming back here. I will, though, I promise.

– Be nice if you did. You can go to the other side of the world easy enough.

– We could all come over. Me, Chris and Clem.

– Forget Chris. Fuck him.

Clem was surprised and looked at Joe who shrugged, but before either of them could speak the door opened and the lead sportsman and his muddy sidekick appeared, the latter's trousers smeared brown and green in a camouflage mix of bark and grass. Dave had his back to the berks as they approached the bar, the dirtier of the two deciding what he wanted to drink before heading for the Gents. The remaining sport ordered and inspected the pub as he waited, saw Joe looking over but didn't recognise him. Clem had seen the hunter and was about to say something, but Joe nudged him with his knee, slowly moving his head side to side. Dave had his back to the bar and for now was oblivious.

Clem didn't want any trouble either, not in a pub full of witnesses, and anyway, he had made his point and his anger was gone. He used The Plough and didn't believe in pissing through your own letterbox. Dave was going away and didn't have to worry about the consequences of any aggro. It was odd the sports weren't long gone, that they hadn't fucked off out of the area, and Joe wondered where they had been, what they'd been doing. Looking out through the window at their car he saw that the front was smashed in, guessed they must have panicked and ended up in a ditch or hit a tree, and he smiled as the film played in his head.

– What's funny? Dave asked.

– I was thinking about those two wankers running off through the trees, Clem replied, thinking Dave was talking to him.

Joe shut his eyes.

– They got off lightly, Dave said, his face clouding over. Deserved more. Fucking look on their faces when I did that ghost impression, though.

– Yeah, proper monster mash, Clem said, reaching into his pocket and taking his own torch out, sticking it under his head and turning it on and pulling a face.

– You're right, Dave said. It frightens me now looking at you, and we're indoors surrounded by people.

He raised his glass to his mouth.

– Thirsty work tracking down cunTs, he laughed. Nice pint of bitter this.

The sport at the bar was looking around the pub again and saw Clem, and this time he made the connection, took in a staring Joe and the back of Dave's head. The man shining the torch into his face seemed different to before, and he realised it was the one who had been holding the shotgun. Next to him was the silent, unarmed man. The psycho with the axe was facing the other way which was a stroke of luck. He paid the barman and left the drinks on the counter, went into the Gents and came back out with his friend, their faces lowered as they hurried out of the pub. An engine sounded and tyres screeched.

– Someone's in a hurry, Dave remarked, unable to see the car concerned from where he was sitting. They serve a good pint in this pub, don't they?

The lights faded and the night closed back in, Joe cheerfully reflecting on how quickly peace could be restored. The Plough was warm and comfortable, the beer well kept and the clientele friendly. A low rumble of conversation rose up, the older twang of the Saxon shires essential to the Estuary sound as town and country fused. He thought about the box of spoken-word albums he had at home, the sentences that could be broken into words, small snippets of sound speeded up and slowed down. Subliminal recordings. He preferred sentences. Grand speeches and quiet asides, young and old and middle-aged voices. He wondered what it was like for a medium, people like Lou, if they could turn the voices on and off.

– I'll have another one of these, I think, Dave continued. Or maybe try a local ale. They've got a good selection.

The landlord had gone round to the other side of the bar and seeing that the sportsmen's beer was going to go to waste Joe went over and collected the glasses, carried them back to their table, thought it only right they have a drink on the deer hunters. He passed one each to Dave and Clem, looked across the room to see if anyone was bothered, which they weren't. He told Dave this was another pint he should try, and when he finished his Directors this is exactly what he did, sitting in a country pub on a cold night not bothering to turn his mobile back on, talking and joking with his pals, the three men pleased with a good deed done while Martina wondered why the naked selfies she was sending were getting no response.

CRACKERS

Spring, 2017

RUBY JAMES STOOD at her bedroom window, forearms on the sill, net curtains draped around her shoulders as she looked out past the bungalows opposite to the field beyond, marvelling at how the frozen dew sparkled as morning broke. She hoped the frost wouldn't kill her rosebuds, but couldn't stop the same rush of excitement that came with snow, ice, mist, fog, thunder, lightning. She loved drizzle and she loved the driest of dry days. Black clouds and blue skies. A downpour was a miracle when she had somewhere to shelter and for a split-second she heard the repetitive beat of torrential rain on a bus-stop roof, the sound replaced by the silence of the moment.

Charlie Boy came out of the house, treading carefully as he did his best not to spill the hot water in the saucepan he was carrying, Ruby with him as he moved down the path, and when he reached their car he began pouring the water out along the top of the windscreen, steam rising as it slid down and melted the frost. Islands began to form where this was thickest and he went back to clear these, saving enough for the side windows, the back ones covered in a white powder that could be removed with the wiper. When he was done he returned the saucepan to the kitchen and Ruby heard Ben barking excitedly until the front door clicked shut once more.

Back outside, Charlie stopped and looked up and waved to Ruby who blew him a kiss in return, and she saw herself through his eyes, a blank face at the window, the nets around her head a wedding veil or a funeral shroud, and because the curtains were white and clean and smelled fresh and alive she chose marriage over death. Charlie started walking, passing the car and continuing along the street, off around the bend and out of sight. Ruby stayed where she was, returning to the field and the chestnut trees on its far edge, the wider world waiting on the other side.

The sun was bringing the first dreamers back and in an hour or so thousands of curtains would be opened and radios turned on. There was going to be brushing and washing and dressing, the eating and drinking of cereal and toast and tea and coffee, the leaving of homes and setting off to work and school through streets lined with houses and flats planned, built, maintained. These citizens carried the remembered and the forgotten, happy and sad times, good dreams and bad, and among their many destinations were factories, offices, shops, warehouses, showrooms, depots, car parks, a bus and a train station, libraries, garages, service stations and later pubs and clubs and churches and halls where speakers spoke and listeners listened.

There was religion and politics, givers and takers, police and thieves, the public and the private, the living and the dead in cemeteries and one big crematorium where the buds in the rose gardens were covered in a killer frost Ruby saw as beautiful, nearby graves under headstones and burials with no markers, dead flowers and living trees full of birds and squirrels eating berries and nuts, horses and donkeys chomping grass, mice and rabbits in hedges and burrows, rats searching dustbins and black bags, dogs and cats watching through windows imagining woods and meadows but preferring warm rooms and regular meals, and beyond the cracking brickwork and concrete pigs and goats there were flesh-made deer and foxes and badgers, the bigger fields further out, heathland, woodland, wasteland, reservoirs, power stations, a bitter loneliness in winter that was skin-tingling in its brutality, and in all of this there was the energy, creativity and hope that meant Ruby felt fantastic as she stood leaning forward at her bedroom window.

It was true that in the town and the country and the places in between crimes were being committed, but justice was inevitable. Ruby believed in heaven and karma and love, in looking on the bright side, dazzled by the light bouncing off the crystals across the road, the uncut diamonds of nature. It didn't matter how dead the land seemed or how low the temperatures fell because there were billions of seeds waiting to burst into life when the conditions were correct. There were good deeds to be done and she thought of the wards she had worked on, her change of direction, the variety and responsibility it had brought, promotion within the structure, something she owed to Christine Ballard, Ruby disciplined and proud to be part of the NHS – always.

Stepping back and standing straight she lifted the curtains as she went, rearranging them so there were no folds and the bottom edge was even against the sill. She took extra care, the same as she did when they were being washed and ironed, conscious the material was easily torn. Mum used to say that these nets were better than any alarm or guard dog as she knew when a window had been opened by the way they were left. Mum's old curtains... Ruby heard footsteps on the stairs and turned her head as the door moved, Ben's breathing on the other side of the wood, waited for him to come in, but he changed his mind and she followed his paws on the landing carpet, the sound growing fainter until they were replaced by the creak of a hinge.

She tugged the duvet back and brushed the sheets flat and tucked the edges under the mattress, shaking the pillows and stacking them three on each side, returning to the duvet and pulling it up again, smoothing the surface and spreading a red blanket with white polka dots over the top. Once the bed was made Ruby went onto the landing and into the bathroom, closed and locked the door, took her dressing-gown off and hung it on a hook and started running a bath, brushing her teeth and using the toilet, removing her top and pants and leaving them on the floor. She undid her locket and placed it carefully on a cabinet shelf where it would be safe, lowering herself into the bath and turning the taps off.

Easing back, Ruby propped her neck against the edge of the bath and stretched her legs out, appreciating the luxury of hot water, looking past her feet and painted nails to the bubble bath and oil behind the taps, next to them her shampoo and conditioner, two bars of soap, a rubber duck with an Elvis quiff and a plastic mermaid called Daphne. The mermaid had long blonde hair that covered her breasts, a silver lower body with runs of blue and purple scales. Elvis squeaked when he was squeezed, while the sound that came out of Daphne was more like a smoker's cough.

The tiles above the bath were whiter than she could ever remember seeing them, reflecting sunlight magnified by the window's frosted glass, a pane of frozen dew that never melted. She watched the glass nuggets twinkle as steam rose and thickened and became the mist that turned the room into a sauna, and she thought about Charlie Boy walking the two miles to work every day so she could use the car, the two miles back when he was finished, and at this very second he was out there in the freezing cold while she was inside in the warm, but he insisted it was fine and she believed him, would have done the same if their positions were reversed.

Charlie didn't mind the snow when it fell as even though it slowed him down it made the journey more fun, his childish excitement returning, while when Ben saw it for the first time he'd bounced into the air he was so surprised, lifting all four paws at the same time to escape the bite, and when he landed he'd backed up and stepped forward and tried again. Ruby wasn't sure which Ben she was seeing, if she was a girl or a woman, and it wasn't long before he loved running around in it, lifting the snow up with his nose and tossing it above his head and barking.

Lowering her head into the water, Ruby's ears hummed as a rubbery film slipped across her cheeks, and she kept her nose in the air as her body vibrated, density and elasticity linking, moving a hand behind her ear to touch the skull bone, imagining she was Daphne swimming with blue whales and spinner dolphins, those wonderful creatures she had seen on *Blue Planet*, the sound of David Attenborough's voice soft and crackling in the depths. That man had lived such a brilliant life, but only a few people could, because there would be no society without the workers, and Ruby was proud to be a worker, proud to be a public-sector worker.

She believed in the structure and planning needed to care for a community, and while there was no age when it came to a person's soul she felt everyone reached a crossroads at some point, went through something that could change the way they saw the world and lived their lives. This was a belief based on experience, and while the memory would always be there she was strong, her strength deliberate. She had changed, but refused to become cynical, more interested in the politics of healthcare and her union and the future of the NHS.

Ruby was melting into the water, a mermaid matching temperatures, wanted to stretch her limbs further, roll over and swim buoyed as she'd done in the hospital's hydrotherapy pool, one of the physiotherapists letting her try it when it was closed for the day, after they'd discussed flotation tanks and the brainwaves they released. She liked the hospital when it was quiet, and if Charlie had picked up the children from Mel and there was time she would walk over and see one of her friends working on the wards where she had spent so many years. Most of the people she knew were still in the system and would probably stay there until they retired, and that was a good thing, her other family dedicated and firm.

When she was a little girl they'd had two goldfish, and when their tank was being cleaned Dad would fill the bath with cold water and let them loose so they could race up and down, and it has seemed amazing at the time, watching them speed back and forward, but now it was just sad, as that was the nearest they'd ever come to being free. She felt cramped suddenly, returned to the heat rather than the idea of space, thought again about the frost outside and her rosebuds in the back garden, roses given to her after Mum died, memorials for a woman who had lost her memories years before. The stems had thickened and the thorns sharpened as they grew bigger and stronger, sending out roots that reached deep into the earth, and Ruby had learned how to care for them with compost and water and her secateurs.

After ten minutes drifting she sat up and reached for the shampoo, tipped out a handful and rubbed it into her hair and scalp, the smell of lavender filling air that was clearer with the mist thinning, the light coming through the window even more powerful than before. She closed her eyes to avoid the glare as well as the sting of the shampoo, a minute later using the shower head to clean it off. These morning baths were her luxury, a mental as well as a physical cleansing that set her up for the day ahead.

She could let the children sleep for a while. It was early and the house was still warming up. Ben would be snuggled up with one of them, turning sleep on and off as dogs did, everyone at peace. This was her private time and as the bath cooled she topped it up with more hot water, listening for the flare of the boiler and the echo of the pipes, the house alive and looking after her family. She adored their home, the place where they were safe and together, didn't ever want to be alone, overwhelmed by the love she felt for her husband and son and daughter and dog.

There were moments when she was waking up or falling asleep, relaxed like she was now, split seconds when she wasn't sure if her children had been born yet, and she wasn't scared when this happened as really it made no difference, they existed and that was that. Maybe one had been born and the other was waiting inside her, and she wasn't sure if her boy or her girl had arrived first, or they could both be in her belly, these spirits she had always known, present in her mind as well as her genes. This house and the steam and the mist and the fog... She wasn't mermaid Daphne and Charlie wasn't Elvis, and definitely not since he'd been forced to sell the Cadillac. That had broken his heart, but they would buy it back one day, she was sure they would.

The fact that her day was planned gave Ruby confidence and security, the support she needed for the work she did, and this was non-stop, each person and situation unique. There were plenty of downs with the ups, and being part of a team made it easier to cope with such a stressful job. Charlie had compared her to Ben, said she jumped out of bed every morning like a dog excited to be alive, as if the day ahead was her first on the planet, that this was a rare quality. It was true as well, because she did look forward to what was going to happen next. She would see Charlie and the children and Ben and her friends and workmates and meet people for the first time and the tenth time, hear their stories, opinions, hopes.

Ruby would dress and go to her children soon, lean down and kiss their foreheads, open the curtains to let the light in, tell them about Jack Frost, coax each one awake and out of bed, ask them to wash and dress so they wouldn't be late for school and she could get to work on time. They might complain at first, but she was patient and would tell them that one day they would wish they were in a classroom learning about history and geography and even maths, and while they were getting ready she would make breakfast, check Charlie had remembered to give Ben his biscuits and a bowl of fresh water although he had never forgotten to do so.

Their children were good natured, happy and perfect. They would eat and brush their teeth and put their shoes and coats on and find their bags and say goodbye to Ben and off they would go – the three of them – out into the cold air. Ruby always said the same thing if the kids moaned, that it was refreshing and good for them and they'd soon warm up walking, and down the side of the field opposite they would go, through the houses and across the road with the help of Tracy the lollipop lady, past the shops where they asked for sweets. It would take ten minutes to reach the school, and here she was going to hug her son and her daughter, whisper in their ears that she loved them, they must never forget she loved them, and she would hug their little bodies to make them understand, watch as they trotted into the playground and found their friends. She would stay by the gate for a minute or two, in case something happened, even though she didn't know what could as the teachers were so alert, and sometimes she would become absorbed in the noise and movement of the yard, finally remembering that the time was passing and turning for home, saying hello to parents she knew, smiling at those she didn't, returning the way she'd come, climbing into the car Charlie had cleared of frost earlier, so she could stay indoors and keep warm.

Ruby washed and rinsed her hair with the shower nozzle, added more water to the bath and lay back down, dizzy from the heat, the strobe-like flashes popping inside the window creating a nightclub effect. She felt as if she had been dancing and drinking, time out of sync again, looking forward to seeing her friends at the end of the week for her birthday. The dizziness didn't last, and she lowered her head below the surface, brain pounding with those underwater vibrations. She had ten minutes before the rollercoaster ride began, a brand new day in the eternal life of nurse Ruby James, the excitement building and bursting, a huge rush of joy that would drive her on and on and on.

At times like these I forget where my body begins and where it ends... it's as if my spirit swells with each new breath until it is too big for my skin... stretching the stitches that hold me together... but these threads can never be broken... I am invincible... the joy flows through my pores and into the world... merging with essential oils and salts... slicks of soapy goodness that circle back and wrap themselves around my arms and legs and torso... turning me inside out... foggy vapour fingers... a body cocooned in a soul... and if I want maybe I can stop breathing... live on the air in my lungs... and yet breathing is one of life's wonders... eases the tiredness of working... moving through darkness... dealing with fear... mobiles and doorbells... old folk waiting on chairs... children in their beds... scared women and men hovering... treatment... explanations... advice... reassurance... cups of tea and stories told... heard... repeated... I drive home through green streets and blue fields... talking animals at fences... whispers in stereo speakers... under the beat... Charlie my soulmate... standing behind me at the window... arms around my waist... he lowers his head to prop his chin on my shoulder... sees the world from my angle... our faces in the glass... distorted by the nets... when something moves in the road I lift the curtains and we step forward... see a fox... a big one... well fed... it must live in the town... it senses us and stops... zooms straight in... I can't tell if it is a vixen or a tod... and we are excited... warm in our house... the home we share... the life we have built... bare feet on new carpet... luxury... two years to pay... soft and deep... the fox keeps staring... hears a noise... continues through the icy-white houses... hard to see properly... but the frost must be heavy... our car is covered... I hope the engine will start... Charlie kisses my neck... beautiful Ruby... thinking life is bigger and better than it is... always seeing the best in people... Charlie... he engulfs me... in our bedroom... in this bath... smelling him like I smell our carpet... shaving cream and shampoo... the soap and toothpaste we share... aftershave I bought for Christmas that he rarely uses... when he comes home he is exhausted... smells like a different man... he has a bath... comes back to me... we hold each other up when we start to sink... keeping our heads above water... I tell him that people are *good... that life* is *bigger... better... remember the tickets you bought... David Hockney... Polaroids taken in a desert... sketches on an iPhone... blown up and framed... a mobile phone like we might own... paintings the size of walls... we were small in comparison but I felt huge inside... thought I was going to burst... so did you... remember... just seeing what one person can achieve... purple trees and upside-down roads... that's how I feel... cameras on a car driving down a lane... trees and hedges across the seasons... the artist went back to live with his mum... Hockney... you do remember Charlie... you must... how we felt... he nods... says of course I do... at the time... continues we've never been anywhere... never lived in another town... another country... seen a desert... left and returned... and I feel myself fading... my stitches will snap... the sadness in his voice... he reminds me of the broken old men who have given up... cancer... heart disease... unfulfilled dreams... looking back on wasted time... no reason to live... we all need a reason... some sort of mission... I tell Charlie we're young and can do anything we want... there's no rush... he says he is a small man... nothing much... my light flickers... oxygen mask stuck to my face... cylinder empty... why does he have to say these things... and why do I think of it now when we are happy... Charlie walking to work in the cold... a beautiful frost... me in the bath... hopelessness pushes us over the edge... off hilltops and bridges... in front of trains... Charlie promises me he is fine... just wishes we had more money... that life could be easier... I tell him it is perfect... it's the same for everyone... and the moment passes... we have our jobs and our house where we raise our children and care for our dog... one day our boy and our girl will grow up and leave home but we love them and they love us and they will live nearby... we will have grandchildren and won't that be fantastic... it's something we are looking forward to even if it is far off in the future... we have*

time... lots of time... why wish the years away when we are
happy... and we really are happy... life is beautiful... we are
lucky... I can't pretend I never think about the other questions...
which are important... but how can we dwell on those things when
we are busy... we all have our stories... ways of telling them...
human lives... fantasies... trying to persuade ourselves... but
Charlie is real and our children are real and our dog is real and the
kids need to get up soon so they can go to school... and lifting my
head out of the water I reach for a towel and dry my hair...
humming a tune... singing... the child I am... morning breaking...
the first morning... blackbird speaking... sweet rain... sunlit from
heaven... the first dewfall... the first grass... and I feel reborn as I
always do... pulling the plug and lifting myself up to sit on the side
of the tub and using the shower head to rinse away the suds...
standing up and wrapping myself in the towel... wiping con-
densation from the mirror and seeing my face with the wall behind
lit up by the light from outside... as if the frost has spread and
turned the tiles into those precious stones... bath emptying... and
in the silence that follows I hear footsteps on the landing... I have
daydreamed too long... there are paws as well... on our soft new
carpet... small hands knocking on the bathroom door and calling
Mum –

Ruby hadn't seen the locket slip out of her shirt, hadn't noticed it
dangling over her glass, shifting forward when Carole beckoned
with a red nail thinking she wanted to be heard more clearly over
Adele and the roar of the pub, had a secret she needed to whisper
even though they were alone with Grace in the loo and Dawn at
the bar. When Ruby was close enough Carole reached across the
table and she followed her hand and saw the silver case as it was
lifted up, Carole letting it lie flat in her palm so she could look at
it more closely. She said the locket was beautiful and very unusual,
that she had never seen it before, would have remembered if she
had.

This was because it was meant to be private, maybe even secret, and Ruby asked her to be careful as the chain was old and delicate and would easily break, moving back as Carole allowed it to slip through her fingers, gently lowering her hand to avoid the jolt that was going to snap one of the links. Ruby tucked the locket back inside her blouse, between her boobs where it belonged, doing up the buttons so it was extra safe as Carole asked where it had come from, if Ruby had just bought it or was it a present from Charlie, something left by her mum that she only wore on special occasions? It really was a lovely piece of jewellery.

Ruby was slow responding, shocked to find herself staring at the ring tied to Carole's wrist by a piece of string, the one Steve had worn the same way, a gift from their daughter. Carole never took it off, and its history had become blurred, but now Ruby was remembering where it had been and what it represented. She wasn't going to lie to Carole, just needed to choose her words, replying that the locket had belonged to a friend, which was the truth. She paused for a few seconds so it wasn't obvious when she changed the subject, even if that was easy to do after three drinks in a noisy pub.

This is what started Ruby thinking about Jeffreys – Carole reaching for the locket he had stolen from Pearl, breaking into those boxed-up memories so Ruby focused on the ring he had taken from Steve. Jonathan Jeffreys – the monster responsible for the murders of Pearl, Steve, Ron and Danny and how many other people she did not know. Jeffreys deemed a psychopath by the authorities. A lunatic acting alone. Both of these points had been emphasised, but there was more to it than that, his motives far deeper, a playing out of prejudices that went back centuries, an arrogance denied but still driving the rulers and their followers today. A psychologist had mentioned a split personality, that the possibility couldn't be ignored, but what he'd meant was the split in society, just didn't realise, his thinking short-term and individual rather than long-term establishment. It was easier to decide Jeffreys was insane. A lone wolf. That had been the official verdict, the final judgement on the man who told Ruby he was working for the state as he set about killing her.

He was easing the burden on the NHS, taking the tough decisions politicians shirked, his message one of sustainability and tolerance, and here he came, Jonathan Jeffreys strutting as he emerged from the shadows, breaking out of the cell where Ruby had placed him, a cardboard box sealed with willpower. He was revived, slipping through the curtains and moving towards the limelight, feigning modesty as he neared centre stage. It was Mr Austerity himself, talkshow political, his younger days as a hanging judge denied and lawsuits threatened, this caring expert keen to adapt to every change that lead to success. He respected the ideal of socialised medicine, loved it, in fact, but the masses mustn't be scared of the private sector and what it had to offer. The old class politics were dead and it was time to move on. People should ignore the past and even the present, look only to the future, and this master of language was wowing the watching millions as he disarmed the Andrews Neil and Marr, charmed Laura Kuenssberg and Jon Snow, calmed Emily Maitlis and Piers Morgan. Vetted audiences whooped and applauded the progressive, liberal-minded Mr Jeffreys, this casual yet smartly dressed, media-savvy, Facebook-friendly, Twitter-dynamic libertine. His years in the margins of Ruby's mind meant he was cautious in his arguments, and yet hadn't he been too easygoing in the past? His beliefs had moved into the mainstream and this was his time. He only wanted to help.

Carole was laughing about whatever she was talking about, pulling Ruby back into the moment, and while she smiled and nodded she couldn't hear enough words to make out sentences as their glasses were raised and lowered, the energy filling the pub a release from the working week, and Ruby was happy seeing Carole dolled up and glamorous, returning to the ring and remembering how she had gone under when Steve died, turning into Candy and selling sex to survive, too proud to ask for help, buried in her grief as Jeffreys moved through the hospital, a virus that mutated as it passed along the corridors and entered the wards collecting details, souls, trophies – a locket, ring, watch, dice.

There had been an inquiry and recommendations made.

Lessons would be learned and the chair offered assurances. Every life was precious. Each individual deserving of respect. It was essential that the public trusted those charged with their care. If that trust was lost the wider society would suffer. Ruby agreed with the woman saying these things, believed she was sincere and became interested in her story, how she had started as a nurse like Ruby and Dawn, in time gaining confidence thanks to the encouragement of an older colleague, taking courses and changing direction, always dedicated to the NHS and what it represented. She spoke the same way as Ruby and the people she knew, believed it was Jeffreys' accent and bearing that had shielded him, that and the sheer self-belief of the self-entitled.

At first Ruby wondered if Christine Ballard would be taken as seriously as the posher members of the panel, but while softly spoken and reflective, she had a presence that meant any bias was overcome. It was Christine who had inspired Ruby, made her realise that she had to push herself if she was going to survive. Ruby didn't believe there was a conscious cover-up with Jeffreys, as those she dealt with were shocked by what he'd done. The police treated her well and were disgusted by the video Jeffreys had played as he attacked her, the film that had given Ruby the extra strength to fight and kill her murderer. Later, she decided she would force herself to keep believing that people were decent and life was special, the world a wonderful place, but in truth her heart had always ruled her head and her faith in humanity naturally returned.

Nothing Ruby or anyone she knew did would ever be good enough for Jonathan Jeffreys and his kind. While there were his parents to consider, the way he had been raised and educated, his actions came from a wider hatred. Ruby, Carole, Dawn and Grace were the scum of England as far as he was concerned, the white trash he had discovered on the outskirts of one of the greatest cities on the planet. His London was about wealth and prestige, architecture and institutions, property as investment. Snobs such as Jeffreys hid their selfishness by denouncing the mob – hooligans and whores, their parents and offspring, the idea of the suburbs, satellites, provinces. This new breed of controller insisted the masses were racist, uneducated and stupid, the elderly a burden stuck in a past that had to be erased, and Ruby was hearing Jeffreys' poison spouted openly on TV and the radio, his spite pouring from the mouths of politicians and journalists and a long line of celebrities, the rich and famous obsessed with this thing they were calling Brexit.

Culling the crackers wasn't enough for Jeffreys, as while he needed clean kills never suspected, a subtle euthanasia through syringe and special medicine, it was important that he chose his victims' afterlives. Everlasting peace was an obscene reward for a worthless existence. Where was the justice in that? Lessons must be learned and examples made. He had taken as much satisfaction deciding where the peasants would spend eternity as he did removing them from society and saving the state the cost of their care. The same rules had applied to Ruby, but he'd got everything wrong. She pulled back and willed Jeffreys back into his box, wondering what he would say if he could see her sitting in this pub with her friends – Ruby in her heaven and Jeffreys in his hell – imagined his fury and was pleased.

Grace came out of the Ladies and glanced over before heading towards the bar, Ruby watching her before returning to Carole and trying to read her lips, this mother who Jeffreys had visited privately, and she felt the tears welling up. As if murdering Steve hadn't been enough... Candy on her knees, Candy's mouth open, Candy gagging on the controller's urine. Carole had sobbed when she told Ruby, once Jeffreys was dead and exposed. Now she was urging Ruby forward again, beckoning with that long red finger, asking if there was a picture of Charlie in the locket, and Ruby nodded. This wasn't a lie either, just it was Pearl's Charlie and not her Charlie Boy, and all this fed into the tears she was finding it more and more difficult to hold back.

Ruby hadn't told anyone about the objects she'd reclaimed from Jeffreys, the trophies he'd stolen from her friends. She knew why she had taken them and was glad she'd had the presence of mind to do so, but the job of passing them on to a loved one had been left half-done. The shocks that followed Jeffreys had comes in waves, moving from short and sharp to a long-drawn-out attrition, and when she returned to work the sadness had been overwhelming. She saw the ghosts of her friends and played out their murders in her mind, a spiral of what-ifs, and this meant she'd had to fight even harder to forget and survive, and so the watch and dice she had taken were hidden at the back of a drawer and left there as she drew on Christine Ballard's example for strength, but those tasks left half-done or not even started always came back to haunt a person in the end.

She had given the ring to Carole and kept the locket for herself, as that was easy and where they belonged. Pearl had never married after Charlie's death, and while she'd taught thousands of children over the years she hadn't had a family of her own, which must have been tough once she retired. While the woman would never have thought of herself as lonely, Ruby's heart had melted when she heard Pearl's love story. Ruby was close to her when she was alive and Pearl's death hadn't broken their bond, the locket a symbol rather than a psychometric tool. Like Steve's ring, the locket had gone to the person who was going to cherish it most, but Ron's watch and Danny's dice were still in her drawer, wrapped in a hanky and sealed with a ribbon. This was her unfinished business, the chink that had allowed Jeffreys to march back into her mind. Passing the watch and dice to the right people was what Ruby she knew she had to do to be properly free.

Carole mouthed sorry as she lifted her phone up to concentrate on a message, Ruby taking the chance to look across the pub and enjoy the space, coming to Dawn and Grace at the bar. They were picking up the drinks and turning in time, side by side, and when they saw the birthday girl watching they started dancing to the music, and with the drinks on the table the four women huddled together so they could hear each other speak. Ruby was told to close her eyes and not to peek as Dawn took the cake she'd bought out of its box and arranged it with a candle in the middle. Ruby's present was placed to the side of the cake by Grace while Carole lit the candle, Dawn telling Ruby she could look now, and once her eyes were open they started singing happy birthday, the rest of the pub somehow hearing and joining in. Dawn told Ruby to make a wish in her direct way, then said to hurry up and blow the candle out or the wax was going to run into the chocolate. It was important to Ruby that she made the right choice, which she was sure she had as the flame was extinguished. Her present was moved over and Ruby commented on the wrapping and bows, which was the work of Grace, and took her time unwrapping rather than ripping the paper apart.

They had bought her a pair of hiking boots. These weren't cheap, and Ruby was touched as well as excited. She had been wanting some for ages, but money was tight and they weren't a necessity. She'd long thought to walk the Ridgeway from Ivanhoe Beacon to Avebury, start near the hill where she'd watched the snow falling with her daughter, let the path take her to the stone circle. After that she would walk the London Loop, begin near the bridge where she had looked at reflections in the canal with her son, head from Uxbridge in an anti-clockwise direction through Kingston and Ewell. The Outer Orbital was the walker's parallel to the raver's M25, and she reckoned she was both of these wrapped into one, the same person who could dance and sleep in the stone circle at Avebury, more like three, four, five individuals, and maybe there were others, an infinite number of characters she hadn't yet met.

Grace was explaining how she'd checked the size, make and colour of the boots with Charlie, but the receipt was in the box if they needed changing. Overcome by their kindness, Ruby cried her bottled-up tears, Grace and Carole aahing while Dawn told her not to be such a silly cow. Ruby dabbed her eyes and watched Grace neatly fold the paper and collect the ribbons and slip them into her handbag, stared at her friend's bracelet and wondered how many people in this pub had similar reminders. It wouldn't just be jewellery they carried with them, but the objects on their shelves, boxes of photographs, furniture passed down and kept as a way of hanging onto the dead. Grace's bracelet reminded Ruby of how they'd met, the tale Grace had told her in the early hours when the ward was still and silent but full of thoughts and dreams altered by fear, sedatives, morphine.

Ruby saw Grace's story in familiar locations and drew on memories than ran from solid to half-remembered to imagined, and while the film altered with the passing of time and her changing moods, the woods remained the same. Danny had gone to the same place to pick mushrooms, but only during the day, wouldn't dare enter the trees at night, although Grace hadn't had a choice. That peasant fear of forests and the dark was inside them all, could easily turn to terror for a man with acid in his brain. Ruby wondered if she could persuade the others to stop at Danny's local, The Green Man, but it could be rough at night, and they'd already planned to go to Nuggets and dance. She promised herself she would start her search for the person who loved Danny in The Green Man, and this made her feel good inside as she cut the cake and put slices on plates supplied by the landlord, and before long their lipstick was smudged with chocolate and they were singing along to Ed Sheeran and thinking about one more round before they headed off.

Ruby realised she was drunk when they were standing outside waiting for the cab to arrive, and when it pulled up Carole knew the driver and sat in the front while Ruby, Dawn and Grace got into the back. Hawkins had worked with Steve at Estuary and swapped hellos with Carole, the skinhead asking about her family and wasn't it mad how fast children grew up, and she replied in kind, got on to the Union Jack Club, wondering if there were any good nights coming up, Ruby unable to hear the answer over Dawn going on about her sister-in-law and Grace asking if Ruby was sure the boots were okay.

Holding her present tight, she was thrilled by the future, and as she was sitting in the middle of the other two she found herself with a tunnel vision of the roads leading to Nuggets, moving away from the pub through houses and onto the main road and under the motorway and finally the quiet drive skirting the reservoir to their lit-up destination at the end of the dark one-lane approach. Every so often Hawkins's shaved head bent over so he could hear

Carole above the racket coming from the back, listening in an attentive manner, clearly a gentleman capable of protecting his passengers from bandits, which is what every woman wanted from their cabbie.

They paid Hawkins and then Des on the door and were inside Nuggets with Ruby buying the drinks and as Carole knew the barman she was able to leave her boots behind the counter for safe-keeping five minutes later dancing with Grace and Dawn as Carole stood by a table minding their glasses talking to a couple she knew holding her phone in the air showing off pictures on a screen that seemed like a sunbeam to Ruby although she accepted her senses were heightened along with her emotions she was even happier than earlier seeing Carole bubbling and in overdrive these last few years she supposed it was the same for lots of people who reached that crossroads and were at breaking point the ones who refused to let their melancholy win sadness was an addiction and weren't there too many religions rooted in misery little more than death cults and Carole had resisted and taken her path and so had Grace and so had Ruby each in their own way and whatever worked had to be good.

Dawn was pressing up close chanting through Botox lips talking faster pupils dilated she was tougher than the rest of them hard as nails happy working on the same wards appreciated the routine and familiar surroundings going out as many nights as she could drinking too much too many drugs called herself a tart and laughed at the description Boxer her only romantic weakness half-platonic and Dawn and Ruby were friends for life like Ruby and Carole and Ruby and Grace they were all friends forever Ruby lucky having these people who would always help each other and were getting stronger as time passed the sisterhood of the grape and the hop and the E on occasion Grace a loner she was different never going to fall in love even if it would do her good she refused Grace gorgeous but mad as a hatter nutty as a fruitcake and who could blame her they all had their foibles.

These thoughts blurred into the rhythm of the song the hymn the worship of a congregation their voices beat-matched to fit fresh meanings Ruby speeding to the sounds of Satellite tripping on her breathing weightless in water and in the sky her essence in the shades of blue the fables told in stained glass read by an illiterate peasantry that dug for victory dug for potatoes parsnips turnips surviving the winter on root vegetables stored and gallons of disease-free ale the seasons changing their moods each one of them beautiful she couldn't remember what came first if it was birth decay death rebirth hopefully it made little difference as she hiked overland to the barrows and a stone circle those rotted wooden crosses and church windows that carried the big answers to the big questions history myth legends explaining good and evil the miracle of creation and the superman who sacrificed himself so others could live accepting his crucifixion rewarded with resurrection and eternal life.

She prayed that one day Charlie Boy would be able to do the things he loved again thinking of Satellite FM and On The Parish and those nights with Joe and Alfonso even though regular money a grown-up wage was more important than the dreams of boys and youths and men of all ages it was right that he had a nine-to-five job and did all the overtime offered the same as Ruby when she wasn't celebrating her birthday like this and they were happy together she was certain of that the sacrifices weren't really sacrifices they'd made their choices and were making do and doing their best everything worthwhile when you had a son and a daughter yet she felt odd tonight despite blowing out that single candle in the pub Ruby a child sitting at the living room table with her friends a little girl in a party dress Mum and Dad bringing plates of sandwiches and jam tarts she was a teenager in bare feet and a mother dancing the link to Charlie and her children loosening every attachment doomed to end in loss but worse was to never have loved or lived life to the full – surely?

Ruby was surfing waves of sound cutting through mist collaged from faces closing her eyes and touching the ceiling and seeping through cracks in plaster and brick and slipping into the night a burst of fog in chilled air a wisp of spirit in the heavens defying gravity one of those fancies where she was immortal floating above the housing estates and factories travelling with the chopper coppers tracking her younger self with their scanners she was looking down on Satellite this magical place picking out shapes and shades of grey and green manmade meets nature familiar land-marks the beam of lights and straight lines circular tracks trying to decide what belonged where an albatross gliding over the terraces and cul-de-sacs and commons and industrial parks the woods and orchards and caravan sites and park homes kites reintroduced breeding spreading out across the shires and into the suburbs watching gardens searching for pet rabbits and small dogs as well as wild peace-loving mice and smaller birds and chicks Ruby didn't like hunters whatever their species it wasn't personal just she was made of love the sweetest part of nature booming from the speakers she was back in Nuggets bass drum techno jungle down-beat the sounds of the machine the electronic throb that didn't need spoken words rarely meant or lived Ruby sweating soaking her clothes heart beating inside her skull full of echo and reverb the smell of drink and drugs eyes closed eyes open closing and opening Ruby the birthday girl breathing perfume and deodorant and smudged lipstick traces of chocolate and sugar rushes melting mascara the lager and ale and stout and gin and vodka and whisky and wine the fainter flavours of speed and ecstasy and the heave of skunk these she resisted a working mum with children and people depending on her Dawn and Carole and all these brains full of she didn't know what couldn't know what they were seeing everyone had their journey Ruby knew her path was a simple one it had to be straightforward the road chosen as she danced like the gene-rations had done on sprung and hard floors the great-grandmothers and grandmothers and mothers and daughters and sisters and children and little girls skipping on a chalked pavement and in the playground Ruby's son and daughter her little boy and little girl hopping Ruby stumbling Grace and Dawn holding her up she bent down their hands strong took her shoes off unzipping her handbag stuffing them inside best she could returning to the dance the music drenched soaked in a bubbly bath until the others pointed to the side of the room and they went over to Carole and Grace said she'd buy a bottle of so they could sit on a couch and drink in peace and dry off and catch their breath and Ruby was pleased heard their hearts beating in time synchronised and thought that was nice.

After another drink she needed a pee and went to the Ladies, unsteady on the shoes she had put back on, removed from the support of the crowd, her friends who would pick her up if she fell down, the music that kept her balanced. She had work in the morning and needed to sober up, had to be fresh and positive, couldn't let anyone down. A big part of her job was raising spirits, providing hope and friendship as well as medical support, and she achieved so much more going to a person's home. She needed a clear head, a full charge of energy, and when she came out of the Ladies she was hit by the heat and felt claustrophobic, decided to go out back for some fresh air, Dawn there talking to a man about boilers, the best-value makes. Ruby left her to it as she sat on a chair near the smokers' hut, thinking but not telling those puffing away what they were doing to their lungs, that they should learn about heart disease and strokes, spend half an hour with the COPD sufferers, never mind a visit to a cancer patient, or come with her to a dying person's home, someone who wished they'd never touched a cigarette. Like Dawn, she had first-hand knowledge of these things, but couldn't say too much when she was out socially.

Dawn left the boiler man and came over to Ruby, asked if she was okay. Ruby was fine. Dawn was shivering and she her to go back inside, that she'd catch her up in a minute or two, needed to clear her head, and when Ruby was alone she moved away from the smokers, spent too long with her thoughts so when she went back inside she couldn't see the others, danced for a while and searched again, took her phone out of her handbag but the battery was flat, decided she needed to go home.

Walking along the lane that led back to the main road, the sound and light faded as Nuggets shrunk to toy-town size, Ruby realising it was going to take her a lot longer than she'd thought, that if she could cut across the fields she would save herself a lot of time. When she saw a stile in the wire fence to her left she used it, removing her shoes again and crossing the grass flanking the reservoir, climbing the slope and stopping at the top. The water was still and beautiful and reflecting the moon, and when she looked into the sky she was surprised by the brightness of the stars, how visible they were away from the houses. She turned to those next, the twinkle of thousands of lights, was struck by the silence, wished she could stay for a while, but her teeth were starting to chatter and she had to keep moving, started down the slope on the other side of the reservoir, a handful of sheep watching her pass.

Once she reached the field below she walked to the far end to avoid the lorries parked in the lay-bys, climbed over the fence and followed the road next to the motorway, knew she could cross this further down and work her way home. Her head was clearing and she could feel the ache in her legs, was tired and cold but forced herself to speed up, wished she'd charged her phone properly and could let Charlie where she was, call for a taxi, and if she couldn't get one maybe he would come and pick her up, put the kids in the back seat asleep as they couldn't be left alone. She was miles from home and unsure of the time, Pearl whispering that she shouldn't worry, everything would be all right, but she was still barefoot and needed to put her shoes back on, that it had been raining and her feet and hands were covered in mud.

Ruby stopped in the middle of the bridge crossing the motorway. She was exhausted and needed to rest. A camera stared at her from the far side, but she had done nothing wrong, placed her forearms on the wall and watched the traffic which was thin and moving fast, the noise louder here than when she sat in her chair on the embankment. It had to be well past midnight and she was sitting on the side of a moonlit hill with her daughter, standing on a humpback bridge looking at a reflection in water with her son, telling them to be careful because they were young and might fall. Ruby hovered on the landing of her house listening to her grown-up children talking downstairs in the living room. She lingered at the window in her bedroom watching the frost form. When Ruby's legs stiffened and cramped she lifted herself up and sat on the wall, and when the pain eased she turned and dangled them over the side, stayed like this for a long time.

A blue light flashed and she wondered why an ambulance was stopping on this quiet little bridge disturbing the peace on such a beautiful night suddenly concerned she'd been called to an accident and had forgotten to put on her uniform needed blood and oxygen maybe a drifter had fallen from the crossing their lungs drowned bones broken brain burned narrowing her eyes and peering into the light as a black shape formed and came out of the revolving shades but the vehicle was too small for an ambulance it must be an RRV a life-saving paramedic on hand Ruby surprised when a policewoman appeared she seemed hesitant took slow steps unsure nervous something not right Ruby startled when another shape appeared from the margins she was distracted had to concentrate a policeman forming and smiling he was moving slowly as well maybe he was out for a stroll just happened to be passing the policewoman must have hurried forward because she was next to Ruby and had a firm grip on her arm asking if she was okay love and why didn't she lift her legs up and turn around and stand and move away from the wall the policeman was next to her now a strong arm around her waist moving behind her back when she swivelled his other hand on her wrist the arm moving to her shoulders as the two police officers breathed relieved easing Ruby upright and away from the wall towards the flashing blue as they got closer she saw their patrol car with Thames Valley markings the man reaching inside and turning the light off while the woman kept hold of her arm offering a bottle of water releasing her grip the water tasted fantastic Ruby thirsty and they said go ahead drink as much as you want finish the bottle if you like.

The policewoman asked Ruby if she was Nurse James. This surprised her, and so did the fact that the man and woman were called Toni and Tony. This was confusing for the first few seconds, and the three of them laughed at the coincidence. They promised to look after her, which was very kind, as the walk home was too much and she shouldn't have stopped on the bridge and let her muscles seize. The police officers asked her to sit in the back of their car with the door open, and they didn't seem in a rush, wanted to chat, asking odd questions, spoke about the CCTV and a night worker concerned for her safety. Ruby didn't understand why, even though she thought it was nice of a stranger to be worried about a stranger, even if everything was fine. He had called the police and they'd hurried to the bridge, and Ruby was overcome that these people cared this much, at the same time felt guilty for causing a fuss. She'd drunk too much and it dawned on her that she had done a dangerous thing, even if it hadn't felt that way at the time. Later she would realise that they'd thought she was going to jump and kill herself, and that shocked her, as she would never do such a thing, couldn't see the point.

Ruby was comfortable in the back as Tony drove – *I sit at the front of the church with Lou* – Toni was next to him but had turned around in her seat so they could talk face to face – *we listen to the last lines of the hymn together* – rather than speaking to the windscreen and its ghost – *I don't see the locket slip out* – Toni remembered Ruby from the hospital – *I don't notice it dangling* – the times she'd gone there with Mum to visit her grandfather – *the chain is old and delicate* – that was nearly ten years ago and this nurse had been extra kind – *easily broken* – she'd taken the time to talk to Granddad at night when he was alone and probably scared thinking he was going to die although he'd never said that to Toni – *fragile links* – Ruby was a good person – *Lou admires the case* – the small kindnesses matter – *thinks it is beautiful and unusual* – Toni told her about Granddad – *she closes her hand over the locket* – nearly ninety now and fit as a fiddle making every day count – *Lou searching for vibrations and the sound of my voice* – hearing this made Ruby even happier than she already was – *Pearl's memories and messages* – she remembered Granddad but not Toni – *whispering* – but she was in her mind somewhere and would come back – *Lou doing her best to hear through the static* – Toni's voice softened and Ruby was asked again about the bridge and the drop and the cars below doing seventy and eighty and some even ninety miles per hour and why was she sitting on the wall on her own late at night – *there are suicides on this side and that side and*

*what a terrible thing for a person to do to themselves but much
worse is what it does to those who love them and the despair
doesn't magically vanish with death at least I don't think it does
although there could be forgiveness and peace I'm not sure my
thoughts confused with someone else's the search for meaning
maybe* – Ruby explained how she'd been out with her friends for
her birthday and had decided to walk home when she couldn't find
them she'd forgotten to charge her phone which was unlike her
she'd had too much to drink and misjudged the distance been
dancing stopped on the bridge to rest it was a beautiful night with
the still water of the reservoir and the moonlight and the stars and
the sound of the traffic was hypnotic she'd been in a sort of trance
*– she wants to pass me a message from someone in the church
these outlines I can't make out and I'm wondering who* – Toni
glanced at Tony and seemed relieved *– stars burning on the altar –*
they wished her happy birthday *– our crucified saviour–* was she
still working at the hospital? *– the monster can't hurt us Lou's
hand hot as she squeezes the locket Pearl close by sure she is with
her Charlie* – Ruby's role had changed *– how has the locket ended
up with Lou did I give it to her or maybe it was Carole* – it must
be difficult work like policing *– I ask her to be careful as the chain
is old and delicate* – serving the community *– it will break if she
squeezes too hard I know she is doing her best I feel her apology
hope she doesn't take it the wrong way she won't and doesn't
wishing I could remember if I bought it or if it was a present from
Charlie or if it was left to me by my mum something to wear on
special occasions a lovely piece of jewellery* – Ruby spoke about
the changes *– reminders of the past and the future* – Toni reached
over and held Ruby's hand and said it was hard dealing with some
of the stuff they saw but at the same time it made their lives
worthwhile and she loved her job and the driver agreed that he
wouldn't want to do anything else.

When they reached her house Ruby was surprised by the relief
she felt seeing that the outside light had been left on as this would
guide her home. Maybe the protection of these two angels had
made her aware of the dangers she faced. She was trusting and

disorientated and easy to lure off the path. Ruby thanked Toni and Tony and hauled herself out of the car, and when she reached the front door she realised they were waiting to see her safely inside.

It took a while to find her key, and when she did she struggled to get it into the lock. Ben was waiting and barked when she was too slow, waking Charlie who'd dozed off watching *Pulp Fiction*, and he came and let Ruby in, saw the police car which flashed its beams and pulled away. He laughed as he asked if she'd had a good time, while Ben jumped up and licked her hand and then her face when she kneeled down in front of him and nearly toppled over, Charlie helping her up and into the living room.

She was struck by the warmth of the house, felt the sweat that had dried on her skin, the dirt on her hands and feet. Charlie had made her sandwiches and she wrapped her arms around his neck and hugged him tight, asking if the children were okay and had they gone to bed on time. Everything was fine and he was glad she was home, but why had she come back in a police car? Ruby explained how she knew one of the officers and they'd given her a lift after she lost the others and realised her phone was dead and had started walking home. She was tired and going to go upstairs and could she have a big glass of Diet Coke and her sandwiches there please?

Once she was in their room she sat on the side of the bed and started to undress, took her shoes off and remembered the walking boots, couldn't believe she'd forgotten them, her panic easing as she remembered they were behind the bar in Nuggets. She could pick them up tomorrow. Her feet were black and she tiptoed to the bathroom and cleaned and dried them, sprinkled some talcum powder, washed her hands and face and wished she could have a bath but would wait until morning. She brushed her teeth and returned to the bedroom, took everything off but her locket and once she was under the duvet she held this in her right hand and squeezed and floated between the two sides, from half-waking to half-sleep. Ben had been waiting for her to settle down and he jumped on the bed, and as she stroked his head she could hear Charlie starting up the stairs with her sandwiches and drink and was suddenly starving, put on her T-shirt and was sitting up straight when the door opened, ready for the perfect end to the perfect night out.

I didn't find out that Lou was a medium until later... when I first met her she was coming into the hospital every visiting time... on the ward as soon as she was allowed... in the evening and twice on the weekends... stayed until one of us went around asking people to think about going home... and during the day... Monday to Friday... she came in on her lunch break... that was when she was working for the council... before the cuts... it was a ten-minute drive each way plus the time it took to find a parking space... more stress... but Lou made sure she walked through those doors smiling... believed in the power of positive thinking... she was determined to convince this world and the next that Barry wasn't ready to die... he was twenty-five years old for God's sake... had his whole life ahead of him... would live into his eighties or nineties if he could just get through this... they both would... Lou had no room for doom and gloom because if she went down that path he would die and so would she... moods shaped events... altered outcomes... that's what she told me later... after we became friends... when she arrived on the ward she would always ask me... or if I wasn't at the front one of the other nurses I suppose... if there was good news today... standing there rubbing sanitiser into her hands... rubbing and rubbing... and when she carried on through the ward she made a point of saying hello to everyone who looked her way... if I was in the section where Barry had his bed I saw how when she reached him she kissed his forehead and leaned in close and whispered into his ear for what seemed like a full minute... I had this idea she was reciting a prayer but I could be wrong... I have never asked... wouldn't intrude... when she was done she sat in the chair next to his bed like visitors do... holding his hand and urging him to get better... perched at the front of the chair... expectant... but there were also times when she fell back and closed her eyes... as if the hope had drained out of her... she turned from

143

a young woman into an old woman... the change was dramatic...
half a century added in a handful of seconds... her body
shrivelled... the skin tight and dry... she lost her colour... that first
time I saw it happen I thought of a corpse... she heard and looked
over... beamed... positive again... as if energy had been pumped
into her system... but after a couple of weeks she didn't know what
to do with herself... brought a book in... Finnegans Wake... this
was during the day... quieter than the evening... it was a surprise
seeing it... that title next to a man fighting for his life... a still body
under white sheets... she told me Barry had planned to read it since
before she met him... Ulysses had been hard enough and Finnegans
Wake was meant to be even harder... but he was tired after work...
it needed his full attention... so Lou was going to read him a few
pages each visit... maybe she had given up on prayer... thought to
bring him back this way... but the idea didn't last long... Barry
would have to read that mad book himself... she laughed when she
said this... sure he could hear her and was laughing too... Lou
settled back into holding his hand... perched on the edge of the
chair... didn't flop back and age again... at least I never saw her if
she did... she was resisting the chaos... another challenge... the
ward's lack of privacy... extremes of emotion... arrivals and
departures... scared families... relieved families... it was easier for
me and the other nurses as we were used to it... we'd grown thick
skins... joked that we had become institutionalised... unem-
ployable in the normal world... Lou stopped going home between
the weekend visiting hours... bought a coffee from the stall inside
the entrance... if it was warm enough she went outside... sat and
watched the people... the whole world passing... staff and patients
and visitors... their different ways... but it was in the day room at
the end of the ward where I got to know her better... when Barry
needed changing or something else done she walked down there
and bought a can from the vending machine... sat in one of the
high-backed chairs and stared into space... I would say hello...
we'd have a quick chat... I had work to do and couldn't hang
about... we talked longer if I was on a break... she didn't believe in
chance... at least not in their case... she'd met Barry when she

drove into the back of his car outside the off-licence… she wasn't going fast… never had a crash before… there was a bang and a jolt… she couldn't believe it… out he got with that calm look on his face… despite what had happened… they pulled over to the side of the road and exchanged details… spoke on the phone… went for a drink… married… that's how it was… and six weeks after he arrived in hospital Barry opened his eyes… three weeks later ready to be discharged… he insisted on having a shave before he left… it was a transformation… they made and make a smart couple… life was renewed and has been good ever since… Lou and I bumped into each a year or so later at the church… my first time… that was a surprise… we recognised each other straight away… she greeted me like an old friend… her memory of that time when she came to the hospital every day is a positive one… she is grateful for the care Barry received… and we have a lot in common… I'm like an older sister… that's what she says… we agree on most things… hear each other clearly… believe that a person has to make the most of their second chances… that it is important to shape our memories… Grace is the same… an example… all us ladies together… witches on the boundary… we know life is too precious to do anything else –

It took Ray ten minutes before he found a parking place, frustration turning to relief as he filled the space and turned his engine off. He was twenty minutes early and stayed in the car as The Angry Agenda piled through 'Us And Them', his anger soothed but festering as the engine cooled. Nick Parker was one of only a handful of modern writers with something original to say, a free thinker who didn't give a fuck about the thought police. The band had put out two blinding albums in *Here Comes Trouble* and *Society*, and Ray had seen them play a good few times in recent years and never been disappointed. Too many bands were churning out see-through slogans, either in it for the pose or too scared of being slated on Facebook. It was pathetic.

More important was this problem with hospital parking. It

broke his heart seeing his mum on a ward, this frail version of her younger self timidly asking when she could come home. He promised it wouldn't be long. Acted cheerful and positive when he visited. Kept smiling. Cracked jokes. But it was hard pretending there was nothing to worry about. It was fucking depressing coming into the hospital, and the last thing he needed when he was already on edge was having to fuck about with the parking. At least he cheered Mum up. She wasn't short of visitors, but he was the person she depended on. The man of the house. Always had been. And she believed him when he said that everything would soon be back to normal. He gave her hope. Everyone had to believe that things were going to get better.

Ray understood that the hospital had been built when there were fewer cars and fewer people about, but it would have been easy to get rid of the double yellows on the road outside or rent and open up the field opposite. He didn't blame the hospital. It had to be the council and government responsible. The firm running the car park. Charging taxpayers for something that should have been free. Yet it wasn't the cost doing his head in. More the lack of empathy. The laziness. Pettiness. A private company should be nowhere near the NHS.

He had crawled around the car park for fifteen minutes yesterday, ready to thump someone by the time he went back out through the barriers and around to the other side of the hospital, past the nurses' blocks as he searched for a space. It was full there as well and he'd ended up parking on a grass verge near the psychiatric ward, across from the maternity unit where his daughters had been born. It was an empty strip of land doing nothing, but when he got back from visiting his mum feeling like shit there was a ticket on the windscreen. If he'd seen the person who'd put it there he would have struggled to control himself, even though he knew he couldn't be lamping people with Mum relying on him.

The cars near him had got tickets as well and he thought of the money the company was making and the immorality of this when there were all those nurses and doctors nearby working long hours trying to save people's lives. That's why he had arrived early today and was sitting here listening to The Angry Agenda, couldn't be driving up and down when he had arranged to see a doctor before she started her shift. He couldn't be late. Hadn't slept well and was expecting a death sentence. If life was a series of ups and downs then he was at one of his lowest points. Every success followed by a kick in the balls. And when you hit the ground every gutless cunt going stuck the boot in. But he would stay strong. Show no weakness. He let *Here Comes Trouble* play to the end before he got out of his car.

Walking into the hospital through the main entrance, he followed the corridor to his mum's ward and at the reception desk asked for Doctor Sanchez. He sat down and waited ten minutes. Followed her into a side room when she arrived. Table and three chairs. Cheap furniture. Functional. Posters on the walls. The effects of smoking and causes of strokes. Cancer, COPD, heart disease. Grim reading. They sat down. He knew Anna Sanchez wouldn't be seeing him if Mum wasn't terminal as it was murder trying to talk to a doctor, didn't have time to settle before she smiled and told him there was good news. His mother had responded well to her treatment and the new medication and would be discharged the following day. In the morning if she could be collected. He listened to the rest of what this wonderful woman had to say and left the room elated. Mum had problems, but was going to be okay.

While it was too early for visitors, the nurse on the desk said he could go in and see Viv if he was quick. When he told her she was coming home Mum's joy made him want to cry. She was happy like a child. His little girl. Their roles had reversed as her world shrank and he had become her father. He would work through the day and do a big shop tonight, seeing as she had people visiting this afternoon and evening, and he asked what she wanted most when she came home, thinking food and drink, but she replied a hot bath. With lots of bubbles. First she would wash her hair. It must stink. He would need to make sure her bath seat was charged up so she could get into it, and that he mustn't forget. If he did she would beat him up.

When Ray came out of the hospital he didn't care about the car parking or the money he was charged when he paid at the machine. Tomorrow they would get on with their lives as if nothing had happened. He felt great and wanted to get back to work. Drive his minicab as he liked to do. And back behind the wheel he contacted the office and Carole had him picking up a Gareth Williams at the railway station. He did a left and a right and followed the road into the centre of Slough to the sound of 'Breadline Britain', and this time he found a place to park straight away. He switched off his engine. Went through more of his Angry Agenda favourites, thinking how he could murder a pint and needed to celebrate. And once he was through the next few days that was exactly what he was going to do. When the weekend came.

He scanned the crowd leaving the station when the first train arrived, trying to guess where these people had come from and where they were going, if they were locals or lived somewhere else. A huge man with a bag over his shoulder had spotted the Estuary sign and was coming over. Ray paused 'Boot Boy Till I Die' and lowered his window, confirmed this was Mr Williams from Cardiff. The Welsh giant squeezed himself into the back seat and tested the car's suspension, Ray making sure he had the right address before pulling away.

– You a Chelsea supporter, then? Gareth asked, seeing the Standing Lion Rampant sticker on Ray's dash.

– That's right. London's finest.

– Did you go to the semi-final then?

– Wasn't going to miss that. Doesn't matter how many times we beat Tottenham, it always feels good. Straight line from Uxbridge. Wembley's like a second ground for us. They should keep it for the finals really, but it makes life easier.

– Cardiff, me. We've had one or two lively days out in the past.

– Can't be denied. It a shame we don't play each other more often. Once every ten years if we're lucky. Same with Millwall. More like twenty now.

– It's for the best with all the cameras. I'd rather have a drink with you lot these days. Mind you, I'll drink with anyone. Apart from Swansea.

– Same here. It's not just the CCTV, though, is it? Everyone's got a camera on their phone. What's all that about? But we're older and wiser.

– I know a few of the Swansea lads, to be fair. Worst mob has to be the Scousers. Liverpool not Everton. Well, they're the same I suppose, but I fucking hate Liverpool, me. Cowards with their Stanley knives. Proud of their blades, they are. That and the thieving.

Ray liked the Welsh. The men could drink and were good company, while the women seemed to sing when they spoke. The Taffs didn't go around slashing people like ponces either. Like Scousers. The country twang that ran from East Anglia down to Cornwall was his favourite accent, and maybe that's why he liked the Welsh. They had a sense of humour as well. Weren't up themselves. Didn't have chips on their shoulders. It was the same with the Geordies. A lot of Welsh had come to Slough to work when the factories were built and had settled locally. They'd voted for Brexit as well. Proper people the Welsh.

– Same here, Ray agreed. Chelsea rent boys this, Chelsea rent boys that. They've got gays on the brain in Liverpool, which isn't a surprise, I suppose, coming from a city that fell in love with the Village People look. Remember the big bushy tashes? Ian Rush, Terry McDermott, Mark Lawrenson? There's that poofy Scally style as well.

– Wasn't it Robbie Fowler offering his arse to Le Saux that started the rent boy stuff?

– He did it right there in front of a full house as well. On the Stamford Bridge pitch. No shame, Fowler. Graeme rightly declined.

They were both laughing.

– If anyone's rent boys it has to be the Scousers. They're denying their inner queer. Like they deny being part of England. What's that all about?

– They're a confused lot those Liverpool supporters, don't

know the difference between history and success. Been living on past glories for decades. Haven't won a league title in nearly thirty years. The only ones Chelsea hate more are Tottenham.

– Handy firm, though.

– I suppose so.

– Chelsea are doing all right with the Russian, aren't they? I love John Terry, me. Don't understand him leaving.

– Conte's not playing him. He's thirty-six, but I'd keep him. They made the same mistake with Frank Lampard.

– Another great player. All that team that started with Mourinho.

– That's what upsets the Mickeys. They think it's their right to win every trophy going, but they've won fuck all for years. Reckon they're the only working-class support in England. Like West Ham in London. All the Premiership clubs have got their glory hunters and numpties.

– Is Slough a good place for a drink? Gareth asked, changing the subject.

– There's a few decent pubs, but tell you what, come over to the Union Jack Club. The boss of Estuary Cars runs it. My uncle Terry. You'll get a good drink at a fair price. Tell them you know me. I'm Ray. You won't find it online, though. Thinking about it, if you want to go best let me know and I'll tell them you're coming. It's not really open to the public unless there's some music on.

– What sort?

– Skinhead reggae. Ska, bluebeat, rocksteady. Terry controls the jukebox. Laurel Aitken, Prince Buster, Desmond Dekker.

He gave Gareth Williams his number so he could message him, had to repeat it a couple of times.

– You in Slough for long?

– I'm staying with my brother for a few days, then I've got some work in Hayes for a couple of months. Maybe longer. I'll see how it goes. A mate over there is putting me up, but I'll be back. It doesn't take long on the train. My pal likes a drink. He'll have pubs he knows. My brother too. But I'll give the Union Jack Club a go. Sounds good.

– It's a Brexit sort of place, Ray added, taking a chance, interested to see what the Welshman had to say.

– Even better. What do you think of our prime minister, then? She's MP for Maidenhead, isn't she? I went through there on the train.

– I don't trust her, but they weren't going to replace Cameron with someone who wants to leave the EU, were they? I mean, they should have done, it makes no sense not to, but the Tory Party is pro-EU.

– Fucking clowns the lot of them. Corbyn's a wanker as well. McDonnell too. MP for Hayes. Terrorist scum the pair of them.

Ray thought to say something about Corbyn and McDonnell, but held back as there was no arguing against that IRA and PLO stuff. He hated the anti-Englishness in parts of the Labour Party, the student element and their obsession with identity politics, the sheer ignorance when it came to the socialist case against the EU. Why Corbyn didn't say what he thought about the European Union, Ray did not know. Appeasing his supporters would ruin the bloke in the end.

– At least May's invoked Article 50 now, Gareth continued. That's something.

Ray believed in fair pay and equality, the nationalisation of core industries and proper resistance to globalisation and the multinationals. He didn't trust party politics, those right and left labels that stuck people in boxes. A mixed economy. Support for small businesses and the self-employed as well as the public sector. A free and independent UK. Like George Orwell, Clement Attlee, Michael Foot, Bob Crow.

– You'll like the Union Jack, he said. Slough's not expensive, though.

– That was a day to remember. When we voted to leave the European Union.

Ray felt the same. Seeing the referendum results come in on June 23rd had been one of the happiest nights of his life. And that wasn't an exaggeration. He had surprised himself with the elation he'd felt. It was the end of a journey. As if he could finally relax.

Maybe it sounded odd thinking of it that way, but it was the truth, and he could summon up that elation with ease. That was unusual. He found it hard to explain the strength of his feelings and why he had them, but the joy was real and important.

– We finally got our way on something, he said. A straight vote and a simple majority.

– I'm just surprised the difference wasn't bigger than one and half million. Nobody I know believes in the EU, but Project Fear meant a lot of people thought they were going to lose their jobs the next day.

Ray thought about all those who had died feeling betrayed, because despite what the establishment said they had existed in numbers. Even so, he'd felt no sadness on June 23rd or the days that followed. He had been on a one-man mission for years, doing his best to wake people up, spreading the word, trying to convert his punters as well as his mates. Some people listened, some thought he was a crank, some agreed but said he was pissing in the wind, some didn't care. Like Gareth, he knew no EU-lovers. Once the subject was in the news a lot more had wanted to leave than stay.

Terry had rented a massive TV on the night. More like a small cinema screen. He'd had it installed in the Union Jack and forty or so purists had gathered to watch the results come in, joined by the same number again as the night progressed. It was no mad piss-up, with coffee available as well as beer, Angie and some of the wives and girlfriends arriving at midnight after a trip to Asda, bringing everything needed for the mountain of sandwiches they set about making, while industrial quantities of Bombay Mix, crisps, peanuts and corn chips were put out. Terry had become more and more interested in the months leading up to the referendum, reviving first-hand memories of his dad George and his old man's pals, how they'd felt about the traitor Heath taking the country into the so-called Common Market, what many regarded as Germany's third attempt to create their European empire.

One of the bonuses was seeing the mouthier remain politicians and public big heads suffering along with the presenters and journalists who were meant to be impartial but had done everything they could to swing the vote in the run-up. Once the result was known they had seethed for a day or two before the biggest sneerers lost control and the insults went into overdrive, a tide of spite that showed them up for the cunts everyone knew they were. The scorn oozed from these closet fascists, and while part of Ray still enjoyed seeing them suffer, it had become harder to hear as time went on.

Brexit means Brexit? It was a con. The word Brexit was an invention. Didn't mean a fucking thing. Made up to distort the real arguments and give the knobs the chance to play for time: 'But what does Brexit actually *mean*?' Next they split their invention. So there was Hard Brexit and Soft Brexit. The same thing had happened under Heath. The European Community became the Common Market. People used the term and swallowed the lie that it was a trade deal. Ray had voted to leave the EU, not some poxy Brexit. It wasn't difficult. Not really.

Then there was that wanker Khan telling anyone who'd listen that London was a remain city, that he wanted to team up with the SNP and stay in the EU. His London stopped at the M25, took no account of that older, traditional culture that was about people rather postcodes. The SNP were rooted in Ireland. Anyone but the English... Ray knew his anger meant little. He had no power. And yet he was happy. The elation he had felt after meeting Doctor Sanchez remained. Mum was his priority. Another sort of anger came with the fear of death, and that had vanished.

Once Ray had dropped Gareth off he called the office, pulled over as he waited for his next fare, moved from The Angry Agenda to the East End Badoes and Gonads, didn't have to wait long as Mrs Pepper was going to West Drayton. Mrs Pepper and her parrot Peter. They were regulars and he was always asked for by name. Peter only behaved when he travelled with the skinhead driver called Ray. Who took this as a compliment. He turned up the volume on 'Oi Mate' and was on his way.

David Bowie died and Joe Martin cried, and more than a year later he was still trying to get his head around the news. Bowie was meant to live forever. He had been back making records with Tony Visconti as well, first *The Next Day* and then *Blackstar*, released two days before his death. Joe had pre-ordered this on black vinyl, but when he found out Bowie knew he was terminal while making it had only listened once before returning the album to its sleeve. To sit there and enjoy it felt wrong, but a few days later he put the record back on his turntable where it belonged.

A lifetime of lyrics were swirling around Joe's head as he was transported back and playing 'We Are The Dead' in a Spiritualist church at the end of the Uxbridge Road. It was as if he'd held his own remembrance service early, time and the order of things cut up and rearranged as they had to be. He'd cried again listening to *Blackstar*, and yet the more personal crisis facing Chris saw him dry eyed and strong and doing his best to help his friend who'd had a breakdown and spent a month in hospital before returning to the house Joe was staring at now.

Standing in the back garden in the sunshine, breathing crisp, clean air as the trees and earth rumbled back to life, the sadness left him and he couldn't help feeling like one of the luckiest people on the planet. He was fit in his body and mind and had plans and dreams to spare, but he did need to play his own trick on time. He'd been connecting Bowie and J Dilla, how Jay had made his *Donuts* album in a hospice as he was dying, Bowie driven in a similar same way with *Blackstar*, these big last pushes to get their thoughts out into the world. Joe had to learn from them and inject some urgency into the ideas he'd let drift, knew he lacked drive, more interested in thinking about his songs than putting them together. He should be panicking, but wasn't.

His parents were well and he had a sister and nephews and nieces, his friends and interests and hobbies, and with the last of these he'd been trying to learn from *Donuts*, beats it had taken him forever to hear right. Bowie kept remixing in his brain, as if his sounds and words had lives of their own, which he supposed they did, and if those records meant so much to Joe how much more had they meant to their creator? Bowie was confronting the horror the best way he knew, and while it was said this showed he had accepted death Joe wasn't so sure, as wasn't rejecting it what made a person want to produce something solid to leave behind? Death had to be the cause of the inner turmoil that cursed every human being. If it could be proved there was an afterlife there would be no more competition, exploitation, anger, crime or war, yet where was the official body dedicated to finding that proof?

Maybe he had known what was coming a month earlier, unnerved by Bowie's 'Lazarus' video on YouTube, and looking back it was a clear warning, the lyrics as haunting as the film. Bowie's eyes were covered in bandages with buttons for pupils, like pennies on a corpse. If Joe felt this way about someone he'd never met, he hated to think what he was going to be like when one of his parents died. He thought about his friend Ray and how worried he was about his mum, and Joe had had none of that yet. It was impossible to imagine, and while he tried to convince himself that he had to get the death of David Bowie into perspective, it wasn't easy.

He checked the time, wanted to finish this bed before he had his break. He'd broken up the earth with a fork and turned half of it with a shovel, the soil in good condition as far as he could tell, with lots of worms and a robin loitering, and he pushed himself hard, knew to use exercise and physical labour to clear his mind. He was sweating and his muscles ached, but when he reached the end he could look back at his work and feel the familiar surge of some old-school satisfaction. He would plant the bed up after he'd had his lunch, went over to get his jacket and bag, walked down to the end of a garden which was wider than the house and well over a hundred feet long.

There was a wooden contraption with a table in the middle and a seat on either side here, and he adjusted this so he was facing the sun. He felt the chill more now he had stopped working and pulled his Harrington on, placed the sandwiches he'd made on the table along with a bag of mixed nuts and a bottle of water. He started eating, put his sunglasses on as the light grew stronger, as soon as he did the clouds closing, and as he sat at the bottom of this garden near the compost heap and shed, shielded by shrubs and bamboo, he was at peace, tucked away in a hidden corner of a strip of land that while manicured still had its wild patches. Joe was happy to be serving the masters in this big house, seeing as his bosses were Chris and Carol.

Poor old Chris had been on a serious downer for nearly four months now, the trigger going back further to an acid attack on a young woman that had destroyed her face. As he'd struggled with some of the things he'd had to deal with during his first stint in the police, it shouldn't have been a surprise he was affected by this, but what *was* surprising was how he had become involved. His new role was supposed to be easier, Chris working in an office rather than on the streets, but it hadn't worked out that way. Along with another officer he'd been accused of assaulting the attacker, the man concerned claiming racist and Islamophobic motives. They had both been suspended and there was an investigation in progress. The case had been targeted by an anti-police group with Chris's name circulated on social media, and he had made the mistake of reading some of the abuse that followed, much worse for his mental health the threats made to his family.

Joe had been going round to see Chris two or three times week, and while they just sat in his room and talked and drank tea, last time Joe had managed to dig out his friend's turntable and vinyl and got him listening to the reggae and dub he'd always loved, along with some punk from the likes of Steve Ignorant and Sub-culture to try and liven the bloke up. Chris could talk differently with Joe than he could his wife, and he'd started to laugh again, sparking back to something like his old self briefly when he was offered a tenner for his record collection.

Dave had called from Palma a couple of times to ask how Chris was, but hadn't tried to talk to him in person, which didn't seem right, and then he'd gone and left a long, rambling message for Joe on his voicemail. Dave had obviously been drinking, but even so, it was a mental rant as he referred to himself in the third person, saying how Dangerous David had always known Sherlock Chris was insane, wasn't that obvious in him becoming a copper after all the things he'd got up to when they were young, it showed he had a split personality and who could ever believe anything he said, it was like Chris was two people, what the fuck had he been telling the doctors and the psychiatrists in the looney bin, or whoever the fuck that righteous ACAB cunt was seeing, the government pumping him full of drugs, maybe one of those truth serums that brought out all the stuff you had lodged in the corners of your brain the things a person heard but didn't hear didn't remember at least not on the surface never responded to or commented on but they never forgot the secrets and confessions and the doctors and police might be tempted to believe the lies he told didn't they make a living that way there was this rigid idea of right and wrong and Chris was a bullshitter Dangerous David had always suspected that but wasn't sure and too polite to say so but now he was certain sitting here after closing sitting in his bar one last drink one for the road one last Heineken anyway it was time he went back to the apartment Martina was missing him life was better here much much better he just hoped Chris was sectioned and stuck in an asylum soon or died and if he wasn't or didn't then Dangerous David – yes that was his name, remember – then Dangerous David would have to get an EasyJet flight over and pay extra for the luxury of being able to have a piss or was that the other company he wasn't sure but it didn't matter how he got there he would put Sherlock Holmes out of his misery that was the kindest thing to do to a worn-out horse a knackered detective in a fucking deerstalker.

Joe had tried to speak to Dave, but he wasn't picking up, deleted the message but had the hump as drunk or not it was no way to talk about someone they'd known since they were kids and who was ill. Dave had a problem with Chris for whatever reason, most likely jealousy as he'd done well for himself, but so what? Chris had worked hard and taken chances, and while he might have got lucky with the changes in technology they should be pleased. Dave was a bitter, competitive wanker, and Joe just thought fuck him. They'd clashed over the years and this was the end of it as far as he was concerned. Dave was a moody part-time punk, a jazz-funk soulboy who walked around with no socks on in the middle of winter. People didn't like that sort of behaviour round here.

Joe had spent December and half of January in India and come home to find Chris in hospital, and while this had brought back memories of Hong King and Smiles's suicide, the repetition hadn't left him feeling guilty, only relieved Chris was still alive. After two weeks in Kolkata he had taken the train from West to East Bengal for five days in Dhaka before returning to Kolkata and continuing to Patna and Bodh Gaya. While a shorter trip than before, it had been intense and special, and he was thinking to visit Kerala and Tamil Nadu next, travel up to Varanasi from Chennai in the south. He had read a lot about Varanasi, the great Hindu holy city on the Ganges, and he wanted to go to nearby Sarnath as well, again drawn by its connection to Gautama and Buddhism. If he could save enough he might even fly to Sri Lanka and start from there, see Colombo and go up into the hills before taking a plane to Thiru-vananthapuram. That was his plan.

He loved India and the Far East and the time he'd spent in Australia, but couldn't live without the seasons, even if he wished winter didn't start in the autumn and run into spring. The funny thing was, he wasn't a big fan of hot weather, preferred days like today when it was bright and breezy, got bored if he was in the sun for too long with nothing to do, and that was why he travelled in the countries he did, as there was that focus on religion which really meant philosophy, a Hindu-Buddhist way of looking at the world that was totally different to that of the West and probably the rest of the world. Even so, India had an eccentricity that reminded him of England and made him feel at ease.

When he'd finished his sandwiches and nuts Joe sat back in the chair and shut his eyes and listened to the birds talking, and despite Chris's problems and Dave being a wanker and Bowie dying, he felt happy. Chris would be okay. He was sure he would recover. Dave was Dave and Bowie had stayed strong until the end. In a minute he would get back to work and was looking forward to planting the bed. He'd tried to get Chris interested but failed, been told to do whatever he wanted, taking Carol with him to the garden centre to choose plants, and thinking about her made him open his eyes and turn his head and there she was standing next to a miniature apple tree.

– A penny for your thoughts, she said.

He had known Carol – Minty – for years and was godfather to her eldest. She walked over and sat down on the grass. Chris liked his garden, before his breakdown finding it a good way to forget work, but it was going to end up overgrown if they weren't careful, Joe offering to help out, thinking this would stir Chris. They had to get him outside. So far he was resisting, but Joe enjoyed coming over for a few hours at a time, imagining what he would do with the garden if it was his, the way he would arrange things and the plants he would buy and because it was long he had this idea to break it up into a series of rooms.

Minty lowered her head and started talking about Chris and how she had seen him like this before, back when he first left the police, which had worked out well for them as he'd started selling and seen his chance with the changes going on, and they'd been able to buy this fantastic house and set themselves up for life, and while she knew Joe was aware of all this nobody but her knew how he had been before he got started, the way he had felt about the victims of the worst crimes he was dealing with and those who had committed them, especially when they escaped justice or their punishments were too lenient. She'd been pleased when he'd left, and yet he had missed the job, felt as if he'd failed, and eventually she'd come round to the idea of him returning, like Joe thinking it was going to be easy working in an office on cyber-crime, but if anything it was worse as he was on the dark web, seeing terrible things he wouldn't tell her about, wanted to be out there making arrests and dealing with the scum in person. The case that had led to this trouble wasn't even one of his own, but to do with an old mate from his time in uniform, someone she didn't know.

Joe sat forward and said that Chris needed to mow the lawn. It was getting too long and the weeds would take over. Minty thought about this and nodded. It was true, her husband liked a tidy lawn and had been feeding and treating it all through last spring and summer, had bought a strimmer and enjoyed using it as much as he did the petrol-driven mower. He needed to want to do it, though, couldn't be asked, so Joe said he would concentrate on the bed he was planting and go see Chris before he left, mention the lawn in passing, how it was a mess and he didn't have time to do it now but would come back specially. Minty nodded again and smiled, stood up and walked towards the house, a minute or so later Joe following her, resisting the urge to look up at the window of the room where Chris was living as he went.

He is a good-looking boy... must be fourteen or fifteen years old... maybe the youngest of the grandchildren... and as soon as he opens the front door I see the likeness... it is a shock... knocks me back... I just stand and stare at this teenage version of my murdered friend Ron... which of course makes him uncomfortable... he looks at the floor... mumbles nobody is home... Mum has gone to the shops... he doesn't know when she will be back... has a thought... raises his eyes and asks me my name... says he will tell her I was here... she can call... but we've already spoken on the phone... this can't wait... it is important... more so now that I have seen him... Ron's watch is in my pocket... this boy's grandfather's watch... burning a hole... I explain that his granddad was a friend of mine... I knew him when he was in hospital... at the end... I am a nurse... but he can see this from my uniform... we spent a lot of time together... he told me about his life... how he was twenty years in the merchant navy... travelled all over the world... saw more than most of us can ever imagine... and the boy is interested... curious... will know something about his granddad but not too much... I imagine... these stories are easily lost... never told... heard... stored... passed on... Ron's children won't know a lot either... not the way I do... and I tell the boy I would like to wait for his mum... if he doesn't mind... she knows I am coming... I am early... that's all... he thinks and says okay... if you want... stands aside so I can enter the house... shuts the door and leads the way down the hall... and once I am sitting in the living room he wants to phone his mum... but I say best not to bother her... let's give it fifteen minutes... she's probably at the checkout right this second... won't appreciate a call when she's in the middle of packing bags...

he sees the logic... and this boy is the person I want to give Ron's gold watch to... now I have met him... this teenager who looks so much like his granddad... at the very least I will tell him its history... some of the stories I have in my head... he has good manners... asks if I would like a cup of tea... some of his mum's carrot cake... she's a very good baker... a very good cook... but he supposes everyone says that about their mums... and I agree... do my best to match his smile... it is true though... even if it's years since my mother made me dinner... and I realise I can't remember how her spaghetti tasted... the pies she made with the extra-thick pastry... mushroom gravy... roast potatoes... Mum serving with a flourish... telling me to eat up... you're too thin... I was the same when I was young... no meat on our bones... wait until you have children... I am excited to see her... she hugs me at the front door... we talk as she stirs the sauce... boils the pasta... all the things we want to say... it is too easy to forget... remember... her sadness after Dad went... the fear... anxiety... dementia... Mum's own death... but she is with me... always... I know that... Ron stands by the door... nods... and I tell this boy that a slice of carrot cake would be lovely... thank you... no milk in the tea please... no sugar... he is pleased that I want to try the cake... and he doesn't have to think of something else to say... walks back along the hall to the kitchen... I follow him... mentally... hear a tap being turned on and off as the kettle fills... feet moving to the counter... two faint clicks as the kettle is slotted into its base and switched on... a cupboard opens... crockery rattles... a drawer rubs... cutlery clanks... a lid pops as it is removed from a tin... I stop... leave him alone to cut the cake and make the tea... my attention on the room... this happy house... clean and tidy... bright colours... that's what I see... feel... standing I go to the shelves and look at the ornaments... a strong smell of polish... no dust on the wood... a wall-mounted television... frozen heroes... controller on the couch... game interrupted... paused... I pick up a framed photo... the family together... see the boy and what must be his sister... Mum and Dad... cheerful faces... and there are other pictures nearby... Ron and his wife Anne... another one where he looks exactly as I remember him... his children... the boy's mum among them... I put my hand in my pocket and feel the watch... Wally made a speech when Ron retired... the gold watch a present... Wally his mate... Ron had lots of friends... Ron Dawes who survived a storm off Cape Horn... lost two friends overboard... I can't remember their names... that's terrible... they will come back to me... I am sure they will... one was from Penzance... the other Glasgow... he was stabbed in Argentina and nearly died... if he had there would be no grandson making tea in the kitchen... different people living in this house... that's how it works... mothers and fathers... brothers and sisters... a little boy... a little girl... growing up... Ron changed... wanted to be local... to have a local... that was important to this post-war socialist... a brave new world... he could still be here now if it wasn't for his murderer Jeffreys... pushing one hundred... a letter from the Queen... he liked a bet on the horses did Ron... to relax in the bookies... after he retired... life was good... and he had that tip... Caped Crusader... Charlie Boy bought the Cadillac on the back of it... I'd forgotten... funny what comes back once you start thinking... Ron told me it took a long time to get the wanderlust out of his system... to settle down... there's a restlessness in some people... an inner loneliness... but Ron was content... moved by this gold watch... the turnout of people... knowing he was loved... which he was... and is... I want to tell his grandson this... everything I know... not sure how to start... maybe the watch is enough... and I must have been looking at these photos for a while as I don't hear the boy return... smell the tea and cake... turn... see him standing in the doorway where Ron is standing... holding a tray... waiting... can I clear the table please... and once the tray has been put down we sit opposite each other... remove the cups and plates... he props the tray against the side of the sofa... we eat and drink... the boy asking me about the cake... I say it is fantastic... because it is... he is more confident... every so often looks at the television screen... his controller... thinking about the game he is playing... remembering his manners... I place the watch on the table... the ticking loud in my head... time clicking... and I am at

peace as I start telling Ron's grandson what he needs to know...
fulfilling a promise... completing the first part of my mission –

Joe caught the fast train from Slough into Paddington and took the tube to Oxford Circus, was approaching The Ship on Wardour Street when he heard his name being called, turned to see Ray walking behind him flanked by two of the younger Chelsea lot he'd seen around but didn't know. The skinhead moved with confidence, a big man in a blue Fred Perry and black MA-1 flight jacket, on his way to the same pub after an early kick-off and post-match pint in The Clarence. Joe stopped and waited for him to catch up, and when he did they fell into step.

– How's your mum? Joe asked.

– Glad to be home and straight into the bath. I thought she'd drowned she was in there so long. Washing the smell of death and decay away. Her words... She's staying with my aunt for a few days. She hasn't done that for ages.

– That's good news, Ray. I'm pleased.

– Yeah, me too. She's tough. Got another twenty years yet.

– It's a result. Nice one for Chelsea today as well.

– I'm looking forward to tonight. It'll round off a proper Saturday. Football, beer and punk rock... To quote one of England's finest.

Like Ray, Joe was a big Knock Off fan and looking forward to seeing them later.

– I haven't felt this good in a long time, Ray continued as they entered The Ship.

He'd been buzzing since leaving home this morning. First he'd gone round to Terry's for a haircut and some breakfast, and while Angie liked to keep her hand in and still looked after some of the Estuary drivers, this was a private, family session. Terry was freshly cropped and looking sharp in a white Ben Sherman when Ray arrived, his uncle keen to get started on one of his famous fry-ups. Angie was going shopping in Staines with a friend and once she'd sorted Ray out the two men soon had the place to themselves.

When they'd finished the Full English they retired to Tel's luxury armchairs to drink another cup of coffee, this one with an Irish twist. Terry was as much a friend as Ray's uncle, and growing up he was the nearest he'd had to a father.

– Your mum got off okay?

– I took her over last night, then had something to eat with Chelsea and April.

– Where did you go? George's?

– We had a pizza. Their choice.

It had been a nice evening. Ray'd always got on well with his daughters, even if looking back it must have been difficult for them at times. He regretted that, saw his anger simmering in Chelsea, something he must have picked up from his mum and passed on through either his behaviour or genes or more likely both. As far as he could see Chelsea had none of his actual rage, and that was a relief. April was quiet and determined, loved animals and nature, didn't eat meat and worried about the planet dying. She enjoyed reading, and he'd given her a copy of *Nineteen Eighty-Four* for her last birthday.

He wasn't sure if she'd get as much out of it as he had, seeing as Orwell hadn't predicted the internet, but none of the old authors had. It was always going to be odd for those who'd never known life without the web to read about a future where it didn't exist. For his part, Ray felt George Orwell was more relevant than ever as doublethink and thoughtcrime became real, and when his birthday arrived April had returned the compliment, giving him *The Circle* by Dave Eggers. This was a brilliant novel. Special. A contemporary take on Orwell. Social media as digital dystopia. Liberal masks. Big smiles. Everyone wanted to be liked and there was nothing new or wrong in that. To keep a good job and progress through the system. But the pressure to conform was huge and the way it was achieved had been refined. Shaming was the new tool. Mental violence. Globalist, technocratic, post-democratic.

His daughters had started asking how he was feeling. If he was okay. They had become protective since the divorce. It was an odd one. But nice. He was proud of his girls. Loved them more than anything. They had their views and he listened to what they said. Felt he was learning things. The world was changing and so were some of the rules. The conventions that were never written down. There were good as well as bad sides to this and Chelsea and April took notice of what he had to say as well. It worked both ways. He was a lucky man. Sometimes he forgot. Too often.

From Terry's house Ray had got a lift to the top end of North End Road with Ian Stills and some of the lads in Bob The Builder's van. Walking through the market to Fulham Broadway he stopped at the *cfcuk* stall across from the station. There were always a small crowd of seriously loyal Blues here. Chelsea fundamentalists who'd been going home and away for years. Some as far back as the Tommy Docherty and Dave Sexton days when Jimmy Greaves and Terry Venables and then Peter Osgood and Alan Hudson were scoring the goals and running the Chelsea midfield.

He'd felt as if he'd wandered into a writers' conference earlier. The Chelsea School was out in force with David Johnstone, Martin Knight, Tim Rolls, Mark Worrall, Walter Otton, Neil Smith, Mark Meehan, Neil Beard, Kelvin Barker and Martin King among those milling around. *Cfcuk* had ruled the fanzine scene for years and *still* only cost a pound. Ray had tried persuading the Sheditor to double the price, but he had a punk-rock soul and refused. This was something Ray respected. Everyone liked the fact that the cost of *cfcuk* never changed. The Chelsea School included the great Alan Hudson, author of *The Working Man's Ballet*, as well as men of letters such as Nick Brown, Rick Glanvill, John Moynihan and BS Johnson, editors and statisticians like Albert Sewell and Ron Hockings.

– Fucking hell, that was painful, Ray said when he had paid for their drinks, the two younger men with Ray having gone down to the other end of the pub to talk to people they knew.

– You still get some good music in here, Joe noted.

There were plenty of Human Punk regulars in The Ship.

– It's like these West End pubs are putting their prices up every week, Ray continued.

– We can go to The Champion or that other Sam Smith's pub behind the 100 Club. They're a lot cheaper. The stout's okay.

– The Blue Posts?

– There's a lot of Blue Posts around here, but that's right. I used to go to the one over the road, but last time they were charging even more than in here.

– The blue posts are where we're meant to leave our horses.

– Jesse James and Billy The Kid... You can be Jesse.

– I don't mind the Sam Smith's stout, but it's nowhere near as smooth as Guinness. A properly poured pint, I mean.

While most of the original buildings remained, these last few years had seen Soho changing at an incredible speed, its atmosphere a world away from the bonkers place Joe had got to know as a teenager. There had been a lingering villainy in the run-down streets that included a big fruit-and-veg market on Berwick Street, English cafes and Italian coffee bars, plenty of record shops, traditional and modernist tailors, walk-up red lights and sex clubs, discos and film-business offices, the theatres on Shaftesbury Avenue and the cheap little restaurants in Chinatown. Then there was the Marquee for the herberts, Madam Jo Jo's for the perverts, some great boozers for a sherbet.

Joe saw Soho as more Harry Fabian and Wide Boy Willetts than Billy Hill and the Krays, and this scruffy area with its nooks and crannies and oddballs had resisted gentrification longer than most of Central London, which was surprising given its position right off Oxford Street. The chains were moving in now, and a plastic, corporate edge was being promoted, while one of the worst things that had happened to the West End had to be the closing down of the 12 Bar on Denmark Street.

– We'd be in there right now if it was still open, Joe said wistfully.

– It's a fucking scandal the 12 Bar going. Good music, good prices and Barnet was the best guv'nor in Central London.

It was Barnet who'd made the 12 Bar special, and Joe had been buying up the singles in the *12 Bar Legacy Collection* he'd started on his London Callin' label, the first release featuring The

Bermondsey Joyriders and the third including Barnet's band The London Sewage Company along with Runnin' Riot. He knew everyone in the music-meets-football world, was a much-loved and respected face and of course part of the wider Chelsea School.

– I've got a Brexit test for you, Ray said, when a student wearing an EU-flag T-shirt passed by.

– Go on.

– I'm an Orwell man, as you know. Read everything he wrote. More or less. I might have missed some of the journalism, but I know the important essays. So I asked myself which way would he have voted in the referendum if he was alive. With all the propaganda and him working for the BBC. I mean, would he have risked his job? And would he have been on Twitter? Instagram?

– Taking selfies with Huxley and Camus.

– There was only one answer, Ray continued. At least for me. You're into Bowie and The Clash. That's right, isn't it?

– Other stuff as well.

– I know, but David Bowie and The Clash.

– You can't do much better than them, can you?

– Decent, I agree, but not exactly Cock Sparrer, Sham, the Rejects.

– I wouldn't criticise any of those bands, but Bowie and The Clash...

– Anyway, Orwell and Bowie, plus Joe Strummer representing The Clash. They're all in the big league and know what they're talking about. Right?

– Right.

– How would those three have voted in the referendum then? George Orwell, David Bowie and Joe Strummer. Think about it for a minute.

Joe was fed up hearing about Brexit but knew it was fixed in Ray's head, that he'd been talking about the EU for years and wasn't one of these people who'd just started thinking about what it meant this last year or two. Ray was ahead of his time. Bowie, Orwell and Strummer?

– George Orwell would have wanted to leave. No doubt about that.

– Definitely, Ray agreed. He was a socialist and a patriot. No other way he could have voted. What about David Bowie?

– Bowie as well. I'm sure he said something about the EU back when it was the EC. Before they changed the name. You can't write a song like 'Big Brother' and be pro-EU. He loved Orwell's writing as well. *Diamond Dogs* is the soundtrack for *Nineteen Eighty-Four*. Did you know that?

– I didn't. Interesting, though. I wasn't sure about Bowie, but thought he'd probably have wanted to leave. How about Joe Strummer?

– Remain. I love Strummer, and The Clash were brilliant, but he was a hippy and part of that middle-class Notting Hill scene. Don't get me wrong, his reasons would have been sound. He wouldn't have gone against the grain, though. Writers are different.

– How many authors wanted to leave, though? At least the ones we know about?

– You haven't got writers like George Orwell now. It's all corporate cock-sucking these days. At least that part of the arts with the money. Means of production, isn't it? But there's a few around. People like Tony Parsons, Julie Burchill, Garry Bushell. I think Parsons wanted to leave. Don't quote me, though.

Ray and Joe wanted to see the support bands, but it was easy to forget the time when you were drinking and talking and getting another round. Nowhere in Central London came close to the 100 Club, a friendly, family-run venue that had been going since before the war. It was a venue they loved, and coming down the stairs and paying Dong on the door while Steve and Big John looked on was part of the Human Punk experience, being met by the sounds of Doctor Vinyl on the decks or one of the bands if they were onstage, and tonight they walked in with Knock Off going at it full tilt.

In this little basement club in the middle of a city whose core was being gentrified in the cloned style of every other Western metropolis a more interesting London lived. Those present had travelled in from the four corners and beyond, and for all those with their family roots in that older London maybe it felt as if they were coming home. Those running things didn't really want the plebs arriving from the suburbs and new towns, preferred a well-heeled population with no ties to the traditional, and this social cleansing was hidden behind endless sermons about a version of diversity that was only ever skin deep.

In some ways the 100 Club reflected the pull of the bigger football sides, how they had become focal points for a displaced population, the descendants of London families who'd moved out across the decades, their memories passed to the new generations. That older industrial class had been driven away by poverty, bombing and rent increases, at the same time drawn to better houses with gardens, the chance of a fresh start. In the case of West London it was Metroland, yet the pull of that Dickensian city and the spirit of the Blitz remained. There was a lot of latter-day romanticism involved, but it was these people's history and the bonds were real.

The controllers hadn't just stolen the bricks and mortar and the land on which they stood, but had been steadily working their way through the culture as well, football long taken over and rebranded, the prices charged more social cleansing. It was the same with the pubs and the cost of a pint. Football, beer, punk rock… Too often sanitised and turned into another airhead fashion with fixed rules applied by keyboard warriors operating through the very corporations they supposedly despised, there were still some bands around with original thinkers in their ranks, and that was what made these Human Punk nights so good.

It was putting proper punk and Oi back into the centre of the town where it had started, which was good news for Joe and Ray. It had only been going a couple of years, but they'd already seen Sham, Ruts DC, the Cockney Rejects and The Professionals along with a nice selection of up-and-coming supports. Ray was already thinking ahead to The Last Resort and the Boots Boys Knees Up at the end of the year when his phone began to vibrate. It was Priscilla. And because he'd had a drink he was tempted to take the call and go outside so they could hear each other, but he resisted. Let it go to voicemail. Would delete the message if she left one.

It was two years since they'd bumped into each other in the pub, and even though he'd wanted to, he hadn't called, letting his feelings drift and fade, then yesterday he'd gone to pick up a fare and there she was waiting. They'd talked and joked all the way. Instantly clicking. She said he was looking good and he told her she was still gorgeous. Wished he hadn't used that word again as it would only lead her on. They'd watched each other in the mirror and maybe talking to a reflection had let him tell her about his mum being in hospital. Some of what he'd felt. The relief when she came home. Priscilla rested a hand on his shoulder. Squeezed. Removed it when the ending was a happy one. He explained that his divorce was final but he couldn't leave his mum. A single mother. Two small boys. Shouldn't have said that either. Kept talking. He worked as many hours as he could. Liked driving. His music. Football. Having a pint. With the boys. Grown men. And Priscilla listened. Let him ramble. She knew. And when the journey ended she asked if he was seeing anyone. Which he wasn't. She repeated what she'd said in the Queen's Head. Ray should give her a call. Mustn't be scared. When she was outside she tapped on his window. He opened it and she leaned in and hugged him. He wanted to kiss her on the mouth. Resisted. She whispered that it was right he cared for his mother. She turned towards her father's house. Where she lived with and looked after her dad. Pausing at the door she blew Ray a kiss. And standing here in the middle of London he pushed these thoughts away. The temptations. Had to be strong.

He reminded himself that he was living the life. A proper Saturday. Standing in front of a mirror. Hair cropped. Grade 2. Running a hand over his bonce. Feeling brand new. The Full English with his Uncle Terry. Irish coffee. A strong one. Ian Stills and the lads in Bob The Builder's van. Strolling down North End Road. The Chelsea School. 'Liquidator' booming as he entered Stamford Bridge. The brilliant green of the grass. Victorious. Carefree. The famous CFC. Drinking in The Clarence. Heading off to Wardour Street. The tube from West Ken. Meeting up with Joe. A little older. Wiser. Drinking in The Ship. Human Punk. The 100 Club. Football, beer and punk rock. The only thing missing was a good woman. He didn't need the aggro. The attachment. Priscilla's madness. Ray was happy. These were his rewards at the end of the working week. Football. Beer. Punk rock. The crowd. People like him. Bricks and mortar. Knock Off. The joys of Oi. The sounds of London Town. London Country.

Davinda closes the curtains... pulls them tight... makes sure there's no gaps in the material as she shuts out the world... the shadows in the dusk... comes and sits on the sofa... full-lotus position... spine dead straight... I can't do that... only the half-lotus... for a while... stay in my chair... it's not a competition... we are warm and relaxed in her ground-floor maisonette... husband at work securing premises... patrolling perimeters... the only light a lamp in the corner... looks like a rabbit... I think... we're two old friends who've worked hundreds of shifts together... days and nights... the highs and lows of life and death... she's been trying to persuade me for ages... mindfulness of breathing... says it will help the anxiety... long-term aftershocks... stop thinking for even a few seconds and bubbles rise from the depths and burst on the surface... expand the conscious mind... Joe Martin reckons it's like a waking sleep... minus the dreams... confusion... but it's a lot more difficult than it sounds... to really stop thinking... Davinda meditating since she was a girl... the best sort of teacher... it comes from within... patient... easygoing... breathing in... breathing out... focusing on the air as it moves through my nose and into my lungs... out again... chest expanding... contracting... and I know what to expect... mind games... trickery... Jack O'Lantern... come with me... another room... lungs as balloons... the smell of rubber... blue ribbons and pins pushed into the ceiling... a child's birthday party... Mum and Dad... my friends... Ben... a cake with six candles... lemon drizzle... presents on the table... round faces and pointed hats... another room... Charlie Boy is selling the Cadillac...

heat and light more important... food on the table... clearing debts... but at least it's Elvis who comes to our house... hands over the cash... thanks to Grace... the King driving our beautiful car away... we console ourselves... a good home... remembering it was Ron's tip that changed Charlie's luck... won him the Cadillac... and I've done right by Ron... met his grandson and daughter... passed on the watch... stories... history... both of them overjoyed... friends for life... only Danny left now... unfinished business... the years pass and fortunes change... different stages of life... children to raise... it's the only thing we can do... not many people get to drive a pink Cadillac... let alone own one... not here in England... but losing it dents Charlie's confidence... worse is coming... another room... Alfonso's funeral... family and friends... Davinda's voice... gently reminding... ease any thoughts away... return to my breath... follow it... slowly... Alfonso's cancer... his treatment only works for a while... I know what's coming... seen it happen so many times before... it breaks my heart... Charlie Boy's heart... his bigger dream is the one he shares with Alfonso and Joe... decks mixer speakers van... the sounds of Satellite... Charlie and Joe don't continue... wouldn't have been right... it must be five or six years ago... Davinda... I have to stop thinking... for a few seconds... longer... but the undertaker smirks... Jonathan Jeffreys... my monster... have to concentrate... focus... the surprise on his face... the rage as he fades... it is a good feeling... seeing him vanish... emptying my mind... Davinda's voice –

Joe was on the road by half-nine, the M25 moving smoothly after the usual delay coming off the M4, but he'd been more interested in the new Ruts DC album *Music Must Destroy* than the traffic – 'Psychic Attack', 'Kill The Pain', the title track with Henry Rollins. It was a cracking album, a bold move in new directions as Segs delivered the words while maintaining his bass-and-drum alliance with Dave Ruffy, the three-strong line-up completed by guitarist Leigh Heggarty from The Price. This album was another of the many bonuses in Joe's life, and he thought about The Ruts and the venues he'd seen them in as a teenager, how it was right that he was able to hear these fresh recordings and watch them play as a man in his prime.

He had his health, family and friends, wheels, money in his pocket, routinely mixing business and pleasure, buying records to sell and save, crate-digging for sounds, and today was one of those when the stars were aligned and he was doing the rounds in style. His route had been plotted and provisions gathered, the plan to circle London with stops in Epsom, Brentwood, Stevenage, Luton and Southall, an anti-clockwise trip through Surrey, Kent, Essex, Hertfordshire, Bedfordshire and Middlesex before ending up back in Berks via the southern tip of Leafy Bucks. There would be little doubling back with the right records being sold by the right people in the right places at the right times.

Taking the chance to make a couple of calls he paused 'Second Hand Child' and tried Chris, went to voicemail but didn't bother leaving a message, instead phoning his mum who answered straight away, breathlessly telling him she was at the allotments with Dad, that they were planting the potatoes. There were the runner beans to get in as well so she couldn't stop, but yes, it was fine to come round for his dinner on Sunday. Joe had already dug the soil ready for the main crop, thought he was meant to be helping put them in, but Mum insisted they could handle this themselves, wanted to get things moving. The difficult bit was breaking up the earth and adding compost, and they were doing the fun part together. As soon as they finished talking Chris rang back, and he was outside as well, about to take Joe's advice and mow the lawn. These two calls made Joe even happier than he already was, further proof that this was one of those days when everything was going to go right.

His first stop was a character called Barry Desmond who'd sent him the same list of records four times, each one amended in red biro to show a sale made on eBay. This list arrived by second-class post rather than email. The envelopes included a sheet of paper where Barry outlined what he described as the provenance of the sold record, along with several lines describing his thoughts on the buyer. These were apparently extensions of his eBay feedback. There was also a photocopied note emphasising that he was a huge fan of The Seekers and would therefore *not* be selling their work as he prized each album he owned dearly. However much pressure a purchaser might apply, he would resist, but he did have some interesting LPs and singles he would like to move on, obviously depending on the terms and conditions offered. There were also items he had inherited which he never listened to and the time had come to let others enjoy the pleasures they offered.

When they spoke on the phone Barry outlined the parking arrangements in detail, and once Joe had left the M25 and worked his way into Epsom and was approaching the bungalow, the man himself was waiting outside on the pavement, walking into the middle of the empty street to usher him towards a specific spot. Barry examined the position of the car, motioning for Joe to move forward slightly, then back a little, nearer to the kerb, before giving him a thumbs-up. Joe had been to the Derby a couple of times, but apart from that he didn't know much about Epsom apart from its horse-racing pedigree, that it was next to the North Downs, home to a number of well-known Chelsea faces and a traveller stronghold similar to his own patch.

Barry was a friendly chap with a soft, sticky handshake that Joe put down to excess soap not properly rinsed off after washing, which tied in with the spotless bungalow. His host suggested he pop into the kitchen and make a pot of tea, that with his guest's agreement he planned to serve this with the homemade butterfly cakes presented to him by a neighbour yesterday evening, Joe noting how the pristine-yet-dated decor of the living room was matched by Barry's movements and use of diction. There were albums, singles, CDs and cassettes arranged on the dining table, but Barry asked if Joe wouldn't mind waiting until he returned as that way they could peruse them together. He was keen to highlight those covers which were creased and the two records slightly scuffed and therefore only meriting a very good plus rating. He believed most were in excellent condition, with several verging on mint.

Once the tea and cakes had been arranged on the table, Barry sat opposite Joe and asked how his journey had been. Barry had never been to Slough itself, but he *had* flown overseas from Heathrow Airport, although he had to admit that he preferred the smaller and more intimate aerodrome at Gatwick. He was wistful as he mentioned the arrivals area. But did Joe know Uxbridge? He did? Barry was impressed and detailed how he had driven there via West Drayton and become fearful at a red traffic light on the high street. A gang of youthful thugs began staring at him so intently from outside a takeaway that he worried he had forgotten to lock his doors – he hadn't – and was relieved when the green allowed him to progress and collect a lady he was taking to dinner in Beaconsfield. He had searched online for a suitable restaurant in Uxbridge, but could find little other than chains and the ubiquitous Bangladeshi misleadingly described as an Indian. She was a fine-looking woman, but sadly unavailable when he called the following morning and requested a second date. Barry's face reddened and he began talking about traffic flows and the state of the Epsom approach roads.

While Joe had quickly warmed to Barry, could see that he was a decent if slightly odd man, he had a schedule to keep and eased him back towards the records, which they started going through. Barry again stated his love of The Seekers, how nothing of theirs was open to negotiation whatever the price offered, but Joe was more interested in Elton John's classic early albums which were in excellent condition, as were LPs by Kate Bush and Michael Jackson. These were all worth money, but there was a lot of middle-of-the-road stuff that was hard to sell for even a pound in the country's charity shops. Best of all were the soundtracks, the main reason for Joe's visit.

He had never thought about these too much in the past, like a lot of people failing to separate the music and effects from the moving images they brought to life. It was silly of him, as a year ago he'd come across the cassette *Shut It! The Music Of The Sweeney* in a junk shop, bought and played it and been amazed it was funk driving scenes that documented a scruffier and much

175

more exciting London. He already had *The Battle Of Britain*, *A Clockwork Orange* and soundtracks based around the work of Gerry and Sylvia Anderson at home, but hadn't listened to them properly, with *The Sweeney* realising these soundtracks were gold-mines. It wasn't just the audio nuggets either, but the part these productions and others like them had played in his life.

Joe was checking *Psycho* and *Zulu*, the work of Bernard Herrmann and John Barry, vinyl that looked as if it had never been played, while *Mary Poppins* and *Chitty Chitty Bang Bang* clearly had been but still weren't far off excellent. He'd been surprised that as well as his long-term partnership with Alfred Hitchcock, Herrmann had written the scores for science-fiction classics such as *The Day The World Stood Still* and, years later, Martin Scorsese's *Taxi Driver*. There was a track to be made using Herrmann breaks alone, probably an album's worth, while the first of Barry's soundtracks would also work well together, a mix involving the murderer Norman, heroic British redcoats and the Zulu Nation, a white witch called Mary, a flying car and second spoken-word appearance from chimney-sweep-cum-inventor Dick Van Dyke.

When he reached the singles Joe found Wire's 'I Am The Fly' and Gang Of Four's 'At Home He's A Tourist' in with the charity-shop staples. These were out of place, and Barry was unable to account for their presence. This worried him briefly before Paul Hardcastle's 'Nineteen' appeared and he began imitating the stuttered delivery of the number concerned. 'I'm A Wanker' by Ivor Biggun And The Red-Nosed Burglars was next, and Joe held it up, said he'd forgotten this one had ever existed, even though it had done so well in the charts. This wasn't surprising as it focused on a hobby everyone enjoyed when they were young and even into old age. Barry smirked and gave Joe another thumbs-up, seemingly acknowledging that while the 45 had been a hit it wasn't worth much as so many copies were available. When it was time to work out a price Barry became agitated, but Joe made him a good offer that was gladly accepted.

Back on the road, he was cruising the London Wall once more, entering Kent and an area that boasted a punk tradition that ran through South-East London. He had The Business and Last Resort on his mind, particularly Micky Fitz who was fighting cancer, broke the silence with 'Harry May', Micky respected and loved by a lot of people, among them Ray as well as Joe. This part of the world was also home to Oi The Godfather, the originator Garry Bushell, leader of the notorious Gonads.

The approach to the Dartford Crossing was slow, but he had allowed for this and once past the toll booths he was moving at a modest speed, rising up into the sky on that surreal arch linking Kent and Essex, struck again by the scale of the London sprawl, how the sounds he was collecting reflected the nature of its people, their heritage as well as their tastes. He had five plastic boxes at home marked *North*, *South*, *East*, *West* and *Central*, and was slowly adding vinyl bought in these areas. The more popular music was universal, and he avoided most of that, interested in the unusual and local as he collected the pieces for his jigsaws.

Next stop was one of the West Ham lot who went to the Human Punk shows at the 100 Club. Bobby Cohen was an old-school Hammer, as big and brash as Barry was small and timid, and yet despite the East End bravado Bob was probably the one who could be most easily conned. He was selling an impressive Oi collection, and Joe was excited by what was on offer. Bob insisted he needed the space and was happy with Spotify, but Joe suspected he was skint and in need of the cash, and for his part was willing to pay more than was needed to help the bloke out. Coming from Essex and being West Ham, Bob was naturally drawn to the East End's finest in Cock Sparrer and the Cockney Rejects, as well as Canvey Island's Doctor Feelgood, three bands Joe loved just as much and maybe more.

Once he had left the M25, Joe followed his SatNav to the Brentwood address and parked outside. The estate was as quiet as Barry's street in Epsom, but there was no one waiting to advise him on his parking. Joe walked up the front path and rang the doorbell, waited before trying again, finally used the knocker. He banged this several times before taking his phone out and calling Bobby who answered right away and said he was in the back garden and on his way, a few seconds later his voice booming from the side of the house.

The cheerful man Joe was used to seeing in a checked claret-and-blue Ben Sherman was standing next to the semi-detached in a blue-and-white bowling shirt, and when he reached him Bobby said he was sorting through the records he was selling in the garden as he could spread them out on the picnic table. They went through a gate that would only needed one kick to smash, making the barbed wire weaved through the trellis above it like clematis pointless. Bobby closed and secured the gate with a padlock and invited Joe to have a gander while he made them both a nice cup of tea. Unless he fancied a proper drink? He had some of those Belgian beers in the fridge, the small ones you could get in Asda now instead of doing the cross-Channel run to Calais.

Joe stuck to tea as he was driving, saw the state of the turntable, amp and speakers piled up next to the table and felt his heart sink. He knew what was on offer vinyl-wise and the gradings, but it was easy for a one-off seller to get those wrong. Going on the state of the gear he feared the worst, but looking at the condition of the album sleeves and then the records inside he was relieved to find they were as described. The singles hadn't been graded and some were pretty battered, but he wasn't too bothered about these, the bonus not mentioned previously a box of rock 'n' roll 45s, among them American classics by Chuck Berry, Jerry Lee Lewis and Little Richard. They were in excellent condition and Joe guessed they'd belonged to an older relative, most likely Bob's mum or dad, but maybe an uncle or aunt.

As they sat at the table drinking their tea, Bobby made his pitch, and Joe was fine with his more bullish market-trader approach, already knew what he was going to pay. Some sellers had a firm price in mind, others wanted to see what he offered, and while every job lot had its risks he rarely lost out. He listened and said what he could pay and Bobby was pleased, Joe agreeing to take the gear even though he didn't want it, and with the business side done Bobby Cohen was soon into his tales of famous Bridge House shows, ICF away days, how his old man had named him after a certain West Ham and England captain who had lifted the World Cup at Wembley. Joe asked if it was true Bobby Moore's middle name was Chelsea? Bob winced and admitted that it was.

Bobby was a big fan of the East End Badoes as well as those bands from south of the river The Business and Last Resort, and they discussed the rivalry between West Ham and Millwall, the idea that the river was an iron curtain between the two clubs, and yet there were plenty of West Ham living south of the water, and wasn't the Poplar boy Terry Hayes a Millwall supporter? Bobby felt these things were complicated, and when Joe had to get going he thanked him for coming over. It was a long way. He'd see him in The Ship before the next Human Punk probably. Or one of the Sam Smith's pubs? The price of a pint in the West End was mental. His handshake was firm and dry and very different to that of The Seekers fan Barry Desmond.

It was half-two by the time Joe got back to the M25, but he would be fine if the traffic kept moving, and with the easy driving he was able to start his picnic. There was the hummus sandwiches he'd made before leaving, a bag of mixed nuts generous with the Brazils and almonds, a pecan-flavoured energy bar. He had brought two cans of root beer along, but resisted these, realised he should have used Bobby's toilet before leaving after drinking tea there and in Barry's bungalow. There was a programme on the radio about the new American president Donald Trump, someone he hadn't heard of until last year, and while it was like Alan Sugar becoming prime minister, this was the same country that had elected Ronnie Raygun. The Democrat candidate Hillary Clinton seemed to belong to the same metropolitan elite that had infected the Labour Party, while Trump and his protectionist promises were always going to appeal to the workers Clinton had dismissed as deplorables, her insults along the same lines as those directed at the English working class after the Brexit vote. It was the same old bollocks, and after a while he turned the programme off and put on the Stone Roses instead, 'I Am The Resurrection' one of those uplifting songs made for driving, when it finished going back to the start of their debut album and 'I Wanna Be Adored'.

By the time he turned off the M25 and took the A1 up to Stevenage he needed a wee. Sandra Hall lived in a four-storey block that looked as if it had been built in the 1930s, a stylish building that was well maintained and shone in the afternoon sun. Once he'd been buzzed in and was on the second floor he got a taste of what he was here for as he approached the open door of her flat. He knocked and 'Don't Look Back In Anger' ended with the scratch of a needle followed by muffled swearing. Joe waited, didn't want to just stroll in even though he was on the verge of pissing himself.

A beautiful blonde in a short white dress appeared, Sandra out of breath as she tiptoed towards him saying she'd been having a last dance before her records were taken away and gone forever. She was having the flat redecorated and wanted a more minimalist look once the work was done. Her records took up too much space. She hadn't played them for years, but setting up her record player and giving them a spin had made her emotional. She hadn't seen that coming. Anyway, would he like a glass of wine? Joe said he'd better not as he was driving and asked if could use her bathroom, wondered why she was having the flat decorated when it looked perfect.

Sandra's bathroom was more like a dressing room, one that belonged to an actress or a model with its rack of laundered dresses and a long row of scent and lotion bottles at the back of the marble surface either side of the sink. An extra touch of class was added by a framed print of Kurt Cobain, but the mirror that took up most of the main wall made Joe feel uncomfortable as he used the toilet even though he was alone, while worse followed when he washed his hands and stood there facing his reflection. Magnified this way he seemed worn down and scruffy, but Liam Gallagher's voice returned with a bang and he was a carefree herbert once more, out on patrol and living the life.

Back in the living room Sandra was sitting on the floor with ten albums spread out like a pair of wings, five on each side of the 'Just Like Honey' single by The Jesus And Mary Chain, which acted as the bird's shrunken head, the bulk of the records on a glass table by the room's main window. Sandra sipped wine and he wondered if she really was an actress or model, more realistically a designer of some sort. He saw her as part of the Britpop generation that had seen and taken its chance under New Labour, not to the same degree as the Gallaghers or Tracy Emin, but she seemed to be doing well for herself. She smiled and flapped a hand and he guessed she was on more than just the drink, which made him nervous. With the music so loud it meant there was no conversation, and that was strange and only added to his unease. At least the price was already agreed and he had the cash in his pocket.

Sandra put her glass down and stood up, scooped the records off the floor and made sure the pile was straight before handing them to Joe, and with his hands full she planted a kiss on his forehead, went over to her turntable and replaced Oasis with Blur, dancing along to 'She's So High'. She looked over her shoulder and smiled, and Joe made an executive decision, knew to take the kiss as a side effect of whatever she had taken rather than a sexual advance, had to accept that this was as good a way as any to buy secondhand albums, would study the grooves like a nerd as Sandra moved across her polished floorboards, and this he did, sitting at the table and going through Oasis, Blur, Verve, Ride, Nirvana and what seemed like every decent Britpop band from the Nineties, as well as the more electronic Orbital, Prodigy and Underworld. He moved fast, on the lookout for the left-field nuggets he was sure were waiting, hoping that the raver Sandra would keep dancing.

Barry Desmond had given him the soundtracks for his own use, Bobby Cohen the rocking 45s that were good for business, and here was Sandra's bonus at the bottom of the pile – seven records featuring Royal Marine and Army bands, drum and bass and brass from the parade grounds of England. They were worth little in terms of money, but he would see what he could dig out of them, and anyway, wasn't military drumming the foundations of the popular music most people had been listening to for the last century? Joe had no time to think about this further as Blur cut off and Sandra was asking if he wanted to buy her turntable and amp as she had no use for them now and they took up space. It was quality gear, but hardware wasn't his field and she would be better off selling the lot on Gumtree or eBay. He could ask this bloke Jack he knew if she wanted, but there would be other buyers out there and she would get decent money. Sandra thanked him for his honesty, said she wasn't stoned or drunk like he maybe thought and would he like to go with her to a Nineties night in King's Cross on Saturday?

His next stop was Vinyl Revelations in nearby Luton, which was the best record shop in the country as far as Joe was concerned. Andy Chesham – aka Doctor Vinyl – was the boss, and while Joe would have driven the short distance just to drink more tea and natter with a man whose kettle was always on the boil, Vinyl had been on the lookout for good sampling material and had just bought a job lot that included lots of BBC *Sound Effects* albums among gems like the gloriously titled *Out Of This World: Atmospheric Sounds And Effects From The BBC Radiophonic Workshop* and the much simpler but equally moving *London Airport (Heathrow)* seven-inch. As he drove he thought how The Jam's *Sound Affects* album played on the words as well as the BBC cover designs, a recognition of the importance of the series. Vinyl was already holding the second and third *DJ Food* albums released by Ninja Tune, as well as various other goodies which weren't far off making Joe's mouth water.

After he had parked at the back of the shop and phoned from his car, Mrs Vinyl opened the door and let him in, the Doctor polishing off a big hardcore sale as more tea was offered. After another wee Joe opted for black coffee. Andy was another cheerful character, someone with a long pedigree when it came to live music, DJing and running his own club nights. The Attic had been a mad three-floor sweaty mess with bands downstairs, a chill-out room playing dub and DJ Shadow, a full-on rave dealing in hard house, trance and techno. Cheeba Cheeba was based at a Jamaican club where the old boys loved their dominoes, the music a clash of ska, reggae, funk, soul, hip hop and drum 'n' bass. Then there was Mayhem with its Britpop, alternative rock and dance. Club Ska, meanwhile, was where Andy had hooked up with Geno Blue and

Duke Dale. While Bobby was naturally West Ham, Doctor Vinyl was an Arsenal supporter, another example of how affiliations spread out from their London core.

Joe would hang around until closing before heading back down to the M25, didn't want to get stuck in the rush-hour traffic more than was needed, had some flexibility with his last stop as the Patels would be in all evening. Maybe he was being a bit devious, but Joe was hoping that if he got his timing right Auntie would have some food on the go. His journey into West London via the M25 meant coming back in on the Uxbridge Road, but this was faster than he'd thought, his decision to avoid the North Circular the right one as he dipped into some of the big trip-hop records – *Blue Lines* by Massive Attack, *Dummy* by Portishead, *Maxinquaye* by Tricky.

The cars were jammed bumper to bumper in the Patels' street and he wondered if they'd been lifted in by a crane, but he eventually found a space five minutes away and was soon removing his shoes and being welcomed into the living room, his nose twitching as something wonderful cooked in the kitchen. While Joe knew a bit about jazz he had never been able to get into the music, and yet hip hop drew heavily on its breaks, which, as he learned more, had made him want to try again. Sections of *Kind Of Blue* by Miles Davis and *Pithecanthropus Erectus* by Charles Mingus had stuck, but he struggled to stay interested. While this was frustrating, they'd led him to Miles's *Bitches Brew*, which was special, and from there to *Lift To The Scaffold*, a soundtrack composed as the film played.

He'd listened to a fair bit of Gene Krupa, and if he had a favourite instrument it was probably the drums. Weren't Ruffy and Esso meant to have been inspired by this sort of drumming, along with John Bonham, Charlie Watts and Ginger Baker? The guitar solo was said to come out of jazz, and he couldn't think of many in rock 'n' roll, but then there was the deeper, more traditional British, Irish and American folk with their fiddle, banjo and mandolin breakdowns. Joe discussed this with Ricky once they were tucking into Auntie's okra, chana masala, dhal, rice and chapattis.

It turned out Ricky Patel was into Misty In Roots and The Ruts like Joe, which was logical given he'd grown up in Southall, while the classical Indian CDs he was selling were from ABC Records on the Broadway. The devotional cassettes had been given to him by an uncle when he was trying to persuade Ricky to stay on an ashram in Wales for a week or two, hoping it would get him off the punk and reggae, which the same uncle said was the real snakebite, not that cider-lager mixture Ricky and the homosexuals with peroxide hair were getting drunk on. This was in the 1970s, and the cassettes had sat in a box ever since. With his uncle dying early, Ricky felt sad whenever he saw them, but couldn't throw the tapes away or give them to a charity shop as that would seem disrespectful.

A price was easily agreed and Ricky asked about the shadow puppets Joe had brought home from Bali. He had no plans to return yet, but Ricky reckoned he could sell a lot of them going on the reaction when they'd been given as presents at Diwali. It was something to think about, and when Joe left Southall just after nine he took the Uxbridge Road through Hayes and down Hillingdon Hill, past the RAF base sold off for housing, and when he came to the roundabout where the Protestant martyrs had been burned he had a thought and took the first exit, did another left and drove up the empty one-way street to the Spiritualist church he'd decorated two years ago, stopping to look at the black building for a minute before continuing. He wondered what Helen was doing and thought about giving her a call, but he had things to do, started listening to *Music Must Destroy* again.

He passed the Dolphin, General Elliott and Pipemakers and left Uxbridge, rising up over the M25, his perfect day confirmed as he saw the traffic below at a standstill, the motorway he would have been on if he'd taken the Western Avenue and tried to circle round to the M4 rather than using the backroads. Once through Iver Heath he put his foot down on the dual carriageway, the woods closing in on either side, slowing for the cameras at George Green, the allotments to his right, Major Tom walking next to the wire fence, and he pictured Mum and Dad at home, knackered after a good day's work, the same well-earned tiredness Joe was feeling after his day on the road.

Reversing right up to his lock-up, he turned the engine and Ruts off but stayed where he was, lightheaded and wondering if he could leave the unloading until tomorrow, knew that was asking for trouble. He checked his phone, found two minds out of three syncing – a message from Chris included a picture of him standing next to his lawn mower and a big pile of grass while Mum had sent a photo that showed her leaning on a fork next to rows of soil where the potatoes had been planted. Ray, meanwhile, had treated him to an unsettling shot of his face next to the mug of a parrot called Peter. Joe thought to call him, but it was too much to be talking about right now. Peter frightened Joe. What the fuck was that all about?

He got out and opened the garage door and turned the light on, and while nobody seemed to be about he was still conscious that his treasure was on show. With the boot open he transferred the day's haul as fast as he could, shut it and went inside the lock-up and closed the door behind him. It was cold and stark with the breeze-block walls and a cavelike smell mixed in with cardboard covers and boxes, yet he felt at home as most men did when they were alone in their shed or garage, a box room at the back of the house, the small shunned spaces nobody else was interested in. Clem took this further with his caravan, sitting outside with his mugs of tea and packets of biscuits, a can or two in the evening, a portion of chips if he'd been out drinking. There were empty buildings there Joe could rent off the Webbs that would be make a better set-up than this one, but the garage was fine for now, a hideaway that had none of the loneliness of the country.

He was the marionette Joe 90, Joe Analogue, Joe Public Calling – a vinyl-loving scrap-metal rag-and-bone man standing in a lock-up in the middle of a silent block of garages on the edge of a massive trading estate, the home of Supermarionation and the Mars bar, his mind moving to the Satellite scores of *Thunderbirds* and *Captain Scarlet*, factory bass and the pulse of 'Are "Friends" Electric?', the rumbling throb of Sons Of Slough's 'I Can't Hear

The Stereo'. He was facing a mountain of music and assorted merchandise that teetered but never fell and crushed him, a trove of the briefly new and long forgotten. It was his curiosity shop, an anti-fashion dreamland that might have lacked glamour and glitz but pissed all over his ex-mate Digital Dave's bland, single-beat summerland.

The memories buried in here were personal, secondhand and third person, and while he was briefly overwhelmed by the possibilities, he quickly returned to the excitement of the challenge, started sifting through the records he'd just unloaded, shifting what he wanted to take home and play with into an empty box. When this looked like it was going to turn into two he became more choosey, didn't want to be filling the boot again, saw himself going back and forward between his car and lock-up, mental trips around and around the M25, up and down the Uxbridge Road, never-ending journeys, lost inside his own giant sample, which on reflection he might not have minded.

She's full of life... bursting with joy... sitting in her garden with a blanket around her shoulders... watching the birds... a table and a feeder... five-star dining... naked oats and red millet and maize and chopped peanuts... striped sunflower and black sunflower... sunflower hearts... other seeds Viv has told me about but whose names I forget... there's no fancy decking or paving... that doesn't help the wildlife... these birds have to take care... make sure it's safe before they eat... need places to hide... where they can see the lie of the land... in the long-term nest... there's a stone bath... giant squirrel gnawing an acorn... and while Viv's garden is small it is busy... her granddaughter's idea to create this haven... after Granny tells her about the starlings and thrushes and sparrows... how she hardly sees them these days... birds she remembers... humans spreading out... covering the world in concrete... spraying insecticides... fewer and fewer places left for the animals... short-term thinking... and this garden shows Viv's soft side... she is a tough woman... I wouldn't want to cross her... especially when she was young... but she likes me and I like her... her son leads me through the house... my fifth visit... the first time since she came home from hospital... it is a good sign she's outside... a beautiful day... bright and crisp... earth humming as the soil starts to warm... stems pushing towards the light... pods cracking and buds exploding... eggs hatching... babies born... Viv beams when she sees me... mentally tough but physically frail... this is how I know her... but she looks great today... reborn... a hundred times better than when I was calling the ambulance... and later... on the ward... her blue eyes blazing... pure happiness... innocence... she opens her arms so I can lean down and give her a hug... the smell of long soapy soaks in bubbly hot water... steam-cleaned... rosy resurrections... she's wearing her best perfume and I understand... a new start.... there's another chair next to her and she tells me to sit down... dear... would you like a drink... a nice cup of tea... no thanks... are you sure her boy asks... I'm fine... thank you... he goes indoors... gives his mum her privacy... independence... he's a good son... I know this... looks after her... lives in the house... cares... the same surname... and we are two girls together now... can speak freely... how are you feeling... Viv runs her eyes over the garden... stares at the back of the house... end of a terrace... her bedroom window... up the stairs I go... along the landing... through the door... pictures of her mother and father on the wall at the foot of her bed... lots of family photos... a dressing table... necklaces hanging down the left side of the mirror... rosary on the right... a bedside lamp... books of prayers and wise sayings... a Bible... the heavy flap of wings brings me back... wood-pigeon clatter... landing on the table... blue grey pink plumage... Viv is looking at me as she explains how some people call them ring doves because of the white feathers around the neck... she loves these birds... the veg growers aren't so keen... wood pigeons eat their brassicas... no sprouts for Christmas... she doesn't care... hates the bloody things... returns to my question... she feels content... knows that's a silly answer and not what I was asking... but she's as near content as she's ever been... this house... coming home... she can lock the doors and shut the windows and knows she's safe... it's true what they say... her home is her castle... her sanctuary... where she belongs... her life is there in the bricks and cement and tiles... her DNA in the wallpaper and paint and carpets and curtains... she is everywhere... this is where she raised her children... did her best... it wasn't always easy... and I take the hand she stretches out... brittle bones... thin skin... thick veins pumping... a strong beat...sunshine on her face... Viv radiant... glowing... her colour has returned... plus some... she wiggles her fingers... showing off the nails... they look fantastic... another granddaughter does them... works in a nail bar... and after a while chatting I get back to work... check her blood pressure... pulse... she says she's tired today... been staying with her sister... they drank two bottles of whiskey... between them... went for a walk each day... watched films and ate chocolate in the evening... listened to music... singing along to The Dubliners... cheerful numbers... crying through 'Four Green Fields'... two elderly sisters... my fine strong son... my boys... what harm can a drink do at this stage of our lives... more sad songs... 'Skibbereen' and 'Grace' and 'Spancil Hill'... Luke Kelly and Ronnie Drew... Guinness Export and Deliveroo... we like our country and western too... Dolly Parton and Waylon Jennings... but three nights is enough... she misses her bed... especially after the hospital... she'll go and see her sister again in a couple of weeks... but to be back in this house with her bits and pieces means everything... protected by her son... she laughs and jokes with him... that's the meaning... children... grandkids... and I think about my own boy... still a child... he has gone into the playground but not the world... a split lip... has to fight his own battles... doesn't want his mum coming into school... I know that... but why can't people just get on... there are enough problems in the world... enough illness... I fear for my son... I really do... when he is older... my daughter as well... different dangers... I say this to Viv... maybe I shouldn't... unprofessional... but she insists every mother feels exactly the same... she's survived... Ray's a fucking nutter... laughing... excuse my French... heart of gold... he's come through the bad times now... everything works out in the end... you'll be fine

Ruby... trust me... and Viv changes the subject... points out a blue
tit... the robin watching from the fence... there's a goldfinch... that
ball of colour... they love the small black niger seeds... a
greenfinch... male... green and yellow... Viv tells me to listen...
the trill of a wren... she talks like this until I gently bring her
back... has she felt dizzy... no... out of breath... no... unsteady on
her feet... no... we run through her pills... the doses... this part is
easy... the mechanics... and while it's right to tell a patient what's
going on too much honesty can be a bad thing... it is important to
be positive... essential... to offer hope and raise a person's spirits...
which can mean exaggerating... fibbing... but so what... and with
Viv no white lies are required... when it is time to leave I stand up
and she goes to do the same... but I tell her to stay where she is...
I can find my own way... Ray will show me out... and she
stretches out an arm... we hold hands... something cold in my
palm... she leaves it there... a silver cross... for helping me... for
saving my life... for being you... it's nice when you come and see
me... I think of Danny's dice... one day I will find the right
person... but not yet... I don't know why... tears in my eyes as I
thank Viv... tell her the cross is beautiful... is she sure... of
course... we hug again... bubbles and perfume... back in the house
I tell her son he can stop worrying... his mum is doing well... but
I'll be keeping an eye on her... write the details of my next visit on
the card I give him... he thanks me several times... and when I am
out in the street I feel so happy I could run and swim and dance all
at once... instead walk to Lou's house at the other end of the cul-
de-sac... ring her doorbell... she's expecting me... at home looking
for work... Barney barking at the shape behind the glass... pushes
forward... sniffs my legs when Lou lets me in... thumping his tail
against the wall... I pat his head and he licks my hand... we follow
Lou through to the kitchen and into another back garden... a table
in the sun... lemonade in a jug... citrus in the air... cupcakes
waiting on a plate –

LOST SOUL SAVED

Summer, 2019

RAY ENGLISH FELT as if his head was about to explode. The bricks were baking and the air was burning and his brain was banging and if that cunt on the other side of the wall didn't turn his engine off in the next ten seconds he was going into the garage and getting a hammer and smashing his windscreen. If the driver got out of his car to complain he'd do him as well. It was selfish. Fucking selfish. Just sitting there with the motor running like he was the only person in the world. The M25 was half a mile away, but this one car was worse than all its motorway traffic put together. Up close. Personal. Exhaust pipe pumping fumes straight into the garden where Ray was doing his best to stay sane with a mug of tea and a packet of custard creams.

The sound was as bad as the smell. A nagging, clanking drone. He could hear his mum telling him to turn his engine off when he was a kid, Ray sitting out in front of this same house waiting for a song to end. Did he want to be gassing people? Of course not. Life was about give and take. That's how things were meant to work. Treat others as you wanted to be treated yourself. And while part of him had probably thought she was being fussy, the better part would have known she was right. It was simple stuff. Basic good manners. Too many people only thought about themselves these days, and it had nothing to do with age or sex. Selfish cunts came in all shapes and sizes.

It started at the top. He was sure of that. Saw himself reaching the car and finding Theresa May or Philip Hammond behind the wheel. Clegg or Chukka in the passenger seat. Bob Geldof and that wanker off the radio whose name he could never remember sitting in the back. Rudd, Campbell, Soubry. His stuck-up Lordship Vince Cable and the hedge-fund yuppie Gina Miller. Animal-killer Heseltine. Especially Heseltine. Ray would drag them out and bash their heads in. It wouldn't make a lot of difference in the long run, as there were plenty more of these people waiting to step into the limelight, but it would release some of the pressure in his head. Stop it exploding.

Maybe he'd get lucky and they'd all be there, crammed into the back of a white van. Lady Nugee wouldn't like that, not Emily Thornberry and the snobs busy looking down their noses at the plebs. But he couldn't be braining her or any other woman. And what if it really was a bird in the car? He was going to look like proper scum threatening a woman with a hammer. Even if it was by mistake. There again, they didn't leave their engines running like men did, tended to think about these things more. No. He needed to control himself. Had enough problems. Ten seconds passed. The sound of the motor dipped. Faded into the background.

Ray was pleased. It was important to make allowances. To do things in democratic fashion. Consider alternative views. Find a consensus. Respect the majority. He believed in society. In democracy. It was the greatest experiment ever attempted by human beings, and he wasn't a fool, knew the odds were stacked and the choices limited and a privileged few still ran the show, but what was the alternative? The system was meant to get better as time passed. Fine-tuning. Straight lines. Yet the middle ground had been corrupted. The engine was being revved. Tony Blair and John Major were sharing a milkshake. Banana flavour. Two straws. One of them had a foot on the accelerator. Hundred-pound shoe pressing down. Part of a pair. The machine roared. Ray was never going to live these minutes again.

Moving forward in his chair he turned his head towards the sound, stared at the wall separating garden and street, saw bricks rattling and cement crumbling and sections collapsing along with the house, terrace, estate. The rubble was being flattened by steamrollers. Space cleared for an Amazon warehouse. Before that happened the fumes were going to kill the bees and butterflies he'd drawn into the garden with lavender plants. Next would be the robins nesting in the ivy. It was selfish cunts like this driver responsible for wiping out the insects and hedgehogs, filling the oceans with plastic, burning rainforests, melting ice caps, fly-tipping in ditches and fields – bin-bag mountains, rotting carpets and splintered wood, cracked plasterboard and broken glass. He thought of the selfish cunt he'd passed last week. Late morning down a local lane. Shade and light. England at its best. Perfect. A track leading into the trees. Ray had stopped, reversed, turned his engine off. Got out of his car and strolled over. Had a word.

The haters didn't want you to be happy. Something positive happened and they had to make it look dirty. That sort of thinking dripped down and bred more pond life. A small plot like this garden for fuck's sake. He'd bought the lavender on special offer at the garden centre. Three pots for the price of two. He'd taken six and felt good about himself. Clean. The lavender was for Mum. For April. He was clued-up thanks to his daughter. It was right to consider the needs of the individual. The different plants. Shade-lovers for the shade, sun-lovers for the sun. Cater for a range of tastes. Grasp the bigger picture. He'd seen a frog in the border. Tiny little thing it was. Diesel, gasoline, petroleum. Its skin would blister. Poppy eyes pop. It was wrong. All wrong.

Ray put his mug down on the grass, stood up and walked along the side of the house, pushed at the door to the garage, bottom corner jamming where the wood needed sanding. He pressed against it with his shoulder. Three soft bumps and he was inside and swearing he'd get on with clearing the garage out, something he did every time he came in here, but Ray knew where to find what he needed. Weighing up the hammer in his right hand he realised he was going too far. Couldn't stop himself. The switch in his brain had clicked. Nutty Ray... Oi The Nutter... Another person. Fucking right. His head was tight and he saw the doctor prescribing those pills last year. It was the same feeling. But different. Not the same. He was alert. Naturally high. No drugs required. This was normal. Natural. Better. Much better.

For two weeks his thinking had narrowed. Tightened. It was as if he couldn't turn his head. He was stuck in a stone tunnel. Imagined water but couldn't look down to see. One morning he'd woken up early and the tunnel walls were made of glass, his relief brief as he realised he was on the Underground, alone in a carriage in the foundations of London. The train was waiting outside a station. Red light holding it up. He was worried the oxygen would run out. Another morning the walls were made of earth. Tree roots jutted out. Became fingers. Bones. He was in some sort of burrow. Or a grave. Further out and in the past. The future. A crumbling skeleton. The doctor had meant well, but Ray threw the pills away. He'd been weak. Should never have taken them in the first place. Nobody apart from the doctor knew, and that was a relief.

The air in the garage was suffocating or refreshing depending on his mood, but he was on a mission and didn't hang around trying to decide which. First he was going to break the car's lights, dent a panel, *then* do the windscreen – keep the best for last. Save it up. He wouldn't hurt the driver unless he had to, and then it would only be in self-defence. Not with the hammer, though. He didn't want to kill the bloke. But he doubted it would come to that. Only in an emergency. Ray was a reasonable man. Nobody could say he wasn't fair. Or that he hadn't been provoked.

He went to open the main door, a panel raised by a cable that was always sticking. He eased, rocked, finally thumped the flimsy metal, and while it vibrated and his blows echoed it wouldn't budge. Doing his best to stay calm he held the cable straight with one hand and after several gentle attempts with the other managed to raise the door, the warmer air and bright light bursting in. He was quickly on the pavement. Paused to look this way and that, seeing who was about. Nobody. He turned to his left and was standing on the corner. The hammer fitted his hand. It could have been made specially.

Ray heard the silence before he saw that the car was gone, but kept walking as he eyeballed the empty space, rich black tar and a bleached grey pavement, light-green weeds and tiny yellow flowers sprouting in the cracks, darker plants thriving along the base of his garden wall. Tiny buds and a straw-like grass whose seeds had spread in the wind, last year's crop landing in front of the house facing the end of his terrace. Once pristine, the small patch of lawn was a mess of grass and weeds that made his own garden seem manicured. The downstairs windows had been boarded up by the council. Mr and Mrs Wicks and their son had moved in when the houses were built in the early Seventies, but they were gone now, the small family of three dead and buried together, their happy home run-down and empty.

Colin Wicks was another one who liked to sit in his car, but outside the house where he lived with the engine turned off, smoking his drugs away from his parents as he listened to Motörhead, Hawkwind, Deep Purple. Colin was a gentleman. Thought of other people. Ray only heard his music when he was passing, the Wiltshire bass and sweet smells seeping past the rubber lining the car's windows. Colin nodded his head in the mist. Drank in his local. He made good money as a toolmaker and for a while he'd been going to a Grand Prix every year. He was a teenage headbanger grown up. Still a boy. Lived with his parents until they died. Stayed. Never left home.

When Ray reached the spot where the selfish cunt's car should have been he stopped and breathed deep. There was no breeze and the fumes remained. Noticing tobacco in with the petrol he looked at the fag ends left by the drivers who stopped here. There were a lot of them, men who chose this spot off the trunk road, but they were respectful and turned their engines off. He swore out loud. Squeezed the handle of the hammer. Shook his head and closed his eyes. The sun blazed. He could smell his skin burning.

– Are you all right, Ray?

May and Hammond? Clegg and Chukka? Bob Geldof and that wanker off the radio whose name he couldn't remember? What the fuck was he called? The one who was always whining about Brexit. Smarmy cunt. England-hater. One of the snobs Orwell wrote about. He could see the face. No. If he left it the name would come back to him later. Then there was Rudd, Campbell, Soubry. The rest of them. Gina Miller. As if any of that lot was ever going to stop for a fag break here. Wouldn't even stop for a flat tyre. They didn't get punctures. Heseltine? One of Thatcher's ministers. The media were all over him, rebranding another arrogant snob as the voice of reason.

– Ray.

Maybe the driver was a teenager getting used to his first car. Loving the freedom. His reward for stacking shelves, lugging bricks, answering phones, loading lorries. Those first wheels were something a boy never forgot. It meant he could get out and about, collect his mates and put his foot down. Crank the volume right up. Or a man in his early twenties stopping to call his girlfriend. Sitting there with a hard-on. Counting the hours. Or a romantic pushing thirty who believed in true love and was sure he'd found his soulmate. Or a new middle-aged driver who'd passed his test at the seventh attempt half an hour earlier. First time out on his own. He was naturally nervous and had pulled in for a minute. Hadn't thought to turn off his engine. Unaware of the effect it had on others. Fair enough. People made mistakes. It wouldn't have been very nice for any of them to look up and see some nutter waving a hammer about. Ray was watching Ray through the glass. The boy and the man. It was the middle of the day. Working people trying to earn a crust. Tiredness kills. A break was good.

– What's the matter, Ray?

A delivery driver stopped to eat a sandwich, keen to get stuck into their coffee while it was still hot. Their Coke while it was still cold. There was no sign of Blair and Major. No banana milk-shake. It was a plumber, electrician, carpenter. A nurse doing her rounds. A carer helping the sick. The elderly. Sellers working on a commission-only basis. Big dreams. Small returns. These men and women were looking forward to their petrol-pump picnics. Their homemade sarnies. Exhausted souls were scared they would doze off. It only took a second. Then there were the drivers who made wrong turns and ended up lost. Swerve, crash, die. Every single one of them craved peace and quiet. Wanted to be left alone. But a looney appears out of nowhere. Starts smashing up their cars and vans. What was he thinking?

– RAY.

He opened his eyes. Lou was staring at him. His neighbour. Mum's friend. Like a daughter. Lou seemed worried, but not Barney. He stepped forward and lowered his head and started sniffing Ray's bare feet and flip flops. Retired Old Bill, Barney was never fully off-duty. Ray was embarrassed Lou had seen him standing here with his eyes shut and the hammer in his hand, dressed in a frayed Ben Sherman and baggy shorts, muttering fuck knows what. Had his thoughts made it into the air? Probably not. But he wasn't sure. At least he was clean and shaved. Every morning. Hair cut three days before. Number 2. He wasn't marching up and down with a big bushy beard like one of those jihadi nonces. Or a Wild West frontiersman slaughtering the Indians and buffalos.

– Can you hear me?

Barney finished sniffing Ray's feet and raised his head, opened his jaw and ran a huge tongue over his nose, teeth inches from the skinhead's balls. The dog tilted his head sideways and looked into Ray's eyes. What did the dog suspect? Know? Ray came back fighting. Reached down and patted Barney on the back of his head, relieved when the tail started to wag. Slowly. For a few seconds only. Even so, it showed that while Barney might have been Old Bill, he was friendly Old Bill. *Former* Old Bill. It was only right he enjoyed a long and peaceful retirement, but his law-and-order instincts were still there. Once a copper, always a copper. Barney would have dealt out some rough justice in his time. It was the nature of the job. Ray had seen mobs scattered by the likes of Barney. Pubs emptied. Streets cleared. He stepped back. Put some distance between his balls and those teeth. Smiled at Lou.

– I've been mending the trellis, he explained, lifting his hammer and pointing it towards the ivy running along the top of the wall.

Lou turned to look.

– Some of the nails were coming out and it was starting to sag. Don't want it to get too loose or the whole lot will come down. There's more to do. I need to cut the ivy right back as well. Can't do it at the moment because there's a nest in there.

Barney took no notice. Kept watching Ray.

– Robins...

Lou nodded and Ray changed the subject.

– Did you get your car fixed?

– Barry went to the place you told him about. Wouldn't know it was there, would you?

Webb Autos was hidden away down a track off a lane off a nearby B-road, the garage operating out of one of the old farm buildings passed down through the family.

– It's a shame Flynn's retiring. He's been there for as long as I can remember.

Flynn was selling his garage and bungalow to the builder Harrison. He was seventy-one years old and had been working on cars since he was fifteen, but arthritis and a bad back meant he'd had enough. Good luck to the bloke, that's what Ray reckoned. He needed it with a son like Adam. The daughter made up for that waste of space, though, and Flynn was going to live with Mary and her family over near Bracknell. There was talk of a caravan on the coast. Winter holidays in the sun. The working-man's dreams. The land had to be worth a bit and at least Harrison had grown up in the area. Ray would stop by and see Flynn before he left.

– He kept working after Maureen died, Lou said. If he was going to pack it in I'd have thought it would be then.

– She was a dinner lady at my school.

– It's for the best, but still a shame.

Lou glanced down at Barney, who sensed this and turned his head.

– How are you getting on with your mum's stuff?

– It's slow, but okay. Have to do it sometime.

– If there's anything I can do to help, you only have to ask. You know that, don't you?

– I do, but it's fine. Honest.

Ray started back towards the house, moving slowly as he chatted with Lou, making sure he was slightly ahead of her but not so she'd notice. This meant he was also in front of Barney. He was conscious of the dog's sense of smell. And angry at himself for leaving the garage door open. When they reached the end of the wall he said goodbye and nipped up the drive, Lou with no choice but to keep walking, Barney sniffing and trying to follow him, the lead meaning he could do no harm. Ray folded his arms and watched them go.

Relieved, he went inside and pulled the door down, stood for a while staring at the wardrobe by the back wall. Hearing nothing, he put his hammer on the workbench and returned to the garden, leaving the side door open so the air could circulate. He sat down in the chair just as Mum liked to do. She'd raved about this seven-pound bargain from the market in Uxbridge. There was even a hole in the arm for a can or a bottle. He glanced at her bedroom window, half-expecting to see her standing there looking out at the world. The smell of her perfume still filled the room and was strongest in the morning.

A bee hovered in front of him for a few seconds. A robin landed on the V of the shed. The bird table and feeder had been cleared of seeds while the water in the bath was evaporating in the heat. A white-winged butterfly passed near his head. The robin darted into its nest. Picking up his mug, Ray found a drowning ladybird. He dipped a finger into the tea and waited for it to cling to his skin, and when it was attached he held his hand up so the sun could dry its body. At first the ladybird seemed frantic, but then it was still and waiting, the body starting to split. Armour separated. Plates opened and wings vibrated. It flew away and Ray felt good. He had saved a life. It was a small exchange for what was to come.

Tipping the remains of his tea into the grass, he ate more biscuits and stretched his legs out. He had to calm down. Think clearly. Took his shirt off and put his sunglasses on. Eased as far back in the chair as he could. Let the sun pound his body. He saw Ray Winstone in *Sexy Beast*. It was hot. Too fucking right. That would be the life, sitting by a pool in your own little villa, and he wondered how Joe was getting on. He hadn't been excited about the trip. Said it was going to be boring, and Ray supposed he knew what he meant. He was fine here in his garden. Concentrated on the sweat flowing through his skin. Covering his face, chest, arms, legs. He was gammon on a barbecue. That's what the haters called white men. Linked it to the older honky insult. What did these racists have against pigs?

Ray's mobile rang. The chorus of 'Football, Beer And Punk Rock'.

– Handsome…

– What are you doing? his friend asked.

– I'm sitting in the garden as a blonde bird in nothing but a G-string dances up and down her portable pole. There's a remix of 'England Belongs To Me' playing. Urban version. Lots of treble. Hold on, she's taking her G-string off and coming over. Sorry, mate, going to have to call you back.

He turned his mobile off. Waited. His phone rang again.

– I'm sitting in the garden, Ray said. Thinking.

– What are you thinking about?

– Selfish cunts who leave their engine running when they're parked on the other side of my garden wall. A garage door that won't open. Old police dogs sniffing my balls and trying to read my mind. Bees, robins, butterflies, ladybirds. Politicians who say one thing and do another. Telling us two and two equals five. George Orwell. The sneering classes. People who look down their noses at us. Democracy. The pecking order. Excuses. Personal responsibility. How we can't always blame being a cunt on the cunts at the top. I'm thinking about all those horrible fuckers out there. The polluters. Sneaks. Thieving cunts who have no respect. That's it really. And I'm building up a thirst baking in the sun. Need to rinse my brain out before my head blows up.

There was a long silence.

– Not thinking about Brexit again then? Handsome said, trying to lighten the mood. We'll have a pint on Tim Martin and cheer you up.

Fucking hell, he'd only called Ray to see what time they were meeting.

– You still there? When are you coming out to play? Seven?

– Up to you. I'll have a couple local first.

– I could meet you at six if you want.

– Suits me.

– I'll check with the others and see where they're starting and let you know. Probably be Wetherspoons. Right, I'm off, can't be fannying about listening to you all day.

– You called me.

– Some of us have got to work to do…

Ray focused on two vapour trails in the sky. The planes queueing for the airport were more easily seen at night when they had their landing lights on, coming in from the east in a slow-motion column. There were cranks out there who swore they were spaceships, worse than them the nutters who insisted they'd met extraterrestrials. Been abducted. Experienced encounters that were somewhere between the two. They became upset when they weren't believed. If jokes were made. Were you probed by a Martian? Women cried. Or shouted. Cried and shouted. Taking the piss was wrong. He was getting hotter. The heat stung.

He was Gammon Man burning. The evil white male. Working-class scum. Pink skin smoking. Pig eyes melting. These sunglasses would only protect them from the sun for so long. He sat forward and concentrated on the garden. The grass was long and he pictured the Wickses' house, a stabbing sadness that was slowly spreading through the estate. He wanted to mow the lawn despite what Mum and April said, that if it was left to grow wild it would turn into a meadow. This might be tiny, but more insects, birds and frogs would come. Even hedgehogs. The countryside had been ruined by short-term thinking. Quick profits. England's animals were being exterminated. Farmers poisoned the fields and builders ripped out the hedgerows. Greedy, selfish cunts. It was strange how he'd never really thought about any of this before.

April was the one. First through his mum and now to his face. She admired this Greta Thunberg character and while men his age didn't like a gurning teenager with pigtails lecturing them it was terrible some of the stick she received. Fair play to these kids for having the guts to stand up and not accept things. It wasn't hard to see that some little fucker running his engine in the street or a big lump fly-tipping down a country lane was ruining things for everyone else. It all connected, like Joe kept saying, but while his punk mate believed in circles and loops and fuck knows what else, Ray was a skinhead and dealt it straight lines. Fist and boot. It was why the grass bothered him. He needed order. And Joe had sat right here and agreed. At least it seemed like he had. Everyone needed some sort of clarity in their lives. Or a place they could go. Just found it in different ways. Joe had told Ray about his friend Chris. The copper. Tidy garden, tidy mind. Chris and Barney. He wondered if the man was as suspicious as the dog.

Ray was under pressure. It was the law of the jungle. Survival of the fittest. He returned to the garage to get the mower, stood looking at the wardrobe for a full minute. It was big and heavy, the varnish buried under layers of paint – the white he'd known as a boy, followed by pink, sky blue, crimson, finally chipped yellow. Small plastic Teletubbies. Worn out figures. He had used stripper and a putty knife to clear a patch and find the original surface. The wardrobe had been passed down, something he'd only realised when he saw it on the pavement outside his brother's house waiting for a homeless charity to collect it in their van. His memory jogged, but it was the names written on the back that had really made him think. He had claimed it and given the volunteers who came a donation, organised a van to bring it to the garage where it had sat unused until early today. The doors were almost closed. He didn't want anyone suffocating.

Moving through the boxes, bags and stacked furniture he opened the doors and looked down at the selfish cunt sitting inside. The left eye was closed and swollen, the right one open and staring. Black masking tape sealed the mouth. String looped hands and legs. A washing line was wrapped around the man's waist, fixing him to a pole in the centre of the wardrobe. Ray glared at the man who'd crept into his house at two in the morning to steal from his mother. Scattering clothes and letters. Rifling drawers and pocketing jewellery. Robbing a frail old lady who had worked for everything she'd ever owned. A single mum who'd done right by her sons. It was the final insult. Where was the respect? The common decency?

Thieves stole your money, your belongings, your work, your vote, your memories, your lives. They took what they wanted and walked away laughing. With them went your belief and confidence. Most of these people were never held to account, while the law protected those who were arrested from a rougher sort of justice. The police and magistrates seemed to think burglary wasn't such a serious crime, but they were wrong. When one of these toerags mucked up like this, chose the wrong house at the wrong time with the wrong person unable to sleep in the next room – well – they got to pay for all the thieving scum who'd escaped justice in the past. Untouchables at the top. Invisibles at the bottom. This wasn't strictly fair, but he didn't give a fuck.

The burglar was in his mid-twenties and would have a story to tell if he was given the chance, but Ray didn't want to hear what he had to say. Nothing could excuse what he had done. Ray couldn't give a toss if he was local, English, foreign, alien. A loner or part of a dodgy family or a gang. And with his anger starting to bubble up again he wedged the doors open and went back out into the garden, forgetting the mower.

He had to make a decision, and whatever he did there would be consequences. If he let the man go he'd have to deal with the police or a revenge attack. And he couldn't let either of those things happen. What would his daughters think if he was done for assault and kidnapping and sent to prison? And this was his mother's house. Full of her possessions. He was responsible for keeping them safe and couldn't be having some lowlife cunt and his mates smashing the place up or burning it down. Mum had always kept her dignity in life. Even when she was sick and dying. Where was that dignity now she was dead? The respect?

April was right. The grass looked better long. He wasn't cracking up like Joe's mate Chris and could live with the rough edges. The garden was beautiful. It would be stupid to cut the lawn and kill the wildflowers and insects. Daisies, dandelions and buttercups were familiar to Ray, and for this reason they'd always been his favourites. Mum and April knew the score and he liked the idea of a miniature meadow. It didn't mean the house would become run-down and derelict like the Wickses' place. He was sure about this and felt relieved. A decision had been made. And while it was a small one and he had bigger problems to sort out, at least it was a start.

*

Lou stared at Barney and Barney stared at Lou and Barney cocked his head and Lou's heart melted. He usually did this when he was trying to understand something she'd said, but she hadn't spoken and he suddenly looked worried, as if he needed an answer to a question he couldn't ask. It was also odd how he was just standing there still and quiet after they'd come into the house after a walk. There was a chewy waiting for him in the kitchen, and normally it was the only thing on his mind as he wagged his tail and tried to hurry her up. She wished she could hear his thoughts but knew this was silly as she doubted they'd be in English or any other human language. They might not even exist as images. She had her feelings, the intuitions and premonitions, a clairaudience others called her gift, but Barney was operating on another plane. He was a clever dog and never going to forget his treat, more detective than constable as Barry liked to say.

Barney sat down and rolled his tongue over his nose, fidgeted and straightened his head, the thought of his chewy too strong as he stood and bounced forward, jumped up on his hind legs, front paws resting on Lou's tummy. She took his collar off with the lead still attached, hated the idea of him wearing it indoors. Next to the road she was on full alert and held it as tight as she could, relieved when they reached the field behind the church and she could let him go. Recently she'd worried there as well, hearing about these gangs who were meant to be going around stealing dogs and holding them to ransom, and yet that was daft as well. Barney might have been an older dog, but he was big and strong and nobody was going to kidnap him. They would be mad to try. He gave her an urgent nudge with his nose and she realised she hadn't rubbed the back of his neck.

When she'd done this for long enough he pushed himself away and was back on four legs, glancing towards the kitchen and then concentrating on Lou as she hung his collar and lead on a hook by the front door, pressing against her legs when they left the hall, tail thumping the wall. She opened a cupboard and took his chewy out of its bag and handed it over, Barney turning and heading for the living room and his chair by the front window, the one with the torn blanket and pillow, his toy pig Sam and a strong smell of dog. There was a thud and she knew he'd arrived.

Lou opened another cupboard and took out a bottle of Gordon's, poured herself a large one, added tonic and ice and followed Barney into the front room, removed her mobile from a back pocket and sat down on the recliner. She was hot after their walk and took a refreshing sip of her drink, placed the glass on the table next to the chair and turned on her phone, found a picture from Barry and winced. His face was wedged between a pair of lampshades that were pink, frilly and horrible, and she messaged him *don't you dare...* quickly, in case he was on his way to the till. She doubted he would buy these shades without her agreeing, but couldn't be sure as he had previous when it came to bringing home tat.

She could never be annoyed with her husband, not after their near miss, and she thought about his most recent bargain buy, the three lava lamps that could have been nice if they weren't cheap, badly made rubbish. The boxes were thick with dust and grit, which should have warned him, things only getting worse when they were opened, the lamps built from an ultra-thin plastic that had warped and cracked, while the coloured wax formed ten-second blobs that rose up and then sank to the bottom and stayed there. Barry was easygoing and generous and people saw him coming, so Lou had returned the lamps herself and got his money back.

Twenty seconds later *only joking* appeared and she placed her mobile on the table, looked over at Barney, who was holding the chewy in position with his front paws as he gnawed away. Lou had another sip of gin and pulled the lever so the recliner tilted back, careful to keep the glass flat on her stomach so her drink didn't spill. The peace that closed in on her was sweet, the only sounds Barney's chewing and her breathing, and she smiled as she considered the ugliness of those lampshades and how much she loved Barry, closed her eyes and absorbed the magic of the home they shared.

Everyone needed a place where they could be themselves, and she thought of the souls who spent their lives searching for peace, a search that could continue into spirit, knew she was privileged to have found hers so early. Nothing was nicer than cuddling up on the sofa with Barry and watching four or five episodes of a drama after one of them had cooked. They'd have a drink or two and later he would go back into the kitchen and make two big bowls of popcorn, half the time burning the pan and coming in to confess he'd done it again and apologise even though he didn't need to, not thinking that she already knew from the smell.

It was warm here in the winter and cool in the summer, and they were like two squirrels who'd moved into an old woodpecker hole and never wanted to leave. She thought about Flynn and how many years she had left with Barry, but despite what had happened before, neither of them was ever going to die. She felt sick at the memory of his illness and remembered the terror she'd felt, a shock given her beliefs and more importantly her knowledge.

She still felt sorry for Flynn, on his own and selling the bungalow where he had raised a family, the land next to it where he'd worked for so long and so hard to make ends meet and later get ahead. He could never have believed Maureen was going to die – *pass over* – not really, not until she was ill and her treatment was failing, and even then there would have been hope, the deeper human belief in immortality, the certainty submerged yet nagging. He was leaving their past to be bulldozed, or at least the physical memorial, but it was the correct thing to do, Lou knew that, their spiritual life everlasting.

She thought about Ray, how he'd moved in with Viv and looked after her, a good son who had stayed strong and seen things through to the end. When she was unemployed Lou would invite Viv round for lunch or walk over and sit in the older woman's suntrap garden when the weather was nice, and once Lou was back working she'd made sure they kept seeing each other. Viv was thrilled when Barney came to live with them, spoiling him with treats she bought specially, and it was sweet how he had sniffed the air and pulled towards the garage earlier, smelling and remembering Viv and maybe seeing her looking out from the shade or maybe standing at one of the windows.

Viv and Maureen were happy in spirit, and Lou wished Flynn and Ray could know and believe this and not be sad and miss them as much as they did, even though she appreciated it was a lot harder when the person was close and loved, would never ever forget how she'd felt with Barry. There was doubt in even the most devout of people, but not every single one, and it was attending the funeral of a Spiritualist friend of her mother's when Lou was sixteen that had changed her life. The service was light and positive, and those she'd talked to at the house afterwards were true believers who regarded death as nothing more than the moving between rooms. There was no sorrow, just joy, and this had been a revelation.

Seeing Ray holding a hammer and talking to himself in the street had knocked Lou off balance for a moment or two, but it was such a beautiful day she was never going to dwell on this or feel negative as he was mending the fence and nothing more. She was a naturally happy person with meaning to her life, had her gift and the security and solid foundations to be able to use it to help others. She had recently turned thirty while Barry was only a year older, everything Lou needed and wanted right here in this house and its garden, the streets outside and the nearby fields. She didn't crave anything more than the routines of their cul-de-sac life, the small estate in this village that wasn't even a village, more a series of clusters attached to the major roads, the perfect location with their house hidden and protected, surrounded by good friends and neighbours.

There was the clocking in and the clocking out, the measuring of days and nights and the times when she couldn't sleep and lay there listening to the breathing of Barry and Barney, full of wonder as her husband and dog jolted in their dreams, and now and then she would listen for voices. Most souls were at peace, but some were lost, the faint noise of the damned far away and easily blocked as she knew they couldn't be let into her mind. Lou was never scared or sad as there was an etiquette, and for the most part she maintained boundaries, worked in the church or one-to-one, at the right times so as not to be overwhelmed. She was disciplined, but needed that regular structure in order to focus. She was a bridge between the living and the dead who weren't dead at all.

Lou sat up and finished her drink, remembering how she'd been after she lost the job she loved, the meaning and wage and regularity, how during the months that followed her confidence dissolved. She was tired all the time, as if a massive iron deficiency was shutting her body down as well as her mind. The voices distorted and faded. She was no good to anyone. Barry had helped her through that period, encouraging her to go for long walks with him, and then there was Ruby and Ben, and that was when they'd thought about getting a dog of their own. She'd kept applying for jobs, gone for interviews, done her best to be positive, but it was when Barney came to live with them that her strength returned, and before long she had found work.

Looking over at Barney she found her lovely boy watching her, sure he had heard his name mentioned, and she blew him a kiss and heard the muffled tap of his tail trying to wag. Reassured, he returned to his chewing while she checked her vibrating phone. It was another picture from Barry, this one showing his face next to that of a rabbit with blue-velvet fur and green eyes. One of its front legs was raised and there was an empty socket in its paw, so she guessed this was a lamp. It was a mad-looking rabbit with a half-price sticker on it, and she thought why not and texted YES.

The church bell rang and a shadow skirted across the front window, a grey blur that seemed to snag in the nets and darken before breaking apart and drifting towards the front door. Barney sat up and growled, jumped off his chair and ran into the hall where he barked several times, Lou telling herself she'd never have to worry about burglars with him about. The letterbox clicked and the blur reappeared as a departing postman, Barney coming back into the room and over to Lou who reached down and stroked his neck. When he returned to his chair he saw Sam on the floor and gently lifted the pig up in his mouth, a toy from his previous life that he loved and never damaged.

Ruby had found Barney for them through a friend of a friend, and when Lou first met him he'd been carrying Sam, just knew they'd been together since he was a puppy. Sam was his bond with a time that had probably vanished as a conscious memory, yet he wouldn't go to sleep at night without him. Humans were the same, held onto the past through objects, Ray's garage a classic example, full of the things Viv had kept of her parents and children, stuff of her own she'd never got around to throwing away. Lou didn't envy Ray sorting that and the rest of the house out, but he would do what was needed, as apart from the heat getting to him earlier, he was strong and in control.

Now she'd cooled down Lou wanted to get back into the sun and work on her tan, went upstairs and changed into her bikini and was soon back in the kitchen making herself another gin and tonic, took this out into the garden and arranged the lounger and herself, leaving Barney to follow when he was ready. Her phone was silent, and Barry would be returning to work. He hadn't messaged her about a shade for the rabbit lamp, which was good as they could choose one together. Lou enjoyed her own company, but was looking forward to her husband coming home and the weekend they had planned, happy for now sunbathing on her lounger, safe in the cul-de-sac, enjoying the sensation of melting, evaporating, joining the spirits in the sky.

Ray sat at the picnic table in front of The Crown and watched the rush-hour traffic pass, leaving his pint to settle longer than usual as he built up the expectation. This was his first drink in five days and he was pushing things to the limit. Barmaid Jan could be floating in the clouds one minute and drowning in a ditch the next, but it didn't affect the way she poured his Guinness. She knew her craft and never let him down. He took a few extra seconds to admire the head and body, this black-and-white stout sold at black-and-white prices. Three pound twenty it cost here, while pubs in Central London were charging a fiver. Different clientele, of course. Business and media whores. The rich and famous. Tourists and students. Day-trippers. He had a thought. Took a picture of his pint, added some words and sent if off. When he couldn't resist any longer he raised his glass and took a mouthful off the top. Perfect.

Putting his drink back down on the table, Ray returned to the road and considered the shrinking size of the newer cars, the bigger SUVs that balanced things out, computer motors mixed in with the older models that were slowly disappearing. This route saw plenty of vans and lorries driven by men operating outside the repetitive journeys of the nine-to-five majority, and away from his garden he didn't care about the noise and smell. These things were about time and place. Something else. On the other side of the road the Co-op drew in locals who parked on the edge of a crumbling pavement where children hung around eating sweets, pensioners studied the noticeboard and dogs waited patiently on leads tied to railings.

He had another mouthful of Guinness and felt his anxiety starting to ease. This was probably wishful thinking, but so what. He wanted to forget yesterday's conversation with his uncle. It was hard enough dealing with the house never mind being banned from work and told to sort his head out. To calm down. Ray had made life difficult for Terry and was embarrassed. Ashamed. What choice did his uncle have? He had to maintain discipline within the firm. Said so often enough. Work wasn't the boys on a beano. He was running a company and there could be no slacking. No battering the male customers. No shagging the ladies. His drivers had to be smartly turned out and polite. There was no room for slobs or rudeness or aggro. Unless a fare refused to pay or tried to do a runner. High standards were essential. Especially these days with the online reviews that could lumber Estuary with a bad reputation overnight and cost them dearly. It wasn't like his uncle disagreed with him on Brexit either.

Terry was the one who'd organised the big screen in the Union Jack on the night of the referendum. And once the result was certain he'd made the already cheap bar free to everyone who'd stayed until the end. He had toasted his father – Ray's granddad – and his old man's mates from the war, every hero who had fought for their country, the wider generation who'd stood firm and been betrayed from within by Ted Heath and his Conservative Party. Terry was as happy as Ray about leaving the EU, but like most people a week or two passed and he had got on with his life, confident the government would do what was required to honour the people's decision.

Ray was less trusting and increasingly angry as the snobs who despised him and Terry and everyone they knew added a 2+2=5 approach to their smear campaign, fiddling the English language in true Orwellian style, slapping a People's Vote label on their demand for a second referendum. As if the masses were too thick to see what they were doing. These fanatics regarded the UK, and especially England, as a fascist nation. They really did. Preferred to side with Germany, Italy, France and Spain. With countries that not so long ago were being run by Hitler, Mussolini, Pétain and Franco.

Worse than this was waking up in the early hours and finding a thief going through his mum's belongings. They said bad things happened in threes, and maybe he should have expected a burglar, been ready for this final insult and not counted Brexit which was a slow mental torture that had been going on for three years now. Ray couldn't do anything about Parliament and the media, his mother's death and the aftermath, Terry suspending him from work, so the selfish cunt who'd broken into his mother's home was going to have to pay for the lot. He would deal with him tomorrow. The bloke could piss and shit himself meantime, crave food and drink, ache from his bruises, because Ray wasn't running a hotel. This was a zero-tolerance situation. But he couldn't dwell on any of this as it would ruin his night out, and he needed a good session to rinse the nuttiness from his brain.

Digging out his phone and earpiece he chose a favourite song, turning the volume up on Knock Off's 'Football, Beer And Punk Rock', because that's what life was about when it came to the crunch. He loved his football and he loved his beer. Not sitting alone in front of the telly swilling from a supermarket can or poncing about in a bar sipping craft ales, but having a pint with the boys in a public house. And he loved listening to a little bit of punk and Oi – to quote the great Lee Wilson – but these were Andy Town's vocals, the music going straight to his head and revving Ray up, the Chelsea man the owner of one of those distinctive voices that instantly set a band apart.

Coming out of Watford, home to Argy Bargy, The Angry Agenda and Tear Up, there had to be something in the water over that way. Knock Off were leading the charge with four albums released in a mere five years, a band that took no prisoners sonically and lyrically. Released on the Human Punk label, 'Football Beer And Punk Rock' was a terrace gem, while their most recent album *You Get One Life* was probably their best yet. Knock Off kept on improving, a dynamic part of an Oi scene that remained one of the best things in Ray's life.

It was going to be a good night. He could feel it in his bones. That earlier anger was behind him as he entered a more reflective mood. He'd sat in his garden surrounded by nature. Made the most of the weather. Dozed in the sun. Walked to this pub. Had a drink in his hand and a tune in his head. He was living like the other half lived even if the split wasn't exactly fifty-fifty. More one percent to ninety-nine percent. The wealthy bubblehead zones were full of people he was never going to meet but had heard about. Aristocrats, landowners, bosses, bankers. Their sons and daughters. Grandchildren. Young royals. Those at the top of the political tree. Trump and Xi Jinping. Merkel and Putin. The billionaires Bezos, Gates, Zuckerberg, Musk. Globalisers. Isolationists. Dictators. The masters of Big Oil, Big Pharma, Big Tech. But he only ever met functionaries. Servants carrying out orders. Men and women with bills to pay and families to feed. And then there were the collaborators. The believers. He thought about the wider planet. Human systems built on class, caste, tribe, race, sex. There were bullies, bigots, liars and cocksuckers everywhere. A worldwide jet set.

He agreed with the slogan *For The Many Not The Few* if not a lot of those repeating it, the left-wing snobs who thought he was scum the same as the right-wing snobs did. He was a working man. White, middle-aged, heterosexual. He was patriotic. For this he was denounced by classist, sexist, racist, ageist, England-hating numpties. The insults were the same as they'd always been, but the attacks were constant with any pretence at fairness abandoned. These tossers preached diversity, but their version was skin deep. George Orwell had written about them in the 1940s.

He saw the cab he'd ordered indicating right as it waited for a gap in the traffic, let through by an RAC van, pulling into the car park and turning in a tight circle so it was back facing the road. Stan was driving. His arm resting on the frame of the open window. Ray drained his glass and grabbed his Harrington and phone, tapped on the pub window and gave Jan a wave, would normally have taken his empty inside and said goodbye but couldn't keep his driver waiting. Nearing the cab he realised Stan was listening to Tear Up's 'King Of The Car Park'.

– All right, Ray?

– Not bad, he replied, getting into the front passenger seat.

The work suspension was strictly between Ray and his uncle. He wouldn't have called Estuary if anyone else had known.

– I thought you'd be in the Union Jack having your Friday light ale, Stan said. You had the day off?

– Yeah, I've got to sort the house out. Hate doing it, but I can't leave it forever. Good choice, by the way. Cracking band Tear Up.

Ray liked the younger man sitting next to him. He was a cheerful character. Worked hard, supported Chelsea, loved his Oi. Stan was one of the new breed, interested in Ray's suggestions, the history of the music and the wider culture, which was always going to warm the nutty man's heart.

– Good news about Frank Lampard, Stan said, once he'd crossed the near lane and was through the mini-roundabouts and on the road to Uxbridge.

– It's what we've been waiting for, Ray agreed. Nothing against Mourinho or Ancelotti or Conte, but Frank's another Di Matteo. It feels like we're getting our club back.

– Hard to believe he started at West Ham.

– Same part of the world as John Terry and Joe Cole. You know,

Joe was a ball boy at Stamford Bridge when he was a kid. Always been a Chelsea supporter. Even when he was playing for West Ham like Frank. Chelsea here, Chelsea there…

– I'm buzzing.

– Worked out well for all three of them. It's a state of mind.

– A way of life.

– Imagine not being a Chelsea supporter.

The traffic slowed down and backed up, Terry Hayes taking over from Jamie Flanagan and steaming into 'Proud To Be English'. Hayes was the PM as far as Ray, Stan and Gal Gonad were concerned. Another of Ray's favourites was 'Poplar Boys'. He loved that song and Terry's delivery. The Millwall man came out of the East End, an example of that cross-Thames drift denied by the dedicated of Bow and Bermondsey. It was a position Ray understood. Lines had to be drawn.

– Let's hope the transfer ban holds, he continued.

– Why?

Stan was surprised.

– Means Frank can bring in the youth. He knows the importance of home-grown players, so if Roman can't go around flashing the cash it gives him the chance to play the youngsters.

– I suppose so.

Stan didn't sound convinced. He liked the marquee signings.

– Trust me, there's loads of talent at Cobham that can't get a game, and we'll see more Chelsea supporters in the side. It'll make a big difference in the long run.

– It's nice getting one or two top players in during the summer, though, Stan said. Just hearing about who might sign livens things up when there's no games on.

– You bring the young players through, and they're like new signings. Look at Mason Mount who Frank had on loan at Derby. He's done well there and scored ten or eleven goals last season from midfield.

– I don't know a lot about him, Stan admitted.

– You're young, Ray laughed. Been raised on the Premiership and known nothing but success. This Mason Mount, he's the next

Frank Lampard. He'll play for England one day. Then there's the right back on loan at Wigan.

– Who's that then?

– Reece James. He's done the business as well. Could be another first-team player. I reckon he'll play for England too.

– They can't all play for England, Stan laughed.

– I bet you twenty pounds Mason Mount and Reece James play for the full England side one day.

– Go on then.

They shook hands.

– Whatever happens, I can't wait for the season to start, Stan said.

– We're a long way behind Man City. Have to be honest. I love watching City play.

– They're a quality side. Down to Pep, isn't it.

– Barcelona were mainly home-grown. Man City are the Chelsea of the North. That's what we used to say and it's true again. Money and trophies.

– Best thing was City beating Liverpool to the title.

– Last day of the season as well. Liverpool losing their seven-point lead. Brilliant. Fucking Scousers.

As they came down off the heath into the valley, crossing a bumper-to-bumper M25 on the way, 'Motherland' from the new Old Firm Casuals album took over, and these tracks Stan was playing were blending with Ray's early pint, charging him up for the night ahead. *Holger Danske* was another fine record, and Ray had nothing but respect for Lars and how he remembered his roots and promoted the original Oi bands.

Once Stan had pulled up in front of the pub, Ray paid and jumped out, quickly inside and spotting Handsome at the bar ordering. Gary, Young Ian, Darren and Two-Ton Tony (From West Drayton) were nearby. Two-Ton saw Ray and nodded. Didn't make eye contact. Ray forced to recall how he'd had a go at him the last time they'd been out. Tony was one of the few remain voters Ray knew. Terrified of losing his job, he'd been seriously spooked by that Bullingdon ponce Osborne and Project

Fear. The same George Osborne who was now editor of the *Evening Standard*. You couldn't make these things up. But Ray had been more aggressive than he'd intended and regretted his behaviour. Felt terrible as the memory intensified.

– You timed that right, Handsome said as Ray reached the bar. I bet you were standing outside waiting for me to finish my pint and get a round in. Peering through the window. Planning your entrance. We need to get you on *I'm A Celebrity*.

Ray was confused.

– I was out there for twenty minutes you're drinking so slow, he said.

– The usual? Remainer cocktail with an EU flag and double shot of spite?

– You forgot the Rich People's cherry. Stick that on top will you?

– How are you? Tony asked when Ray moved towards him.

– I'm good, he replied.

Ray meant it as well. He strolled into a pub at the end of the week to meet up with his mates and left his worries at the door. They could seep back in later in a drink-dulled form, and seeing Tony was filling him with guilt, but he was going to sort that out. Make amends. A glass was passed to him and he raised the Guinness to his lips. He took a step backwards and motioned for Tony to follow.

– Look, I'm sorry about last week, he said. It's not an excuse, but I'd had a lot to drink.

– What are you apologising for? an earwigging Ian butted in, only half-joking. He needs to be told.

– No, Ray said in a firm but friendly tone, I was wrong. Out of order. They were all fair points you raised, Tony. Seriously, I'm sorry.

Ian knew Tony better and could take the piss without threatening him, but kept quiet and stepped away.

– Honest, Tone, Ray continued. It was that cousin of yours who wound me up. Went and changed my mood. I had a go at you when I should have had a go at him. No offence. I know he's family. Just I've got things on my mind. You know…

– He shouldn't have said what he did, Ray. He's always putting his foot in it. Doesn't mean to, but it's like he's got Tourette's or something.

Ray had met a fair few people like that over the years. There were the ones who always had to push things and knew exactly what they were doing. It was there in their eyes. Voices. The words they used. Within that lot there were the chancers and the psychos. Mainly chancers. There were also those who didn't realise what they were doing. It was as if there was another person in there stirring. Ray put Tony's cousin in this last category. Not at the time, but now. After listening to Tony.

– I think he gives it the big one to cover up his shyness.

The bloke dealt in furniture and did house clearances for stock plus the extras he could sell on, and Ray had heard him talking about people he'd done these for in the past. How they didn't care about their dead relatives' possessions. Which was good for business.

– I can speed things up, he'd cheerfully told Ray. I'll bring the van round and sort out a skip. We can knock it out in half a day. I've got a couple of big gypsy boys who'll do the heavy lifting. You decide what you want to keep, and I'll go through the rest. Rubbish for landfill, whatever I can sell in the van. Most of it will be junk, believe me. I've done enough of these clearances over the years. People hang onto all kinds of shit. Proper tramps a lot of them.

– That's a bit insensitive, Ray had said as he stepped forward.

Handsome moved between them and ushered Tony's cousin away. He'd then left the pub. Later Ray was talking to Two-Ton, wasn't going to refer to the incident as he wasn't responsible, but they'd got onto Brexit and Ray had lost his patience hearing the same old trade-deal bollocks repeated yet again. From Ted Heath to Theresa May. It was important for Ray to play his part and make democracy work, but he'd over-reacted to another opinion. Calling Two-Ton a fucking traitor wasn't right. He just didn't believe the country was going to be dismantled. Heath's lies lived on and Tony Benn's truths were ignored.

The EU a common market? Little more than a trade deal? This had driven Ray round the bend for years, and yet he had to remember that the likes of Tony were innocents. Two-Ton had never been interested in politics and wanted an easy life, but suddenly he'd been bombarded with propaganda and like so many feared for his future. And so Ray apologised at length and Tony seemed happy. Good relations were restored. Any bad feelings kicked back outside where they belonged.

– What do you think about Frank Lampard then? Ray asked, moving on before things got too mushy.

– First English manager in over twenty years, Two-Ton replied. It's fantastic.

– I don't know, Gary butted in. He hasn't got a lot of experience, has he? He'd have been better off waiting a few years. Stay at Derby and finish his apprenticeship.

– The chance to manage Chelsea might not come around again, Ray said. He's got to take the job when it's offered. He did well with Derby. Got them to the play-offs.

– Didn't win promotion, though, did he?

– At least it was Villa who beat them, Tony said. That has to be good for John Terry. He'll be Chelsea's manager one day as well.

– You know what the Russian's like, Handsome observed. A few bad results and Frank will be out.

– He wouldn't do that. It's not like Frank's come from nowhere. Wouldn't fucking dare.

– JT's looking at things long term.

– Maybe, but Frank went to Derby and Gerrard's at Rangers and what's John doing? He should be managing.

– Fucking Scouser, Gary remarked with a smirk.

– We'd have loved Gerrard if he'd come to Chelsea, Ray replied. Scouser or not.

– Of course we would.

Gary's mum was Liverpool born and bred and one of the nicest people Ray had ever met. Salt of the earth. Proper values and a heart of gold. The boys said they hated Scousers same as the Scousers swore they hated Cockneys, and at the football there were few grey areas, but in real life things were different. Football was a soap opera that would continue forever.

– You recovered from Baku yet? Ray asked.

Gary had travelled to Azerbaijan with Paul for the Europa League final against Arsenal. Taken the long route to save money, but it hadn't worked out that way.

– My credit card hasn't, Gary replied. Can't believe we did that journey. The whole trip was mental.

– Over land and sea.

– And Leicester.

– Worth it, though. Had to be done. Nearly two days each way.

Ray admired their dedication. They rarely missed a game. Every club had fanatics who kept going year after year. Decade after decade. Home and away. Chelsea versus Arsenal in Baku and UEFA doesn't change the venue? What was that about? Well, he knew. Money. It was the way professional football had gone and people could either pay the high prices or pick their moments. Ray enjoyed the livelier European games, but not a rip-off in somewhere like Baku. Terry had travelled direct and offered to pay for him, but no way could he accept. It was nice seeing Arsenal get thumped, even if it was never going to be enough for the Cup final and that Sanchez handball.

– Funny they didn't wear rainbow laces for that one, Ian said.

– When it comes to money the lectures stop, Handsome agreed.

– Gary Lineker and Gary Neville... What's wrong with the Garys, Gary?

– Not really Garys, though, are they? Gary replied. Not proper Garys.

Ian Stills had come up through the ranks at Chelsea and built a reputation for himself. Ray had come to like him, the earlier distaste he'd felt knowing Ian had stabbed his father fading as Ray got older and started thinking how his own dad had fucked off and left Mum to it with no real consequences. It was a terrible thing to do to your flesh and blood, but Ian had balanced out over the years and had a good head on his shoulders. Darren was harder to work out, while his mates Stan and Matt were good-time boys who enjoyed a drink and made Ray smile. Ian looked as if he was on one tonight, finishing his pint early and pushing the pace.

The drink was soon flowing and the serious stuff forgotten, their laughter growing louder, especially when Handsome and Gary tried to chat up a couple of thirty-year-olds. Handsome was feeling confident as they headed off to the Ladies, at least until Darren claimed to have had a blow job off the better-looking of the two a couple of weeks earlier. And Ray pointed out that Handsome and Gary were old enough to be their dads and should be ashamed of themselves.

– Listen to him, Handsome said. It's not like they're teenagers.

– Or underage, Gary emphasised.

– She didn't just swallow it either, Darren continued. Rinsed and gargled first.

– I don't believe you and I don't care.

But Handsome did believe Darren and he did care, even though it made no difference, as when the women reappeared they saw them talking, Darren waving over so the other men turned and stared, instead of returning, the ladies in question walking away down to the other end of the pub to find their friends.

Two pints later, Ray and the others left the pub, and after a quick drink in a filling-up Whelan's and three more in a busy Three Tuns, they arrived in the Queen's Head. The football had been discussed at length, the beer was flowing and he wondered who would dip into the wonderful world of punk rock.

– Right, Handsome said, once they had been served and his memory stirred. Getting back to what I was saying before I was interrupted earlier. We're in charge of the next *I'm A Celebrity Get Me Out Of Here* and we've got the beer and bush tucker sorted out, but still have to choose the contestants. We get to pick one person each. Who would you have?

– That bird who gave me a blow job, Darren decided.

– You want her drinking from a puddle and eating dead snakes?

– It's going to be hot and steamy in the jungle, and I'd rather see her sweating in a wet T-shirt than Harry Redknapp.

– She's not famous, though. I mean, not nationally.

Darren paused, tempted to nominate Theresa May as he enjoyed watching the BBC's Parliament Channel and especially the current prime minister. He found female MPs a huge turn-on, loved seeing them squeezed into a packed House Of Commons, used iPlayer to replay the earlier live feeds, even freezing certain Right Honourable Members when they were asking a question or making a statement so he could wank over them late at night when he was unable to sleep. Mrs May was reserved yet glamorous, a classy lady whose success increased her appeal, and he would never masturbate over Theresa as it would have been disrespectful and even perverted. He couldn't stick her in the jungle with a bunch of glory-hunters as she would find it demeaning, and it was going to spoil the romance if he saw her covered in sweat without her make-up and sexy shoes. He also felt it would be risky going down the Theresa May path with the others as they were bound to start taking the piss, plus it was only going to set Ray off on one of his Brexit rants.

– Charlotte Hinchcliffe then, he said. Emily Atack…

– Good choice, Ian nodded.

– She's already been on the programme. But fine…

– Gary?

– I don't know. Jeremy Corbyn?

Corbyn wasn't popular with most of the boys for a variety of reasons.

– What about you, Ian?

– Saint Gary. Stick that wanker Lineker in there.

– Another good choice.

– Gordon Ramsay, Two-Ton Tony (From West Drayton) offered.

His dislike of the chef was well known to the others.

– Who would you put in there, Ray?

– I don't know.

– Must be someone.

– John Lydon. Stick some punk rock in the jungle to liven things up. Or Andy Town. He'll eat anything that moves.

– Which one? John or Andy?

223

– Andy Town. The jungle won't bother Andy.

– So we've got Charlotte Hinchcliffe, Jeremy Corbyn, Gary Lineker, Gordon Ramsay and Andy Town. Interesting that three are punishments, one is Darren perving over a nice pair of tits, while Andy's in there to cause havoc.

– What about you? Ray asked.

– Ricky Gervais, Handsome replied. We need some humour. The man's a genius.

– Good call, Ray said.

Everyone else felt the same way. Ricky was a diamond. Him and Peter Kay. North and South. England united.

By his seventh pint Ray was feeling the effects earlier than usual. He wasn't legless or even properly drunk, more like mellow and muddled, but in a nice way. He moved away from his friends and sat on a stool at one of the high tables to gather his thoughts. Couldn't manage it and let them unravel and float away.

– Hello, Ray.

There were fingers tapping on his shoulder and he turned to find a gorgeous woman facing him.

– It's me. Priscilla.

She was grinning.

– Do you remember me?

He wondered how long she'd been standing there. More importantly, if she was real. The last time he'd seen her was in this same pub. No. It was in his cab. Maybe he was hallucinating, but he could smell her perfume and thought of his mum, felt the energy surrounding Priscilla, saw how she was full of life and recovered.

– Don't be daft. How could I forget you?

– I thought you had. I'm still waiting for your call.

She bit her lip, reached out and touched his arm.

– I'm only joking. How are you?

– I'm good, he lied.

It didn't feel like a lie, though, not since he'd had his first drink, not since he'd met up with the lads, especially not now he was looking at Priscilla standing there even more beautiful than he remembered.

– Are you sure, Ray?

– Just working and that. I'm all right.

– I've been in here a few times since I last saw you. I wondered if we'd bump into each other. What I would say.

For a moment he was worried, imagined her as a stalker, which came out of that story she'd told him, the one that had scared him off. But it was a stupid thing to think, as she had to go out and this was the place they'd first met, a pub they both used. People ran into each other. That was normal. And Priscilla was normal. Well, not exactly normal, but then neither was he sometimes.

– How's your mum?

– She passed away last year.

Priscilla's smile sagged and she took his hand, and after a moment's hesitation she hugged Ray, squeezed tight so he thought of his mum again and how she had started doing the same thing towards the end of her life, in the last few years when she was slowly dying and he wasn't noticing, hoping for the best and those endless new beginnings. And he remembered how she wanted him to be loved and settled, worried about what would happen after she was gone, his brother Ronnie married and safe watching TV. Not like her lump of a little boy Ray. The nutter.

– I'm sorry, Ray. You were a good son to her.

He had been sitting with Mum at two in the morning on the night before she died when a nurse came through the curtains they'd let him pull around her bed on that tucked-away ward full of the old. A depressing, heartbreaking place most people would end up in eventually. How the hospital staff stood it he did not know. This nurse who came in had said the same thing – that he was a good son. And he had felt an odd sort of pride that he had never surrendered. Never hidden. Gone the distance.

– I didn't meet her, but I know how much you loved each other.

The nurse was young and wore a hijab, and he'd felt at the time that her comment meant more because she was Muslim. They looked after each other. Turned up for visits in big numbers. It was the same with the gypsies. The English family had all come. Mum hadn't lacked visitors. They'd all done their best.

– I really am sorry, Ray.

He heard Priscilla's voice breaking and pulled her in close. His friends at the bar were leering like the overgrown teenagers they were, Handsome with his tongue in the side of his cheek mimicking a blow job, which was disrespectful and would have been embarrassing if Priscilla had turned suddenly and seen. Ray glared at Handsome and the others, shook his head very slowly as he eyeballed them so they looked away and left him alone.

– Were you with her? Sorry, that's too personal.

– It's okay. Yes, I was there when she died. We all were. It would have been terrible if I hadn't been.

– That's private, I shouldn't have asked, but it's good you were. It was the same with me and my dad.

– Sorry, I didn't know. When did he die?

– Nearly six months ago. It was sudden. I came home from work, and he was sitting in his chair. His eyes were closed. He just went to sleep and never woke up.

Ray saw Priscilla's body heave as the shock returned, that moment when the worst happens and everything else is unimportant, all the arguments and anger meaningless, just a huge waste of precious time. She stepped back and they were two people again as she opened her handbag.

– What a pair, she laughed.

Priscilla dabbed at her eyes with a tissue.

– Has my mascara run?

She tilted her head so he could see, and Ray was struck by the sparkle in her eyes that even that terrible memory couldn't ruin. And he looked at her mouth and wanted to kiss her and forget the madness and take Priscilla home.

– It's a bit smudged. Not much, though.

– I'll sort it out in the Ladies. Tell me something good, Ray. Make me laugh.

Ray thought about the burglar in his garage and the fact that he had to kill him and dump the body, the trouble at work and how he'd let his uncle down, the state of the nation with Westminster refusing to carry out the will of the people, and he couldn't find any words. Yet he didn't panic. He had always felt easy in Priscilla's company. At least until that night outside her house. Otherwise she was perfect. Beautiful in her white summer dress.

– I didn't mow the lawn, he blurted out. It hasn't been cut for ages.

– That's good news? Priscilla asked, laughing.

– I was going to cut it, but I forgot to bring the mower out of the garage, and then I sat down and looked at it again. I saw the daisies and dandelions and thought about what my daughter says. How the insects and birds are dying. Mum used to talk about the sparrows and starlings. That she missed seeing them. April says we need to make these miniature meadows in our gardens. Change things for the better.

Priscilla was close again. Her head cocked so she could hear what he was saying. Battling the noise of the pub. Her right breast brushed against Ray as she changed position to speak. The material was thin.

– That *is* good news, Ray. You look sad, though. Sorry, I have to tell you. I'm honest. You know...

– I know.

She moved closer still and Ray raised a hand so she kept coming, slipping his arm around her shoulders as she lowered her head and leaned it against his chest. He felt the heat of Priscilla's body seeping through his Fred Perry. Breathed in the smell of her hair. And it struck him that her honesty was part of her madness and that maybe there was little difference between the two.

– You're the most honest person I've ever met, he said, even though the thing that kept them apart wasn't true.

But she believed it was and that meant she was honest. Like Two-Ton. He had been hard on Tony and Priscilla. With one he had said too much. The other he had ignored. Yet with Priscilla it was more than just a difference of opinion.

– I have to go, she whispered. My friends are waiting outside.

The best liars enjoyed the easiest lives. There was no insanity in conforming. Only rewards. Jobs, money, respect. He wished he could go somewhere quiet with Priscilla. Sit in a corner of a room and hold her hand and talk, but she was easing away and kissing his cheek.

– Can I take a picture of us together, she asked. So I don't forget what you look like.

Ray knew this was the end. He nodded and she took her phone out and stood next to him and took the photo. He felt terrible and pulled a face to pretend that he didn't. She looked at her phone.

– Let's try again, she said. Come on.

This time he smiled, and she was pleased.

– Goodbye, Ray.

Leaving the pub, she waved through the window and was gone. Hadn't even asked him to call. This was the last time he would ever see her, and it was his fault. He'd had enough chances. Felt stuck. Couldn't move.

It took Ray a while to sort himself out. Two-Ton had gone back to West Drayton leaving Handsome and Gary talking by the bar, Young Ian and Darren near the open pub doors looking at one of their phones. Ray placed his mobile on the surface of the table and plugged in, filled his head with music, adding some punk rock to the scene. The real punk known as Oi. He listened to The Last Resort, The Business and Infa-Riot and was strong once more. The straight lines returned. He finished his drink and felt revived, put his phone away and went over to Handsome and Gary and ordered another round.

The trees shelter Grace... the ferns mean she's hidden... safe from predators... and she's doing her best to keep still... not make a sound... quiet as a mouse when an owl barks... but she can't help the wheeze of her breath... the ticking in her chest... curls up like a hedgehog... tight as she can... half acorn... half pine cone... protecting her face from the cold... a ball studded with quills that prick the noses of a boar and a bear and a wolf... interested spirits of animals past... Grace in the darkness with her ear to the ground... hears the planet sigh... a drawn-out yearning that presses her heart... buried seeds waiting... the air loaded with woodland narcotics... hovering... circling... closing in... tiny psychedelic bursts... fractal swirls... invisible colours in a monochrome set... she's never felt this tired... exhausted... must stay awake... to stay alive... fall asleep and she'll never wake up... drift forever... back through the centuries... she has to fight... listen for the hunters... the king and his lords and their butchering men... this plague on the land... human blight... raping and murdering... peasants and animals... it makes no difference... nothing can stop the monsters when the law doesn't care... priests swear it is the Devil sending his beasts under the canopy... that dirty old pervert is scared of the trees... witches and witchcraft... green men... the Devil is a coward... there's nothing romantic about that bed-wetting nonce... hexed by the poor he fears our gods... pagan magic... highwaymen come to tax the rich... the king and his lords... their retribution brutal if they catch our heroes... Robin Goodfellow... Dick Turpin... outlaws roam the shires... force the fiddlers to stand and deliver... their money or their lives... and Grace glimpses these things as her breathing slows... wet bark and dry ferns... spores in her lungs... a head full of scent... moss and fungi... lichens and berries... needles bleeding into the soil... dead leaves rotting... enriching the earth... intoxicating... a sweet decay... she is sinking... sighing with the planet... dozing... her heart stops... vibrations... electro-convulsive... fronds unfurl... she is awake... excited... could be a fairy... dragonfly wings... a pixie family outing... their boots on a twig... she's sitting in bed as her mother reads... Germanic words... Saxon stories... a house on the edge of a forest... Grace a child... Grace an adult... the vibration continues... separates into footsteps... she scratches at the earth like a rabbit... breaks a nail and a claw... the hole she's made releases more scent... ancient... cloven hooves on the path... the steps stop... she waits... silence... lifts her head and peers through the leaves... a muntjac stares back... this deer as special as a fairy... close enough to reach out and touch... she resists... doesn't want to scare it away... neither of them move... their eyes locked... the deer curious not frightened... like the boar and the bear and the wolf... Grace sure *it's a girl... the doe trusts her... she'll never forget that... something moves... another muntjac... this one is bigger... also curious... more cautious... the doe looks at the buck... who moves forward... back... unsure... his head turns... ears rise... listening... the doe turns at exactly the same time... alert... in tune... two seconds... a decision... they are off in the opposite direction... moving deeper into the trees... Grace kneels... watches them go... towards a light she hasn't noticed... they know the woods... the paths to take... that something dangerous is coming... her body already bruised... dead worms in a muddy ditch... rigid frogs... Grace semi-conscious... crawling and stumbling and staggering... she has made it this far and can't stop... has to keep going... be strong... brave... follow the muntjacs... she stands... the space between the lowest branches and ferns is flat... as if it's been pressed from above and below... her head is squashed... briefly... popping back into shape... broken body mending... stones in the mix... jutting from concrete and timber... bolts... stems... but the way the air is being squeezed means she understands the light... it isn't human... she's sure of that... moon bouncing sunshine... she crouches as she moves... narcotics disturbed... fractals warping... leaving the pines behind... hazel and rowan... a cluster of oaks... their skeletons don't scare her... she can walk upright here... crossing grass... the woods closing in... undergrowth thickens... blends as the path thins... trickles... it is hard to see... she trips on a log... breaks its casing... trunks tortured... skinned... brambles scratch... holly cuts... red ink clots... a dead end of colourless green... an overgrown weave of trees and bushes... some sort of wall... willow... coppiced maybe... she is certain the muntjacs came this way... uses her hands... feels her way... pushes into looser conifers... tumbles... a corridor where she can't see a thing... the smell of so many perfumes mixing is incredible... nearly knocks her out... sparks... an opening... she stands at the edge of a clearing soaked in moonlight... a hidden enclosure bordered by trees... tall black screens... it is a beautiful sight but she's easily seen... a target for longbows... crossbows... Grace drops to the ground... hides in the ferns... starts humming...*

imagines she's the doe... the muntjac... frail but fast... senses honed... and peering into the clearing she panics... eyes adjusting... three hunters... except they can't be men as they are huge... outlines... she lies on her tummy and cups her chin... watches these giants but none of them move... they are wooden... struck by lightning... she feels foolish... metal patches... confused... silver linings... the earth yawns... its yearning stronger... she is soothed by the light... the king and his lords and their butchering men can't enter... sanctuary... the white quivers... intensifies... murmurs... the buzz of the universe... hibernating bees in a honeycomb mind... she stands and walks into the middle of the clearing and lies down on the grass... damp seeps through her clothes but she doesn't care... inside she is dry and warm... nobody can harm her... she is protected... spreads her arms and legs out to form a cross... a star... absorbing the moonlight... sunlight... starlight... boughs creak... pine and hazel... rowan and oak... an hour passes... she is no longer alone... winter will pass and soon it will be spring... summer... our meadow... her dream and my dream... Grace standing... returning to the trees with the man from the stars —

Joe came back from the bar and placed the three pints of Estrella he was carrying on the table, sat down and filled his mouth with lager. He wasn't keen on these flat European beers, but at least it was nice and cold. He was feeling rough and needed refreshing after last night's session and the fry-up they'd just eaten in an English-run cafe, and while he'd known much hotter days they weren't usually this muggy. Mind you, he wasn't drinking a lot of alcohol when he was down near the equator, on his own and away from the local temptations and his herbert pals sitting opposite, his skinhead mate Ray who'd sent him a picture of a pint of Guinness on a picnic table with the caption *Wish You Were Here?*

He wiped his forehead, sweating lager dregs and the shots Dave had insisted on pouring in the early hours once he'd taken him and Chris back to a closed Vista. Drink was one of their bonds, consumed in the places where likeminded men gathered, the mead halls of Valhalla a vision of what heaven could be if they were lucky and believed in a pissed-up afterlife. Their love of public houses went with the English climate, and it didn't matter what the season was as each one had its own charms, the changing conditions a lot different to those he found when he was alone in the East.

He was remembering a two-day train journey from Chennai to Varanasi in particular, when it was over a hundred and twenty degrees outside according to the guard, and yet he'd felt a lot more comfortable than he did right now. It might have been baking even in the shade of his carriage, but the heat was dry and he was sure he had hardly sweated, and definitely not like he was at the moment. It was more humid here and he imagined worse in England, could smell the petrol and freshly poured Guinness, hear the hum of industry and the airport and the crisscrossing motorways, the voices of the mischief-makers and law-abiders, couldn't wait to get back to Slough and have a proper pint, start going through the cassettes he'd bought off O'Mara, return to the tracks he'd been working on, the breakdowns and versions he found so addictive.

Joe had been to India three times in the last six years, and while he loved its energy and flamboyance and the animal magic of the Hindu pantheon, his romanticised view of the country had changed since his visit on the way back from Australia. It was easy being an outsider who didn't have to worry about caste or sex or religion, ignorant of what was being said and done around him, the sheer effort it took the majority just to stay alive. He might have felt the heat during that journey to Varanasi, but it was nothing to what the workers had to endure as they laboured in the sun, even worse the lives of those who didn't have jobs or were sick or old, left to beg or starve.

Like most people he feared unemployment and ending up on the streets, yet he had a welfare state to help him, a cooperative system that had been fought for not given, the remnants of a post-war socialism that had reappeared in the shape of Jeremy Corbyn and John McDonnell but was nevertheless being dismantled. He was glad he lived in England, the memory of earlier lessons learned still with him, driven home when his train to Varanasi stopped at a station whose name he would never know.

A crowd of hawkers had bundled aboard to sell chai and samosas and Ganesh statues to the travellers, a skinny figure in a heavy brown coat rushing along the aisle of Joe's carriage and turning into his doorless compartment, standing above him and staring down. He'd wondered how the woman could wear such a thick coat in the heat, how her body must be sweltering as she held out a hand and asked for baksheesh. These thoughts were vague, lazy like the realisation that the coat was a cloak, made from a rough material that could have been an army blanket if it didn't have the black buttons. Something clicked, and he focused on her face and expression, saw what he at first thought was hatred, embarrassed as he realised it was desperation, shocked when she opened the cloak to show the scars where her breasts had been. She pulled at her skin which stretched and came loose from her body as if it was a vest. He gave her the rupees in his pocket and she turned and hurried off the train, another passenger explaining that the woman had leprosy.

– We're blessed, Joe said. You know that, don't you?

Dave and Chris looked at him and Dave nodded. Three chums on holiday. Boyhood pals and their merry japes. Friends forever. Not a care in the world.

– Hot weather, cold beer, intelligent conversation, Dave confirmed. What more could a man want? Apart from a blow job off one of these tanned lovelies strolling up and down searching for cock. Once the drinking's done I'll be happy to oblige.

– We're luckier than most, Chris admitted in a more sombre tone.

– We need to find you a woman, Dave announced. You're out on parole and only got a week of freedom. There's this new barmaid working tonight. She's not exactly Scarlett Johansson, but good enough for you. No offence to the missus, Chris, but you need to get your leg over. I'll be servicing her myself soon, so you'd better get in there quick because first or last she'll remember me best.

– Same old Dave, same old lines, Joe said.

– One up the bum, no harm done.

– Remixed and versioned.

– Let me have a go on this, Dave said, too quick for Joe as he reached over and grabbed his Volca Drum, left in a bar last night and recovered an hour earlier.

Joe didn't mind Dave trying his luck. It was murder figuring out how to use his new drum machine, even if he was finally getting the hang of the controls. Dave wanted a reaction and was disappointed, while Joe'd already had some fun at Chris's expense with the preprogrammed patterns, using the pitch attack and tempo to drive him round the bend when he was in the shower and unable to turn it off. Dave as well, last night when they were out, and he had played the two rhythms he'd made, which while basic didn't sound too bad. He was excited by the Korg, reckoned that whoever invented these machines had to be in the genius class, and maybe that was why they were unable to write a set of simple, easily understood instructions.

To be fair, he probably wouldn't have been able to work those out either, and it felt right that the boffins responsible seemed to be following their intuition as much as the science, maybe even working out sounds by ear. He didn't know what went on inside their studios and heads, only that he admired everyone from the Japanese inventors and BBC sound engineers to the likes of Blackbeard and Adrian Sherwood and local sparks Electric Jack. Thinking about them made Joe want to get out of the sun and sit in a dark room with his rabbit lamp lighting up the yellow pads of his customised MPC, his mind focused and clear as the hours passed in a matter of minutes.

– I can't be bothered, Dave said after a long look at the Volca, and pushed it back. Here you go, Gary.

Joe hadn't minded the Gary Numan comparison when they were drunk last night and he didn't mind it hungover this morning either, but he wasn't going to risk losing his drum machine again.

None of them were the sort to have one drink, and while he was suffering and it was a bit early to start again, he was on holiday and would do what was required. First he had to deal with the Volca Drum. The apartment he was sharing with Chris was a short walk away, and he was going to put it in there now.

– I'll be back in a minute, he said, drinking half his remaining lager. I don't want to lose this again. Might not find it next time.

He had a thought and decided to put some pressure on the others and drained his glass. The Estrella would only be warm when he returned and he enjoyed the hurt look on Dave's face while Chris merely sighed. Back at the apartment, Joe wrapped the Volca inside a clean shirt and put this in his bag, went into the kitchen and cut up an orange, put the slices in a bowl and sat outside on the shaded balcony. He took his time with the orange as he considered the ten-minute track he'd been building before leaving England, a series of sentences used whole, chopped into phrases, words and sounds, the speed of the latter adjusted and the results warped and reshaped. He'd used vinyl recordings that included Winston Churchill and Eric Morecambe before stretching his rules and adding clips taken off the internet, his focus the great Don Logan from *Sexy Beast*.

Don had summed up how Joe was feeling this morning, missing the buzz and the bolt of his own culture, perplexed by the expat life. It would have been wrong not to have dropped some of Ben Kingsley's lines from *Gandhi* in as a mark of respect for the actor's range, and this he had done. There were seven versions of this verbal bastard pop on the go, and he was taking things to the limit with *Unsaid*, the voices no longer human, key words dismantled and turned into the smallest of breaks. He wished again that he was hunched over his MPC instead of looking at another session. It was a tough old life, but he'd manage somehow.

On his return, Dave and Chris were arguing the toss over Brexit, and while Joe liked repetitions in music, knew a good song depended on them, there was nothing musical in what they were saying. At least they had seen him coming and a fresh pint was waiting, and he started on this and thought about his surroundings again, could sort of see why someone would want to move here, but was still with Don. After three days Joe was restless, missing home in a way he never did when he was in the East. He wasn't complaining, glad they'd made it over at last, and it was nice meeting Martina who'd taken a day off to drive them around the island to see the sights. It was a beautiful place with friendly people and he shouldn't be feeling bored. He tried not to listen to what the others were saying, but it was impossible not to tune in.

Dave was pissed off because he lived in the EU and the UK leaving meant paperwork and hassle, plus he made money bringing tobacco into England and there were bound to be restrictions on that as well. He doubted he'd be deported, but you never knew with the Spanish authorities. It wasn't like living in England. Brexit was pointless, an angry vote when the rest of Europe was loved up. He didn't give a toss if Brussels was undemocratic, didn't care if the EU became a dictatorship one day as he would be dead by then. It was a price worth paying if it meant Europe could stand up to China. Borders were wrong, or at least those between European countries, and hadn't Fortress Europe done a good job keeping non-Europeans out? The benefits were clear and outweighed the costs.

Chris was insisting the UK needed to tighten its borders not loosen them, that they had to control the numbers coming in. He had nothing against those who worked hard, there were just too many of them, and they were changing the culture as well as driving down wages. Sure, he had used Poles to put in his new kitchen. So what? They'd done a good job at a nice price. Look at the amount of people arriving from the Middle East and Africa. What the fuck was Merkel thinking? England was a soft touch. It was on his doorstep. Russian and Albanian gangs, the Romanians robbing Indians of their dowries and trying to take over the scrap-metal business. What about Clem? The time they pulled out the squirt? He hated the scum who splashed acid. Fucking despised those cunts. What about the terrorist attacks? Manchester? FGM? The grooming gangs?

– That's the Pakis, Dave pointed out. Fair enough, kick them out, but not the East Europeans, not those Polish birds, not the lovelies. None of the EU countries want the Muslims. Not the people, anyway.

Joe reckoned leaving the EU was good for democracy and bad for business, and it wasn't going to suddenly make everything right. The same establishment would remain in place and in time push for a return. He hadn't been as shocked as Ray by the reaction of those with their fingers in the pie, although he *was* surprised at how blatant the insults had become. They had talked about this at length and agreed that the real arguments had been sidelined early on, the rubbish that followed a reflection of everything they'd known during their lifetimes.

He hated the focus on immigration, the way it had been manipulated by elements on both sides and exploited by the media as a form of clickbait. Those who wanted to remain in the EU should have stated the truth up front, said they believed in a EU superstate and technocratic government. Likewise the leave side should have stuck to the fact that the EU was a political project and not a trade deal. It was three years since the referendum, and the worse the attempts to overturn the vote the more pleased he was that the majority had rebelled, but he was sick of Brexit, lacked the passion and anger that was driving Ray round the bend.

It was depressing that even the BBC had lost the plot. He believed in the BBC, the ideal of a publicly funded organisation that wasn't driven by the profit motive and could be truly independent in its reporting, dedicated to a non-biased presentation of world affairs, would hate to see it privatised, but it needed a clear-out. The BBC was meant to represent Britain and the honesty of an analogue world, but the internet and the dumbed-down nature of social media was destroying impartiality, and even the BBC had become infected.

The Labour Party was fucked as well, had missed its big chance and been destroyed by the posh element that had been hollowing it out for as long as he could remember. Even the anti-EU Corbyn and McDonnell had been shut up, and after the Blair years ran into Cameron and Clegg and the rise of the internet, he realised that the class war had been sidelined. These were his best friends sitting here and they were talking bollocks, and he thought about *Unsaid*, words broken down to a drone, suddenly excited to do the same with the EU question, take the voices of May and Juncker and Farage and put them into his MPC, add Macron and Merkel and Tusk and one or two celebrity big mouths. He was quickly lost in the permutations, brought back by a change in tone, didn't know if it was Dangerous Dave or Sherlock Chris getting angry, knew he had to change the subject and move them on.

– Are you going to drink those? he asked, pointing at their glasses. Come on Chris, it'll get you in the mood for when you meet Dave's new barmaid.

– She's a darling, Dave said, Brexit instantly forgotten. You'll love her. Got to sort yourself out, mate.

– And what about you? Joe continued. When are you coming home? Bring Martina. I'll talk to her if you like. There's no reason to stay here. That other business was sorted out in B&Q, remember. Why are you still living in exile?

– I'm set up, Dave said, looking at Chris and thinking about Gary Wells.

It had been a while since he'd thought of that bullying cunt Wells. Good fucking riddance. He had no regrets apart from blabbing to Chris. That was four years ago, and he had stopped worrying as soon as he was back behind the bar in Vista, but here they were together again and his memory had been well and truly jogged.

– What does Martina say about you servicing the barmaids? You can't be that serious about her if you're shagging everything that moves.

– *Anything* that moves, Chris added with a grin.

Dave had only strayed a couple of times even though he gave it the large one around his friends, as that's what they'd done as kids and it was part of the humour, but more than that he liked to wind up Buddha Joe and that righteous tosser Saint Christopher. True, the first of those two women had been on the receiving end for six months, but the second was a one-off and he'd only gone and got caught doing the nasty. She was this little raver of a barmaid from Hull, off her nut as soon as she left work, and this one time she'd finished her shift and they'd been alone in Vista and he'd had too much to drink and began serving shots once the shutters were down, sharing several lines of the coke he'd got back into for a while. He'd been careless, was doing her from behind when the boss turned up looking for her mobile.

– One up the bum, no harm done, he mumbled, as if on remote.

Martina didn't go berserk the second she walked in and saw what was happening, instead paused and looked around the bar before calmly walking over and taking a Heineken bottle from a crate of empties. That's how she explained it later as he hadn't seen her enter, and she'd even removed her shoes so he didn't hear her walk up behind him, doing her best to shove the bottle up his arse. It would have done a lot more damage if it had been the full insertion she'd intended, but what she managed was bad enough. Fuck knows what the gays saw in that sort of thing. Martina had twisted the bottle while Dave screamed and tried to pull out of the barmaid, which meant him backing into the glass, and while he hadn't felt lucky at the time later on he'd thanked God it was an empty and hadn't had the metal cap attached.

– Except for the screaming.

– Screaming? Chris asked.

– What she doesn't know isn't going to hurt her, Dave said with what he meant as a confident expression, although to Joe and Chris it seemed as if he was grimacing.

The real screaming and shouting had been saved for the barmaid from Hull, who was punched and kicked out of Vista while Dave stood there in his shirt holding his bum with his hands not knowing what to do, if he should leg it or try and calm Martina down. She started hitting him next, and while he moved his hands round to protect his balls he let her get on with it, the pain nothing compared to his aching arse. Anyway, he was used to her violence, the blows that didn't hurt that much, and he didn't care about her rages as they always made up after, Martina full of guilt and eager to repent. He knew this was different, that he had

239

gone too far and regretted shagging the barmaid, just wished he didn't have the coke in his system and could get rid of his hard-on. Martina was threatening to kill him when a strange thing happened.

– You don't understand women, that's your trouble, he said as his cockiness returned. Neither of you do.

Martina stopped shouting and stared at his erection in silence, and then started laughing. Dave assumed she was becoming hysterical, but she'd only gone and pulled a chair over, sat down and gently moved his hands away and cupped his balls, and after making a show of licking off the barmaid's juice – *that filthy English slut of a whore* – she'd given him the best blow job he'd had in his life, even better than the one he'd got off a Soul Patrol girl outside the Community Centre when he was a teenager. Martina hadn't let him off the hook, but he could live with her moods just as he could live with his own. Life was sweet apart from this Sherlock Holmes business, the strange case of the wanker Gary Wells.

– No offence, but there's only one of us here who's shagging regularly.

Fucking Chris the coppering cunt who'd never said anything about the big secret Dave had shared. Fucking Chris sitting in judgement when he wasn't exactly a QC or a DI or even out on the beat. Fucking Chris perving on the internet. The bloke was never unfaithful to his missus even though they hadn't had sex for fuck knows how many years, not even a kiss, he bet, and that was a suspicious way to be carrying on.

– Why don't we go to that place we passed last night, Joe said. The bar with the reggae playing.

– Sounds good to me, Chris replied.

– They've got those palm trees outside. Lots of shade. I'm going to shrivel up and die I'm sweating so much. There's something wrong with the sun here.

– You're a fucking heathen. Pasty punk-rock skin.

– Fuck off, cunT.

– CunT.

– You two can sunbathe and I'll sit under the palms.

– They do a Sunday roast, Dave said as they strolled along the promenade. No good for you, though, Joe. Like I said, this isn't England. No vegan options here, mate.

– We've only just had breakfast, Chris remarked.

Dave glared at Chris and Joe wondered why as it was a fair comment, even his own version of the Full English served without the bacon and eggs was making him feel heavy and tired. Maybe he was ill, didn't understand why he was suffering like this when the others seemed fine, why he was bored and even homesick. He had been on the other side of the world for months at a time and never been bothered. It made no sense. They continued in silence until a woman in an Indian headdress stepped out in front of them and held a hand in the air.

– How! she exclaimed.

The three herberts stopped and listened to what she had to say, her spiel delivered in what was probably a Dutch or Belgian accent.

– We have a two-for-one promotion until two o'clock, and before midday you will also receive complimentary olives and walnuts. Can I tempt you?

Dave tried not to leer as he ran his eyes over shapely tanned legs, white shorts and a tight orange top, Joe waiting for the inevitable comment, surprised when it didn't come.

– Why is the bar called Dances On Water? Dave asked.

– It is my name. I love the water. Swimming, but also surfing.

– Two drinks for the price of one? Do you have draft lager?

– Fosters, Carlsberg, Stella Artois. Heineken in bottles only.

Dave frowned and seemed to be considering the options.

– You like Heineken I think, Dances On Water said. You are a Heineken man.

Dave looked more closely at the woman and wondered if she knew the barmaid from Hull, had maybe given her a job, but no, Claire had only been over for a couple of months and had gone home. He'd met up with her once more before she left and ended what he'd started that night when Martina did him up the jacksie. He didn't count it as being unfaithful, just completing a half-finished job. He giggled, which confused Dances On Water and worried Joe and Chris.

– I used to like Heineken, he explained, but I've gone off it.

He turned to the others.

– What do you reckon, boys? Fancy a pit stop?

Chris nodded and Joe shrugged. It was an interesting little bar, but why it had the Indian theme wasn't clear, especially with this talk of swimming and surfing. Joe doubted there were many Pawnee or Cheyenne riding the waves off Hawaii.

– My name is Mighty Wolf, Dave announced, extending a hand which was shaken.

– The famous English humour, Dances On Water remarked.

Joe noticed the look on her face as she addressed the smooth-talking, jazz-funk-loving soulboy and was sad to realise they were flirting. It was fucking typical.

– This is my companion Peaceful Buffalo, he said as he indicated Joe.

Dances On Water reached over and Joe shook her hand.

– And finally our confederate Sneaky Serpent.

Chris started, wondering where Dave had got Sneaky Serpent from, didn't like being compared to a snake or described as sneaky. He would rather have been a buffalo like Joe or a wolf like Dave. Why did he get to decide? Who made him the fucking chief? Even so, he was happy to make the most of the promotion and sit in one of those comfortable-looking chairs in the outdoor area he could see to the side of the bar. The owner shook his hand and they followed her inside, Dave telling him it was his round, which Chris knew, irritated by his tone as much as the reminder but letting it pass, brooding instead on his Indian name as the drinks were ordered and poured.

Grace comes out of the trees… stands by the side of the road… cars and lorries thudding past… one more step and they'll smash her to pieces… but she wants to live… knows how to survive… breathes… the metallic pong of the dual carriageway… its petrol and oil and rubber... curious changes for the traveller within... the man from the stars... and while Devil's Ditch has long been filled in and sealed the past seeps back... pollutes and confuses... this smart black strip of tarmac rising out of the town and cutting through the green... splitting the bigger wood in two... linking satellite and suburb... four lanes... a central reservation... same faces... different times... Satan styles his hair... powders both cheeks... leers... hunts easy meat... rabbits and deer... locals walking home late at night... lone hitchhikers... fragile souls he can entice into his carriage... charming... convincing... instilling trust under cover of darkness... vulnerable creatures who can't defend themselves... the starman sees... humans are the dominant species... but divided... O is here to help... to save Grace... but the desire to live must come from within... she turns and starts walking along the pavement next to the road... it is hardly ever used these days... nettles spill out from the trees... narrow the space between her body and the traffic... she can't hear the planet... its murmurs and sighs... yearning... the dozing seeds and dreaming hedgehogs... squirrels in their nests... toadstools and ferns... fungi kingdoms that spread for miles... somewhere between animal and plant... Grace unsteady... one mistake and she'll fall to her death... the wheels of a lorry... there's a wooden lamppost... old and forgotten... reassuring... smudged yellow light... the machines come in waves... a break in the flow... she can smell the woods again... a surge of pine... damp trunks and composting needles... strongest is the fur of the doe... a car lined with leather... stripped skin... two worlds fizzing as they meet... Grace knows... she's been scratching at the earth like a rabbit... psychedelic soil leaking acid... she's startled... the body of a fox... torso crushed... neck twisted... head untouched and propped against the kerb... stiff open jaw... blazing white teeth... staring eyes... O is learning about the human condition... life and death... good and evil... Grace sways and nettles burn her legs... she vomits... wants to sit down but has to keep moving... reach the town... there's a bend in the road and she runs down the slope as the pavement widens... nothing coming in either direction... dual carriageway deserted...

the moon lights its surface... illuminating fields... there are cows to her right and they call out... stand and watch... Grace wonders if they know... and if they can sense the alien... wants to stop and stroke their noses... but there's some commotion up ahead... across from the petrol station and opposite the allotments... the land before the houses begin... the first estate... blazing lights... music and voices faint at first... a big wheel... but the pain is spreading... an overgrown ditch full of brambles and plastic... dock leaves on a bank... she stops and picks the biggest... there's a pile of logs... rough bark softened by the rain... split by ice... moss means they've been here a while... struck by lightning... chopped up... left to rot... Grace sits on these and hopes she won't get splinters in her legs and bottom... the dress she's wearing is thin... she's lost her coat and pants... bare feet cut and dirty... can't remember which shoes she was she wearing... she's even lost her handbag and wishes she hadn't... rubs her legs until the leaves crumble and she has to pick more and start again... rubbing harder... ripping at the skin with her nails... breaking three more... panicking... she has to scrub the pain away... O hums... softly... and she is calmed by his wisdom... the lessons she has learned... pain can pass... she shouldn't be scared... but he wants to understand the spectacle... the lights and sounds... Grace transported... she is moving through the fair... confidence soaring... strength in numbers... the power of the people... anything is possible... everything... she's thrilled by the intensity of what she is seeing and hearing and smelling... the radiant faces with galaxy eyes... ancient heads smooth and new... tattooed make-up... earrings necklaces lockets crosses... neon promises always kept... nothing wicked will this way come... humans magnificent... magnified... wood steel flesh giants held together by iron joints... nuts and bolted bones... shapes shuffle... circles squares triangles oblongs splinter... create forms that can't exist... Grace sees marionettes dancing and puppets smooching... strings attached and cut... targets and teddy bears... hand-painted stalls... electric reds blues greens... lions and unicorns... rides that float and sink and twist inside out... a breathing donkey... spinning toy horses... swinging tin monkeys... Shrek beaming... years *decades centuries rest inside each other... boys and girls running to the next amusement... coming back around in big looping circles... following their middle-aged selves... soulmates hold hands and she envies the love that lasts forever... and Grace is thrilled by the intensity of what she is hearing... waves of sound that rustle her hair... every note separate yet part of the whole... songs play in a single second... fairground favourites Elvis and Eminem... Trojan and Motown... David Bowie and David Essex... Major Tom scratching Joe 90 notes... bubbling babies children teenagers adults... their thoughts as three-minute pop songs... fermenting... and Grace is thrilled by the intensity of what she is smelling... everything has its fragrance... the skin of the people and the hair on their heads and the coats of their dogs and the dung of the donkey... every thought and wish and dream... smoke from a fire... logs coal and paper... simmering soup inside a gas-warmed caravan... cabbage and potato... tomato from a can... popcorn and chips... chestnuts roasting... gears and engines... rumbling generators... the curiosity of mice and rabbits and the faeries in the crowd... Grace's senses raging... she's never felt so alive... coming here since she was a girl... for as long as she can remember... there is a charter... traditions pass down... locals and travellers... often the same... and Grace is thrilled by the history... most people never move far from where they are born and grow up... and those who leave often return... need to come back... an ancestor of her father's won money here boxing... he fought a gypsy man... doesn't know much more... he has told her about the Finnegan brothers buried in Iver... Jimmy Stockins living in Iver Heath... Joe Smith in New Denham... her dad boxed when he was young... from the city... from the plough... he saw Henry Cooper fight Muhammad Ali... tells her his stories again and again... if he doesn't for a while she'll ask... and most of all Grace is thrilled by the intensity of O... his positivity protects her as she leaves the clearing and passes through the woods and walks by the road and moves through the fair... they ride the dodgems together... the merry-go-round... sit on a single horse... visit the fortune teller Lola... and I feel as if I am with her... the two Davids... Bowie and Essex... the two Es... Elvis and*

Eminem... the Ronettes and Roy Ellis... and as Grace leaves the carnival she is transported again... lands in the town... thrilled by the love of her mother and father... her classroom and teachers... friends made and the games they play... the clothes she wears and the people she meets... the work she does and the life she leads –

The picture was fuzzy and the sound distorted, but the Guinness was honing Ray's senses and he realised that he was in the 100 Club watching The Last Resort steam through 'Never Get A Job'. Roi Pearce was flanked by Beef and JJ Kaos, Ray's royal-blue Fred Perry soaked in sweat as his head nodded to this and some early Resort classics – 'King Of The Jungle', 'Red White And Blue', 'Rose Of England' – which after a while fused and became 'Freedom'. It wasn't only songs off *A Way Of Life* either, but tracks from the more recent *You'll Never Take Us* and *This Is My England*. He loved all of these albums – *Skinhead Anthems I, II* and *III* – just as he loved the annual Boot Boys Knees Up night at Human Punk.

Ray took his shirt off and wrung out the water, put it back on and was behind the decks with Doctor Vinyl, the Human Punk DJ spinning 'Harry May' as he lead the crowd in a singalong tribute to Micky Fitz. The Business moved past heading for the stage where David Dong, Max Spartan, Danny Boxall and Big E stood either side of the steps while guest vocalists Roi, Mike Brand, Lee Wilson and Sebi – who'd flown over from Germany – waited nearby. It was a right royal turn-out of Oi Oi legends who would take their turns joining Steve Whale, Steve Kent, JJ and Micky Fairbairn throughout the set. Ray was back in the crowd singing along to 'Get Out Of My House', 'Justice Not Politics' and 'The Truth, The Whole Truth And Nothing But The Truth', and again these songs merged, became 'Real Enemy'.

The nutty man's mind was busy with some of the writers who meant the most to him, and this demanded a big dose of Lee Wilson. Infa-Riot were delivering 'I'm More Punk Than You', 'Boot Boy' and 'Punk And Oi!', the choruses, verses and rhymes of a very English wordsmith moving into 'Proud'. This lifted Ray up because like all of the best lyricists Wilson rejected the official pecking order, those naff categories of left and right, had no time for the regulation stereotypes, snobberies and prejudices, restrictions of wealth and language, insisted it was right to be proud of yourself and proud of your culture. Ray cheered Infa-Riot as the lights came on and they left the stage, Dr Vinyl playing Wire's 'I Am The Fly' especially for Lee.

Ray had left the venue and was on his way home, taking the Bakerloo line from Oxford Circus to Baker Street, the Metropolitan line out to Uxbridge. Tony Smith was with him and they discussed his record shop in Ruislip Manor, the Outer London manors and a culture never reported but going strong thanks to places such as Tony's brilliant Sounds Of The Suburbs. Leaving Uxbridge station, Ray was knocked down by torrential rain that carried him into Windsor Street. He tried to swim to the Queen's Head, but the current was too strong and he was washed against the doors of The Metropolitan. Uncle Terry pulled him inside and spoke to the landlady who looked like Jan, handing her a five-pound note before leaving without speaking to or even looking at his nephew.

Sitting at a table drying off, Ray was struck by the blue eyes of the old men who had gathered to watch him drink his stout. They were all here, the descendants of families from the Danelaw and Wessex and the Irish navigators who'd helped build the railways and Metroland. There was a car parked outside with its engine running, but it was Terry behind the wheel with Lol sitting next to him so Ray let it go. More important was the thieving cunt handcuffed to a radiator, and despite the masking tape covering his mouth he was chanting *nutter* and turning the heads of the regulars. Ray had to shut him up, but before he could decide how the door crashed open and his mum was inside shouting at him, really screaming her head off, and he was shocked as he didn't know why. Priscilla followed her in and stood there crying and shaking her head. He wanted to stand up but couldn't, asking them what had happened. Had he done something wrong? Something terrible?

Stirred by the sunlight filling his room Ray sat up in bed. He'd had a lot to drink and was briefly worried he'd got into a fight, been caught on CCTV, but the fear faded as he realised he'd behaved. He remembered walking down Windsor Street to George's, but by the time he got there it was closed. That was before a late drink in The Crown. Was that right? How had he got there? Couldn't picture any of the Estuary drivers picking him up. It came back to him. A black cab outside the tube station. He must have gone back up there and found it waiting. He'd talked to the driver about Brexit. A man who shared his anger. Ray wondered why he hadn't called Estuary, the conversation with his uncle returning and making him jolt. Yet nobody apart from Terry and Ray knew.

There had been a light on in The Crown and he'd asked the driver to drop him off, had this idea there was a lock-in going on and the chance of another drink. He was facing a bolted door. The pub empty. Lights left on by mistake. He'd turned to walk the five minutes home, taken a few steps and heard a noise by the pie-and-mash van. A rat going through a bin bag. Clapping his hands he watched the shadow of a fox moving into the car park that ran down the side of the pub to the beer garden. It was a big one. Huge. More like a wolf. The fairy lights were still on in the garden. Maybe someone he knew was out there. He went to have a look and found Jan sitting at a table. She had a glass of wine in front of her and was smoking a cigarette. She deserved her time alone after finishing work and he went to leave. Ray was pleased. He had done the right thing. Didn't need that extra pint.

Except she'd seen him and called his name, and he'd gone into the garden through the open gate in the rickety little waist-high fence. She told Ray to come and sit down and have a drink, went into the pub to pour his usual. There was rustling in the bushes and he stood up and clapped his hands again, much louder this time, heard the fox heading towards the far end of the garden where it was overgrown and there would be a quiet way out. It was the kind thing to do. If the fox started trusting humans it would be in danger. There were some evil people out there. Scum who hurt animals for fun. Sadistic cunts. They progressed to women, children, anyone they could bully into silence. These things connected. Liberties were taken. Look at politics. It was the same with drugs. Puff, speed, coke and finally heroin. And thieving. Shoplifters became the muggers who became the burglars who could easily turn into rapists and the murderers of pensioners and even kids. Fucking nonces the lot of them. Lines had to be drawn. Standards maintained.

Jan had reappeared with the perfect pint of Guinness and several packets of crisps, and he remembered the taste of these as clearly as the stout. Yes, she knew her craft all right. The landlady was an artist. And she wouldn't let him pay even though he offered. He'd been hungry after missing out on a curry and even after the amount he'd drunk, the heat of the night and his heavy head, he could have murdered a ruby right now. If there was a carton of leftovers in the fridge he'd scoff the lot. The same went for the Full English. He'd have loved one of Terry's notorious fry-ups, but it was too early to call him, and anyway, he needed to keep his distance for a while. The sadness was overwhelming. He had let his uncle down. Maybe that was what his mum was angry about. Why Priscilla had been crying and shaking her head.

He'd sat in the beer garden for a good hour talking with Jan and her husband Ken when he turned up. There was a second pint. He couldn't remember much of what was said, but everyone was happy. The good weather made a difference. He had this idea that Jan wrapped her arms around him in the middle of the garden, started rubbing against him. He had a hard-on. Then and now. But he had never thought of her like that, and she was a married woman who loved her husband. From a distance she looked like someone else. The garden was full of people and the clouds were dark and low. He was in the Queen's Head. It was Priscilla, not Jan.

His memory was clearing. He'd bumped into Priscilla. The same pub as before. Or was he imagining it? That's what he'd thought at the time. It was like a second replay of the first time they'd met. Third time lucky. Things always happened in threes, and that could mean the good as well as the bad. For a moment he'd wondered if she'd come looking for him, but Priscilla could have thought the same thing. That he was a stalker. But she didn't. Priscilla was with her friends and said she was leaving. Again, the same as before. That was odd. It didn't matter. She looked even better than he remembered. Her dad had died. He'd only met him once. Briefly. Hello and goodbye. From what she'd told him, Elvis was a character.

It was hard to believe he'd only gone out with Priscilla the three times, including that last night at Shepherd's Cross. Sitting outside her dad's house it was as if he'd drifted into one of the fairytales he used to read Chelsea and April when they were small. He was on the edge of a great forest. There were witches and wolves in the trees. It was pitch black and lonely. He was a logic man who preferred order and company. He pushed her words away and concentrated on Priscilla leaning against him in the pub. His cock was rock hard, but it was more than just sex. He tried to separate his dreams and memories and wishful thinking but it was impossible.

Ray looked for his phone and found it on the floor. Checked the time. Half-six. He must have opened the window to cool the room down and could hear the faint hum of the motorway, the weekend meaning it was quieter than normal. He went through his messages and found one from Priscilla. Could hear her voice.

– I loved seeing you, Ray. Look after yourself, darling.

She had added a kiss and he looked at the pictures she'd sent. There they were – Ray and Priscilla Nutter. Two nut-nuts in a pod. They were glowing. Fitted each other. That's what it looked like to Ray. There was another photo where he had his eyes wide open in pretend surprise. He was an idiot. A big kid. Knew he was asking for trouble if he saw her again, but everything else had gone wrong and Priscilla was a positive. Maybe he had to change. Consider the impossible. No. She was a temptation that had to be resisted. Perhaps when the house was sorted out and he was back at work they could go for a drink and talk, but he couldn't think about that right now. He was holding a man prisoner in his garage.

Ray had a shave and a shower, went downstairs and made

himself a mug of strong black coffee and some toast with apricot jam, went into the back garden and sat in his mum's chair, felt the sunshine on his skin, the sense of peace it brought. It was going to be another hot day, and when he'd finished eating he returned to the kitchen and filled a jug with water, brought it out and topped up the bird bath, added seeds and nuts to their table and feeder. He made a second cup of coffee and returned to his place in the sun. And the birds came. Lots of them. He felt good. For a while looking forward to the carefree day ahead. Until the reality returned and he had to become another sort of person. Someone he wasn't. It was his duty to protect his mother's house and her belongings. His girls. Which meant defending himself.

The condemned man was waiting in the wardrobe. It was mental keeping him tied up like that as a kicking might have been enough. Or he could have called the police. But his temper had got the better of him. Again. Let the selfish cunt go and he would return with his mates or family. Burn the house down. He could still talk to the police, but the burglar would want revenge, and Ray was going to be charged with kidnap and assault and fuck knows what else. The last option was brutal and final and not his style but made sense if he wanted to survive. That was what mattered.

Standing in the middle of the garage he started moving boxes and furniture towards the back, built a wall in front of the wardrobe while clearing space at the front so he could reverse the back of his car inside and transfer the thief to the boot without the neighbours seeing. He checked the condemned man, his head raising along with the smell of piss and shit. Dirty fucker. There again, what was he meant to do? But there were no excuses. Ray had to be strong. Decisive. This selfish cunt had no respect. No shame. He deserved what was coming.

Ray's phone pinged. It was a message from his neighbour Lou. Her dog Barney had gone missing and she was asking people to keep a look out for him. To check their gardens, sheds and garages. She was outside the Co-op where he'd last been seen. He felt bad for Lou as she really did love that dog. Barney had worked hard and deserved a peaceful retirement. It wasn't fair if something had happened to him. And Lou had been good to his mum. Invited her round for lunch. Came with Barney and brought a cake or buns. They'd talk for hours. Mum liked Barney and Barney liked Mum. Lou and Barry were decent people. Unselfish. The best sort. Givers not takers. They didn't have a bad word to say about anyone. Ray stared at the wanker in the wardrobe for a while and decided he could wait.

Grace lifts me up when I'm on my knees... back at work but struggling... the man in the white coat returning... that first time... the last time... before this time... marching back into my head... refusing to leave... and he has brought his special medicine... the syringes... Jonathan Jeffreys... social cleanser... collector of souls... trophies... stolen treasures... and each day is harder than the one before... my body aching... head sore... throat clogged... hearing fractured... vision splintered... everything I touch feels flat... there are no more textures... the smell of the hospital has changed... it reeks of failure and decay... hopelessness... every sort of cancer... infection... rotting hearts and clotting blood... damaged brains... amputated limbs and offal... blocked toilets... incinerators that char and turn to ash... my world shrinks with the bodies of the sick... faint pulses in frail wrists... thinking slow... no more dancing... no Satellite sounds... just this sluggish thud in my chest... a funeral march... and it dawns on me that I am more dead than alive... a ghost haunting the wards... drifting along the corridors... sitting alone in the chapel at two in the morning... stuck in limbo... neither here nor there... trying to remember my burial... the prayers said and hymns sung and eulogy spoken... Charlie Boy crying... our children unborn... Jeffreys has killed the magic as well as my friends... his is the final face... my murderer... the dead dogs and dead people... I wonder if I am weighed down in a reservoir... buried in the woods... motorway bones... the foundations of a new house... dissolved in acid... I wish I could change what happened... create a new truth... but that's not me...

and there is this sense of unfairness that will be with me forever...
not enough has been said... the authorities... yet at first I am
strong... put the beast in his box... strong and positive... examine
what has happened... take my time... deal in facts... confront the
reality... make myself look forward not back... and it works... for
a while... but not long enough... cremations and burials... Charlie
does his best... it isn't easy... Dawn and Carole love me... Davinda
and Sally... Boxer... everyone is so kind... I fight to survive... do
my job... can't let the patients down... but their faces flicker...
fade... and it is Grace who brings me back... she saves my life... I
am sure of this... by talking the way she does... her conviction...
anything is possible... everything... Grace reminds me of who I am
and what I believe... she's shown the man from the stars our
world... and he has shown it to her... a fair exchange... that's her
view... she lowers her voice but speaks with certainty... the wood
and the fair... it worries me at first... I am scared for her... this is
in the early hours when it's dark outside and the other patients are
asleep and dozing and tripping... and whether Grace's story is true
in the normal sense doesn't matter... I have faith in what she is
saying... want to believe... the fear leaves me... we're all living our
own fantasies... every human being... it takes an outsider to remind
us... these identities we create... poor Grace... lucky Grace... I
mean I know what has happened... more or less... not the details...
not then... not now... she has been on the ward for a night and a
day when I first speak to her properly... but I've seen her brought
in... the police... there are two versions... the one untold by
Grace... sort of unknown... unreal... that story makes me sick... so
angry that I shake... I'm not the only one... Jeffreys... Grace is
younger than me... gorgeous... innocent in the best way... pure...
and before she goes home she thanks me for helping her... saving
her life... at first she thought she'd died... that I was a spirit...
leaning over her bed... but she feels me squeeze her hand... and
what has made her live is having me listen... and eventually...
telling her my own story... she laughs... there's strength in
numbers... the fact that I believe her... or at least think it is
possible... and I know Grace in a different way now... she is my

friend... her dad calls her Priscilla when he comes to visit... but she will always be Grace to me... the bracelet on her wrist... belonged to her gran... the name Grace engraved in flowery letters... and I think about the fake minicab... West End prowler... his friends... men from the city... could have been anyone... the police have no pictures... perverts mix with perverts... sexual predators... not the first time and not the last... those sort of people... rarely caught... punished... and I believe in the spacemen... her man from the stars... O... because they are better beings... godlike... and it is a nicer tale... makes Grace happy... me as well... means we can live –

It was five years since Priscilla had decided to tell Ray about her encounter with the aliens and their leader O. It was nearly eleven and he was driving her home, his lights on full beam as he negotiated the tangled lanes leading to Shepherd's Cross, and as they moved through the darkness it struck her how comfortable she felt with this man, more at ease than she'd ever been with a member of the opposite sex. That included O, although he wasn't male in the normal sense, had merely adopted a human opposite in order to link more easily with the female whose life he wished to save. There had been nothing sexual about Priscilla's time with O, but she was attracted to Ray, and her desire was increasing as they went deeper into the night. She was thrilled by the intensity of what she was seeing, hearing, smelling, feeling inside.

It was only ten days since they'd met and this was the third time they'd been out together, yet she already knew she could trust him with the truth. She didn't expect Ray to believe her right away, just needed him to listen and not try to shut her up. It was important he accepted the possibility of something better than the horror, a grubby story too many had been quick to believe. Priscilla knew she was probably making things difficult, but believed in this nutty character who rejected the Nutter tag and the way his own history had been rewritten.

Ray made her laugh and feel good about herself, told her she was gorgeous when she was sure she wasn't. He didn't mean it as some cheap chat-up line either, and she hoped he fancied her as much as she fancied him. He'd been honest and told her he was married, joking that he must be a nightmare to live with in that way people did when they worried something was true. Ray and Liz were living apart and wouldn't get back together now the children were older. He had his beliefs and interests, a passion that excited Priscilla, and while she could see how that might cause chaos at times, it only added to the appeal. She wanted to be as honest as Ray had been and would talk to him about O when they reached the house.

The only person she'd properly discussed her abduction with was Ruby, a nurse at the hospital where she'd been taken after a couple walking home from the pub found her sitting on the kerb disorientated and bleeding. Her face was bruised and she'd lost her handbag and everything inside it, didn't know her name or where she lived or how she had ended up on the pavement. The woman sat with Priscilla while her husband phoned for an ambulance and then the police. After being examined by a doctor in A&E she was moved to Ruby's ward as detectives set about trying to identify her and work out what had happened.

Priscilla wasn't aware of this until three days later, and when she found out what was being said she was shocked. It was disgusting and mad. She had tried to explain the truth to the doctors and the police and her dad, but this only seemed to upset them more. She was sent for scans and a counsellor came to see her, followed by a psychologist who asked all sorts of odd questions. The fact that spacemen had landed in the woods and saved her life and that as an act of friendship she had taken O to the fair and shown him where she used to love going with her parents when she was a child had made her father cry. These attempts to explain what had really happened were closed down and before long disputed, the effects of her concussion openly discussed in front of her, and this made Priscilla feel increasingly confused and alone.

They could accept the idea that she had been abducted on a

night out in the West End after losing her friends, that the man posing as a minicab driver had attacked her in an isolated spot once they'd crossed the M25. They were fine with that and the lie that two other men had been involved, leaving her for dead in the woods between Uxbridge and Slough. What sort of imaginations could conjure up this filth? It was perverted. As if she wasn't going to remember such a terrible thing happening, and if it *had* happened she would have killed herself.

Priscilla was the one who had been there and knew, but after a while she realised she was going to have to stop disagreeing for the sake of her safety. Her mental health was being questioned, and there was no way she wanted to end up sedated or sent to live in an institution, branded delusional or even insane, had to keep her mouth shut. She also needed to protect O and his friends. The less the authorities knew about their visit to Earth the better. They might want to return one day, although she doubted they ever would.

She had tried to talk to her dad again a year later, sure it would help him if he knew what a positive encounter it had been. If he could believe her it would stop him torturing himself, but he'd become upset so she backed off. While the years since had dulled his pain she wished she could rid him of his sadness. Priscilla had a fresh way of looking at the world and had never needed to question what had happened, more than happy to accept her good fortune. It was Dad who suffered. She lived a quiet life with him now, liked it when they walked through the beeches on the week-ends but had never been back to the woods where she'd met O. It would have been a mistake to try and find the clearing. If she did it might break a spell.

Priscilla was at peace, and this was largely thanks to Ruby. She'd needed to tell her story to someone who would understand, couldn't have kept it all bottled up inside herself forever. Later she wondered about making contact with others who'd been abducted, but their stories sounded far-fetched and often mad and she was settled, going out locally with friends who lived nearby, staying within a certain distance of Shepherd's Cross, mindful that her dad was vulnerable following his stroke.

Ruby was one of the nurses monitoring her in those early days when her mind was recovering from the intensity of her experience, and after she returned to the moment Ruby took the time to stop and chat, coming to sit with her at the end of a shift or when she was working through the night and the ward was quiet. She listened – *really* listened – genuinely interested in what Priscilla had to say. Ruby knew the woods and spoke about a friend of hers, Danny Wax Cap, the other people she knew who had been killed by a real monster, not some figment of the police's imagination. They had become friends and to this day had a special bond.

Ruby was a different sort of character to Ray, someone who had been attacked and nearly murdered, a terror Priscilla couldn't imagine, the very thought making her feel dizzy, and yet while Ruby was bound to have her moments of doubt, the darkness that had to come with such a trauma, she only saw the good in people. Everyone had their ways of getting through life, and Ray raged at the unfairness and refused to surrender and she loved that quality as well. What right did anyone have to decide how another person survived? Both Ruby and Ray had energy and drive, but if Ruby was the cheerful woman from the public sector who refused to dwell on the grim realities then Ray was the angry self-employed man who couldn't let things go.

Autumn was Priscilla's favourite season. She enjoyed seeing nature close down for the bitter months to come, and nowhere was this more obvious than in the trees. She loved the way the leaves changed their colour and shape, crumbling and falling and rotting into the soil, feeding the roots ahead of spring. She had been telling Ray this earlier and he'd wrapped an arm around her waist and pulled her close and she'd felt a surge of emotion as her body tingled, and that was the moment she decided she had to tell him about O.

Ray was into the last of the lanes, hedgerows rising high on either side, and she could see her Mini up ahead, hoped Dad was okay and asleep. His stroke could have been a lot worse and he had recovered well, but she would never leave him to live alone.

Not that she wanted to move, content in this house he'd bought when it was derelict, and being a builder meant he'd brought the place back to life and done it up to a high standard. Ray and Ruby needed to be around people and have things going on, but while Priscilla was no hermit, she enjoyed the solitude, reckoned she had the best of both worlds. It was true that opposites attracted and Ray could make her whole.

He parked beyond the front windows of the house and turned the engine off. They had kissed, but that was it, and even though Priscilla wanted to it was a long time since she'd had sex with a man, not since before she'd met O. That was over ten years ago, and it had seemed ridiculous after the insights she'd gained, a ritual without meaning if it wasn't to create life, yet she wanted to be with Ray, and when he reached over she responded, feeling his hands on her breasts but easing back in her seat as she needed to tell him about the aliens first.

While it was dark with the lights off, there was enough of a glow feeding through the trees from the moon to show the outlines of their faces as they sat sideways facing each other. Priscilla announced that she had something to say and he said she could tell him anything as long as it wasn't that she didn't want to see him again. Priscilla knew she was going to sound mad at first, would have thought so herself before O, and she had read about similar cases since, knew there were patterns and shared experiences but also fantasists and liars, people who were genuinely insane, but that wasn't going to stop her telling the truth.

Priscilla dived in and said she had been abducted by aliens and Ray laughed. She was prepared, stressed that she wasn't joking, had encountered beings from outer space, men from the stars. Ray asked if she meant ET, and again Priscilla was ready, didn't get upset, paused for a moment, wishing she could see his face clearly. He seemed to be smiling. Wasn't taking her seriously. And why should he? She continued, explaining that the term *abducted* was loaded, suggested a kidnapping, something terrible, and it hadn't been like that at all. She'd had no choice at first as the aliens had to act fast to stop her freezing to death or being killed by hunters, but once she was safely through the trees and standing by the side of the dual carriageway the leader became an observer and she had made the decisions.

There were evil spirits in the pines that night and she'd hidden in the ferns and become a scared rabbit. Two deer came and showed her a light in the distance and this had drawn her to a clearing. It was hard to reach, hidden away like another dimension, and once she was there she'd waited at the edge of the magic ray filling the field, out of sight in the ferns. Her vision had adjusted and she'd seen three giants. These were the spacemen. It was then that she realised the hum she could hear came from a hovering spaceship she'd thought was the moon. Or maybe it was when she had walked into the middle of the field.

The tallest of these travellers was the leader and said she could call him O, but only if she wanted, as it would make their mission easier. Consent was essential. If she said no her choice would be fully respected. There were no names on his planet as every being knew every other being and they practised telepathy while at the same time respecting boundaries. O was one of the letters from her language and the shape of human heads, eyes and mouths. Earth was an O, as were the other planets in this universe and beyond. O also meant zero which was nothing, and he found this quaint. There was much to learn and he wanted Priscilla to help him achieve insights into the ways of humankind, although their time together would be short.

Ray hadn't spoken, and Priscilla was quick to reassure him there was nothing sexual about the hours she'd spent with O. There were no sexes in his world, no need to reproduce as new life-forms were never required. There might be small updates to a casing every so often, but that was rare, as his kind were eternal and near enough perfect. In his natural state O looked different to anything that could ever be imagined by humans and to operate outside his craft he needed a physical form that was loosely familiar, although this would only protect him for a while before he had to either link with Priscilla or return. As their thoughts merged it felt as if he was inside her bones as well as her mind and nervous system. Did that make sense? She knew what she meant, even if it was very difficult to express in words.

She explained that to appreciate O he should be seen as an extraterrestrial saint with the curiosity of a child. He came from a world that operated beyond birth and death, a planet where there was no fear or hatred. Only harmony. There was no violence. Not even a nightmare. Priscilla felt a rush of sickness she managed to control, her voice dipping as she asked Ray why people had to make jokes about these encounters, talk about intimate probes and extended examinations, the use of force and cruelty? It hadn't been that way. Totally the opposite, in fact. What did Ray think? Wasn't it fantastic? But she didn't wait for an answer.

It was true O had asked about her breasts, if it was right that once a boy reached puberty he became attracted to what suckled him as a baby. Priscilla had never looked at it in that way, but O was correct. He asked if he could touch them and she had replied no, but wasn't angry as this was a research request from a non-sexual being who intended no harm, and it had to be remembered that he couldn't *physically* touch them. O had asked about her vagina, found it odd that the male's reproductive organ planted its seed in the same gateway from which the small humans the bonding of genders created emerged. Could he explore this area? Again, she had said no, and while she knew this sounded strange O was a researcher not a predator. He had accepted her refusal and asked about her mouth. Was it true that the DNA of the male was wasted here and the term blow job applied to a sucking motion considered highly desirable to the recipient? Before she could answer this question he had asked about her bum, if it was true that the area invented to excrete the remains of nutrients eaten in order to maintain human life was used for sexual gratification? If so, could he carry out an experiment? This had stretched Priscilla's patience to the limit and she had shown her annoyance when refusing permission. O had apologised and become thoughtful. Ray remained silent and Priscilla stifled a sob.

Why was she talking like this? What was she thinking? Had she lost her mind? She was focusing on the wrong things. It was as if she was trying to justify the lies Ray had never heard. He knew nothing about the police's theory and the insanity of an investigation that led nowhere. How her truth had been dismissed. It was important to move on, reach the fairground, take Ray with her so he could feel the excitement of what she had experienced, the way her senses had gone into overdrive, the joy that followed.

Did he know the fair she was talking about? She had been going there since she was a little girl. He nodded and said he had been there as a boy. Maybe they'd seen each other. It was a nice thought, but Priscilla had to make him understand the power of O, explained how the alien had shown her the world more clearly than she had ever seen it before, given her an appreciation of life she would never lose. She mentioned the smells and shapes and sounds and sensed Ray drifting away. He would be more interested in the questions O asked about everyday life, the smallest things she had never considered, and these came flooding back, exchanges she hadn't remembered until this second, but she couldn't express them in words, tears forming and running down her face, pleased Ray wouldn't see them in the dark.

After sitting in silence for a while she asked Ray what he thought. He was honest and said he didn't know, reached over and held her hand, didn't squeeze it or try to kiss or even hug her, and although she was sad it wasn't a shock. The important thing was that he had let her speak. Only Ruby had listened like this, and it was merely a matter of time before he accepted the possibility of what she had said. He was scared, that's all. But when he said he'd better get going as he was working early, had a job picking up at the airport, she felt as if her heart was going to burst. They kissed now, but only briefly, and she felt the intensity of his being and was thrilled and revived, certain that it might take a while but in the end they would be together.

Joe was wide awake by seven, had a shower and got dressed and headed for the kitchen, poured himself a glass of orange juice from the carton in the fridge and took a handful of figs from the box he'd bought in the market, went out and sat on the balcony. The air was cool and refreshing and he remembered how he'd suffered in the heat yesterday, felt a lot better this morning, clean and revived after pacing himself last night. He had left the others drinking in a Eurodisco bar and hadn't heard Chris come in, knew he'd made it back in one piece when he heard him moaning in his sleep in the early hours.

There was a sprawling courtyard below with succulent beds and palm trees, metal tables and chairs, lots of loungers, a hatch that served drinks and snacks, a swimming pool and hot tub. This space was enclosed by three six-storey apartment blocks and a high south-facing wall. It was a peaceful, private hideaway, and he wondered again what it would be like to live in the Mediterranean, and in this complex in particular where Dave had spent a year before moving in with Martina, if the visitors interested or irritated the long-term residents.

Twenty minutes later he was passing the empty pool, the only other person about a cleaner in a Lionel Messi shirt, a skinny youth with a broom in one hand and a phone in the other. Joe felt the musty warmth lingering at ground level and guessed it was going to be another hot day, left paradise through the main entrance and was soon in that bigger paradise beyond, walking on the promenade, after a few minutes missing the rush of the gym, decided to jog until he reached the stall where he'd bought his coffee two days earlier. Once this was handed over he continued until he found an empty bench facing the sea and sat down, took a sip and winced.

Gunpowder must have been blended with the beans to create a bigger version of the small Turkish cups he'd drunk in Istanbul, a muddy potion brewed to blow a person's head off. He was heating up again after his short run and the coffee, pictured himself as seen from the deck of one of the boats leaving and returning to the port to his right, Bowie's black star lit up by the greatest star of all, drums thumping inside his chest, echoing through his skull, the rush of adrenaline and caffeine and heartbeat, Bowie the prettiest star, always calm, always collected.

Joe's mood had changed and he was happy spending these easy days with two people he'd known for most of his life, and despite the tiffs with Dave over the years they were brothers who always made up in the end, the three of them on the best of terms. He thought about Smiles and his suicide, Luke and Gary Wells, everything that had happened, but was way past dwelling on this as he had done nothing wrong and had no regrets. Dave could live with his actions, and while he had that level of violence in him, killing a man was a one-off he would never repeat. It was a subject they didn't talk about. Joe wondered why he was thinking about this now, sitting in the sun without a care in the world.

He wouldn't say he was content as that would mean he'd lost his ambition, even if it was centred around some wonky interests such as his love of music, pulling it apart and putting it back together again, a sonic jigsaw that kept on expanding, but even so, he was feeling like nothing mattered, had heard that as a person got older the anger faded as experience showed the bad times would pass, that apart from death there didn't have to be any dead ends. This didn't apply to everyone, but maybe he was one of the lucky majority, and while he was still looking forward to going home, the time was passing and he would make sure he enjoyed what was left of his stay.

He had bought a double cassette deck off eBay that had been delivered the day before he left and he was excited to get it properly hooked up, the sort of thing he'd never been able to afford when he was a kid. He loved how those old C30, 60 and 90 tapes were back in fashion with young people sick of the digital world. They were often the ones showing his generation the way, coming in with fresh attitudes, and he saw Luke and Jack and the enthusiasm they had as they went through the stages of his own life already lived, the frustrations that arrived around the thirty mark, controlled and channelled in their cases, and he wished he'd been as clued-up, maybe hiding some weakness in himself by living alone, never marrying or having children, losing himself in music and the pub and the gym and the friendships that came from those before bailing out for a month or two and going off travelling.

Chris was still asleep as Joe sipped his coffee and reflected, deep inside dreams he would never remember. He was on a psychiatric ward, but instead of the caring souls who'd helped him in the past the doctors and nurses had been replaced by automatons called Alex. These had been born out of Fritz Lang's *Metropolis*, while the smaller models that cleaned the rooms and mowed the lawns came from Martin Scorsese's *Hugo*. When Chris asked which of these machines was male and which was female an official screamed abuse and threatened to cancel his membership of the human race. He would be deleted. Or added to the sex-offenders' list. How would Chris like that? To be labelled a nonce, a splasher of sperm and acid. As a Sherlock he would have to investigate himself and every decision was going to be checked and amended until it was correct. A nurse stretched out a silver arm and red wires shot from the fingers and delivered a shock that raced to his brain where the searing pain nearly knocked him out. He could smell singed electrics as his cells burned and feared fire would break out inside his head and spread through his hair and kill the other patients on the ward. It seemed obvious that his memory banks were being cleared and his individuality erased, which according to the same official was worth the agony. There was a room where he could sit on his own if he wished, but only for one minute, and he knew when it was time to leave as *The Killing* began playing on the walls and he was transported to a Scandi noir universe, an evening in front of the television with Carol. He was pleased to be seeing his wife again and regretted his errors, had missed the freshly popped popcorn waiting for him in huge plastic bowls, the work involved in this new murder case and the satisfaction he'd have when he nailed the perp.

Some time had passed and he found himself in an interview room, the robot element replaced by the very human curves of DI Williams. Chris was very conscious of the erection he was carrying and the bulge in the front of his strides, didn't want her to think he was a crude sort of chap. His name was Sherlock 'Chris' Holmes and he would remain professional at all times. Williams was on duty and wearing a uniform despite being a detective, explaining there was no longer a need to remain undercover, that it was finally time to bring their affair out into the open. She knew he had been a thief when he was young but didn't care as Chris had repented and paid his dues to society and she admired his moral strength. She removed her tunic and skirt, stood before him in crisp white stockings and bra, Chris impressed she wasn't wearing panties, the realisation that she had clearly planned this encounter and ensured the cameras in the room had been switched off exciting him so much he feared he was going to ejaculate before he could reach the DI. He needn't have worried as when she turned her back and walked to the desk and assumed the position he slid into DI Williams with ease and was informed that he could last for as long as was needed. There was no rush and when he woke up later it was with a throbbing hard-on and no recollection of what had gone on.

Dave had barely slept, his mind and body refusing to settle, Martina telling him several times to keep still, eventually sitting up in bed and punching him hard in the side of his head. Sloping off to the living room he stretched out on the couch, but the realisation of what he had done was becoming clearer as the drink slowly wore off. Joe and Chris coming to see him in this new life of his had been emotional, the confusion he felt jumbled further by the amount they'd drunk, stirring memories and loosening his grip, meaning he'd only gone and repeated his confession of four years earlier. Left alone with Chris after Joe went back to the apartment, he had explained in detail how he'd killed Gary Wells, staring at the face opposite and waiting for the expression to change, for the bloke to say something – anything – but there was nothing. Chris had heard him loud and clear, there was no doubt about that, but he refused to respond apart from a slow nod, the finishing of his food and drink, a brief *goodnight*.

Dave couldn't believe what he had done. There was no righteous dub playing this time, no Prince Far I, just him confessing to some-one who sat there eating his pizza and refused to speak. What had happened to Chris? Why had he become a copper? Had he turned religious? Was he like that when they were young? It was hard to remember clearly how things had been. Was he going to have to kill Chris to shut him up? He'd done it before and had no regrets, never felt any remorse, but Wells wasn't a friend and he deserved to die. There'd nearly been a second time, and he couldn't pretend he hadn't hurt one or two people over the years, but murdering Chris in cold blood? If it was a case of his own survival there would only be one choice.

He had drifted into a dreamy half-sleep around five o'clock, his mind a tangle of vague threads, but he was clear that Martina had come into the room and joined him on the sofa. She was crying and apologising, sorry she'd hit him, would confess when she went to church even if it was different when a woman beat a man, that it wasn't as wrong, but she still felt terrible. She was naked and kissed Dave's forehead when he said that he forgave her, licked his face and chest, ran her tongue down his body and was soon sucking him off. Dave leaned back knowing these make-up sessions were well worth the odd punch and kick, wasn't so sure about the old Heineken-bottle treatment.

When Dave saw Joe approaching Vista a few hours later he was relieved, stood up and went to the entrance and waved. He couldn't keep his mistakes to himself any longer, needed to tell Joe even though he knew he'd do his nut. That was nothing to what was coming when he told him what he was planning to do to Chris. It would have to be humane – quick and unexpected – and having spent time in prison as a freedom-loving man who went off travelling for months at a time surely Joe could be persuaded. It wasn't as if he wasn't going to be in trouble himself. However it went, there was no way Dave was going to jail, and thinking about it, life was just one long endless trial, the troubles you thought would fade away lingering and returning even when you went and lived overseas, homesick but making do in order to survive.

As Dave brooded over Chris, the man himself was having a shower and rubbing soap into his balls, moving to his cock and building up a rhythm, thinking of DI Williams, the spunk bubbling up and spurting into her before he pulled out and splashed some over her bum. She fucking loved it when he rubbed it into the crack of her arse and then her clit, in real life and right now in his imagination. He supposed their affair had been so erotic because it was secret and morally wrong, but normally he refused to think about those times and wondered why he was this morning.

Once Chris was dressed he checked the fridge for food, found it empty apart from a carton of orange juice and three cans of lager, and looking around the kitchen he definitely didn't fancy the figs Joe had bought, needed something more substantial. He left the flat and was blasted by the heat when he entered the courtyard, passed the swimming pool and loungers, followed the promenade towards Vista, planned to stop at one of the restaurants on the way. Martina made good French-bread sandwiches and milky American coffee, but she wouldn't be there yet and he couldn't wait.

Martina seemed to be a soothing influence on Dave. It must have been difficult living with his moods, but she seemed to genuinely like the bloke and the rubbish he came out with some-times was probably lost in translation. It was hard enough Chris knowing what the bloke was rambling on about when he was on one, so good luck to them. There were bad things going on in the world, but a lot more that was good. He was content strolling by the sea on such a beautiful morning, his dark days of depression and hopelessness in the past, settling into this long stretch of concrete and feeling unstoppable if hungry, despite the time fancying a big bowl of pasta with an order of chips on the side, followed by an early shandy with his pals.

These are the good times... the best days... all of us together... Charlie and me and our children and dog... in the green between old and new settlements... an orange sun in a turquoise sky... this blooming meadow heaven on Earth... and we came here in the car... it took less than ten minutes... singing... parking... winding our way through the pines... following the path that leads to our field... dry earth... rampant ferns... crumbling stumps spilling ants... a giant puffball... the spirt of Danny Wax Cap... and we leave the shade and come into the open... sunlight throbbing... it can never be too bright for me... never too hot... we walk to the middle of the meadow... spread the blanket out on luscious soft grass... wildflower drifts... currents in an ocean... I sit down... Charlie Boy stretches out... his mirror shades reflecting my white face tanning brown... blonde hair bleaching white... our children go off to explore... searching for grasshoppers... know not to hurt the insects... anything... we are raising them properly... love and respect... good manners... they are the most important things in our lives... innocents in a field... on top of a hill... a humpback bridge... an English village... summer... this meadow... yes... these are the good days... the best times... Ben sniffing... rabbits and deer... mice and voles... foxes and badgers... lemonade through a straw... pink plastic cups... surging joy... the children safe... playing... laughing... we will live forever... nobody is going to be forgotten... Mum and Dad watching from the edge of the trees... the shadows... machines break down... that's all... Ben stands between them... Ben runs with our children... Ben spreads out next to my husband... soulmate... while I squeeze my locket... Pearl and her Charlie... here but there... somewhere else... the same place... riding on a motorbike that never crashes... the truest love... eternal... following my breath... lungs inflating like birthday balloons... hearing the dragonfly before I see it... hovering above the basket... special occasions... sandwiches fresh this morning... favourite fillings... silver foil... crisps and nuts and cakes and samosas... the coleslaw I made... two types of biscuit... chocolate and plain... drinks in a cooler... cold and fizzy... and I sit here daydream believing... souls as drivers... bodies as cars... moving... drifting... speeding... respecting time... memory... living in the moment... making every second count... tripping on life... Danny's dice... I know what to do... one last task... time to eat... call the children... Charlie Boy picking up the basket... laughing at the weight... the feast inside... we sit in a circle and I hand out the plates... children cross-legged... copying their mum... full lotus... I am their mother... it is hard to believe... the wonder... they wait for me to open their sandwiches... explain what's inside... it's only right... Mum makes the picnic... up early while they are still asleep... Ben licks his lips... sniffs... don't worry... I haven't left you out... yes... the good times... the best days... our family together... the sun beating down... our bodies... souls... blazing light... heaven... this meadow –

Ray met Lou in front of the Co-op in the exact spot where Barney had gone missing. Along with Barry she had been searching for him from ten last night until two this morning and again since seven. She looked terrible and had clearly been crying, said her husband was driving around blaming himself as he was the one who'd tied their lovely boy to the railings when he went into the shop for supplies. He'd only been gone five minutes, came out with his cans and tortilla chips and salsa and found the lead and collar still there, but no Barney.

Lou hadn't expected Ray to help search, only messaging him and some of the other neighbours on the off-chance they might have seen the dog and so that they could keep a lookout. Ray listened as Lou explained how much Barney liked him, pulling towards the garage the last two times they'd passed his house, knowing that was the way through to the garden where Ray might be sitting in the sun. Of course, Barney remembered Viv, and animals saw things humans couldn't. She caught herself and stopped. Lou was going to stay here in case he returned. They had friends out searching as well. It was very kind of Ray.

She believed Barney had been spooked by a lorry. It was late when he went missing, with little traffic on the road, so the sound of a driver dropping gears and applying the brakes before accelerating to get through the mini roundabouts by the pub was bound to scare him. He'd pulled at his lead and the collar slipped off. She always worried about putting it on too tight and had reminded Barry before he went out. They didn't want to choke the poor thing. It was her fault, not Barry's. Barney would have run off in the opposite direction and could have gone for miles if he was really frightened, most likely into the woods. His instinct would tell him that was the safest place to hide. Outlaws always headed for the trees.

The other possibility was that someone had taken Barney. Seen him on his own and stopped and bundled him into their car. It could have been one of those gangs who kidnapped dogs and held them to ransom. As Lou said this it seemed as if she was going to start crying again, so Ray got in fast, told her that was impossible. Barney was big. A police dog. Retired, but strong. He was used to riots. Dealing with violent men. He wasn't going to be pulled into a car by a stranger. Ray did wonder if he had been coaxed inside with a lump of steak as dogs were always on the scrounge, but he didn't say this to Lou. Again, he felt it was unlikely. Barney wasn't some pimped-up pedigree. He wasn't worth anything. At least not in terms of money. There would be no point taking him unless the person concerned was a sadist who enjoyed hurting animals. That's where the nonces started. Budding serial killers. He kept this to himself as well. What he did say to Lou was that Barney was no poodle. No Macron. This made her smile.

There were some real degenerates out there, though. Beasts who'd grab a woman walking home at night. Pull her off the pavement and stick her in the boot of their car or the back of a van. Spike their drinks in a nightclub. The lowest of the low. Rapist scum. And if they could do that to a human they would do the same and worse to an animal. Hanging was too good for a sex case. He thought of his daughters and how he could no longer protect them in the way he had done when they were children. Thank God that sort of thing had never happened to anyone he knew.

He felt sick at the thought as any sane person would, remembered something Priscilla had said once about the brutality of human beings. How deviants wanted to live inside their victim's head. Long-term torture. Murder by suicide. He didn't recall the exact words, just that every victim had to decide if they were going to live or die. That it was better to take control. Shape the future. Why he was thinking about this right now he didn't know. Maybe it was meant to help him with the burglar, Estuary Cars, the missing dog. All three.

Lou was still talking about Barney being abducted. He thought about the meaning of the word and felt confused. As if he was missing something. Returned to Chelsea and April. Every parent's fear. Saw his girls as babies. The years before they started school. How excited they were when he came home from work. Pictured himself reading them stories at bedtime. Waving through the playground railings. Waiting at the gate. Helping with their history and maths homework. Taking his girls to see Chelsea play. Sunday dinner. Visiting his mum. Feeding Bob and Molly carrots. Uncle Terry. A pub garden in the summer. Seaside holidays. Watching cartoons and films. Delivery pizzas. Trips to George's. Their first jobs. Coming home drunk. The threat of boys and drugs. Music blaring. The periods when he had been kicked out. Their mum. Finally the divorce. That came later, and it was good they were older. He loved his daughters and they loved him. He was sure of that.

It could have been someone out walking who'd taken Barney. Why did they need a car? But the dog wasn't stupid. He would have barked at the very least. Steamed in. Unless it was a person he knew and trusted. And Ray thought how he had been across the road in The Crown's beer garden last night. He'd walked home drunk and could have killed the dog because he was suspicious. Nosing around the garage door. Old Bill smelling the thieving cunt in the wardrobe. But Ray wasn't that sort of person. And the times didn't match. Barney had disappeared around ten, while Ray hadn't arrived at the pub until two hours later. He was relieved. Which was strange. The remains of the drink.

The lorry theory made more sense. Or maybe the collar had simply come loose. But surely he would have waited? Ray scanned the cars pulling up outside the shops. A van leaving. Weekend runs for bread, eggs, bacon, ketchup and all the rest of those essential fry-up ingredients. The Full English would be on the go. Terry and Ray and Lol. Milk for tea. Newspapers. Men like him arriving. Shorts. Polo shirts. Cropped heads. Women such as Jan, Lou, Priscilla. Magic touches. Lou had stopped speaking. She was staring at the collar and lead. Tears were running down her face.

He didn't know what to do. Said he would start looking. Why didn't she call Barry? See if he'd had any luck? Ray insisted he had a good feeling about Barney, and this seemed to cheer Lou up.

He doubted the dog had gone far. Neither would Barney suddenly decide he wanted to get back to nature. Go live in the woods or a field. He was used to the good life. A roof over his head. Food and water. Warm, soft beds. Endless love. Treats. Ray tried to imagine what he'd do in Barney's position. He would know his way home for a start. Surely. Maybe he had become confused. Disorientated by the thunder of the passing lorry. He would know fear. Loneliness. Every creature did. Even men like Ray. Who should he tell about his sadness and anger? Nobody was interested. You had to stand on your own two feet. All that other stuff was propaganda. The need to talk. Sensitive sides. What a pile of shit. Barney understood.

It made sense that he would have started for home, and Ray went over and stood next to the main road. He might have made a mistake. Headed towards the motorway instead of the houses. He glanced across to The Crown. Barney didn't drink beer. The pie-and-mash stall in the car park hadn't opened yet. They did bacon rolls weekday mornings. Tea and coffee. But mainly it was open in the afternoons and evenings. Wendy's Pie & Mash. Proper liquor. Ray's mouth watered. Barney liked his food. Something clicked. Ray crossed over to the pub, passed the van and continued into the car park, reached the beer garden, entered through the rickety little gate.

There was a black lump at the far end and he started walking over, as he got nearer saw it was definitely Barney. He was lying on his side facing Ray. Body rigid. The old police dog had lived a too-short retirement. It wasn't right. His lead had come loose for whatever reason and he'd wandered off. Cocked his leg. Smelled the van which would have closed an hour earlier. That sensitive nose. He had crossed the road and searched for scraps. Lumps of pie. Mashed potato. But why hadn't he returned to the shops? Must have been distracted. Got lost. Locked in the garden maybe. But he had come back to the van later. Ray thought he was a rat and clapped his hands. Barney ran off and ended up in the garden again. When the gate closed he was stuck. He'd had a heart attack. Hid in the undergrowth as dying animals did. Must have been alive while Ray was talking to Jan. He wished he'd been sober and taken more notice. That he hadn't scared him that second time. At least Barney had come out into the open and died on the lawn.

He felt terrible as he neared the dead dog and hoped Barney had passed away with the sun shining on him. But he'd died alone. That was terrible. Ray shuddered inside. Could hardly breathe. He stopped and looked down at the body. Had to decide how he would tell Lou. Barney opened his eyes and banged his tail on the ground.

It was a short, happy drive home, but Ray's mood was dark as he reversed into his garage. He turned off the engine and opened the boot. Slid the blade of his craft knife out. Inched through to the wardrobe and glared at the thief inside. The selfish cunt clocked the knife and his eyes opened wide. He started to struggle. Ray shushed and slowly shook his head as he kneeled down and released him from the pole, helped the man to his feet and towards the car. He fucking stunk. Ray eased him into the boot. Which he then closed.

Ray drove to the Western Avenue. Dropped his speed from sixty to fifty to forty to thirty. He had considered the different methods and locations. The ways murderers murdered. The places they dumped their bodies. Knives, ropes, plastic bags. Woods, wasteland, railway tracks. Too messy. Too obvious. Cities had their own hideaways, especially further out in the old industrial areas. It made sense to take this well away from the house. Add some distance. The bloke deserved to die. No music. RAF Northolt. No words. The Polish War Memorial.

Ray arrived at the quiet place he had chosen. Executioner and undertaker. Derelict buildings. The ruins of dead firms. Due for demolition. Eventually. Few people came here. Nobody on the weekends. He saw his mum. Priscilla. Shouting and crying. He got out and looked around. Mum was smiling. Priscilla too. They knew him. What he was capable of doing. And so Ray opened the boot and used the knife to free the selfish cunt's ankles and hands, pulled the tape from his mouth, held a finger up when he looked as if he was about to speak, motioned for him to climb out. Reaching into the inside pocket of his jacket, Ray took out a hundred pounds in twenties. Passed it over. Told him to fuck off. That way. Between the signs. Keep going. There's a train station. Don't ever come back. The cunt, the man, the youth, the boy said thank you in a broken voice and walked away.

Ray retraced his route, the traffic moving so before too long he was approaching Uxbridge Circus, taking the next exit and circling back under the start of the M40 onto the Oxford Road and taking the first turning, then a slip road, stopping in a lay-by. Ray turned the engine off. He was no murderer. Had done the right thing. There might be consequences, but he would be ready and deal with whatever happened.

He phoned Terry and apologised. Promised he would leave his passengers alone if he was allowed to go back to work. Wouldn't mention Brexit. He had overstepped the mark. But he understood if that wasn't possible. It was much more important that this didn't come between them, Ray admitting that clearing out the house was doing his head in. All the stuff in the news about the EU. Those fucking politicians. Traitors. Scum of the earth. Sorry… He didn't mention the burglar. That was done. A private matter. There was no need for anyone to know. What could he say? He had been unfair to Terry. Put him in a difficult position. Taken the fact they were family for granted.

The relief and warmth in his uncle's voice brought a tear to Ray's eye. Literally. The *piss off* he received when he said he could go and work somewhere else made him grin. Terry became serious. Wanted to make it clear he agreed with what Ray thought about the EU. All the lads did. He knew that, didn't he? Ray did. Maybe he had forgotten? No, he hadn't. Terry reminded him that George had fought for this country in the war, but they could talk about it over a pint, even though it had all been said. He could start work again tomorrow.

That was all it had needed, and once the call ended Ray told himself he was a fool. He had to learn to listen. Thought of his mum and how she had gone on at him to stay out of trouble. To find a way to control his anger. That he was a grown man and not a child. Shouldn't be running around getting into fights. People called him Nutter for a reason. Nutty was friendlier. Fine lines. But there were nutters and headcases and psychos. A pecking order. Each term loaded. Nutter wasn't so bad. But it was in the past. No more justifications. His father had abandoned the family. Fuck him. Terry was his uncle and his dad. Ray missed his mum. For the first time since the day she died he cried. Relieved he was on his own.

Ten minutes later he called Priscilla. He was half-expecting her answer phone. Would have felt easier leaving a message. But there she was on the other end of the line and he froze for several seconds, said that he was sitting in his car, parked in a lay-by, that he had been glad to see her last night. She asked why he was in a lay-by and he had to think of a reason, couldn't mention the burglar in the wardrobe or the fact he'd almost lost his job, told her about Barney instead. Went into detail. Once he had finished she invited him to come and see her at Shepherd's Cross. He remembered that her dad had died and felt as sorry for her as he had been feeling for himself.

She could make them some food. Or had he eaten? Not even breakfast? He told Priscilla he was starving. She reckoned it was too hot to cook, but could fix some sandwiches if he wanted. There were some bottles of lager in the fridge. It was very quiet out here on her own. She would love it if he came round. It was such a beautiful day. What did he think? Did he remember the house? Of course. He thought about her abduction by aliens. The men from the stars. Their leader O. Priscilla talking. Stifling a sob. And it didn't bother him anymore. She needed to believe. He was excited to see her and on the move, the sun scorching the land as he drove in silence, deciding he would stop and buy her some flowers. Knew the right garage. It was on the way.

*

I roll Danny's dice and see what happens... walk into The Green Man... late afternoon... the landlord shouldn't be too busy... he'll have time to talk... the early drinkers going home... the next wave not yet arrived... that's my logic... it's a local and he'll know his regulars... and I'm hoping he's going to remember Danny Wax Cap... but it turns out the landlord is new... only been running the place for six months... sorry... he says... asks the two men at the other end of the bar if they recall someone called Danny... used to drink in here... they think... shake their heads... I buy myself a drink... sit on a stool... study the people scattered in ones and twos... weigh them up... mainly men... retired... self-employed and unemployed... shift workers finished for the day... most of them old enough... the years have passed... I ask the landlord and he says to go ahead... move from table to table... Danny... he used to come in here... Danny Wax Cap... I tell them what he looked like... one man thinks he might know Danny... decides no... sorry... saw him two weeks ago... thinks I should come in at night when the pub is busier... maybe... I go back to the bar... my stool... the landlord sure there will be someone... his regulars have been coming in here forever... the daytime lot... drink too much... don't eat properly... crisps... peanuts... chips on the way home... kebabs... at night the age falls... they wouldn't know this Danny character... his phone vibrates... he answers... moves away and lowers his voice... I've failed... left it too long... there's no way I'll find someone who loved Danny... I've searched online... nothing... feel sick... lonely... the pub hushed... I didn't deal with this in the right way... stupid... selfish... I've let Danny down... one drink is enough... time to leave... and this is when I meet Bubba... by chance... except it's not as I'm here for a reason... looking for him... but I do get lucky... rolling the dice... giving it a go... standing... moving... waving to the landlord... reach the door and hear that name... Bubba... the sort that sticks in the mind... a good old boy... see him playing pool with Danny... remember it clearly... that table in the corner... probably the same one... I forgot it was round the side of the bar... tucked away... Bubba heading to the counter... needs a refill... the landlord finishes his call... starts pouring before Bubba asks... he sees me staring... frozen... holds up a finger so I stay where I am... passes the pint over and takes Bubba's money... leans forward... talking... Bubba turns... looks at me... sips his drink... walks over... says is that right... I'm asking about his mate Danny... and I'm nodding and saying yes and he motions us towards a table... we sit down... he knew Danny well... mad he was... but in the best way... do I know what he means... asks what I want... listens... I put the dice on the table... he nods... grins... he was all right Danny... liked his drink... his puff... the magic mushrooms... Bubba misses him... it's terrible what happened... the psycho who did those murders... fucking scum... excuse my French... a terrible thing you don't expect to happen... and we swap Danny memories... Bubba reckons there was a girl he was seeing... for a while... but it wasn't serious... probably already over when he was killed... the dice seems so small... fragile... Bubba picks it up and holds it in his hand... the same as Carole did with my locket... the case that belongs to me and Pearl... our Charlies inside... Bubba turns the dice over... closes his palm around it as if he's a psychometrist... maybe... I don't ask... perhaps Lou knows him... this could be the way he sees things... Bubba opens his hand again... rolls the dice on the table... doesn't give it much of a push as we don't want it falling on the floor and getting lost... hoovered up when the pub's cleaned... Bubba knows... respectful... it lands on three... Bubba places a finger on the dice... pulls it back towards him... gently... dirt in the creases of his skin... broken nails... even sitting down this man is big... oversized... silver in his hair... a drinker's gaze... Danny... this was his favourite place... fucking loved it here... sorry... didn't mean to swear again... not in front of a lady... you're the nurse... I thought so... he spoke about you... sorry... can't remember your name... Ruby... he was happiest in this pub... The Green Man... Danny with his mates... Danny talking... at ease... accepted... and it dawns on me that this dice belongs to Bubba... Danny nodding... standing behind his friend who is raising his pint... sipping the nectar... and it all comes crashing back... Danny sitting outside... lemonade... dope... liberty-cap tea... *six months for thinking too much... sentenced for E... heroin inside... a spiritual man who never hurt a soul... music and drugs working together... an addictive personality... wants it all... drugs entering the country's prisons... how can he prove it's official... a cull... the same as Jeffreys... euthanasia... Danny changes... HIV-positive... fights the virus... beats the addiction... straight-edge... eating right... healthy... determined to live... up early and out jogging... people fight back like that... I know one or two... there will be a cure... he lives during the day... asks me what a condemned man feels like... strapped down... sedated... executioner giving him the lethal injection... Danny swimming... regular rhythm of the breaststroke... sinking deeper... breathing... weights... sweating... spores ride the winds like a DJ... England a pagan country... that's what he tells me... Christian separation... body and soul... fermenting potions... rotting fruit and hops... ceremonies... fairgrounds... he loves his mushrooms... grey knight-cap... cornflower bolete... puffballs... chanterelle... earthstar... stinkhorn... spring and autumn... a glut... outside in the foggy streets... we don't want to hear the breaking news... repeating news... reshaped news... additions deletions conclusions... entertainment news... controlled... a film director says that in space... Danny cycles out... gets lost in the pines and ferns... Danny... Grace... autumn and winter... tramps and their lean-tos... shades of black... grey... brown... the pines mean lots of boletes... the main part of a fungus is underground... spores in the tubes under the cap... Danny sees goblins... witches... an imp on a bad trip... summer... a clearing... I remember this now... no way would he ever sleep in there at night... day-tripping... Jack Frost... Herne The Hunter... Will O' The Wisp... Saturday his reward... when the weather is bad it's good to watch sunny films... comedies... Danny never tells The Green Man boys about the clearing... not even Bubba... Paul P... that one syringe in prison... addicted to moderation... he will survive and die of old age... Sunday dinner outside the pub... spliff in his hand... Bubba balancing a pint on his head... Steve Rollins used to come in here... Carole and the kids outside... Carole waving to Danny... that time... and I ask Bubba if he'd like to have the dice... to remember Danny by... he is surprised... moved... struggling to speak... control his emotions... thank you... yes... I would love to have it... are you sure... and I am nodding and crying and very happy... Bubba picking up the dice... turning it... examining the numbers... says thank you again... thank you very much –*

Ray wasn't fussed about being stuck in traffic even though he'd finished work and was on his way home. Nothing could touch him today. He was king of the castle. A very friendly rascal. Hadn't even reacted when a Nissan cut him up and the driver raised a finger. The plum concerned sped off when he saw the skinhead behind the wheel, the shaved head and staring eyes, but Ray didn't give a toss. He wasn't about to chase the cheeky little fucker and box him in somewhere quiet and drag him out and kick his fucking head in to the sound of an Oi Oi special blaring. Make the important point that two fingers was the English way. No chance. The thought had barely crossed his mind. And that showed maturity. Leadership qualities. He was pleased. His life was changing. Changing for the better.

It had been the perfect working day. His last fare a pick up from Denham Station going to the Heathrow side of West Drayton, and this had ended with a three-pound tip in fifty-pence pieces. It was much too generous. Especially from a pensioner who'd clearly had a drink or three too many. Ray started to explain that a pound was enough, but saw the hurt look forming on the old boy's face and stopped. He didn't want to insult the bloke, who went on to explain that he'd had a nice win on the gee-gees and was keen to share his good fortune. He also wanted to get rid of some shrapnel and guessed it was handy when you were driving a cab.

Every job had been a pleasure. Each punter a joy. Ray had been at his charming best. The conversation flowed and he hadn't mentioned Brexit once, thankful to be back at work and not about to risk another row. He was providing a service and mustn't upset the public. People didn't want their driver raving about the enemy within. Traitors blocking the democratic process. Closet fascists who deserved a hiding. He would love to stick the boot in – HARD. Find the sneerers sitting in a van. Sneering. Engine running. Selfish fucking cunts. But he said none of this as Estuary meant more to him than a rant. The firm was in his blood. Family. Work was good for the soul. Essential. The other drivers were his mates. Yes, today had been perfect.

He was listening to Chubby And The Gang's 'Speed Kills', the debut from a band talking about life along the Uxbridge Road. Joe had put him on to this lot when he was talking about his *Uxbridge Road Special*, a mash-up of Sex Pistols, Clash, Lurkers and Ruts records. Bits of Sweet's 'Ballroom Blitz' and 'Teenage Rampage'. He was making *Uxbridge Road Breakdown* by adding Misty In Roots and classical Indian breaks – whatever that meant. He didn't understand Joe's sampler and how it worked, but it was interesting what he'd said about *musique concrète* in the 1940s, the earlier splicing and looping of tape, how hip hop had started with kids raiding their mum and dad's records, trip hop originating in Bristol. Joe had made lots of other recordings apparently, and he'd had the idea for these and several other versions while he was doing up the Spiritualist church for Lou.

He had sent Ray a clip to see what he thought, making him promise to keep it to himself, but he hadn't listened to it yet which was rude. To be honest, he'd forgotten, but he found it now and played it to the end. It was long. Nearly seven minutes. Ray preferred short sharp bursts of raw energy. Straight lines and seething lyrics. Clever verses with a chanting chorus. There were jumps, repetitions, sound effects galore on *Uxbridge Road Special*. He knew the person responsible and his reasoning, and for that reason he liked the track. It represented their part of the world. But Ray was an Oi man through and through. Stuck to the path while Joe wandered off. Ray had his tradition that stretched back to originals like Cock Sparrer, Sham 69 and The Jam. Oi was developing in its own way and getting stronger by the day.

The traffic began to move, and after fifteen minutes spent with the East End Badoes, Arch Rivals, Crown Court, Resistance 77 and Boilermaker he was pulling up outside the house, turning his engine off and music down. He stayed where he was waiting for Sparrer's 'Running Riot' to end, conscious of Mum's respect for the neighbours, her love for this little street the bullying class might describe as nondescript, part of one of those drive-through places that would be dismissed by a Dimbleby on the way to somewhere they considered more important. When the song finished, he went indoors.

Mum told him to go and sit in the garden, that she'd bring him a cold drink and some biscuits to keep him going until his dinner was ready. He must be starving working ten hours straight. Three biscuits and no more. Did he want custard creams, ginger snaps or Jammie Dodgers? One of each? She didn't want him getting full up. Was he seeing that girl Liz later? She seemed nice enough. Go and sit in the garden... This Ray did, saying hello to a father he didn't know, a figure that wasn't there in front of the TV watching the news – Thatcher, Major, Blair, Cameron, May. He passed Mum who was coming into the house when he thought she was in the kitchen. She was ten years older and had her hands cupped to carry the runner beans he hadn't grown this year. She was calling from upstairs. The bathroom. Crying because she couldn't get off the toilet. The bedroom. Standing at the window. Waving.

Ray sat in her chair in the sun and thought about Priscilla, how she'd said it was fine to believe whatever made you happy as long as it didn't hurt anyone. He wasn't sure about that, but she had placed a finger on his lips to quieten him before he could speak. His lemonade was one of the light ales he'd bought off Buster in the Union Jack, but he'd forgotten the opener. Couldn't be bothered to get up. There was no dinner and little food in the fridge. In a while he would have a shower and put on a clean Fred Perry, go and pick Priscilla up, drive over to the Royal Standard. They would sit in the beer garden. Maybe she was a bit bonkers and a nutter in the lighthearted sense, but that had to be a positive. She was a special lady.

The spacemen didn't seem important now, and he couldn't work out why. But he was pleased. It was about something else.

Lots of things were. He had thought this before. And it applied to him as well. He didn't want to dwell on the bad stuff that had happened in his life, and why the fuck should he when he was on the up. Still floating after last night. Invited to Terry's for the Full English at six in the evening. Tel's all-day breakfast. Angie was on her way out when he arrived. Squeezed his hand and kissed him on the cheek. Which had seemed odd at the time.

Once they'd eaten, Terry opened two bottles of London Pride and handed one to Ray, apologised for not having any Guinness left, blamed Angie for guzzling the last two. Ray didn't mind. He could drink anything. They'd gone into the garden and over to the field to give Bob and Molly some carrots, moved to the picnic table and sat down, and for the first time Ray twigged that this was more than just a social. For a moment he was worried, but if it was another warning his uncle wouldn't have been able to draw it out.

Terry leaned on the wood and focused on his nephew, explained how he wanted to take more of a back seat at work. Angie said it was time to enjoy the rewards of his hard work and that was what he was going to do. They planned to take some trips. A cruise to see the northern lights. The fjords of Norway. He'd like to go to Jamaica one day as well, but only if they could see where some of those original ska singles were recorded. And they'd thought about Las Vegas. Book some shows and drive out to the Grand Canyon. Maybe visit California. This meant Angie would be doing less as well. They'd discussed it, and he wanted Ray to become a partner and take over the running of the firm. He would be eased in slowly and they'd still be around, but in time he would be the new guv'nor.

It was only right. Ray was disciplined and conscientious and had never let Terry down – that argument with the anti-Brexit wanker didn't count – plus he was family. Ray could be trusted. He'd been there for Viv as well. Gone the extra mile. A lot of people bottled out. Ray understood and valued Estuary Cars and had earned the jump. Terry and Angie would take their time showing Ray how the management side of things worked. Weren't going to throw him in at the deep end. What did he think? They felt it was the perfect arrangement. A seamless progression. That it was meant to be. And Ray agreed.

Joe was out at the Oaks early, making the most of his Sunday, glad to be home and pleased Dave was staying with Chris for a couple of weeks as he plotted his return to civilisation. He was aiming to find a job and rent a flat so Martina could come and join him, as it turned out she'd dreamed of living in England since she was a little girl, although what she would make of this part of the kingdom... It could go either way, Dave keeping a straight face as he promised her that guided tour of Queensmere and a wine-tasting session in The Moon Over Water, adding that Herbert Manor was a lot more lively than Palma, not saying whether this was a good or bad thing.

Martina's favourite TV series was *Midsomer Murders*, and maybe she was expecting weekly fetes on the village green and regular cream teas at Lady Penelope's country mansion – minus the carnage – while the name of Slough's shopping mall had started her off on the royal family and how much she loved the Queen and Duke of Edinburgh, Prince William and Kate. When Dave told her they would be living a ten-minute drive from Windsor Castle the drunk suggestion of Joe's that Martina spend a few months in England brewed and became a plan in the following days.

It had taken Joe a long time to realise there was serious problem between his two best mates. He was shocked walking into Vista one morning and finding the worst version of Dave Barrows waiting for him, not the dodgy geezer or jazz-funk ponce or digital Euroland dancer but the genuinely dangerous man he'd tried to pretend didn't exist. He couldn't believe what he was hearing. Dave had only gone and told Chris about Gary Wells, and after a sleepless night decided he was going to kill their friend. It wasn't the usual moody moaning either, his voice and eyes piercing and mental, Joe knowing that he had to sort this out fast.

First he needed to calm Dave down by not having a big argument with him, act as if this was a normal thing to say, asking if he could have a cold drink from the fridge and sitting down and waiting for Dave to join him, buying some time by saying he needed to think about what he'd just heard. Luckily Dave was knackered, yawning and going into the back for a rest when Martina arrived. Joe immediately messaged Chris and caught him finishing his breakfast on the way to Vista, walked back along the promenade and found the bloke, sat on the bench where he'd had his coffee earlier and in roundabout way asking what he knew, saying Dave was concerned, worried Chris had been put in a difficult position, discovered he'd known all along, had worked it out as soon as he heard Wells had been killed.

Chris explained that after what had happened with Luke it was obvious, everything going back to that night when Joe and Smiles ended up in the canal by the gasworks. Chris's voice hardened. Wells was a bully. The right judgement had been made and the correct sentence carried out. Then he became angry. What did Joe think? What did that wanker Dave think? That he was going to grass up his friends? People he'd known since he was a boy? He would never betray his mates. Not unless it was a sex crime, but he didn't mix with nonces. Or if one of them had thrown acid in a woman's face. Anyone's face. Chris emphasised that he might be Old Bill, a rozzer in the Sherlock Zuckerberg tradition, but he was still an everyday garden herbert. With that he relaxed. What was that cunT Dave going to do? Kill him?

That's exactly what could have happened if Joe hadn't persuaded Chris to clear things up, to go and talk to Dave and repeat what he'd just said. Joe kept the reality of the situation to himself, saying they needed to put Dave out of his misery as he was fretting and had enough mental problems as it was, while Chris smiled and admitted he had been winding him up by refusing to respond. It was all in the past now, and their world was returning to normal. A weight Joe didn't know he'd been carrying lifted. As Dave said after he had apologised for doubting Chris and trying to hug him like a Spaniard – something Chris resisted, preferring a handshake and a pint – they were all chums again. Always had been and always would be.

The day after he got home Joe had rented one of the empty lock-ups from the Webbs and was going to move his stock over from the trading estate when the lease ran out. He had his sampler and the rest of his set-up here already, a couple of boxes of records from the flat, and while he was tempted to build new shelves he would resist and only bring what he was going to use, ferry a box or two back and forward and maintain his focus. It was quiet even when the main garage was open and he had a lot more space and wished he'd done this sooner. Money was the issue as usual, and he had chosen to rent the lock-up over a trip away later in the year.

This place was a luxury and he had to make the most of it, couldn't be going away for two months and leaving it empty. At least not yet. He didn't want to either, not this year, and while he would travel again it would be nice to be at home through the winter for a change, finish more of the tracks he was building. He should have got into something like this when he was younger and wondered where it might have taken him, and why he hadn't, supposed it was partly down to a lack of confidence and expectations. He wasn't complaining, as while he'd had his ups and downs like everyone else, overall he was blessed.

He would spend Christmas with his mum and dad and sister and her family, which had become more important when people he knew were losing their parents. Again, he had been lucky, felt good about life and what he was doing. There were hollows, a fear of being tied down, but that was his nature. There was so much he wanted to do and never enough minutes in the day. Dad needed help at the allotments with the digging, and he was doing that, drinking lots of tea there as well as when he was on the road buying vinyl, spending time with Mum at the house just talking, taking her to the big Tescos near the train station when she asked.

Another bonus was sitting with Clem outside his caravan in the evening sipping a can or two, and it turned out that this traveller who had never travelled far and didn't want to either had a secret. If he shared it with Joe he had to keep it to himself. No telling Chris, Dave or anyone else. It was strictly between the two of them. He wanted Joe to promise and shake, which he did, but instead of a story about a long-lost relative leaving him millions of pounds, the sort of secret that could be shared in the comfort of their chairs, Clem said they needed to go into the woods. There was still time before the sun went down and he was keen to get going.

They crossed the heathland in front of the caravan which was dry and rock hard, went into the trees along the route that could take a vehicle, after five minutes veering off into the ferns and following a series of trails that became smaller and smaller, eventually coming to a dead end. A wall of vegetation blocked their way, and Joe asked if they'd got lost. What was the secret? Couldn't he just tell him? Clem insisted it had to be seen. Couldn't be described. He walked forward and sideways, found a small gap in the conifers and stepped forward.

Joe, meanwhile, was remembering the hunters they'd scared off a few years earlier, worried they'd come back and Clem had killed them and this was where he'd left their bodies, or maybe he was keeping them prisoner, but that was mad thinking. Dave had been the one waving an axe about while Clem fired into the air above the sportsmen's heads. He had told them to run and let them escape. Clem would stand up when there was trouble and never let those around him down, but he liked a quiet life and animals and was nothing like the psycho Dave.

Clem slipped into the green and vanished and Joe followed him in. It was dark for twenty or thirty seconds as he eased himself forward with branches and twigs jabbing at his body, and then he was through the other side and standing on the edge of a clearing. This was circled by trees and bushes and rhododendrons that had grown into each other in places, with ferns and shrubs thick at ground level. The clearing wasn't massive and the grass was parched, but this wasn't what he was staring at once he'd taken in the scene. How could it be when there were three giants right there in front of him. They had to be at least eight feet tall, with one even bigger, human forms that seemed to combine tree trunks, stumps and planks with sheets and strips of steel and metal, the joints probably concrete, limbs held together with what looked like iron bolts. The carved faces were oversized, smiling, friendly. Clem grinned and Joe went over for a closer look.

Half an hour later they started back as the light was beginning to fade, Clem going into his caravan as he had to be up early while Joe returned to close his lock-up. Clem trusted him and he would never tell a soul. Everyone was creating something from their dreams and imagination and experiences, were just doing it in their own special ways, and like Clem he felt good deciding what to keep and use, what to ignore and bin, pulling life apart and putting it back together, speeding it up and slowing it down, the past and the future this never-ending present they were all living.

He had left his mobile behind, and when he picked it up he found a message from Dave. He was sitting in Chris's garden and they were having a barbecue. Joe was invited. He texted back and was told to get a move on while there were still some cans left. They'd even bought bean burgers. Joe left the Oaks and headed into Slough, and while he had eclectic tastes and loved what he was doing with his MPC, nothing beat a big dose of punk rock, songs that were fast, melodic and lyric-driven, and thinking of Dave and Chris and Smiles and Clem he put on some Ruts and X-Ray Spex, as he often did.

SLAUGHTERHOUSE PRAYER

JOHN KING

When a boy realises the grown-ups are killing animals and that he has been eating their bodies, he gives up meat. But should he share the truth and break another child's heart? As a youth he wants to believe in the ability of words and peaceful protest to end the slaughter, while struggling to resist a desire for revenge. Now a disillusioned man trying to rebuild his life, he must choose one of two paths. Acceptance means security, but those meat-industry adverts keep taunting him and some familiar insults – *smelly pig*, *dirty cow*, *chick-chick-chicken* – fill his head.

Slaughterhouse Prayer deals in human invention and our treatment of non-human animals, the manipulation of language and the corruption of innocence. Society's pecking order is challenged as the story moves to its margins and beyond. A book of dreams, where visions are more real than reality and sentimentality is a strength, it asks a series of questions. Can a person honestly kill without emotion? Could a vegan soldier stay professional and humane? And will we ever confront the terror that surrounds us?

London Books
£9.99 paperback
ISBN 978-0-9957217-2-2